ALSO BY SHARON GERLACH

Malakh (novella)

Office Politics

The Wyckham House

Condemned

Blink of an Eye

Where I Belong

SHARON GERLACH

The Secret Dreams of Sarah-Jane Quinn

RUNNING INK PRESS

A Running Ink Press Novel

Running Ink Press, LLC
1419 N Lee St
Spokane WA 99202

The Secret Dreams of Sarah-Jane Quinn
Copyright 2009 Sharon Gerlach
ISBN-10 0983291268
ISBN-13 978-0-9832912-6-8

Edited by N.L. Gervasio
Cover image Copyright 2007 Adisa
Cover design by Joshua Gerlach

First Running Ink Press paperback print: July 2012

Printed in the U.S.A.

DEDICATION

To Gini Magnuson, whose love for this story made me determined to see it released to the world.

And to the real Stu & Lori, whose happiness together was foretold in this book, despite what seemed like insurmountable odds.

the secret dreams of sarah-jane quinn

1

BET YOU A DIME

"Bet you a dime Stuckey says *umm* nine times while talking to Frannie."

I look up from my copy and in the direction my cubicle mate is pointing. Frannie Harrison, our supervisor, is standing just outside her office door, talking to *her* supervisor, George Stuckey. George appears to be an intelligent man, but when he's in the vicinity of Frannie he turns into a bumbling idiot, which always has some entertainment value.

"Sixteen," I counter, assessing the way Stuckey is leaning against the wall, his hands in his pockets. This could be a long conversation.

"Come on, Quinn—you been smokin' crack?" Coleridge Tate wheels his chair out of his cubicle and half into mine, and we cock our heads toward the Suits to see who will win.

"I just . . . umm . . . think we would . . . umm . . . be better served if we . . . umm . . . stationed a Training Specialist in Customer Relations . . . umm . . . permanently. It wouldn't . . . umm . . . you know, be a reduction of your staff, and the employee would still . . . umm . . . be doing some of the training materials, but they would mostly be . . . umm . . . assisting the customer service representatives. Then your staff wouldn't have to . . . umm . . . keep running downstairs to Customer Relations all the time."

"George, I'm not giving up any of my staff to Customer Relations. I will, however, consent to in-depth training for one customer service representative, who can then train his or her coworkers." A small frown creases Frannie's brow, and I can tell she's clamping a lid on her temper.

"How many times was that?" Collie whispers, leaning close enough to me that I can smell the tantalizing scent of his aftershave. "Seven or eight?"

"I thought it was six."

"No way. I was still closest. Pay up." He holds out his hand, and I rummage in my desk for a dime. Grinning like a pirate with mayhem on his mind, he escapes with his treasure, disappearing into his own cube.

Coleridge Tate would make a bet on how many times his own mother tripped going up her front steps. I don't know if he's a compulsive gambler or if he's just bored out of his freaking mind with his job, but ever since I started working here four months ago, he's been betting me a dime on almost anything, up to and including how many times our pregnant supervisor makes a trip to the bathroom on any given day.

I huck a paper clip over the cubicle wall between us, hoping to bounce it off his head. A couple minutes later it comes back over, holding a paper replica of a dime, which cracks me up. Not everyone appreciates Collie's sense of humor. Take Brooke Fields, for instance. She rolls her eyes at his jokes, makes muffled *mmphm* sounds when she finds him loafing, and is downright cross and impatient when, at the end of the week, she finds he's completed more work than she has in spite of his long periods of idleness.

This same chick, however, wastes no time cozying up to him at company functions or the rare times she joins us for Happy Hour at Tony's, a bar that seems to be a local tradition for the employees at Harper & Lyttle, Inc. For some reason, this job drives many to drink. (Speaking of... Frannie looks distinctly as though she'd like a big-ass margarita herself as she watches Stuckey shuffle away. When he's out of earshot, I clearly hear her mutter, "Moron!" Collie smothers a laugh.)

When I started working here four months ago, I was paraded around and introduced to the rest of the Training Division staff like a prized cow. In fact, Collie calls it "the prized cow tour." I know why they do it—so that you can place in your mind where everyone sits—

but still, it's a bit humiliating. *This is Sarah Jane Quinn, the latest addition to our herd. Make her feel udderly welcome.* Honestly.

Anyway, when I was taken around to Brooke's cube caddy-corner from mine, she flounced her perfect Baywatch-blonde hair and fixed me with haughty blue eyes. "Brooke Fields. I've heard all the jokes, so don't bother."

I didn't—and still don't—know what jokes she's referring to, but the chip on her shoulder is obvious. At the time, I dropped the *bitch on wheels* label on her, and I've yet to see any reason to lift it.

Needless to say, Brooke isn't often invited to our after-hours gatherings. Usually it's just me, Collie, Hannah, Lauren, and Allison, and we've drank more than our fair share of rum. The girls and I usually take it in the form of daiquiris, but Collie claims that's a frou-frou drink. He orders his straight up or in some vile concoction he calls an Acid Trip (rum, vodka, gin, Midori, and tequila. I call it a Get-Down-and-Crazy, and it's just begging for a What-Did-I-Do-Last-Night incident of epic proportions).

Collie kicks the divider between us. "Hey, Quinn, going to the Christmas party tonight?"

"Dunno."

"Come on. I don't wanna go if you're not gonna be there."

"I thought you had the munchkin tonight and couldn't make the party."

His voice lowers. "That's just what I told Brooke to get out of her trying to make this into a date. My parents are keeping Munchkin overnight." Munchkin is Collie's daughter. Her real name is Megan, but since he let her watch *The Wizard of Oz* and dress up as a munchkin for Halloween last year, she only answers to Munchkin.

Okay, I have a confession to make, and you damn well better keep it secret. There's something about a good-looking man in the daddy role that I find sexier than hell—not that I'd ever tell Collie that. It'd make things weird between us, and I don't want that.

I don't know much about the circumstances of his daughter's birth, but I do know that he's never been married and that he learned he had a child only when Child Protective Services contacted him after

Munchkin's mother abandoned her at her daycare provider's. To get custody, he had to jump through a whole bunch of hoops, consent to two years of CPS monitoring, and get a better job, which is how he ended up at Harper & Lyttle, but he apparently did so willingly and with enthusiasm. His daughter is four now, and he's had her for just over two years. CPS lifted their monitoring about three months ago. He's a good daddy, another thing I find sexy as hell—with men in general, not Collie specifically. If you try to say any differently, I'll deny it to my grave.

"Bet you a dime you go tonight."

"Bet you a dime I don't. Why don't you just bring Munchkin over and we can watch classic Christmas movies all night?"

"Sarah," he says expressively. He only calls me Sarah when I've tried his patience beyond endurance. Otherwise I'm just Quinn—or, when he's trying to needle me, Prized Cow. "*Die Hard* is *not* a Christmas movie."

"The hell you say! I'm taking back your Christmas present. For what I spent I could buy the first two seasons of *Dexter* on DVD."

"Then you spent too much on me. You should have spent it on Munchkin."

"I spent more on Munchkin, so there."

"Told you not to."

"You're not the boss of me," I reply, grinning, knowing he'll give up the argument now. And I'm right. He sighs expressively.

"Don't know what I'm gonna do with you, Quinn."

"You'll think of something."

He doesn't reply, but I can't shake the funny feeling that he's sitting over there on his side of the cube wall, grinning—and plotting—like a mischievous boy.

* * * * *

I walk into the party with dime in hand, but Collie is already deep in conversation with one of the programmers from Concept Development over near the buffet table. He's not so distracted that he doesn't notice me; he catches my gaze briefly, a glint in his green eyes. I know he'll be by to collect later.

Lauren, Hannah, and Allison wave to me from a festively decorated table, and I hurry across the room to join them, as much as I can hurry in heels and a dress. I don't ordinarily wear heels, as I'm not outstandingly graceful in stilettos, and come on, be honest—no one wants to watch a girl who walks like a linebacker, am I right? I slide into my seat with no mishaps, and the girls' conversation continues as though there'd been no interruption.

"She said she came with him, but I don't believe it." Allison shakes her head in disgust, sending her auburn curls flying into her face.

"I saw them come in different cars," says Hannah, leaning in toward the rest of us so we can hear her lowered tones over the strains of the string quartet. Harper & Lyttle spares no expense on their parties. In fact, some events live on in company legend, such as the one four years ago that ended in Las Vegas with Sam Harrison married to his vile office manager. I haven't heard the whole story, but I know she attempted suicide-by-Porsche and ended up in a mental facility after shooting him on the company campus. Nothing exciting like that has happened since I've been here. Figures.

"He avoids her like the plague," I chime in, because I know this firsthand. Collie and I are pretty close friends. "He told her he wasn't coming tonight just so she wouldn't try to turn it into a date. You know how she is—she'd have glued herself to his side like a leech."

"I don't know why he doesn't file complaints about her," Hannah grumps. She's a petite American-Asian with perfect, doll-like features and glossy, straight black hair, so cute you want to just put her in your pocket and take her home. We all thought for a long time that she would be the one Collie asked out, but to tell you the truth, I'm not quite sure Hannah even likes men. She never talks about them, anyway.

"Because she's vile and if he filed complaints, she would be even more vile. Sometimes discretion is the better part of valor." I send a look across the dimly lit room where Collie is still talking to the programmer. He's gesturing with his hands as he talks, which makes me chuckle. "I wonder if he could talk if we tied his hands behind his back."

"I'd like to tie his hands to *something*," mutters Lauren. She's going through a dry-spell of dating right now since she gave the last one the boot. She came home from one of our get-togethers at Tony's to find him dressed in her lacy Victoria's Secret lingerie. That was too much for her; she said she could deal with the surprise of learning her boyfriend likes to cross-dress, but no-one—stress, *no one*—wears her undies.

"No lie," I agree with her absently, still watching him across the room. He's wearing a suit jacket tonight, which he normally doesn't at work; it's the first thing to come off as soon as he reaches his cubicle, and by nine-thirty his tie is undone and either hanging around his neck or is stuffed into the pocket of his jacket. It looks like he got his hair cut after work but he didn't shave; he looks handsome and rakish, and I'm not the only one who's noticed.

At the sudden silence around the table, I drag my eyes away, feeling a blush heat my cheeks. "What? I appreciate a good-looking man the same as anyone else."

We all start talking at once as they disagree and I defend myself. Hannah breaks up our good-natured argument by snapping her fingers in our faces.

"I'm out of punch. Let's go get more."

Women never go anywhere alone—you've probably already noticed that yourself, especially when we go to the restroom. A friend of mine says that's because you never know if the stall you're choosing is out of toilet paper until you get inside and settled, and you need someone to hand you a wad under the stall divider.

My own personal philosophy is that many women are so lacking in confidence that they're *afraid* to go somewhere alone, in case they don't know how to do something required of them once they reach their destination. I rather suspect both theories are right.

We go as a group for more punch…four times in forty minutes. I'm into my fifth cup when I realize I'm a little lightheaded.

"Hey—is this stuff alcoholic?"

"Where've you been, Sarah?" Allison shakes her head, laughing. "It's champagne punch, hence the little place-card in front of the punch bowl that said *Champagne Punch.*"

"I didn't see it there. I wouldn't have had so much had I realized." It doesn't, however, stop me from finishing my current cup.

Hannah levels an assessing look at me and nods. "Truth-or-Dare or Truth-*and*-Dare?" she fires at me. The other girls fall silent.

Truth-or-Dare/Truth-and-Dare is a game we've played since we all started hanging out together outside work. You know the basics of the classic truth-or-dare game. Truth-*and*-Dare is a twist we added; if you accept the truth-and-dare challenge, you're dared to show, do, or say the truth of the challenge. I don't think I need to tell you the stakes are sometimes high.

"Oh, come on, not now!" I protest.

"Truth-or-Dare, or Truth-and-Dare?" she repeats insistently.

I huff out an impatient breath. "Okay, fine. Truth-or-Dare."

"You can't," Lauren pipes up. "You took Truth-or-Dare last time. You have to take Truth-*and*-Dare."

Another one of our made-up rules, one I myself initiated. I knew someday it would come back to bite me in the ass.

"Okay, fine. Give it your best shot."

"Okay, this is your Truth-and-Dare. You have to do something that will show us your true feelings for Coleridge Tate."

I skid my chair back several inches from the table, totally unprepared for this particular challenge.

"No way." I've never dodged a challenge before, but this is one I *can't* take. I can't do this; if I open the floodgates on my secret dreams, there's no telling whether I'll ever be able to slam them shut again.

Okay, I'm a coward. Now you know the sordid truth about Sarah-Jane Quinn. If the truth is out, I may have to act on it, and if I act on it, I may be rejected, and if I'm rejected, I may simply die from humiliation and shame. Yup. Coward.

"Honor system, Sarah. You have to accept the challenge, or we can't speak to you for a week *and* you're our coffee girl for that week.

Those are the rules," Lauren reminds me solemnly. She's blonde, like me, only her hair is lighter, closer to platinum (and completely natural); the dim lighting in the convention room makes her hair seem to glow silver.

"Oh, shit," I murmur. Collie's dime is still clenched in my hand, its serrated edge biting into my palm. I ease my grip and take a steadying breath. "Okay. Okay, I can do this."

"I *told* you she has romantic feelings for him!" Lauren crows triumphantly. The other two reluctantly hand over dimes, and I roll my eyes. Collie has everyone betting on everything.

My legs shake as they carry me across the room. My fingers, holding the dime between them in a death grip, have gone numb by the time I reach him. He flicks me a glance as I approach, but the programmer doesn't seem to notice me. He continues on with his droning monologue and only stops—in shock, I'm sure—when I step up close to Collie, hook my hand around his neck, and pull his head down to mine. His hand goes automatically to my waist, either to pull me closer or push me away; before he can do either, I kiss him. My kiss is brief but full on his lips—no mistaking my intent for it to be more than just a friendly peck. When I draw away, he lifts his head, staring at me with an indecipherable expression. The programmer takes a breath.

"So as I was saying, Collie—"

"Excuse me a moment, Henry. I must show Sarah how to do this properly." His hand snakes around to the small of my back, anchoring me against him, and *his* kiss is anything but brief. It's slow and leisurely, thorough and completely devastating. If you'd told me at noon today that I'd be standing by the buffet table at seven o'clock French-kissing Coleridge Tate, I'd have said you were out of your mind.

At last he draws away, his lips lingering against mine for a long moment, still wearing that maddeningly unreadable expression.

"Well, Sarah," he drawls. "How much of that punch have you had?"

"Too damn much." I hold out my dime to him, but he's holding out his hand to Henry, who is digging in his pocket for a dime. "What'd you bet?"

He presses a finger against my nose playfully. "Never you mind. I believe you owe me a dime yourself, Quinn."

I drop it into his hand and he pockets it. "Collie—"

"Now off you go to your table, and do try to stay out of trouble."

"Collie," I try again.

"Sarah," he says, his pirate's grin at odds with his tone of long-suffering patience. "I'm just a man. There are limits to my self-control, so before I embarrass myself in public, you'd best—" He motions toward my table and I nod mutely, taking several steps backward before I abandon all dignity and flee back to my group of girlfriends, who are staring at us, slack-jawed. I wonder what we're going to do now, how this is going to change our friendship. That was not the kind of kiss you give a casual friend. My greatest worry is he'll start the avoidance routine, and that would hurt unbearably.

About ten minutes later, I chance one more look at him, finding him looking back. He winks and I relax. Everything will be fine.

In retrospect—many months later—I'll wonder whether he set it all up, because planning ahead on a devious scale is Coleridge Tate's extraordinary talent.

ALWAYS A BUDDY

I think there should be a federal investigation into dentists. They're the sadists of the civilized world, and they not only go entirely unpunished, they get *paid* for inflicting abject pain and misery on people. If the average citizen went around poking and prodding and drilling and instilling quaking dread in others, they'd be arrested.

Add to the misery of getting three fillings (yes, three, thanks for noticing) the fact that it's the morning following the Christmas party and I have a hangover (I can't *believe* they had a party with alcohol on a Thursday night), I'm drooling down my chin, and I have to face Collie after kissing him last night. It all adds up to I wish I'd called in sick today.

He's on the phone when I pass his cubicle, so I dodge the bullet for at least a couple minutes. As I hang my coat on the hook suspended from my cube wall, I spy the hang-over kit he's left in front of my monitor. I can't help but laugh. The gallon-size plastic bag holds a treasure of items necessary to make it through today: a smaller snack-size baggie holding six aspirin; a coupon for a free burger with purchase of fries and shake at a nearby fast food joint (nothing helps beat the queasies from an over-indulgence of alcohol like a greasy burger); a bottle of spring water; a Mardi Gras mask for whatever reason Collie thought pertinent at the time; and a sandwich bag labeled *After Dentist Kit* with a travel pack of tissues and a straw with a flexible end.

"How's the hang-over, Quinn?" he asks from his side of our shared cube wall.

"Oy." I go for the aspirin first, and down three of them with spring water—which promptly spills down my chin because I can't feel roughly three-quarters of my face. Now I see the necessity of the straw. I wrangle it out of the bag and stuff it into the bottle, and things are much easier from there.

I spin around in my chair—slowly—to get my sunglasses out of my jacket pocket and let out a startled yell. Collie is lounging with one shoulder against the cube wall behind me.

"Jesus, Coleridge! Can't you find a hobby other than sneaking up on people?"

He notices the wet patch on my shirt. "I gave you a straw for a reason. And—ah—you're drooling down your chin." He steps around me and grabs the pack of tissues, and my embarrassment is complete as he mops up my face. As he draws away, his thumb runs over my lower lip in what could have been an accidental caress but, judging from the glint of amusement in his eyes, is nothing more than a wicked reminder of last night.

"You're a freaking tease, Coleridge Tate. You do know that, don't you?"

"Sadly, I've been told that more than once. Sorry about the face-wiping thing; habit from having a kid. You're a mess, Quinn. Why'd you even come in today, anyway? Just like drooling on the keyboard?"

"I didn't want anyone thinking I called in sick because—" I stop, face flaming, mortified that I even brought up the party.

"Ah." Collie scoots onto the edge of my desk and fixes me with a resigned look. "So you're going all girly on me and you want to talk about last night."

"I never said *I* wanted to talk about it. I just don't want anyone *else* talking about it."

"Too late for that, I'm afraid," he laments, sounding anything but sorry. "My...sources tell me it's *the* topic on the grapevine."

I close my eyes and huff out a breath. "Great. So why'd you do it? Just to provide fodder for the gossip mill?"

He leans closer and whispers with absolute delight, "If I recall the chain of events correctly—and of the two of us, I was the most sober, so I believe my recollection is more reliable—*you* kissed *me* first."

"Yes, and you could have just let me walk away, you know."

"Are you kidding? I was the envy of every guy at the party. Besides, no way was I going to let Henry win that bet."

"*What* bet?"

"Well...we noticed how many times you went to the punch bowl—didn't you read it was champagne punch?"

"After I drank five cups of it," I reply dryly. "Do continue."

"I knew the second you got out of your chair what you were going to do. Alcohol makes you reckless, Quinn. But hey, better me than some schmuck who'd take advantage of you, right?"

"And what you did *wasn't* taking advantage of me?"

"God, no." He waves it away nonchalantly, and I repress a sudden urge to sock him in the eye. So what the hell was it—a mercy kissing? "We both woke up alone in our own homes and neither of us had to come to work in last night's clothes, so no, it wasn't taking advantage of you.

"Anyway, when I saw you coming, I told Henry 'I bet she's coming over here on a dare to kiss me.' And Henry, the sly old dog, says 'You're probably right, Collie, but I bet you don't have the guts to turn the tables and kiss her like you—well, *really* kiss her." A slow flush creeps up his neck and into his face as he makes the hasty amendment. I wonder what Henry *really* said to him.

"And so you did. To win a bet."

"A dime is a dime, Quinn. You of all people should know that. Are we done talking about this now?"

"You mean, am I done being all girly?" He grins. "Yeah, I s'pose so."

"Good." He slides off the edge of my desk. "Munchkin wants to go Monte Carlo bowling tonight. You up for it?"

"You're killin' me, Tate," because I'm a lousy bowler.

"But what a way to go. We'll pick you up at eight so we can get a burger beforehand." He's gone before I can protest, and to be honest, I'm glad. God knows what he'd say if he knew how much it hurt to hear it was just a bet.

My problem with guys is I'm always a buddy and never a girlfriend. I listen too well, empathize too much, and understand perfectly why they think they way they do (testosterone). I can work on cars (I changed my own head gaskets last year), I watch football (yeah, the Cowboys are my team, even when they suck), and I bait my own fishing hook. I wear blue jeans and sweats in my off time, can lift almost as much as Collie with my legs, and can catch a fast pitch.

As a result, most guys don't even notice that I'm female despite the fact that I'm slim, blonde, and long-legged. While I may command the respect of a good number of males, I don't attract their amorous attention. But damned if I'm going to become some brainless feminine fluff just to get some man who probably doesn't deserve me anyway…ummm, that was aimed at those numerous faceless guys out there who haven't noticed I'm a woman. Collie totally deserves me; he just hasn't realized it yet. Just so we get that straight.

I actually *do* have work to do, in case you were wondering. It's not all about bets and putative boyfriends. They tell me I'm an entry-level Training Specialist, but it seems I get more training from others than I give. When I took the job, I didn't expect anything glamorous; my skills with word processing and spreadsheets bumped me to the top of the hire list, and since the pay was better than the job I'd lost, I was more than happy to accept. I don't mind what I do—or what I'll *be* doing, at any rate; I test software and write step-by-step instructions of how to use said software. Maybe not glamorous, but interesting enough—more so than my previous employment. I'd been a receptionist for a small insurance company, and there were days I was bored nearly to tears. At least I'm not bored here, and there are few phone calls to deal with. I really detest talking on the phone, so that suits me just fine.

As if in tune to my thoughts, my phone rings. "Training Division, Sarah Quinn speaking."

"Sarah, it's me." Allison. *"What the hell was that all about last night?"*

"Nothing. Just a bet. Why are you whispering?"

"It's called being discreet, which you definitely were *not* last night. Do you know there are bets going on all over the company about whether or not you and Collie slept together last night?"

A blush burns along my cheeks. "Oh, just because we kissed that must mean we're setting the sheets on fire, eh?" I say, more loudly than I intended. Collie's attempt to muffle his laughter is half-hearted at best.

"*Sarah!* Let's go get coffee.*"*

This is a euphemism for having a private chat. Apparently it used to be illegal in Harper & Lyttle Land to request a private chat lest someone else think the chat was about them. Frannie abolished the policy but the euphemism lives on, partly because she, Gretchen, and Stella still use it.

"All right, fine." She hangs up and I resign myself to a whispered Q&A session in the break room that will accomplish nothing.

I grab my coffee mug—still full of hot coffee—and pause on my way by Collie's cube. "You owe me big-time."

He doesn't turn around as he replies. He doesn't even stop keying the training manual he's working on. "Quinn, I did you a favor. I just made you highly popular with the male population at Harper & Lyttle."

"How do you figure?"

He spins around in his chair, releasing the lever that allows his chair to lean back. "Guys want to date girls other guys are kissing."

"Why? Because they think we're easy?" And that was somehow doing me a favor? I really *should* have socked him in the eye.

"Noooo," he drawls patiently. "Because if one man finds a girl attractive enough to kiss, then obviously that girl has some serious mojo going on."

I breathe in sharply through my nose, not seeing that this is any different than making other guys think I'm easy. "I'm going to kick your ass, Collie."

"Yeah, nothing like an ingrate. Have a nice chat, Quinn." With a devilish grin, he spins his chair back around, presenting me with his back. As I edge out of his cube I see him loosen his tie and pull it over his head.

I shush Allison when she starts whispering; the hallway to the break room serves as a sound tunnel, funneling conversations back to the Training Division like an intercom. No way am I going to be the source of Collie's amusement over this incident any more than I have to be.

"What is going on?" Allison demands as soon as we reach the break room, which—unfortunately—is empty. "What happened after the party?"

"Nothing."

"Nothing! After a kiss like that?"

"It was a bet, Allison." She looks back at me with a blank look. "I kissed him on a dare. He kissed me on a bet."

"For a dime," she guesses.

"Precisely. End of story. Now can I get back to all the work I'm not doing because I'm in here?"

She hooks a lock of auburn hair behind her ear, giving me a frank appraisal. "You're so full of shit."

"Not."

"You can fool him, but you can't fool me," she says kindly and waits.

Of my six colleagues, I'm closest to Allison. Hannah is quite self-contained and we rarely see her outside work unless it's a Tony's daiquiri night. Lauren is cruising for a new man, so she goes out a lot with a less attractive friend who already has a beau. I know that sounds harsh, but no girl wants to compete with her good-looking girlfriends for a man's attention. Stella, our Senior Specialist, is outrageously exotic and wrapped up in her wedding plans (and besides, she's probably six years older than me, which might as well be a century when you're in your mid-twenties). Although closer to our age, Morgan is in the office only infrequently, since she works from home. And Brooke is…well, a bitch on wheels. No way am I confiding in her. Allison and I do a bunch of girly things together outside work; it's my one feminine outlet. If I didn't have her, in no time Collie would doubtless have me chopping firewood and hunting and mounting antlers on my living room wall.

"A freaking bet, Allie," I say finally. "For a dime. Henry Perkins from Concept Development bet Collie a dime that he wouldn't turn the tables on me and kiss me back—*really* kiss me."

To my amazement, Allison giggles. "Oh, Sarah." She tries to stifle her laughter and ends up snorting. "He may tell *you* it was all for a bet, but *no* man—not even Coleridge Tate—kisses a woman like that for a dime."

"I'm not hanging my hopes on it, and I'm not going to pursue him like some desperate ho—a la Brooke. I'd rather have his friendship than nothing at all."

"All right, but mark my words…"

"Consider them marked."

We leave the break room and come into the hallway just behind Frannie, who is walking and reading a report at the same time. It's obvious she's been in the bathroom, because she's trailing a five-square length of toilet paper from her low-heeled pump.

"Should we tell her?" Allie whispers from the corner of her mouth.

"Yeah. It's always something—I swear the woman is hopeless."

"Psst! Frannie!" Allison stage-whispers. Frannie turns absently, and Allie motions to her shoe. Fran sighs expressively. With a little maneuvering and some assistance from the wall to maintain her balance, she manages to catch hold of the toilet paper. The bigger she gets, the harder it is for her to do anything. She said the other day that she's almost to the point she'll have to wear slip-on shoes until the baby's born, because she suspects her feet are just a myth; she hasn't seem them in weeks.

"There!" she says triumphantly, gingerly holding the toilet paper by one corner. She smoothes the back of the other hand, report and all, down over her backside. "Thanks, ladies. At least my skirt wasn't tucked into my pantyhose this time."

Shaking her head, she continues on her way, and Allison covers her mouth to muffle her giggle.

"*This* time?" That's a story I'd like to hear.

I slip back into my cubicle and take my chair, finding Collie's tie draped haphazardly over my monitor, which means he tossed it over the cube wall. I toss it back.

"Bet you a dime I beat you all three games tonight, Quinn."

"Bet you a dime you don't." A bet I'll win, I'm sure, because he'll throw a game or two to let Munchkin win at least once…or me.

"Lots of guys at the bowling alley for Monte Carlo."

"Mmmm."

"If you need me to kiss you again to spark their interest, just say so."

"I'll kick you in the shins if you do," I reply, smiling.

A brief beat of silence, then, "Bet you a dime you don't."

"Bet you both a dime you can't shut up for ten minutes at a stretch," Stella calls out in an acidic tone. Collie chuckles.

A moment later: "I'm here for ya, Quinn."

If only.

3

THE DICTATORPHONE

"Bad news," says Frannie, twirling her pencil into her hair. "The coffee maker is no longer under warranty, and we have no money in the budget to fix the damn thing until the new fiscal year. We'll just have to bear with the wheezing and groaning until then."

Stella snorts, either with disgust or to clear her nasal passages; she's suffering a head cold that's making all of us miserable. "Great. Have you tried to work with Lauren when she's had no coffee? She's worse than Morgan."

"Hey!" exclaim Lauren and Morgan in unison. Stella waves her tissue in apology and hangs her head over her coffee mug again, breathing in the steam.

Collie nudges me and writes on his notepad: *Bet you a dime Stella doesn't make it through the meeting without saying "Oh for shit's sake!" at least once.*

I write back: *No bet. It's a given. Got anything else?*

Collie: *Nope. Give me a minute, tho'. I'll think of something.*

"Okay, down to real business. I made a deal with Sam for Production to start using a font point that is readable without the aid of the Hubble telescope."

Everyone cheers, especially Gretchen; she's prone to migraines, and the miniscule print on the reports Production churns out accelerates them.

Fran continues, "I had to sleep with him to get him to agree. You guys owe me big time."

We all laugh because Sam, the head of Production, is Frannie's husband.

"Thanks for taking one for the home team," Morgan remarks, tongue-in-cheek.

"You're so welcome." Fran grins. "Sarah, I promised your services as a transcriptionist to Evelyn Harper; she found a bunch of dictation tapes for which she can't find the corresponding documents. Before she tosses them, she wants to be sure there's nothing on them that needs to be saved."

"Okay. At my desk or in her office?"

"She delivered the tapes to me after hearing you can transcribe. *Somewhere* in the depths of the basement storage room lurks a portable dictation machine. Your first job of the day is to excavate it, test it out—take a tape with you—and then spend the rest of the day recovering from inhaling ten years of dust."

"Take your inhaler," Collie adds helpfully.

Oh, I guess I forgot to mention I have asthma. Environmental conditions can set it off, but usually stress is the culprit. I haven't had an attack in five months—since before I even met Collie—but he keeps track of my inhaler like a mother hen. Must be the parent in him.

"Yes, do," Frannie agrees readily. "And take Collie as well. The basement's creepy. I don't go down there without Sam." She stops, realizing how that could be taken, and flushes to the roots of her hair as we all crack up. "Sometimes we even have legitimate business there."

Collie slants me a look from the corner of his eye. I wonder if he's remembering how he kissed me at the Christmas party last month. I know I am; it's never very far from my mind, in fact. But he's said nothing about it since the day after it happened and far be it from me to bring it up. (Oh, and by the way, I won the Monte Carlo bowling bet: he won a game, I won a game, and Munchkin won a game. He was most reluctant to hand over his dime, but a bet is a bet and I brook no welshers).

"Next order of business," Frannie plows on, squinting at her notes. "The Powers-That-Be are thinking you guys might like a little fun at the office, so they've planned a miniature golf tournament. The holes will be set up in each department—except the Senior Exec level—and the theme is anything Irish. The tournament is scheduled for St. Patrick's Day—"

"Hence the Irish theme," Collie murmurs in an aside to me.

"—and we have to decorate our own departments."

Stella harrumphs. "Oh, for shit's sake!"

Collie and I exchange a look, grinning.

"I know, I know. You'll just have to deal with it, Stel." And then she says, more to herself than anyone else, "At least it's not a freaking pancake breakfast."

And Gretchen replies, also in a low tone, "Or a Post-It conference."

They look at each other and snicker a little, and then Fran seems to realize she hasn't dismissed us. "Okay, folks, meeting's over. I need to stand so I can get this critter's feet out of my lungs."

She pushes on her belly as she stands up, making the baby shift, and heaves a sigh of relief as she joins Gretchen at the door. They talk in low voices as they walk ahead of us to the department, and at one point Fran gives her a one-armed hug and a sympathetic smile— typical Frannie. She's very absent-mindedly affectionate, if you get what I mean, but we all know she cares. There's something very comforting about her pragmatic, straight-forward approach to things.

Collie and I toss our notepads into our cubicles and head downstairs. The lower level of the Harper & Lyttle building is a veritable graveyard of obsolete surplus just begging to be donated to a landfill. It might even have been on Evelyn Harper's To-Do List when she took over running the company, but no doubt she threw up her hands in defeat when she saw the real state of affairs.

The bewildering labyrinth of discarded office detritus stacked on shelving units haphazardly arranged with no rhyme or reason is much like the architecture of the building itself. Blocking one aisle are two desks, stacked one upon the other, and I'm reasonably sure that's the aisle where I'll eventually find the stupid dictation machine. I see a spot where I can probably shimmy my way over the bottom desk, which is more than likely wedged cheek-by-jowl against the shelving unit.

"So where do you want to start, Quinn?"

"Doesn't matter," I reply reasonably. "It's going to be in the last place we look."

He chuckles. "That it will."

More than an hour later, we still haven't found what were looking for, but I *am* halfway to an asthma attack. Collie makes me use my inhaler, gives me an Altoid to cleanse the nasty taste of the inhalant from my mouth, and then insists he carry on the search by himself.

"What is it I'm looking for again?" His voice comes from two aisles over.

"A Dictaphone."

"A *what*?"

"A Dictaphone. It may be some other brand, I don't know. I've heard rumors of such a thing languishing in here, but I've never actually seen it myself."

"So it could be just a myth," he deduces, probably more correct than he knows. The dictation machine I'm looking for will be fairly old by today's technology standards, but I'll need it to transcribe the old tapes. Dictation is rarely used here anymore since the age of technology gave us the unequaled gift of e-mail.

"Very likely."

"Bet you a dime it's down that damn aisle with desks blocking the way."

"That's what I was thinking. I can help, you know."

He pops back into view, brushing cobwebs from his hair. "Nah. What kind of gallant knight would I be? Come on; maybe it's over here."

We head to a new section—Collie calls this "searching the grid;" I think in a former dream-life he was a cop or an archaeologist—but we find nothing but a bunch of aging hanging folders (which obviously escaped the eagle-eye of the former head of Inventory Control) and a selection of mammoth ten-key machines hailing from sometime around the Cretaceous Period. Finally he announces that there's nowhere left to search but the blocked aisle.

"What kind of maniac arranged the storage anyway?" I grumble.

"Probably the architect who designed the building," he replies absently, echoing my earlier thought. "I'm thinking it was Stevie Wonder or Ronnie Milsap. Are you sure this Dictatorphone is supposed to be down here?"

"Not a Dictatorphone, silly." I smother a laugh. "A Dictaphone."

"I didn't know that was possible," he remarks.

"What's possible?"

"A *Dic*-ta-phone," he says, stressing the syllables.

"I don't ge—oh!" I can feel the crimson tide ebbing and flowing in my face. "I am *so* not going to respond to that. We'd better find it soon. My feet are killing me."

He opens his mouth, probably to make a wise-crack, just as the basement door creaks open. We're on the other side of the very large, very cram-packed room, so we don't at first realize we're unwilling witnesses to a very private conversation.

"I don't really want to talk about it, Gus, especially at work."

"You don't seem to want to talk about it at home, either. I think you owe it to me to be straight with me."

She huffs out a breath, and the dull thwack of her heels comes farther into the room—and closer to us.

Collie puts a finger to his lips to warn me to silence, spins a slow circle on the spot to survey our surroundings, and then tugs me over to an old wooden desk shoved close to the wall, perched for unknown reasons on two oak pallets. We duck behind it just in time, his arm around me keeping me anchored safely in place as though he's afraid I'm going to bolt and run into the middle of this domestic disaster.

"Either you're staying with me, or you're going back to him," Gus says quietly. I shoot a look at Collie, my mouth dropping open. I can't imagine *any* woman leaving Gus Haldemann; more than half the women in the company are madly in love with him.

"That's not what this is about!" Gretchen bursts out impatiently. "This is about the girls' father. They deserve to have a relationship with him."

"He tore up his parent card the night he walked out on all of you,"

23

Gus replies implacably. "And a relationship with his children isn't what he's after. He's after a reconciliation with you."

"Gus, you're being silly. It's been two and a half years; why would you think I'd want anything to do with him after what he did? But I have to allow my children an opportunity to know their father."

"Yeah? He suddenly woke up and remembered he had them after two years—two years during which another man had to step in and fulfill his responsibilities?"

"You didn't *have* to," Gretchen says in a hard voice. "You just *did*."

Dead silence reigns for several interminable seconds. I really wish they would get on with it—break up, make amends, whatever—because I *really* have to use my inhaler. Collie's fingers tighten on my shoulder and he shoots me a concerned look.

Gus's voice, when it comes, has lost all trace of anger. It's quiet and full of terrible regret. "Well, Gretchen." He seems to struggle for words. "I'm sorry that my caring for all of you has been so burdensome to you."

"That isn't what I said! Why do you always twist what I say?"

"We've had that argument before and I'm not anxious to rehash it. I have a lot of work to do, so I'd better go back up."

Rapid strides carry him away through the maze of the storage room, and then pound up the stairs. When the door at the top creaks closed again, Gretchen lets out a primal snarl of frustration and hurls something at the wall. The clatter seems tremendous as broken pieces of whatever rain down on the cement floor. She remains for a long moment, breathing deeply to calm herself, and at last the clack of her heels on the stairs and the creak of the basement door inform us we're alone again.

"Wow," Collie finally says. "I'm pretty sure I wanted to know none of that."

"Me too." I fumble out my inhaler and take a deep pull off it as he goes to examine the casualty of Gus and Gretchen's private war.

"Ummm…Quinn, you'd better come take a look."

The last thing I care about right now is the remains of some ancient ten-key. Few people will notice it's gone, and if we scoop the pieces over toward the shelves where the machines are stored, anyone who *does* notice will simply think it fell off the shelf of its own accord.

Collie holds out a fragment of heavy-duty plastic, his expression solemn but his eyes dancing with suppressed mirth. I take it from him and turn it over, looking down at the single, raised word, the silver paint long worn away from the letters: *DICTAPHONE.*

Tales from the Water Cooler

Sunday, January 25
Going Postal: A Career-Limiting Move

Posted by Sarah Quinn

NOTE: Names have been changed to protect the guilty… er…innocent.

Everyone knows an office is not an easy place to work. Different personalities, backgrounds, and temperaments all add to the stresses of workloads, client issues, and administrative politics. An office professional handles oneself with dignity, decorum, and—needless to say—professionalism. Just as there are dress codes (yes, Boss Lady, I'm aware I don't follow ours at all), there are codes of conduct as well:

- If your boss is crabby, do NOT ask what his or her problem is.

- Likewise, if your boss is crying in his or her office, do NOT ask questions. Back away slowly and pretend that you're deaf and blind.

- If the coffeemaker is broken, find an excuse—ANY excuse—to go home immediately. You do NOT want to be a part of an office with no coffee.

- Chocolate. Learn it, use it, offer it to your coworkers. Your office life will be much better for it.

- Do NOT offer to water your office mates' plants. Even if the plants are nothing more than dried sticks with leaf skeletons still clinging to them when you get them, you WILL be blamed for their demise if you so much as approach them

26

with a cup of water.

- And finally, do NOT go postal in the office, no matter what happens or how justified you may feel you are (NOTE: "blowing your buffer" is a synonym for "going postal." I may use each of these terms interchangeably over the course of this blog). Going postal is UNDOUBTEDLY a career-limiting move.

These are just a few general codes of conduct. I'm sure I'll think of more later. I'll discuss some—if not all—of these codes later; for now, simply refer to this list when you feel confused over what your reaction to a particular situation should be. And remember, I'm here to help, so if you're having a situation that have not yet covered, feel free to request guidance.

DID YOU KNOW:

EXCEL TIP: You can copy and paste the contents of a single cell or selection of consecutive cells down an entire column in three easy clicks:

- Click into the cell you want to copy down the column.

- Hover at the lower right-hand edge of the cell until you get the bold plus sign.

- Double-click using the left mouse button.

Your data will copy down to the last row that contains data. You might have to click the little Auto Fill Options for a selection of choices to make sure your data fills in correctly. VOILA!

Blog Archive
    2009
        January
            Going Postal: A Career Limiting Move

About Me
Savvy Sarah

I am an administrative office professional with several years' experience in office settings. I have an AAS in Administrative Office Management and currently work as a training specialist for a software development company in Los Angeles.

THERE'S NO PLACE (TO AVOID) LIKE HOME

I didn't start out hating my family; I'm sure that at some point in my life, I honestly cared for these people with whom I share a blood tie. Now, however, there aren't words eloquent enough to describe my loathing for them. The disgusting part is my loathing doesn't stop my longing for their acceptance, for a normal relationship with them. Sadly, there is nothing normal about them, and I've learned the hard way that they aren't capable of maintaining lengthy associations. I guess their base personalities act as a deterrent to anyone with staying power.

My sister is in mid-sentence when I arrive, and three hours later she's still talking. I don't know why my mother doesn't just tell her to shut the hell up; fifteen minutes into my visit I'm damn near homicidal. But mummy dearest seems riveted, and they yak on as though they're solving the world's biggest problems while preparing homemade lasagna.

Mom is a fabulous cook and a dedicated gardener. I'm sure her cooking is the only thing that kept my childhood from being a complete murky blur of abject misery. The familial estate (two residential suburban lots with a modest reproduction farmhouse set smack-dab in the middle) is just large enough that being hauled out to help with the gardening wasn't a chore but a reprieve. While Mom worked the front—because it had to be *just so* lest the neighbors think ill of her—I worked the back (the vegetable gardens and herb beds), and for the most part I had peace and solitude.

And where, you might be asking, was my darling sister during this time? Out with one of a variety of boyfriends or sleeping under the influence of prescription allergy medications. Unable to contribute to the general chores, she nevertheless managed to miraculously resurrect herself in time for the evening meal and to take in any number of silly television shows with the parental units.

You might think I'm partaking in a large serving of bitter pie, and you may very well be right. I prefer to think of it as being honest. My mother always tells me to keep my mouth shut if I don't have anything positive to say, and for the most part I respect that directive even though it makes me grind my teeth in frustration, which in turn gives my dentist hives. However, we're being honest here, right? So honest it is, then, if not a trifle bitter.

"You're very quiet today, Sarah-Jane," Mom notes with an obvious tone of disapproval.

I'm always Sarah-Jane and never just Sarah, another thing that causes me endless irritation. I've been pondering the absurdity of giving children hyphenated first names, which, in my humble opinion, is only marginally less ridiculous than giving them hyphenated first names followed by middle names. You should see the hummer crammed onto my driver's license: *Sarah-Jane Aubrey Quinn*. Try shouting *that* out the back door at supper time (not that Mother would ever be so crass). Could be worse, I suppose—I could be *Mary-Anne Madison Quinn*. That would be infinitely worse in more ways than one.

"Sarah!" says Mary-Anne sharply. "Mom asked you a question."

"Actually, I believe she made a remark," I correct her mildly. Her mouth thins to an angry hyphen—apropos—and she opens her mouth. Mom steps in smoothly.

"There's no need to cause an argument, Sarah-Jane." I grind my teeth, biting back my protest. "I simply noted that you're very distant today. Are we poor company?"

Yes. "No, Mom. I'm just tired from work."

"Oh yes, the new job." She sniffs. "Mary-Anne got a raise at work, which is phenomenal considering the tight-fisted company she works for."

And they're off again, talking, talking, never asking, never expressing any interest in me whatsoever. Now you know another sordid truth about Sarah-Jane Quinn: I'm unimportant. A coward and unimportant. Wow…maybe I should be cutting myself.

"I'm going to go streaking across the UCLA campus," I say conversationally. Mary-Anne doesn't even pause in her monologue, and Mom shows no sign of having heard me. "And then I'm going to dress up like a hooker and pick up johns on Sepulveda Boulevard, just for kicks."

"Sarah-Jane," says Mom, and I simultaneously quail at the thought of having incurred her wrath while at the same time rejoicing that I finally captured her attention. "Will you set the dining room table, please? Use the everyday dishes, please; I'd hate for any of the china to get broken before Easter."

My shoulders slump. When I try to think of why I came tonight, my mind draws a blank.

The crowning moment of the evening comes after Dad gets home and we all sit down to dinner. Now, a teensy thing about my dear old dad….

"JESUS CHRIST, SARAH! You're twenty-[string of expletives deleted]-six-years old and you can't manage not to smear your dinner all over your shirt?"

Face burning, I look down to find a blob of marinara sauce splattered on my shirt. It happens, you know—and only when I'm wearing white. And only in front of Dad. I think it's because his impatience and disapproval make me nervous. I've never had an unguarded moment around my father that ended well…such as now.

Hastily, I swipe at my shirt with my napkin, only too late realizing I fell into the trap. Oh, it doesn't matter *what* trap; there's always one, cleverly disguised and set to spring at the slightest provocation.

"Sarah-Jane!" Mom gasps. "*My good damask napkins!*" Obviously she's forgotten she asked me to put them on. No paper napkins will ever grace Mom's table, and usually she has a stock of linen ones on hand for everyday use, but she's got them soaking in the washer to get out the stains.

"I'd get you a clean shirt, Sarah, except I moved the last of my clothes to my apartment last week."

31

This is about the fourteenth time Mary-Anne has mentioned her new apartment. She's like a yo-yo, bouncing in and out of the family abode. First, she moved out with a boyfriend, and then moved back home when that fell through. Then she wanted to go to college and couldn't afford to live on her own, so the parents let her move back in long enough to complete a certificate at the local community college. Out she bounced again, this time in with a couple of friends who ended up booting her out (probably for talking incessantly about herself), and back into the parents' house she came, where she's been for the past two years while she pays off enormous credit card debt. Last week she finally found a small apartment she can afford by herself.

The flip side to this particularly noxious coin is that when I left home at eighteen (graciously invited to do so by the parents four weeks into my first full-time job) I was told they didn't have a revolving door. Once gone, forever gone. And they meant it; that job ended when my employer went under, and they refused to let me move back in. I found work at Harper & Lyttle in the nick of time— just as my savings ran out and I was damn near homeless. No hope or sympathy from the home front whatsoever. I managed to keep my apartment, pay all my bills, and not end up with every account I have in collections. And they call *her* the responsible one.

After dinner Mom and I do the dishes. Mary-Anne promptly— and unsurprisingly—vanishes, leaving me to deflect Mom's sharp commands by myself.

I don't make my escape until seven-forty-five, and here's how it goes: I beg off joining them for coffee in the sitting room; Mom walks me to the front door, where I say goodbye and I'll visit again soon blah blah blah and give her a perfunctory kiss near her cheek—and I say *near* because she moves neatly out of reach before my lips touch her skin. I step out onto the porch, turn to say one last goodnight— and the door closes promptly in my face.

That stings, but I don't cry. Another truth about Sarah-Jane Quinn: I haven't cried since I was sixteen and came home from studying at a friend's house to find my sister making prom night arrangements with *my* boyfriend in the sitting room, her new prom dress arranged neatly over the back of a wing-back chair, the plastic wrapper bunched up around the neck of the hanger.

An argument of epic proportions ensued and waged throughout the house (wisely, my *ex*-boyfriend beat a hasty retreat and never set foot near either one of us again). Makeup compacts, hurled in the heat of battle, left multicolored blotches on pristine white walls, their shattered remains littering the polished wood floors of the hallway between our bedrooms. One struck her dead-center in the forehead (I played fast-pitch softball), leaving a perfect red circle that later bruised.

And the coup-de-grâce: a pitcher of cherry Kool-Aid hurled from five feet away, staining silver taffeta and cream damask alike. Mom still has not forgiven me for ruining her favorite reading chair and making Mary-Anne's dress nonreturnable. Did I set out to ruin the dress from the start of the fight? You bet your last mother-lovin' dime.

I collapsed on my bed after the fight, locking my door behind me. From the sitting room my mother's shrieks of fury, my sister's self-centered wailing, and my father's thundering expostulates promising ruination and woe carried up the stairs, but the door muffled the worst of it…the door and my own heartbroken sobs. A cold war reigned in the house for weeks afterward.

It was then that I realized they would never accept me. They would never approve of me. They would never include me. And they would never be the family I deserved because they are totally incapable of thinking of anyone other than themselves. I haven't cried once in the intervening eight years, not even when my last boyfriend called me a frigid ice queen on his way out the door.

Oh, don't pity me. Everyone whines about their dysfunctional families, but you know what? I rather suspect every damn one of us comes from a dysfunctional family of some sort, because "normal" is defined by a bunch of white coats with PhD's in psychology, hell-bent on making us all permanent victims of our pasts with no accountability for our actions and reactions when we don't fit into their neat little Ozzie-and-Harriet boxes. That isn't to say there aren't some crappy families out there, ranging from mildly crappy to complete shit-heels.

There just is no Saturday-matinee perfect family, that's all I'm saying.

I pause before going into my apartment, as I do after every visit to my family. I like to try to shake the negative vibes off; no way is that crew invading my sanctuary. I draw a deep breath and let it out slowly, but it's not enough. Another, and then another…and finally I'm free of them.

My own company pleases me immensely; no one to please (or disappoint), no one to intrude on my reading time. I'm a voracious reader and it doesn't matter if I've read a book eighty-nine times; I'll read it again if there's nothing else or if I get a strong urge to revisit treasured characters. An introvert to the core, that's me.

So when the doorbell rings unexpectedly when I've read barely three pages of a brand-spanking-new novel I just picked up on the way home from my parents' house, I am less than thrilled.

A glance out the peephole and my irritation vanishes. Collie and—

"Sarah!" Munchkin flings herself through the door as soon as I release the chain and turn the knob. She hits me like a whirling dervish and we barely keep our feet. I've gone from Miss Quinn (Collie insisting) to Miss Sarah (Collie relenting) to just plain Sarah (Collie capitulating).

I swing her up onto my hip and grin down at her. She's precious, with gorgeous Latin-black hair and large, dark eyes. Her mother is a naturalized citizen, originally from Mexico, and her Latin blood combined with Collie's Black Irish heritage created perfection in Megan. Smooth, rich *café au lait* skin, dark espresso eyes, a cascade of thick, near-black hair falling in ringlets halfway down her back. Collie's going to have his hands full with this one. I'll bet he already has the shotgun picked out and a draft in the works of the rules for dating his daughter.

"Are we intruding?" Collie asks belatedly.

"Nah. I just got back from my parents' a little while ago."

"I know." He tips me a wink, and it dawns on me that his visit wasn't as spontaneous as I'd thought. I've never told Collie about my childhood, about the emotional neglect and the verbal battering, but somehow—perhaps in the things I've never mentioned—he's caught on to the fact that things are less than okay on the home front. Any time I've mentioned I'm making a visit home, he either shows up or calls afterward. It never occurred to me until tonight that he's been trying to chase away my ghosts.

"We came to make cookies," he says, holding up a plastic grocery bag stuffed with all the necessities. "You up for it?"

"Yeah." I smile gratefully, forgetting all about the paperback I was irritated to abandon. I trail after him into the kitchen and watch as he and Munchkin deftly arrange their ingredients and get to work.

It turns out I don't have to do anything but watch and participate in conversation. Munchkin's a little chatterbox, which means she's sleepy. She gets the chattiest right before she conks out…and sure enough, halfway through the fourth batch of cookies, she's passed out on the sofa, covered with a lightweight velour throw.

"Bet you a dime I can get you in the shower tonight," Collie says with a positively lewd grin.

"Bet I can get you there first."

His grin goes from wicked to satanic, and without warning he scoops a handful of flour out of the five-pound bag he brought and flings it at me just as I grab the wooden spoon from the dough bowl and launch a wad of sticky chocolate chip dough at him. A cloud of flour envelopes me so that I can't see my sweet bomb hit its target. But I hear the satisfying splat and his startled yelp before I succumb to flour inhalation.

"Nice," he says, scooping cookie dough off his forehead and out of his hair—which only makes it worse since his hands are coated with flour. "Real nice, Quinn. That could have been a cookie."

"It was worth the sacrifice," I retort, chuckling and choking. He's a mess.

"You look like a ghost," he remarks.

"I don't know *what* you look like, but I'm pretty sure you got the worst of that exchange."

"Stellar." He holds my gaze, still smiling.

And God knows what comes over me. Call it a random act of boldness if you will. I reach out and take his hand, and lead him—

35

walking backward—toward the bathroom, still holding his gaze, still smiling.

He pauses at the bathroom door as though unsure he wants to follow me in, but in the end he steps across the threshold willingly. I pop open the shower stall door (thanking God I gave the stall a thorough cleaning yesterday) and turn on the water, adjusting the temperature so it's not too hot or too cold.

Collie's smile has mostly faded from his mouth but still hovers around his eyes as though he's wondering just how far I'll take this. I drop his hand and grab the front of his shirt, spinning him around as my fingers slip the first button from its moorings.

He opens his mouth, possibly to protest, and I give him a hearty shove backwards. His foot catches on the inch-high lip of the tiled shower base and he stumbles right underneath the spray with a surprised shout.

"Shampoo's on the rack. You owe me a dime, Tate."

I close the door behind me, immensely satisfied to have bested him for once, gratified to hear his whoop of laughter follow me down the hallway.

EVER NOTICE CUPID RHYMES WITH STUPID?

A strange phenomenon occurs around certain holidays, specifically Valentine's Day and Christmas. People begin acting weird. Conversations are started randomly and sometimes abandoned mid-sentence, an action that would be deemed rude any other time of the year. Men flirt shamelessly with women, and women flirt back with a reckless lack of inhibition.

And oh, how the e-mails flow. PowerPoints with random philosophical anecdotes and precious photographs of fuzzy little animals sweeter than sugar clog e-mail inboxes. Frantic discussions interrupt the work flow to an almost alarming extent, covering such live-or-die topics as what color/style/length dress should she buy and what restaurant/movie/bar should he take her to.

As Valentine's Day approaches—heralded with an anticipatory air of a long-awaited triumph…or a disaster of epic proportions—tempers flare and patience vanishes, and even the most serene employees succumb to the edgy atmosphere in the office. Well, the exception being Sam Harrison, who seems to take every-damn-thing in stride. I don't think you could ruffle that man no matter how hard you tried, and to be honest, if he wasn't such eye candy I'd have to bonk him over the head for being so irritatingly even-keeled. Even Frannie—whom I know loves him passionately—rolled her eyes one day and muttered under her breath, "I married freaking Pollyanna."

Office romances sprout like strange flowers—or mold, in some cases—and just as rapidly dwindle out. Established romances weather sudden flash floods…or don't.

Collie and I already know about one such relationship, and I've been watching it closely—watching it slowly fall, that is, much like the Roman Empire. Gus and Gretchen are on the tips of everyone's tongues, but of course at a moderately low decibel inaudible to either of them. That's how the grapevine works.

It's tragic, really, like witnessing the demise of a mortally-wounded magnificent beast too stubborn to give up and die. They aren't going down in sensational, scandalous flames; I can't imagine Gretchen ever being anything but proper and private, and Gus is nothing but a gentleman. But going down they are, and the last count is coming soon. You can tell by how cordial they are with one another—too cordial, too careful, not like the easy way Frannie and Sam interact.

"Bet you a dime they don't make it to Valentine's Day," Collie murmurs to me in the break room one morning.

I look up in time to see the not-so-happy couple pass by, careful distance between them.

"That's not a bet I want to take part in," I reply quietly, because I'm sad for both of them.

"Yeah," he admits, "I don't really want to, either. Say, what are *you* doing for Valentine's Day?"

"Nothing much. Reading a book or something. Renting some shoot-em-up flicks, maybe."

"What kind of evening is *that*?" He makes a horrified face. "Let's go out to dinner. There's this steak house I want to try. The parents have Munchkin for the weekend; they're taking her to Disneyland."

"Wow. Will they adopt me?" I ask, only half-joking.

He grins. "If you ask nicely; my mom's a sucker for a waif in need. Let's save Disneyland for next Christmas. It's awesome at Christmas. Come on—whaddaya say? I've been cramming fast food down my throat for two months. I need a good steak."

"I thought you'd have a date or something." Well, I hadn't really *thought* he'd have a date; I more *feared* it than anything else.

He scowls at me. "Why would I do a thing like that? We'll go right from here; it's closer than if you go all the way home, and we can get on the waiting list early enough that we can eat before ten."

"That sounds promising," I reply dryly, but inside I'm doing the

Happy Dance. Dinner with Collie at a nice steakhouse on the most romantic night of the year. Even if it's not really a date, I'll still have his company, and I won't be wondering if he's out getting to know the girl of his dreams.

That's my biggest fear, you know—that he'll meet someone and be whisked away from me before I even have a chance. But paralyzing as it is, that fear doesn't stop me from choking back my feelings any time I get a wild impulse to just blurt them out. I get this logjam in my throat when I have any strong emotion about something; everything just stops short of my tongue and piles up, unsaid but felt so strongly that I ache. I spent so much of my childhood choking back my anger and pain that it became instinct to hold everything in. Now I freeze up anytime the situation calls for defending or expressing myself—hence the ex-boyfriend's crowning of me as the Ice Queen when he left for warmer emotional climates.

Back in my cubicle, I've barely resumed my work when Collie says in a low voice (so as not to incur the wrath of Stella): "Bet you a dime you wear a dress."

"Bet you two dimes I don't." I hate dresses. I wear them when I have to, but it's reluctantly and with discomfort. I feel so…exposed when I wear them, know what I mean?

After a moment he replies, "Big spender."

"Will you two knock it off?" Lauren complains, tossing a paperclip over the cube wall at him. "I need to talk to Sarah, Collie, so buzz off."

"*You* buzz off," he replies amiably. "You're supposed to say 'Sarah, let's get coffee' and go to the break room to have your conversation, not interrupt everyone's work so you can have your conversation."

"You weren't working, you were talking," Stella chimes in, her tone acerbic. Hannah and Allison snicker. I can hear Allie typing rapidly, so when I get an instant message from her, it's no surprise. She's faster when she's not keying from copy.

ALLIE: *So…do I understand that correctly? Did Collie ask you out for Valentine's Day?*

Lauren comes into my cubicle and I motion her to wait while I reply. She leans against my desk and reads as I type.

ME: *I don't know what you think you heard, but it's not a date. Just hanging together.*

ALLIE: *Hanging where?*

ME: *Some new steakhouse he wants to try. He said watching shoot-em-ups and reading was no way to spend Valentine's Day.*

ALLIE: *Sarah, you're so naïve. I heard him on the phone two weeks ago asking his parents to take Munchkin this weekend so he could make plans. He might have seemed casual about it, and he might have made it seem like a night of "just friends," but he planned this out.*

I look up at Lauren, who lifts a brow and gives me the thumbs-up.

ME: *Maybe those plans fell through and I'm just the back-up. Ever thought of that?*

Lauren snorts and shakes her head.

"Hey, are you guys talking about me over there?" Collie calls out, eliciting a disgusted snort from Stella.

"Not everything's about you, stud muffin," she says drolly. "I'm going to get coffee. And I mean I'm *really* going to get coffee. If anyone follows me, I'll put thumbtacks in your Hershey's kisses."

She whisks away and we all snicker—in low voices, so she can't hear us. We never know with Stella if she's serious or just messing with us. And she's been a right crab-ass the last couple of months as her wedding looms closer.

ALLIE: *You disgust me. Go talk with Lauren before she has a nervous breakdown.*

Chuckling, I stand up, looking toward her cube. She's standing too; she rolls her eyes and I pretend to scratch my nose with my middle finger. She grins and ducks back down into her chair as Stella comes back. I grab my coffee cup and Lauren's arm, and drag her off to the break room.

"What so important you couldn't talk to me in my cube?"

"I didn't want Collie to hear. He'd try to set something up, and I don't want anyone to interfere."

"Set what up? What are you talking about?"

"What do you know about Stewart?"

"Stewart? Stewart who?" I rack my brain for a mental image to go with the name, but nothing comes.

"*Stewart!*" she repeats impatiently. "You and Collie call him Wonder Geek."

"Oh! Wonder Geek! What about him?"

"Does he have a girlfriend? Or probably more importantly, is he straight?"

Oh yes, that is indeed the more important question. A girlfriend can be gotten rid of; gayness—well, that's not so easily surmountable.

"Far as I know."

Lauren leans across the table, her expression intense. "Tell me everything you know."

"It's not like he tells me all his deep dark secrets, Lauren. I barely know the guy. Frannie knows him better—maybe you should ask her."

"Are you kidding me? You know Frannie; something would *just slip out* during conversation, and the cat's out of the bag."

I see a problem with this way of thinking. "Well, Lauren…isn't the cat going to be out of the bag if you end up getting a date with him?"

Lauren's face scrunches into a frown, and I have to fight down a wave of laughter; she looks like one of those smashed-face cats. "My God, why do I even ask you anything? You call that help?" And she flounces away, stomping back to her cubicle, her temper piqued.

Back in my own chair, I contemplate an act of subtle—or not so subtle—revenge. I even bring up the online employee directory and look up Stewart Drummond's extension. My hand hovers over the phone…and then falls away. What do I think I'm doing anyway? I can barely order pizza let alone spill a friend's secret to a guy I hardly know.

I shake off my irritation and go back to work. Lauren's not the only one who's succumbed to the office tension; the whole damn company feels like a powder keg about to blow. It's nothing personal.

But the e-mail that comes into my inbox a few minutes later *is* personal—*highly* personal. Not to me, but to others in the company. At first I ignore the little e-mail notification in the tray at the lower right of my screen because I'm recording keystrokes for a video training clip. But when Collie gives a low whistle, Allie murmurs "Holy shit!" and Stella exits her cube at top speed, her chair crashing into the partition between her and Collie with enough force to rattle the whole cube farm, I know something's up. She meets up with Frannie and both disappear into Gretchen's office, the door closing behind them with a loud bang.

I bring up my inbox and click on the unread e-mail, which comes up slowly because there's a picture inserted. The subject line says "The Naked Truth," and it's been sent to everyone in the company. Because the addresses are listed individually in the *To* field and not from a system group, it's fairly obvious that they were copied from the employee directory on the company website and that this came from outside the system.

And then the picture loads. My mouth drops open in shock and I'm only vaguely aware of Collie wheeling his chair into my cube.

"Guess it's a good thing you didn't take my bet, Quinn," he says soberly, his eyes on my monitor.

"Guess so."

My screen is filled with an image of Gretchen Clark, but it's a Gretchen I've never seen before—and never had any desire to see. The lighting is intimate—as is her pose: her head tipped back, eyes half-closed, her dark hair swirling down her back in rich, gleaming waves. Her blouse is half-off her shoulder, revealing a spaghetti-thin black bra strap.

And the man with her, his lips pressed to the bare upper swell of her breast, is *not* Gus Haldemann. The date stamp in the lower right-hand corner says the photograph was taken eight days ago.

"Who is he?" I whisper to Collie.

"Not sure. Bet you a dime to a doughnut it's her ex-husband."

"Date stamps can be faked, can't they?"

Collie shrugs. "Sure they can."

I look up at him, glance toward Gretchen's closed office door, and then back at my monitor. I click the delete button, sending the mail to the trash bin. And then I empty the trash bin. The e-mail's left me feeling slimy, dirty, because I found myself riveted to the image in spite of the knowledge that I was witnessing a deeply private moment. The obvious arousal and intimacy in her expression strum a longing deep inside me, a longing for a relationship that inspires that kind of consuming passion.

Collie's hand on my neck, warm and gentle, brings my head up again. He nods at the monitor. "You have a good heart, Quinn," he says softly.

"Did you delete it?"

"As soon as I realized what it was."

Rapid footfalls pass my cubicle, and I look up in time to see Gus Haldemann striding past. His face is completely expressionless. He pauses at Gretchen's office, straightening his shoulders, and then knocks on the door. A moment later, he slips inside, closing the door silently behind him.

"Glad I'm not in there," I say.

"Me too. Let's go make sure there's a pot of strong coffee made. I have a feeling it's gonna be needed."

He pulls me out of my chair, and three steps out of my cube I grab his hand to stop him. "You have a good heart, Tate."

Collie smiles and I swear my heart stops beating for a timeless moment. He links our fingers and tugs me along, half a pace behind him. I have a marginal sense of guilt for feeling so exultant while Gretchen's world is falling apart as we speak, but that's the nature of love. Cupid's a lousy shot sometimes, and I came to the conclusion long ago that most of his shots find their mark in your heart or in your ass.

Guess we all know where Cupid shot Gretchen.

LOVE IS IN THE AIR…AND ON THE ROCKS

Collie's instincts about arriving at the steakhouse early pay off; we get on the waiting list and are told we have only an hour to an hour-and-a-half to wait. The lobby is jam-packed and all the seats are taken—even in the bar—so we have to stand. Luckily, I wore comfortable shoes with my slacks. Yes, slacks. Collie's two dimes are stowed safely in my purse, but knowing him, I'm reasonably sure they'll return to his pocket before the night is over.

We've been waiting for half an hour when we see a familiar face: Sam is shouldering his way through the crowd, Frannie sidling along in his wake. She sees me and grins delightedly.

"Sarah! Collie! I didn't know you'd be here."

"We came early enough to get only an hour and a half wait," I tell her. "Collie planned ahead."

"I always plan ahead. That way I'm not doing anything right now," he admits.

Frannie laughs. Sam motions to her from the hostess station and calls through the buzzing crowd, "Two hours, Frannie. Can you wait that long?"

She looks over the crowd, searching for a seat. There are numerous possibilities if some men would find a little chivalry and vacate a seat for her, but most of them studiously avoid her gaze.

"Do they have those little pager doohickeys? That way we can sit in the car."

Collie tips me a glance askance and I nod. Funny how some people can communicate without words. I see Fran and Sam do it all the time, and for some reason Collie and I can do it as well even though we don't have the same kind of relationship. Perhaps it's just that great minds tend to think alike.

"Why don't you two join us? Your wait will be shorter and we'd love the company. Unless you want to be alone," Collie amends hastily.

"That'd be wonderful!" Frannie exclaims. "We wouldn't be alone anyway. Gus will be joining us."

Gus…but not Gretchen. Collie sends me another glance, this one speaking volumes as he pushes through the crowd to join Sam at the hostess station and amend the number in our party. Apparently he was right, and Gus and Gretchen didn't make it to Valentine's Day. No explanation has been given about the photo of Gretchen; perhaps they thought it was best to have IT delete the message from all inboxes and pretend it had never happened. Easy to do when you aren't faced with a red-eyed, blotchy-faced office manager every day.

"No Gretchen?" I ask lightly, watching Frannie closely.

"No." She worries her lower lip between her teeth for a moment, frowning. "Those two are making me nuts. Just freaking work it out, that's what I keep telling them. Hard-headed doesn't even begin to describe them. You expect it with him—he's German. But her…"

"Is it that bad then?"

"Bad enough. I mean, you saw the e-mail. Turns out the little gal James left Gretchen for decided to exact a little revenge when he left *her.*" Frannie's lips twist into a smile that looks more like a grimace. She checks her phone and sighs when she finds no missed calls or texts. "Gretchen left work early today and hasn't answered my text messages. We made plans months ago for all four of us to go Red Lobster. We decided to come here instead when she bailed on us."

Collie and Sam make their way back from the hostess station and draw us to a small pocket of unoccupied space, where we scrunch together too closely to truly be comfortable.

"I don't understand it," I dive back into our interrupted conversation. "Gus seems like he's a great guy, and he's gorgeous to boot."

Collie glowers, but Frannie quirks a brow and darts a look at Sam, who smiles like he knows a delightful secret.

"Yeah, he is. A great guy, I mean," Frannie says.

More people pile into the lobby, and our pocket of space becomes even smaller. Gus finds us packed together like human sardines. He smiles and chats normally enough, but even a blind man could see the tension coiled inside him. It's in the way he holds his shoulders and clenches his jaw.

We're seated not long after he arrives, which relieves Frannie, whose feet are aching by this time. She orders a virgin margarita (our server, a diminutive blonde with way too much perk, cocks a brow at her and sends a look at her bulging stomach, to which Fran replies dryly, "I know, I know, nothing virgin about me."). I order my traditional daiquiri, and Collie asks for his Acid Trip. Sam and Gus opt for scotch, and Sam looks a little worried when Gus orders a double straight up.

"So how'd you fend off Stuckey trying to pirate away your staff to Customer Service, Fran?" Gus asks once he's downed half his drink in one swallow.

"I told him no way. He seemed to take me at my word."

"It's that look you get in your eyes," Sam says. "That 'don't fuck with me' look."

"Oh, know it well, do you, Sam?" I quip, and everyone laughs.

Sam takes a leisurely sip of his scotch, his gaze on Frannie just a little more intimate than is appropriate in public. "I could no more stop Frannie from speaking her mind than I could stop the sun rising in the east. She's definitely confident." He turns to me, pinning me with a gaze that seems to see too much. "How about you, Sarah? You seem pretty up-front here at the table, but I don't hear anything about you in the admin meetings."

I frown. "Is that bad?"

"Not so much. We used to have regular conversations about Fran."

"Did not!" she protests.

"Did so," Gus chimes in. The scotch has gone a long way toward relaxing him, and one might think he's just out having a casual evening with friends but for the high color the alcohol has put in his cheeks. "George Stuckey thinks you're just too cute for words when you get indignant."

"But Sarah," Sam continues. "You don't hear a peep about her. There must be *something* you're not happy with."

"Lots of things. But bitching isn't going to change them."

"Come on, give just a little," Gus prods. "More vacation? Sick leave? Higher pay?"

"Those are a given. I wouldn't mind company cell phones being brought back. My Verizon bill is killing me."

"Doubtful," Gus replies, twirling his empty glass on the table with a long-fingered, negligent hand. "Too many people throwing other employees' cell phones into garden fountains."

He slants a look at Frannie from under lowered lashes, and then turns his gaze to me, a wicked grin curving his mouth that makes my heart accelerate. For the first time, I notice just exactly how sinfully handsome he is.

"We're too busy spending the money once earmarked for the cell phones on alcohol for the Christmas parties," Sam says idly. Gus shoots him a murderous look, which he pretends not to see. I don't understand the meaning behind the look; obviously alcohol being served at company parties is a sore spot with Gus.

"You might want to skip the champagne punch next time," I suggest tentatively. Collie arches a brow and burning color races along my cheekbones. "Or else have a bigger sign in front of it. A girl could find lots of trouble if she doesn't realize she's drinking an alcoholic beverage."

"I *heard* about that," Gus remarks idly. His gaze bounces between Collie and me.

Sam opens his mouth, but Frannie jumps in first, almost as though trying to ward off something he's going to say. "*Heard* it? Sam and I *saw* it."

"It's okay,'" Collie assures them gamely, stretching his arm along the back of my chair in an uncharacteristic gesture of possessiveness. "I don't let Sarah drink much anymore."

"Funny…Fran has a similar problem," Sam confides.

"Do not."

"Do so," Gus contradicts her again. "I seem to recall hearing about you asking for a screaming orgasm."

"The *drink*," she insists, her face flaming, and she shoots Sam a look that tells us all he's in *big* trouble.

Our server returns and we place our orders for dinner, which arrives rather quickly considering the crowd tonight. Conversation bounces from lighthearted to philosophical and back again. An excellent dinner is followed by an exquisite dessert. Liquor flows freely, and while perhaps it's not a wise decision, we all are glad when Sam suggests we take our gang into the bar and free up a table for someone else. We all seem loath to end the night even though Gus, Collie, and I may all end up taking cabs home because we drank too much.

We wind our way through the tables to the bar, and just short of the door Frannie sucks in a shocked breath and stops dead in her tracks. Gus, behind her, isn't paying attention; he and Sam are lamenting the outcome of the Super Bowl. He rams into Frannie, nearly knocking her off her feet, barely catching her before she falls.

"Sorry, Frannie," he apologizes. "I didn't see you st—" The words die on his lips as he finally becomes aware of the scene before him.

Gretchen, her face white with shock, scoots her chair toward the windows behind her as Gus takes a step around Frannie. The man across the table from her—the man from the illicit photograph—drops his fork, the color draining from his face.

I can't blame them; Gus is a large man, broad-shouldered and strong from weight training. And angry…oh my God, is he angry. Gretchen squeezes the edge of the table, her knuckles colorless, clawing panic in her eyes.

Like a magnet drawn to steel, Gus's forward motion propels him toward her companion. And like moons in orbit around a planet, we're drawn with him. His hand clenches into a fist at his side, preparing to strike, and I don't think twice. I grab his wrist as he brings his arm back. Startled, he whirls around, and I don't think he even recognizes

49

me through the bloodlust in his eyes.

"You can't hit him," I whisper urgently. "Come on, let's just go in the bar. Please, Gus. This isn't the way to handle it."

He turns to find his way blocked by Sam and Collie, and then turns back to me. The bloodlust is gone, and a terrible pain is left in its wake.

"Who..." I trail off, not sure now is the time to ask.

"The girls' father." Strangely worded, as though Gretchen isn't the primary focus of their relationship.

"I'm sorry, Gus. Come on, let's sit down. Please."

But the bar isn't where he wants to go. He spins on his heel and heads toward the front entrance, pausing only to send one last look at Gretchen. His heart is in his eyes, and everyone can see it's broken. Tears spill down her cheeks and—can I be brutally honest here?

Good, because I don't really care if she's confused. I don't care if she's hurting too. I simply do not *care* what she's feeling. I'm watching her shatter the heart of a good man for the company of one who abandoned her and their children, and I can't even pretend to understand her choice. I mean, let's be real, right? On one hand, there's the shithead who ran off with another woman—on Valentine's Day three years ago to boot—and on the other, there's the man who put her heart back together and stood in as a father to her children.

Then he's gone into the chilly February night. Sam hesitates only long enough to have one of those silent exchanges with Frannie, and then he's off after his best friend. Frannie stares at Gretchen, biting her lip.

"Don't worry about it. Enjoy the rest of your night, Gretchen," she manages to say in a neutral tone. Her eyes swing to the ex and she nods once. I can feel a definite wintry chill even though her voice remains pleasant. "James."

And then she ushers Collie and me after Sam and Gus, pausing to draw in a deep breath of misty air—it's been raining. "Well, fuck me running," she murmurs. "I'm sorry, guys. Seems my party ruined your evening out."

"We won't ever say we were bored," Collie says with good humor.

50

"Don't sweat it, Fran. We're all friends here."

"I'd better catch up to Sam and Gus. I'll see you two on Monday." She surprises us both by kissing us each on the cheek. Her belly brushes against mine and I feel the baby kick. Then she's gone, waddling across the parking lot to Gus's truck where he and Sam are talking.

I sigh. This is why I hate Valentine's Day. Drama, drama, always drama.

Collie nudges me with his elbow. "Come on, Quinn. I'll take you home."

He doesn't leave me at the door like I expect. I mean, it's not like this is a real date, right? He follows me inside and pops a movie in the DVD player while I change into a tank top and pajama capris. And yes, I did rent two or three shoot-em-ups in the event he cancelled on me. And yes, I am a worthless blob of low self-esteem. Blah blah blah. I fully subscribe to the Boy Scout motto: always be prepared.

We're halfway through *Lethal Weapon* when I remember I was supposed to text Allison and tell her how the night went. I don't have a landline, so I hunt through my purse for my cell phone and find the battery dead, and remember that I left my charger on my desk. Figures.

"What are you doing, Quinn? *Lethal Weapon*'s on."

"I need to send Allison a text. Lemme use your cell—my battery's dead and my charger's at work." I'll tell Allie not to respond, and I can delete the message before he sees it. I grab his cell phone off my coffee table and let out a startled yell as he makes a grab for it. "What the hell, Collie?"

"I'm almost out of minutes," he protests, trying to wrest it out of my hand. I slide off the sofa and dance out of his reach.

"Bullshit. You just paid your bill three days ago, so you've got new minutes."

"How do you know that?"

"I was in your cubicle when you paid it online, remember?"

I side-step him as he comes off the sofa, making another swipe at the phone. "Stop it—it'll take just a second." I start to flip open the

51

phone, but his hand smacks it in an abortive attempt to seize it. I barely keep hold of it, and I duck under his arm, eluding him yet again.

"Dammit, Quinn! Give me my phone!"

"What's the big deal, Tate? You got porn on your phone?"

Collie's right behind me, reaching, and I dodge away, realizing my mistake too late. The only place I have to run is the bedroom. But I'm determined now to keep his phone away from him, only because he's determined that I don't open it.

"I mean it, Quinn! Give it back right now!"

Laughing, I race down the hallway and into my bedroom, keeping just out of his reach—although once or twice I feel his fingers scrabbling down my back, just barely missing grabbing the neckline of my tank top. A good thing, too—the possibility exists that if he'd managed to catch hold of it, he'd have ripped it right from my body. While that scenario has its definite advantages, I think if he rejected me after seeing me half-naked I'd die from the humiliation.

My tactical error comes from a last minute decision to break right and go around the foot of my bed to the other side. I'm already three steps to the left, so it requires backtracking, which gives Collie a distinct advantage. He sweeps my legs out from under me and I topple to earth—or rather, to the bed. He pounces, pinning me to the mattress just as I manage to flip open the phone.

My laughter dies on my lips as I see the display screen. The angle from which the photograph was taken tells me the photographer stood on the opposite side of the buffet table from us, because they were able to catch Collie's expression perfectly, while my face is turned slightly away. The quality of the photo suggests a fairly high-end digital SLR; I try to remember who had that kind of camera at the party. Funny... I don't remember anyone by the buffet table except Collie. And Henry Perkins, of course, he of the "bet you a dime you don't turn the tables on her and kiss her like you—"

I suddenly remember Collie's speedy change of word choice when he told me about his bet with Henry. This photo was snapped just as he pulled away from me, his lips a mere fraction from mine as he looks down into my eyes. He did not view our kiss with detached amusement like he would have me believe—like I *had* believed. In truth, I'm too close to him, to our relationship, to see beyond my own assumptions and insecurities. The photo gives me an objective perspective I didn't have in real life.

His hand closes over mine, snapping the phone shut, and with reluctance I drag my eyes away from it. I could look at that photograph forever—the photograph I never even knew existed—because there's something in the look on his face that makes my heart race and my hopes soar.

But I look at *him* instead, because I can feel his eyes willing me to. His hand around my other wrist tightens. I let my eyes ask the question, because I can't seem to find the breath for words.

I don't know who moves first. I don't remember, even, the moment we come together in a frenzied kiss. Passion ignites and rages uncontrolled, and I'm the last person in the world who wants to tame it. Collie's hands are everywhere, leaving fire in their wake, and it's endless moments later that I realize he's systematically undressed us both. The only thing between us now is my ladies' boxer briefs.

His eyes open, staring frankly into mine, and his hand slides over my wrist and across my palm. Our fingers twine together. We stay that way for endless moments, our eyes locked in a gaze that I'm insanely sure tells him every secret dream about him that I harbor in my heart.

"Sarah." He breathes my name on an exhale, and it shivers through me, shattering any inhibitions or reserves I might have. And what protests might I lodge, anyway? It's Collie, and I'm pretty sure I love him.

I pull him to me, expressing my willingness without words, and then there's nothing but the physical sensations he's evoking in my body—and Cupid's arrow dead center in my heart.

Tales from the Water Cooler

Sunday, February 15
Faces in the Crowd

Posted by Sarah Quinn

Let's face it: everyone has a role in the office, even if it's not one they particularly find flattering. There may be a Germaphobe, that one peculiar person who despises dirt and is constantly cleaning her office. Or there could be a Creeper—oh, you know who I mean: that person who could not move faster than time in reverse if threatened at gunpoint.

Here are the people in my office. You should make note of their "superhero" names, because for protection of the innocent and the guilty alike, I'll be using these names instead of their real ones.

Boss Lady:	She's large (pregnant) and in charge
Junior Boss:	Second in command
Wannabe:	Third in command, wants to be first
Hot Sauce:	Token male, sexy as hell
Bitter Pie:	Would crab-ass over winning lottery
Happy Wanderer:	We never know where she is
Chicken Little:	Everything's a catastrophe
Tazmanian Devil:	Don't piss her off...*please*
Mother Hen:	Everybody's (annoying) mother
Eye Candy:	Boss Lady's gorgeous hubby
Centerfold:	Most (Sort of) Eligible Bachelor
Prized Cow:	Yours truly

Know them. Keep them straight. I will be referring to them frequently. Pop quiz on Monday. Nah, just kidding.

Okay, I don't really like being called Prized Cow, but it's what Hot Sauce calls me—often to my face—because of how I was paraded around to be introduced to everyone in my first day. My cross to bear.

DID YOU KNOW:

WORD TIP: Don't mouse around! Keyboard shortcuts can cut your formatting time in half--or less. Learn the most common ones, and the chore of select, click this, click that, etc. is no longer as cumbersome.

CTRL+A:	Selects all text in a document
CTRL+S:	Saves the file
CTRL+O:	Opens the Open File dialog box
CTRL+E:	Center alignment
CTRL+L:	Left alignment
CTRL+R:	Right alignment
CTRL+J:	Justified alignment
CTRL+C:	Copies selection to the clipboard
CTRL+V:	Pastes the clipboard
CTRL+X:	Cuts the selection from the document and stores it on the clipboard
CTRL+B:	Toggles on or off bold text
CTRL+I:	Toggles on or off italics
CTRL+U:	Toggles on or off underlined text
CTRL+N:	Opens a new blank document
CTRL+H:	Opens Replace dialog box
CTRL+F:	Opens Find dialog box
CTRL+P:	Prints current document
CTRL+M:	Increases indent
CTRL+Y:	Repeats last action
CTRL+SHIFT+M:	Decreases indent
CTRL+ALT+C:	Inserts copyright symbol

These are just a few shortcuts that can make your life easier.

Blog Archive
    2009
        February

Faces in the Crowd

January

Going Postal: A Career-Limiting Move

About Me

Savvy Sarah

I am an administrative office professional with several years' experience in office settings. I have an AAS in Administrative Office Management and currently work as a training specialist for a software development company in Los Angeles.

MEANWHILE, BACK AT THE OFFICE...

Of course the inevitable had to happen. Collie, damn his black heart, gave me up to the cause and outed my artistic talents to Frannie. To learn I can draw and paint cheered her considerably after she came back from the Adminisphere meeting during which they drew out of a hat assigned themes for the golf tournament ("In much the same way they make executive decisions," Frannie muttered at one point). Our theme is an enchanted hedge maze, and I'm resigned to the fact that I'm going to be neck-deep in leprechauns, elves, and fairies for the next three and a half weeks.

The catastrophe of Valentine's Day only four days behind us, Gretchen looks as though she's in the midst of an emotional maelstrom. I haven't seen Gus; he avoids our floor and if he needs to see Frannie for something, he summons her to his office rather than making the trip up. I'll bet Gus and Gretchen's home-life is tense right now, if indeed they're still cohabitating. I feel bad for Gretchen's girls; I've seen them with Gus and from all appearances they adore him.

Somehow I have to fit in all the decorating for the tournament around my workload, which means I spend most of my off-hours drawing mythical creatures and designing backgrounds of laurel hedges to transfer onto butcher paper with the help of a projector. I also spend a lot of time in the basement storage, wandering the labyrinth of shelves looking for anything that can be of any use.

Which is where I am now, scouring the depths for a roll of black poly sheeting Stella is sure she sent into Harper & Lyttle purgatory years ago. This is the height of frugalness (or cheapskatedness, if you will); poly sheeting only costs about fifteen bucks a roll, whereas the time I'm spending hunting for it is quickly tripling that cost.

So engrossed am I in my search that I don't hear the—what's that? Oh, you want to know about Collie and me. Well, that would be kissing and telling… All right, all right! He stayed the night, we had breakfast at some new neighborhood café the next morning, and then he went golfing with his brother, leaving me with a kiss and a wink and a whole helluva lot of questions and concerns. He has not touched me since, and thank you for asking—nothing like a little salt in a raw wound. Now, back to the present…

So engrossed am I in my search that I don't hear the door of the basement storage open or the footsteps come down the stairs. I'm more than startled when I make my way out of the maze of castoff detritus to find Gretchen sitting on the steps, her arms clasped around her knees and her chin propped in the small dip where her knees are pressed together. She's not crying, but it's obvious she's done her share over the last few days. She doesn't seem surprised to see me, which should have been my first clue that she's sought me out, but frankly I have my own personal distractions so it really should be no surprise that I miss the cue.

"I'm sorry, Gretchen. I didn't mean to intrude on your alone time." I start to sidle past her on the stairs, but she grabs my hand to stop me as I go by.

"Will you sit for a minute?"

"Sure," I say gamely, sitting down beside her and wishing I was anywhere but here.

She lets go of my hand and hugs her knees again. I admit I'm still angry at her, even though it's none my business, but her obvious anguish lets me see her in a more sympathetic light for the first time.

"You think less of me because of Valentine's Day, don't you?" she says at length.

"It's not any of my business, Gretchen."

"It doesn't stop you from forming an opinion," she replies, her tone morose.

I draw in a sharp breath through my nose. "All right. I just don't understand how you could be indecisive about a man who seems as

58

terrific as Gus Haldemann, and even entertain the thought of doing anything but collect child support from the man who ran out on you and your children." I pause. "But then, I have no idea what Gus is like to live with, so…."

She smiles faintly, sadly, her eyes looking into the gloom of the basement but clearly seeing something in her mind. "He's terrific, everything a woman could wish for. He's just not…my wish."

"But why—" I stop, remembering that it's none of my business.

"I didn't go to that restaurant with James. I thought Frannie, Sam, and Gus were going to Red Lobster, so it seemed a safe enough bet that I could have an evening alone. Sometimes you just need time with yourself. Do you ever feel that way?"

"I do." Especially after I've been to see my parents.

"When the hostess asked if she could seat another single diner at my table, it seemed selfish to say no. I never dreamed it would be James."

I study her face in the weak white-yellow light from the fluorescent overhead, noting the way guilt tightens her expression. She may not have known James was the solitary diner the hostess wanted to seat with her, but she was not sorry it was him. Not only that….

"It's not the first time you've been in contact with him recently, is it, Gretchen?"

My quiet question falls between us and lays like an ugly stain in the ensuing silence. Finally, she shakes her head.

"He called me a few months ago out of the blue and asked if he could see the girls. He's authorized visitation in the divorce, you see, but he's never asked before. I told him I would have to think about it—I mean, Sarah, he's virtually a stranger to Beatrice! She was just a baby when he left us. He asked to see me then, said he wanted to talk to me."

"And so you agreed," I deduce.

Gretchen nods. "I can't explain to someone who doesn't have children the connection you feel toward the father of your kids. He's not Gus, he's probably not even half the man Gus is, but…he's the girls' father. He was my husband for almost eleven years." She shrugs.

"Gus worries about the girls, worries James will hurt them again."

"Gretch, what *about* the girls? They've been with Gus for more than two years now. And where was James during all this time? Writing child support checks and living like he has no responsibility, letting another man raise his children."

"I know. But Gus and I...well." She heaves a quavering sigh. "We knew early on it wouldn't work between us, but... I couldn't handle everything all on my own. For two years now we've been nothing but roommates sharing the responsibility of raising my children. And he helped, he didn't mind, he just wanted us to be safe, but—" Tears well up and spill from her eyes.

"I want my life back! I never wanted things to change, but they did and I had to live with it for years and now I have a chance to have it all back!"

She starts to cry in earnest. There's one thing I'm gloriously good at: even if I can't express my own emotions very well, I can manage other people's. I put my arm around her and rub her back with my hand, letting her cry and babble, murmuring soothing responses as appropriate. My heart is doubly torn now for both of them.

"Just be careful, Sarah. That's all I wanted to tell you. Be careful, because Collie's daughter has another parent. Men are strange when it comes to the mothers of their children."

"I don't think they ever had that kind of relationship, Gretch, but I'll take your advice to heart. Are you all right?"

"Well enough." She manages a tremulous smile. "Go on back; I'm just going to sit here for a while."

I squeeze her shoulder as I leave and steal one last glance at her as she huddles on the stair, looking small and forlorn. As I go back to my cube, I contemplate how we sometimes tend to see things in black and white when we're outside a situation, but really there are many shades of grey in between, nuances we can't discern or know unless we're participants. My judgment of Gretchen now seems harsh and flawed, and shame makes me squirm a little in my skin.

Back in my chair, I fire off an e-mail to Stella, copied to Frannie, that I couldn't find the poly sheeting and our decorating budget will just have to take a hit. A moment later Collie whispers, *"Pssst! Quinn!"*

"What?"

"Bet you a dime you need a drink after work."

"No bet."

"Tony's? I'll drive."

"So you can get the DUI instead of me?"

"I'm not the one who needs a drink."

"All right, then." I smirk silently to myself.

Allie pops up in her cube, making kissing motions toward me to tease, and Collie stands up, catching her. She pops back into her chair, face flaming.

"It's all right," Collie calls out to her. "You guys can come too."

My smirk fades, but Collie's already sat back down. I'm starting to wonder if Cupid didn't hit me in the same damn place he hit Gretchen. What can you expect from a freaking naked cherub who flies around shooting arrows at people, anyway? A menace to society, if you ask me.

With a heavy sigh, I release the catch on my seat back, close my eyes, and recline backward as far as I can go—a hazardous act in any circumstances, since the seat can turn on you at any given moment and spill you in a humiliated heap on your cubicle floor. But I'm tired and Collie's distance since Valentine's Day stings more than a little.

When I open my eyes, I find a pair of legs, clad in neatly pressed black trousers, inches from my face. I sigh again. Grey eyes peer at me with mild amusement, sparking some recollection deep in my memory that I can't quite bring to the surface, but the rest of his face remains impassive. I admire Gus Haldemann the control he possesses over his feelings; perhaps it's the emotional reservist in me that recognizes a kindred spirit.

"Can I talk to you privately for a minute, Sarah?" he asks politely. Great—first one and now the other.

"Sure. Er…if I can get upright again, that is," I reply with a rueful smile. Reclining is much easier than sitting back up.

Gus leans down and engages the lever. The back of the seat springs up with force, flinging me halfway out of my chair and into my desk.

"Settle down over there!" Hannah sings out. My cube mates muffle their snorts of laughter—those who laugh, anyway, which is all of them except Brooke, who never laughs at anything, and Collie, who is strangely silent.

"Wow. Who needs Disneyland when we have office chairs?"

"I'm sorry. Sometimes they're a little more forceful than you expect. Are you all right?"

"Yeah. What's a broken rib among friends? Shall we?"

He steps out of my cube and waits for me to precede him (*impeccable manners*, my mind notes for some odd reason). I go a fair distance down the hallway and stop near the water fountain, still within view of Collie's and Stella's cubes. I don't do this because I'm afraid of him, but because I don't want anyone starting rumors about us. I turn my back to the cube farm, leaning against the wall.

Gus clears his throat, looking endearingly uncertain and a trifle embarrassed. It's crystal clear, in that moment, why most of the women in the company have crushes on him.

"I wanted to thank you for the other night. For not letting me hit him. That would have been a bad scene, and I'm sure we all would have regretted it."

And Gus would have regretted it from jail cell, I'd wager, because Gretchen's ex-husband looks like the weasel type who'd press charges rather than take the licks he has coming.

"Not a problem. I didn't want you to do anything you'd need a lawyer for."

He smiles, and some of the weariness falls from his expression. *Gretchen, you fool!* I think with a vehemence that surprises me. I don't know what it is about certain women that makes them go for the guy who treats them like dog shit and shaft the perfectly handsome, sexy, charming man like this one. I vowed long ago, after the prom date incident with my sister, that I would never go for the asshole, and so far I've kept that promise to myself. It's meant not dating very often, but at least it's saved me all the drama and heartache.

"So if there's anything I can do to help," and he flicks a glance at

Collie, "just let me know."

I look over my shoulder at Collie. He's got his tie off again and is leaning over the cubicle wall between us, doing something with the discarded length of silk on my side of the wall.

"I don't think there's anything you can do to help *that* one," I remark dryly, turning back.

Gus takes a step closer, tantalizing my nose with some faint but heavenly musky scent. Another random thought crosses my mind: *a man who knows how to wear cologne*. Don't ask; I don't know. My mind throws these odd things out every now and then. Twenty years from now, I might not even remember Gus's name, but I will remember that he had impeccable manners and smelled delightful.

"How about I stand really close to you while I talk to you? Maybe that will help."

I chuckle. "I doubt he'd even notice."

"He's noticing."

"Well, it may help *my* situation, but I doubt it will do wonders for yours."

He draws in a deep breath and lets it out slowly, adding enticing cinnamon to the musk cologne. Damn, five more minutes of this and I may just forget *Collie's* name. *The difference between men and boys*, my mind babbles.

"There's nothing that will help my situation," he says heavily. "It's only a matter of time before she leaves. I guessed it would end up like this two years ago, but….."

That three-letter word holds a wealth of information. *But* he'd gone the distance anyway. He may play it close to the vest with public displays of his feelings, but he's no coward when going for something he wants.

He shrugs unhappily. "But the girls needed some stability, and Gretchen couldn't give it, so I did what I could. I'm not a naïve man; she'll go back to James. It's just a matter of time before she figures out how to tell me."

"I'm really sorry, Gus."

He stares at me for a silent, intense moment, then replies, "I believe you really are. Thank you for that, Sarah." He smiles suddenly and with a quick nod, walks away. I watch him go, breathing in the fading musk-and-cinnamon until I can no longer detect it, and then slowly walk back to my cube.

My Rubik's cube, that old throwback from the Eighties, has been lynched with Collie's tie from my flat screen monitor. Two sticky notes with hastily drawn eyes sprouting outrageous lashes have been pasted on either side of the tie just above the Cube, which forms the nose of this surrealist work of art.

"Cute, Tate."

"Mmmm. So what did Gus the Great want?"

"Gus the Great? Really, Collie." I can't help but chuckle. "He just wanted to thank me for not letting him pound on Gretchen's ex on Valentine's Day."

"I guess that required standing less than an inch away from you."

"Apparently so."

He's silent for a moment, then mutters, "Lecher."

I smile and tuck the Post-It eyes into my desk drawer.

8

A MEASURE OF WORTH

"Crap."

Collie looks up from my Rubik's Cube, to which he's affixing Hanukkah stickers. Colorful pictures of dreidels, menorahs, and letters of the Hebrew alphabet are now stuck haphazardly over the original primary colors. There is no rhyme or reason to the order in which he's placed the stickers, much like I'm beginning to suspect there's no rhyme or reason to the way Collie's brain works. And before you ask, neither one of us is Jewish. I have no idea why he has Hanukkah stickers.

"What's wrong?"

"I just got an e-mail from Frannie. Performance evaluation today at one. Er…is it normal to have an eval in Human Resources?" I'm mildly alarmed that the meeting is located in HR; easier to give you your walking papers without you causing a scene, I guess.

"Ah. Your probationary period is over. This is the one and only time you'll have an eval in HR, unless you become a disciplinary problem. Which," he adds in a tone of disapproval, "you would never be."

"You say that like it's a bad thing." I click to accept the meeting, and then spin around in my chair to find him looming behind me. There's a sticker of a menorah on his pants leg. He leans over my chair, bracing his hands on the arms, until he's nose-to-nose with me.

"Not a *bad* thing. Just a *safe* thing."

"Safe's not good?" I arch a brow at him, but I'm not particularly interested in his answer. I'm projecting my most powerful *Kiss me! Kiss me, dammit!* thought in his direction.

"I know they say 'better safe than sorry,' but what if you end up sorry that you were so safe? You can be too careful in life and end up never living."

"So, in order to fully live I must be a troublemaker," I deduce.

"It's a start. I say we begin your descent into hoodlumity by wreaking havoc in the basement."

He leans in closer, his nose brushing the side of mine, his lips tantalizingly close. Maybe he's waiting for me to close the gap, but it's not going to happen. I'm still a little annoyed at him for backing off after our night together. Even our bowling expeditions and shared lunchtimes have tapered off.

"Whaddaya say, Quinn?"

"Hoodlumity? That isn't a real word."

"Sure it is. Look it up." He straightens and tugs me out of my chair, glancing around to make sure we're not noticed, and pulls me along behind him into the hallway.

The elevator door opens just as we reach it, spilling out a number of suits and skirts in various shades of somber blues, greys, and basic black. We filter our way through them and into the elevator car, and Collie pushes the glowing B to send us to the basement.

"On what are we going to wreak havoc?"

"I'm pretty sure I saw another Dictatorphone in one of the far reaches of Wild Kingdom down there. If I'm not mistaken, Evelyn Harper still wants to you transcribe."

"She tried to rent one, but the rental companies were fresh out. Bizarre but true. Then she went out of town, so it hasn't been an issue."

"Well, we are going to find it today, Quinn. Do you feel lucky?"

"That remains to be seen, Callahan." Come on, tell me you got that reference. I wasn't even born when that movie came out, but it *is* a shoot-em-up flick and I've seen it no less than eight times in my young life.

Collie chuckles and slants me a look from the corner of his eye as the door slides open. He ushers me out ahead of him and into Wild Kingdom we go.

Our "search the grid" method must not have worked very well last time, because I'm quite sure we never went into this particular corner, although granted, we didn't search the entire basement.

"Where is it?"

"Right here," Collie says, reaching around me to lay a hand on the aging Dictaphone, stuffed between a metal file organizer and an untidy stack of alphabetizers that should have been thrown away roughly around 1985. "I wonder if it even works."

"Maybe. We should take it up with us." I start to grab it off the dusty shelf, but he quickly shoves me forward. "Collie!"

"We'll get it on our way out. I want to show you something else." His hands on my shoulders and the toes of his shoes nearly kicking my heels, he guides me ahead of him and around a corner into an alcove. An ancient metal desk, a relic from the 1970s, is pushed into the farthest reaches of the dead-end, but there's little else.

"There's nothing back here."

"*We're* back here. I wouldn't say we're nothing. Come on—I'll boost you up." He turns me around and lifts me onto the desk.

"What for?"

"Makes this a little easier," he says, lifting a brow, and moves in close. I barely have time to register his wicked grin before he's kissing me. This time there's no Henry waiting to hand over his dime, no colleagues marking every detail to speed along the grapevine. There's just him and me and a bunch of wild, reckless thoughts I have no business thinking while I'm at work.

A long while later, he lifts his head and gives me a typical Collie grin.

"What the hell are you doing?" I force out the words. I'm no confrontationist, but after all the mixed signals he's been sending since Christmas, this is too much.

"I thought that was obvious, but if you're in any doubt, I'd be overjoyed to repeat it." He leans in again, but I push him back.

"Who'd you bet this time?"

He narrows his eyes on my face and nods knowingly. "Ah. That stung, didn't it?"

"I'm going to sting *you*—"

"Whoa, Quinn. You're scaring me. I knew it stung; your smile went all weird when I told you about the bet with Henry. And you've been less than thrilled with me since we…since Valentine's Day. I just thought I'd make up for it."

"You can't just go around kissing me, Collie!"

"Why not? You didn't seem to be objecting. Besides, we did a hell of a lot more than kissing not so long ago."

I roll my eyes in exasperation. "Do you go around kissing and…and…"—I wave my hand expressively—"all your female friends?"

"Going all girly on me again, Quinn?" He takes his hands from my waist and holds them up like a bagged criminal. "All right. No more kissing." Now that isn't precisely what I meant, and by his truly satanic expression, he damn well knows it. "I can see you're going to be high maintenance."

"High maintenance!" I sputter indignantly. "Collie, you've been avoiding me since we…since we slept together." I don't know why that's so hard to say, but both of us seem to be having trouble spitting it out in direct terms. Hot color burns in my cheeks.

"Ah. Come to terms with it, have you?"

"What?"

"You were acting really weird the morning after, so I assumed you were regretting it. Now I admit I don't have the finesse of, say, Cassanova, but I personally found no fault with either the technique or the emotion that inspired it. I admit, however, that it's possible you didn't find it nearly as—"

"Collie!" He shuts up. "I—I—" I draw in a breath, trying to steady my nerves. "I didn't know *how* to act. I've never *had* a morning after." The blush in my face becomes itchy and painful, it's so intense. "The only other guy I've…well…it was the night before he left for boot camp. He was gone when I woke up."

He stares at me, speechless for a long moment. "Well, Sarah. That puts things in perspective." He cups his hand over my cheek, his thumb stroking my cheekbone. "If it makes a difference, I was unsure myself. I didn't plan that. I wanted to go slow. I…Afterward, I worried about how careless I'd been. I was careless once in the past, and the result of that incident calls me Daddy."

"That's not a concern," I hastily interject. My blush is deepening again, and my throat is starting to close up.

His other hand comes up, smoothing my other cheek, and he bends to me again, kissing my forehead. "You're the color of a tomato, Sarah, and you're wheezing. Let's get the Dictatorphone and go get your inhaler. We can talk about this tonight when Munchkin and I come over to watch a movie."

I narrow my eyes. "*What* movie?" The last time they came with movie in hand, I was stuck in Disney princess hell for an hour.

"*Madagascar*, I think. I can recite the entire dialogue if you want."

"Don't ruin it for me, eh?"

He lifts me off the desk and slides me against the length of his body as he lowers me to the floor. His eyes hold mine steadily.

"Let's just be careful, Sarah. 'Kay?"

"Okay. I'd just thought—"

"You thought wrong." He kisses me again, and things are getting truly interesting when we hear the snick of the basement door closing and footsteps coming down the steps. Collie lifts his head and gives me a wry look. "You gotta be kidding."

"Story of my life," I whisper. "Every damn time I come down here, it turns into Grand Central Station. I never knew the basement was such a hot spot."

He grins, tightening his arms around me as he kisses me again. No reason why, if we maintain self-control, we can't remain undetected until the interloper has left. And things seem to be going well in that regard until…

"Shit! Shit shit *shit!*"

The frustrated rage in the man's voice is nothing compared to the physical manifestation of his mental state. Shelves clatter, plastic file trays shatter, a plastic pencil can bounces down our aisle, ricochets off the wall, and rolls to a stop at our feet. Collie turns around, keeping me behind him in case the violent episode spills into our corner.

But with one last item shattered against the cement wall, the outburst ends. The man's labored breathing calms. Collie is about to take a cautious step forward when a cell phone chimes. Horror-struck, he looks at me, but it's neither of ours: mine is in my purse in my cubicle, and his—in his pocket—is silent.

The man huffs out a sigh. "Gus Haldemann."

Collie and I exchange a look of surprise. *Gus?* He of the iron emotional control, just wreaked havoc in the boneyard of Harper & Lyttle? Holy *crap!*

"I'm running an errand, but I'll be back up in a few minutes." He snaps his phone shut with no goodbye and heaves another sigh, probably as he surveys the wreckage.

His footsteps crunch over the debris littering the floor, kicking something out of his way, and then he's gone. Collie peers around the corner tentatively and groans.

"C'mere, Quinn. Get a load of *this* mess."

The devastation is worse than I'd imagined but not as bad as it could have been considering the racks of office equipment and supplies within easy reach.

"Should we clean it up?"

"After your eval, maybe. Grab that evil Dictatorphone and come on."

Sweeping shattered plastic shards out of my way as I go, I make my way to the shelf. Where the Dictaphone sat only a few minutes ago is a clean spot on an otherwise dusty shelf.

"Collie, it's gone."

"What?" He strides back, looks at the dust-free spot on the shelf that's exactly the size of the Dictaphone. "No. That is entirely *too* coincidental."

Maybe it is, but nevertheless, we find the remains of the Dictaphone under a shelving unit where Gus kicked it out of his way.

"Between those two, we're never going to keep one intact." I toe the remains and shrug. "I think I'll just suggest Evelyn send the stupid tapes out to a dictation service. I hate transcribing anyway."

And later, as fate would have it, my evaluation is with Frannie and

Gus. We sit in a small arrangement of wingback chairs in his office, me across from Gus, Frannie adjacent to both of us, and in his expression I see none of the turbulent emotion he let loose in the basement. As he pages through the performance evaluation Frannie has prepared for this momentous event (and why the hell are these things so long, anyway? Either I'm doing a good job or I'm not. Seems to me a paragraph or two would suffice to sum that up), he nods a couple of times, and then frowns.

"What is it, Gus?" Fran asks.

"Has Sarah read through this yet?"

She sends a glance my way and shakes her head. "Not yet. I wanted you to nitpick it first, but we ran out of time before the meeting."

"Yes. I had an…errand to run."

And it could be my imagination, but I'm pretty sure he flicks a glance at me. Frannie pulls a stapled packet from her notebook and hands it to me. I'm getting nervous now. If it was a glowing review, why would Gus frown and ask if I've seen it.

Midway through the evaluation—which is indeed glowing—I find what made him frown. *Learning developed products to the level needed to prepare training materials is not progressing as quickly as anticipated. Sarah should be able to open the programs and teach herself from the ground up, but still requires quite a lot of assistance.* My cheeks burn in embarrassment but the words jam in my throat.

"What's the problem, Gus?" Fran prods, whipping out her pencil and notepad.

He pages through the eval again and shakes his head. "Just thought I'd check again. I don't see the certification that she's been through the development orientation."

"Devel—" Her face goes quite blank. "I could have sworn you did that within your first two weeks here, Sarah."

I swallow over the lump in my throat. "They cancelled the training due to some conflict and said they would reschedule me. They never did. Quite honestly, I forgot all about it."

"I would have, too," Gus interjects. "Sarah, the development

71

orientation introduces you to the software the company writes. Most of the attributes are fairly unique to this company and are used in all of the products. That you've managed to learn what you have so far without the training is more indicative of your job performance than what you *haven't* learned. Would you agree, Fran?"

"Yes. I'm so sorry, Sarah. I didn't realize you'd never received your training. I'm usually on top of these things. I'll amend this right away. Would you like to set up another time to meet, Gus?"

"No, I think we've covered everything that needs to be addressed. Once that's amended and Sarah signs, send it to me for her permanent file." He smiles at me. "Welcome to permanent purgatory, Sarah."

"Gus!" Frannie exclaims and laughs. "You can't say that!"

"I just did. Now, if we're done, Fran, I'd like to have a word with Sarah before she goes back to work."

Fran's smile dims a little and she looks resigned. "Sure. I'll see you back in the department, Sarah." She gathers her stuff and scoots to the edge of her seat. Gus stands and gives her an arm up, and she waddles to the door. I can barely remember what she looks like not pregnant, but she's cute as hell with her round belly and her penguin-like gait.

When he takes his chair again, he levels a look at me, his smile gone. "Your supervisor is responsible to make sure you receive the training. You have the right to file a formal letter of complaint against Frannie for the oversight."

My mouth drops open in shock. "Why would I do that? It was a simple mistake."

"Still, she should not have marked it as fulfilled unless she had written notification of your attendance."

His face is as impassive as ever, and for a nauseating moment I have the strong desire to smack him. I know he feels; I've seen it, and the results of it. But damn, his poker face is extraordinary—and extraordinarily annoying at this particular moment.

"I don't want to file a complaint," I manage.

He relaxes, and only then I realize how tense he was. "I'm glad. This day has been bad enough as it is."

"I'm sorry."

"You keep saying that, but try as I might I can't figure out why you're sorry when you haven't done anything." His smile takes the sting out of his words. "I did want to ask you about something else before you go. You weren't going to speak up about not receiving the training. You were just going to take the eval as it was. Why?"

I shrug uncomfortably. "It's not a big deal."

"I beg to differ. If you're doing a good job, you should receive credit for it. Your measure of worth is something that should be defended, Sarah."

I don't say anything; what can I say, anyway? He's right, but I doubt it will change the way I am—nothing short of years of therapy will, and there's no chance of that. I think shrinks are a bunch of whack jobs.

He lifts his chin, his eyes narrowed on my face. "Mmm. In any case, your evaluation will be amended, and once I receive it I'll send you a packet that outlines the additional benefits permanent employees receive. Do you have any questions?"

"No. Thank you." I'm out of my chair and halfway to the door before his voice stops me again.

"Sarah."

Crap. If he pulls out one of those damn Employee Action Resources (EAR) pamphlets and tells me I can get confidential counseling at the expense of my employer, I'm going to use it to torture him to death. Death by paper cuts.

"Thank you for not saying anything about the basement. I'll clean it up later."

Startled, I look up. His poker face has dropped away, but he doesn't look embarrassed. He looks desperately unhappy.

"How did you know I was there?"

A corner of his mouth twitches up. "Your perfume. Very distinctive scent; I remember it from Valentine's Day. It seems that our talk the other day…ah…helped."

"Yes, it did. How did you know it would?"

"As a man of experience, I'm well aware that men take notice of women other men show an interest in."

"So I've heard."

"Best of luck then, Sarah-Jane Quinn," he says softly, and my skin prickles into gooseflesh at his intimate tone. What is it about perfect, powerful men—and make no mistake, he *is* powerful, at least in terms of the Harper & Lyttle kingdom—that makes women desire them? And I'm not immune, regardless of my feelings for Collie.

"Thank you."

I slip out the door and into the elevator, where I sag against the shiny, stainless steel wall. The metal is cool against my flaming face. It's almost as though I was sucked into a vortex that's turned everything in my life inside out from the moment I saw Frannie and Sam in that steakhouse on Valentine's Day. Up is down, left is right, and then there's this strange pull I feel toward a man who has no reason to notice me but has taken an odd form of interest in me.

I give Collie the thumbs-up as I pass his cube, certain that the worst part of the day is past.

My doorbell rings at half-past seven. I've already made popcorn and a quick batch of fudge for movie time. Munchkin flings herself inside, as she always does, wrapping her arms around my legs.

Collie smiles ruefully and holds up the featured attraction: *Barney's Imagination Island.*

Kill. Me. Please.

9

THAT'S NOT IN MY JOB DESCRIPTION

"Do you think she's going to drop that baby right here?" Allison murmurs close to my ear.

We've been watching Frannie all morning, and she looks tired and heavy, slow in the way that pregnant women are when they're about to deliver. But, being the workaholic that she is, none of us figured she would allow that baby out until after this silly golf tournament.

"Dunno. I've never had a baby before, so I couldn't tell you. But she *does* look like she's dragging ass."

"She's taking it way too easy. You know how she is—right in the thick of things even when she's dog-ass tired. I think she's going to go into labor...if she isn't there already."

"Want me to go ask her?" I offer, hoping she doesn't. Frannie's usually pretty even-keeled (Sam's influence, I'd bet), but pregnant women are unpredictable at best and can turn on you without warning or provocation...much like a rabid dog.

Besides, Gus Haldemann is sitting in the chair next to her, right outside her office, observing the decorating with a keen eye and cracking jokes with Fran. If she wasn't all right, he'd probably be the first—right after Sam—to notice.

"Yeah, why don't you?" she asks, taking my end of the butcher paper we're hanging over the black poly sheeting draping the cube walls.

The department is a mess and no work is getting done because the golf tournament is tomorrow and we have to decorate—and both Stella and Gretchen have taken personal days. While other divisions are scrambling to complete their themes, I'm proud to say everything for the Training Division is completed, laid out, and ready to be taped/stapled/T-pinned into place. Perhaps Frannie isn't the only workaholic in the department.

Gus watches me approach, his expression as unreadable as ever, looking impeccable in black trousers and a black mock-turtleneck. I feel suddenly conscious of my faded peg-leg jeans and prairie blouse, those old throw-backs from the 1980's modeled after Victorian blouses, and not a silly puffy-sleeved concoction, either. This one is white eyelet, form-fitting, with a fairly low v-neck and hook-and-eye closures. I look good, if not a little retro, but definitely not sophisticated.

I scoot into the free chair on her left. "Are you all right, Frannie? You look exhausted."

"Ah," she says with a smirk. "Gus and I were just making a friendly wager on how long it would take my staff to send an emissary to check on my condition."

"We're actually deciding on how long until we mutiny and make you go home," I counter, smiling.

Gus laughs, the sound surprising because he doesn't do so very often anymore. Collie's head comes up and he sends a piercing glare Gus's way. It doesn't take a psychologist to determine that this man is one of Collie's buttons to push. I have no idea why he would be jealous of Gus Haldemann; the man must be thirty-something to my twenty-six. If he's shown any interest in me, it's not on a romantic or sexual level.

Frannie scowls at us. "I'm *fine*. I think I would know better than either of you when this baby is coming." See—without provocation or warning.

"If this was your second or third child, Fran, I might be inclined to believe you," Gus says smoothly.

"Oh?" she rejoins crossly, but there's a glint of humor in her eyes. "And how many children do *you* have, Gus? And how about *you*, Sarah?"

"None," I say as Gus holds up a lazy hand, his fingers formed into a zero. "However, I've had several pregnant friends who look just like you do right now and went into labor within hours."

"And I," he interjects before Fran can protest, "have five brothers and a sister, all of whom have children—one of which I helped deliver because she said exactly the same thing you just did, Frannie."

Frannie gives us both a cold look. "You two are incorrigible."

Gus grins at me. "Like that's a newsflash."

"No lie. Have it your way, Frannie, but if you make me deliver this baby, I'm going to be asking for a big-ass raise."

He laughs again, and Collie looks up again, frowning. It's like he's conditioned to look up and frown when he hears Gus laugh, much like Pavlov's dogs salivating at the bell.

I get up, giving Frannie a stern look before turning to Gus. "Keep an eye on her, will you?"

"Your wish is my command," he replies easily.

Frannie gives him a sharp, considering look which he gives all indication of not noticing. I beat a hasty retreat before she can say anything; she's not shy of saying what pops into her mind without the benefit of filtering it through the sieve of discretion. Their eyes bore into my back as I cross the room to Collie, who bends down to whisper to me, *his* eyes still on Gus Haldemann.

"Why's he always watching you?"

"I wasn't aware that he does," I whisper back.

"Well, he shouldn't. It's indecent."

I chuckle. "Why is that?"

"He's old enough to be...to be..."

"My lover?" I laugh at him outright, leading him out of visual range of our superiors. "Collie, don't be ridiculous."

"He should be ashamed of himself, chasing after a young woman while his girlfriend is packing to move out."

I pause. "Oh, she's moving out? I didn't know that. Poor Gus."

Collie's frown turns ferocious, making me laugh again. Part of my decorating design was to raise the height of our cube walls; with the help of some broken-down wardrobe boxes, I've managed to accomplish this. It's given the added benefit of affording some privacy, and I'm pleased to say Collie's stolen more than one kiss today. I pull him down for another, and then another, until his frown fades away and his old cocky grin is back. I make a mental note to thank Gus again for putting Collie on notice; I wonder how long it would have taken to progress to this point with him had Gus not helped it along. I don't dare tell Collie that he is feigning interest in me for this purpose; I don't want to jinx it all.

"Go back to work. There's still a lot to do." I push him back in the direction of his assigned duties, and he salutes.

"Aye aye, General."

Allie is still holding the butcher paper when I go back, tapping her foot and pretending annoyance. "Honestly," she whispers, "I think I liked it before when you two were just playing footsie."

"Oh, shush."

I take my end of the paper and we spread it out, moving it into place so we can pin it up. I must say I've outdone myself; not an inch of the off-white butcher paper shows through my laurel hedge design. In order to make the scene three-dimensional, the fairies, elves, and leprechauns I've created are cutouts that we'll fix into place using double-sided foam tape (which is what Collie is doing on the other side of the cube farm), with a few drawn into the hedge itself. In some areas, I've made cutouts of the laurel hedge that we'll tape on to give an added dimension. Watching Frannie's eyes light up when I unrolled a section of the hedge for her to see was worth all the off-work hours I spent designing, drawing, painting, and cutting. Collie and Munchkin helped a bit, but most of the work was done by yours truly.

Frannie orders us pizza for lunch. Still reigning from the arm-chair outside her office, her only capitulation to our concerns being that she allowed Gus to drag a footstool out of the basement so she can put her feet up, she declines having any pizza herself and has been sipping on a large bottle of Gatorade all day.

Sam joins us for a slice, exchanging concerned looks with Gus over Fran's head. At one point, when she's otherwise engaged, Gus holds up nine fingers and Sam nods. It takes me a moment, but I eventually come to the conclusion that you probably have already reached: she's in labor, Gus and Sam are aware of it, and the former has been timing her contractions. Unfortunately, the Production Division is insanely busy running manuals for the launch of a new product in the next few weeks, and Sam can't stay. As he's leaving, Fran leans forward to scratch her ankle, and he holds up a hand to his ear like a telephone. Gus nods, and Sam vanishes back to the clatter and hum of his department.

Two o'clock heralds the arrival of Gretchen, her four girls trailing her like ducklings as she carries in additional decorations for the department. She pauses when she sees Gus, but he watches her without expression. It isn't until the girls see him and swarm him, squealing with delight, that he lets his mask slip away. The smallest crawls into his lap, tucking herself under his chin, her tiny, dimpled hands leaving cotton-candy smudges on his black shirt. His embrace is big enough to enfold all four of them, and after he's bestowed kisses and cuddles to them all, he looks over their heads, catching me watching, his eyes filled with a pain so acute that it hits me like a shockwave.

I have a sudden understanding of the lay of this particular land. He told me himself that Gretchen would go back to James; he no doubt long ago came to terms with it, even somewhat distanced himself from it. But losing the children—two of whom probably don't even remember their real father—is killing him. He has no parental rights, can be afforded no visitation. When Gretchen completes the severing of their ties to one another, he loses the children he's been father to and provider for.

"Ah, hell," Collie says at my elbow. "That's enough to rip your heart out."

I give him a look over my shoulder. "What is?"

He nods surreptitiously toward Gus and the girls. "Whatever else, he loves those kids."

"Yeah, he does. Are you done eating?"

"Yup. Why?"

"Get back to work, cowboy. The day is waning."

He leans against the wall, giving me a sultry smile. "Cowboy? That one of your fantasies we need to explore, Quinn?"

I point toward his assigned section. "GO!"

Laughing, he ducks around the corner. I go back to work, pretending not to notice when Gretchen leaves, taking her reluctant daughters with her. I wonder idly what's going on with her and Frannie, because they barely exchanged five words.

An hour later, Frannie waddles past me, moving slowly to the bathroom.

"You all right, Fran?"

"Fine," she grits through clenched teeth.

"You need some help?"

She stops, fixing me with a malevolent glare. "The day I need help wiping my own butt will be the day they lay me in my coffin."

With effort, she continues on her way, and once she rounds the corner and disappears from view, I look at Gus (whose shoulders are shaking with silent laughter) and raise my hands in helpless frustration. He makes a placating gesture and I go back to work, relieved that when she comes back from the bathroom he'll probably try to talk her into going home—or to the hospital.

I've been carefully pinning, taping, and adjusting and have lost track of all time and all sense of surroundings, so when his hand falls on my shoulder unexpectedly, I just about jump out of my skin.

"Frannie's been in the restroom for more than fifteen minutes. Would you mind going in and checking on her?"

I make a face. "Sure. Be prepared to handle triage; I can't guarantee I'll come out in good condition."

He chuckles. "Yeah, her tongue's a bit sharp today."

The restroom is set up so when you walk in the door, you take a sharp left past an alcove with a small sofa and then a right around a wall into the area where the stalls and sinks are. I guess this is so no one catches an accidental glimpse of you adjusting your underwear or something. I hear Frannie before I see her: sharp breaths in through her nose, huffed breaths out through her mouth. She's bracing herself against the sink with one hand, the other clutched to her stomach. As I watch, her belly tightens, and she clenches her teeth until the contraction passes.

"We told you to go home," I remind her with a wry smile. I drape her arm over my shoulders and lead her to the small sofa in the alcove. "I'll go have Gus call Sam so he can bring the car around to take you to the hospital."

She clutches my arms, her fingers biting deep into my flesh. "No...time!" she pants. Her belly tightens again, and panic flares up inside me.

"Holy crap, Frannie! They're a minute apart!" She nods, a jerky motion like a poorly operated marionette, and gasps in a breath as the contraction passes. "I'll be right back. I have to go tell Gus."

She clutches me again. "Don't lea—leave me!" Her face scrunches, her belly ripples. Another contraction, less than a minute after the last one.

"Frannie, I can't deliver a baby!"

"Have...to!" she pants. "Water broke. Lay...me on the...floor."

I stare at her, completely taken aback. Screw this—if I'm going to have to do this, I'm not going to do it alone. I prise her fingers off my arm and rush to the door.

"*Sarah!*" Frannie shouts through clenched teeth, but I'm already running out the door.

I don't have far to run; alarmed that I didn't come back immediately, Gus is rounding the corner at the same time I am, and we collide painfully. He grabs my elbows to keep me on my feet.

"Where's Frannie, Sarah?"

"In labor, in the restroom."

"I'll call the hospital." He whips out his cell phone like a gun-slinger.

"No time. Her contractions are a minute apart. Come *on!*" I tug on his arm to propel him into motion.

"*Me?*" he protests.

"I've never delivered a baby! You have."

"I only helped!"

"Yeah? Well, now you're going to help me!"

I look up and realize we've gathered a crowd. The ladies are all huddled together, whispering amongst themselves and looking scared that I'll ask *them* for help. Collie is leaning negligently against the outer cube wall, narrowed eyes fixed on my hands circling Gus's forearm.

"Call Sam, will you?" Gus says to him. "He needs to call the paramedics and notify the hospital, preferably while he's trotting his ass up here."

Collie salutes and heads to a phone, and finally Gus allows me to drag him away. We come back through the doors as Frannie screams my name through clenched teeth. She's scooted herself halfway off the sofa but apparently wasn't able—or brave enough—to lower herself all the way to the floor. He scoops her up easily and takes her down to the cold tile, resting her head in his lap, smiling down at her to hide his own panic. I kneel beside her but don't touch her; I've heard that women in labor often don't like to be touched.

"Well, Frannie, of all the adventures we've had together, I never expected to be here doing this."

She reaches up and grabs the front of his shirt. "Sam…"

"Is on his way up. How close, Fran?"

"C-Close." She pulls him down closer to her face. "Can't d-do…this, G-Gus."

He shoots me an apprehensive look and barks out a laugh. "A little late now! You have to; there's no time to get you to the hospital." Frannie closes her eyes and nods in resignation.

"Gus, maybe we should trade places. I've never done this before…"

Her eyes pop open, blazing into his. "You are *not* looking down…there no matter how good of friends…we are!"

He slants a grin at me and shrugs. "You heard the lady. At least she wore a dress," he adds helpfully.

"Wise ass," I mutter. And more than that, she's also, at some point in time, removed her underwear. I lean down and look past Gus under the walls of the three stalls. The closest one, the handicapped stall, has a large puddle of fluid around the base of the toilet. I rather suspect she discarded her soaked panties in there after her water broke.

Frannie shudders and tries to roll onto her side and into a ball, pressing her face into Gus's forearm to muffle her scream of pain. I hold her feet to the tile, her knees raised, keeping her in place, and let me tell you, she is *not* thankful.

"I don't think I can do this. Gus, you'd better—"

"SARAH, YOU BETTER HELP ME!" she threatens in her best *Exorcist* voice. I want to set the record straight right here and now: pregnant women in labor are *not* cute. They are *not* radiant and peaceful and serene. Once the contractions start, they turn into demon-possessed, sweaty little dictators with all the self-control of a willful five-year-old.

Her contractions are coming rapidly, and now she's making an odd keening noise punctuated with grunts of effort. Oh great...now she's pushing! I guess there's no chance of waiting for the paramedics now. I chance a glimpse, hoping I never have to admit to anyone how much of my boss I've seen, and...

"Oh my God, I can see the baby's head!" I look up at them, terrified. *"What do I do?"*

Gus glances down at Frannie. The color has somehow drained from his face and into hers. "Catch, I guess."

The restroom door slams open and Frannie gives a growl of aggressive displeasure until Sam skids around the corner, dropping to his knees beside his wife. Gus looks longingly at the door and I pin him with a malevolent glare of my own. He swallows hard.

"Sam, maybe you'd better go meet the paramedics so they know where to come," he ventures.

"Don't you leave me, Sam!"

"Aaaahh," Sam says uncertainly. His fingers, clenched in Frannie's tight grip, are turning purple, and for the first time I notice her teethmarks in Gus's forearm.

"I'll go," I offer. "Sam, can you—?"

"NO ONE'S LEAVING!" shrieks the Exorcist. Her body stiffens, her face contorts, and for your peace of mind I won't even attempt to describe the sounds that herald the arrival of the newest member of the Harrison household. I make it barely in time; my hands slide under the slimy little bundle of *someone's* joy—eventually—just

before the baby touches the tiles.

"Holy shit," Gus breathes. He's paler than before, if possible.

Sam crawls closer to me, the most extraordinary expression on his face as he beholds his...

"It's a girl," I announce. I start to tremble badly and afraid that I'm going to drop the newborn, I thrust her toward her father. Sam doesn't take her straightaway; he's unbuttoning his shirt. He shrugs out of it (unfortunately, he's wearing a white undershirt beneath it; he's eye candy, remember) and wraps it around his baby daughter. The cord, still connected to her mother, pokes through a gap.

Frannie raises her head, looking up at her baby nestled in her husband's arms, and laughs weakly. "Twenty-two hours of labor my ass, Gretchen!"

In the sudden hush after our laughter fades way, the ding of the elevator is clearly audible. A second later the restroom door creaks open and the paramedics pile in with a collapsible gurney. I scoot backward, out of the way, while they clip the cord and pile a disgruntled Frannie onto the gurney, then tuck the baby into the crook of her arm. She looks awestruck.

As they wheel her past me, she smiles, her hand reaching toward me although we're too far away to touch. "Sarah, thank you," she says softly.

"It's all good, Frannie. Congratulations." I offer a tremulous smile, and then she's gone. Sam, meanwhile, has embraced Gus in one of those back-thumping hugs guys exchange, infused with enough testosterone to dispel any suspicions of latent homosexuality. He releases him and turns to me as I manage to gain my feet, leaving bloody smears on the green slate-tiled wall. My legs are shaking very badly so it's probably a good thing he hugs me, because otherwise I might have fallen.

"Thank you, Sarah." He cups my face and kisses my forehead exuberantly, and then dashes out the door, leaving me alone with Gus. I'm not aware of him moving until he catches me when my legs give out.

"Whoa, Sarah." He lowers me onto the sofa, disappears into the sink area, and comes back with a couple of warm, wet paper towels. He drapes one across my forehead and uses the other to wipe the baby slime from my hands and the wall. Then he kneels in front of me, catching hold of my damp fingers, smiling beatifically.

"You did well, Sarah-Jane Quinn."

"*That* is *not* in my job description! *Make training videos, write instruction manuals, deliver supervisor's baby....* She'd better never do that to me again!"

This makes him laugh until tears stand out in his eyes. I think it's belated hysteria, quite frankly.

"We delivered a baby, Sarah. That's something to be proud of. You're really not what I expected at all." Then he cups my face, much like Sam did—but unlike Sam, he kisses me full on the lips.

I can only stare at him, stunned, because the touch of his lips against mine was like an electric shock. He seems to realize what he just did, for a rush of color floods his face.

"I'm sorry. I'm just psyched. Holy shit." He draws in a steadying breath and stands up. "I'll send Collie in."

He's gone before I can stop him, and as the door swings closed behind him, I suddenly wonder if I'm wrong about Gus feigning interest in me just to spur Collie on. But I don't have long to wonder. Like a damn revolving door, the restroom door swishes open, letting in Collie, Allie, and Hannah, and with tremendous effort I push the thought to the back of my mind in favor of the more immediate thoughts of Tony's Bar and copious amounts of rum.

Tales from the Water Cooler

Friday, March 20
Love Triangles: Three-Pointed Pains- in-the....

Posted by Sarah Quinn

Avoid love triangles. I can't emphasize this enough. No good can come of them, so it's best just to refrain from participating in them.

For the sake of example, say you've been madly in love with a guy for some time. Then along comes another eligible bachelor, handsome and successful and oozing charisma. Say this second gentleman offers to help you with wooing your love.

Do not—I repeat, DO NOT—accept such offers of help, regardless of whether or not they are legitimate. Such offers can be extended with the most innocent of intentions, and morph into something else entirely, leaving you bewildered, torn, and stark raving mad. In fact, I am not at all certain that the ultimate agenda of the male of the species isn't aimed entirely at the singular goal of driving the female of the species out of her mind. Why else do we pin such live-or-die decisions upon their testosterone-soaked heads?

So if the opportunity of a love triangle presents itself to you, run. Run like the wind. I'm here to tell you it's like giving yourself a three-pointed enema.

Postscript added 3/21/2009: The "delete" function on this blog is inoperational at present time; I can only add to this post, not delete it. So I just want to say: don't mind me. I'm raving. Just call it contact retardation from being in close proximity to too-high levels of testosterone. Modern medicine has yet to find a cure.

DID YOU KNOW:

ACCESS TIP: No matter what anyone tries to tell you in textbooks or forums, it is NOT possible to have two primary keys in an Access database table when one of the primary keys is an AUTONUMBER field. Do not attempt this, or you will find yourself spending hours in tech forums trying to make it work, only to discover that it is an impossibility. Save yourself the trouble and heed my advice.

Blog Archive

2009

March

Love Triangles: Three- Pointed Pains-in-the…

February

Faces in the Crowd

January

Going Postal: A Career-Limiting Move

About Me

Savvy Sarah

I am an administrative office professional with several years' experience in office settings. I have an AAS in Administrative Office Management and currently work as a training specialist for a software development company in Los Angeles.

10

DON'T CALL ME SIR

A strange thing about when you do something heroic or highly unusual: you obtain a sort of legendary notoriety that skyrockets your popularity. When I come to work the next day, people to whom I've never spoken other than in passing—and some whom I've never even met at all—walk and talk with me as though we're lifelong friends. I've come to the conclusion that people want to bask in the glow of the fame of others…until the glow fades.

The whole company is talking about Gus Haldemann and me delivering the Harrisons' baby in the restroom, but all I can think about is Collie's alarming reaction to my name being linked so securely to Gus's…and Gus kissing me in the restroom. I know, I know—I'm completely contrary. I worked so hard for my relationship with Collie; I have no business dwelling on the attentions of another man, especially one so far out of my league. But damn…come on, tell me you wouldn't be the same way if a man like Gus Haldemann suddenly noticed you, even if it were for the sole benefit of helping along your relationship with another man.

I come in the next morning with a hangover and no small amount of trepidation: after Tony's Bar, we (Collie, Hannah, Allison, Lauren, and me) came back to finish decorating the department. I barely remember any of this; I relied solely on their ability in their various inebriated states to follow my written plans and slurred, verbal instructions. I've placed a lot of faith in Collie on this; since he was the designated driver and thus the only sober one of us, he was also appointed the designated project manager.

"You worry too much, Quinn," Collie says, eyes glinting, when I breathe a sigh of relief. The department is perfect, just as I imagined it would turn out. The walls and the cube farm have been transformed into a hedge maze dotted with magical beings and softly lit with strings of white Christmas lights. Glow-in-the-dark tape arranged into neat arrows point the correct route to the hole, which George Stuckey placed just this morning. A few seconds' effort and a little moss transforms the portable hole's plastic ugliness into a credible-looking rock.

The tournament isn't until after work hours, and we somehow manage to accomplish quite a lot of work in spite of the distraction of being in an enchanted hedge maze. Just after lunch, Gretchen brings me the permanent employee benefits package Gus promised—and silly me, I'm disappointed he didn't deliver it to me himself even as I feel a wash of guilt for it because of Collie and Gretchen.

Gretchen herself looks worn out, her eyes red-rimmed and underscored with purple half-moons. I have a hard time feeling sorry for her, since it seems to me she's brought the whole thing on her own head, but I admit I'm biased toward Gus.

"Are you all right, Gretch?" I ask as she turns to leave my cube.

"Hmm?" She looks blank for a moment. "Oh yes, I'm fine, Sarah, thanks for asking. I just had a late night. I spent a couple of hours at the hospital with Frannie, and stayed up late packing."

"So it really can't be worked out?"

She shakes her head, loosening a few tendrils of glossy dark hair from her messy up-do. She looks like a tragic heroine in some hopeless romance movie. "No, I'm afraid not. It's been a long time since things were good between us. If it weren't for the girls, he probably would have ended it himself a year or two ago."

"He does seem to love them."

"Yes," she replies softly. "He does."

"If you two really loved each other, you would work it out. Love is a choice you make, not a random feeling."

She smiles sadly, almost pityingly. "We really just aren't compatible, Sarah. Besides, I believe I was just a temporary diversion while he was looking for someone. He's only gone through the motions of working things out with me because he loves my kids."

"I know it's none of my business, Gretchen, but it seems sad the kids have to lose him."

"It's something I should have thought over before moving in with him. He gives his all, Gus does, with no conditions." She gives me a thoughtful look. "That's something you might want to remember."

"Me? Why?"

"Why indeed." Her expression is ironic as she leaves.

A second later, Collie wheels into my cube, scooting his chair backwards. "See, I told you."

I give him a shove back out. "Piss off."

"Mark my words, Quinn—"

I grab my coffee cup and step around him. "You two are out of your minds. I'm going to get some coffee and maybe find some intelligent conversation for a change."

He chuckles as I huff off. Perhaps he's psychic and has foreseen that the only conversation I'm going to find is with...

"Oh...hi, Eric."

I try to school my expression so that my distaste doesn't show when I find that the sole occupant of the break room is Eric Edwards from the Sales Division. He isn't one of my favorite people; while he's intelligent enough, his personality is abrasive and, well...sleazy. It's almost as though his every action has been sifted through a how-can-this-benefit-me filter of slime. I'm not a big fan of people who think only about how they can use you to step up to higher ground.

"Sarah, I was just thinking about you." He beams a smile at me, showing big white teeth that remind me of Chiclets.

"Umm...why?"

"I heard you delivered Frannie Free—er—Harrison's baby yesterday. That's incredible!" He turns up the wattage on his smile, nearly blinding me. I rather suspect his dentist used Fluorescent White when he made these babies, for surely they're caps. No one has teeth that white and square and...big. *My, grandmother, what big teeth you have!*

I stifle a snort of laughter and head for the coffee machine at the back counter. "Yes, I did. With some help. It wasn't incredible; it was scary."

"Still, it was very brave," he replies, sobering somewhat as he joins me at the counter. "So, Sarah…what say we go get a burger sometime?"

"I…ah…don't think that's a good idea."

He pretends to suddenly remember something. "Oh, yes. You have a boyfriend. I remember now. The guy you kissed at the Christmas party."

"Yes."

"So that's still going on, eh? Not exclusively though, am I right? Just a burger, Sarah, how about it?"

"No thank you, Eric." I turn to leave, but he has me trapped between the tables and the counter.

"Aww, come on. I promise you'll have a good time."

Now I've heard about Eric's "good times," although I'm reasonably sure much of it is hype. "The answer is still no, but thanks for asking. Excuse me, please."

He leans in, uncomfortably close, until my back is to the wall behind me. "Now really, Sarah, what can it hurt? Until there's a ring on your finger, there's nothing to stop you from going out with me."

Except me. I take a step to the side, and find his arm barring my sideways escape. My breath comes short, and belatedly I remember my inhaler, left on my desk beside the phone. I rarely need it, and honestly, who'd've thought I'd need it for a quick trip to the break room?

"Please move." But my voice lacks the strength of a command, and is easy for him to ignore.

"Come on, Sarah. Just say yes." I shake my head mutely, and his expression turns truly ugly. His voice lowers so that no one coming in would be able to hear him. "There's a dozen chicks who'd give their eye teeth for a date with me. What's your fucking problem? You frigid or something?"

I step to the side again, pushing against his arm with the futile hope that he'll just let me past. This doesn't even border on sexual harassment; it's a full-blown incident, and not his first. He's gone through the required class twice in the last two years; third strike is a firing offense...but I know if he gets fired because I make a complaint, he's liable to serve up a healthy dose of revenge. He's an ugly piece of rampant chauvinism.

"Is there a problem in here?" We both jump as Gus's curt question slices through the tension in the room. Eric's arm falls away and he steps back. "I believe you have work in your own department, Eric, as well as a break room. I recommend you get back to them."

"Yes, sir." The glance Eric Edwards spares me is positively murderous, but he leaves without another word to me, sidling past Gus with lowered gaze. Gus watches him go, his grey eyes narrowed, and then turns to me.

"I expect to see you in my office after your break to discuss this incident." When I don't immediately reply, he pivots on his heel to leave.

"It's not necessary. He was just being...persuasive. He's a salesman."

The fury in his expression as he crosses the room to me is terrifying even though it isn't directed at me, but unlike Eric Edwards, he minds the rules of personal space. It's clear from his agitated gesticulating, however, that he's struggling for patience. "Sarah, he has a very nasty habit of intimidation and harassment. You can't just let him get away with it."

I reach down into my meager reserve of courage and find flippancy. "Yes, *sir.*"

His arm freezes in mid-gesture. *"What?"*

I swallow hard. "I realize you're the HR director." My voice is wheezing, dammit, and I need my inhaler. I hate conflict, hate confrontation even more, but most of all I hate my inability to handle either without the aid of albuterol. "You saw what you saw; you can write it up yourself, but I don't have to be a part of it. I'm the one who has to walk out to her car alone." A frantic breath in; but not enough air.

He holds up his hands in a placating manner. "Calm down, Sarah.

You're having an asthma attack."

"No...shit." *Breathe in, breathe out.* Reminds me of that stupid movie about the kid learning karate, only this is much more serious than *wax on, wax off.*

Meanwhile, Gus's hand dives into his trousers pocket, coming out with his cell phone. With one hand, he flips it open and dials; with the other, he guides me down into a chair. *Oh please, elephant, move off my chest! Breathe, Sarah, BREATHE!*

Gus doesn't bother with a greeting when the phone is answered at the other end. "Bring Sarah's inhaler to the break room." And he doesn't bother with a goodbye either. He snaps his phone closed and pockets it, then swings a chair around to sit facing me.

"Collie's bringing your inhaler. I'm sorry I upset you. But please think about filing that complaint. We can assign security to escort you to and from the parking lot for a while."

I nod, meaning I'll think about it. My slow, steady breaths have paid off and I have some of my lung capacity restored, but I still need that inhaler. The mention of Collie reminds me that I had meant to thank him for lighting a fire under my boy's slow-moving ass.

"By the way, thank you for Collie." *Gasp.* "He's jealous of the attention you show me." *Gasp.* "It worked."

Gus stares at me for a silent moment until he hears the thud of running footsteps in the hallway. "What makes you think it has anything to do with Collie?"

What air capacity I've gained is suddenly gone, and so is he. He relinquishes his chair to Collie, who has my inhaler positioned and ready to trigger. Mist with a nasty flavor fills my mouth, and I inhale gratefully. Moments later I can breathe again. Collie's hand at the back of my neck keeps my head still; his other hand holds the inhaler at the ready. His eyes bore into mine as though he can make my lungs work through the sheer force of his will.

"What happened?"

It's Gus who answers. "It's my fault. She had an altercation with Eric Edwards. I made matters worse by pushing her to file a complaint."

Collie looks exasperated. "Quinn," he says wearily. "What am I gonna do with you?"

"Think about what I said, Sarah," Gus advises. My eyes widen. He'd bring that up, right in front of my boyfriend? He stresses with raised brows, "The complaint."

"I'll talk to her," Collie assures him.

"It's time I was going then. Again, I'm sorry, Sarah."

I grab Collie's hand, pulling the inhaler into my mouth, firing another round.

"Thank you, sir," Collie says gratefully.

Gus sighs. "Sir," he mutters, shaking his head as he walks out.

Collie pulls me forward until we're forehead to forehead. "Silly girl," he whispers. I tilt my head for a kiss and he chuckles. "No way. You said that stuff tastes like shit."

I kiss him anyway. He makes a face when he draws away, but I needed the contact, the solidity of our relationship, because somehow my world has spun out of control. Women like me don't attract the attention of men like Gus Haldemann. He's handsome, experienced, a mover-and-shaker in this company. I'm not elegant or sophisticated; I'm young and naïve and emotionally stunted. What shift in the cosmos allowed this to happen, and just when I finally got my heart's desire?

Forehead to forehead again, Collie smoothes my hair off my cheek. "You all right?" I nod. "Then let's talk about filing that complaint. I'll go with you if you want."

I scoot my chair back. "I don't want to file a complaint."

"Sarah, Gus is right—much as I hate to admit that. You should file the complaint. Edwards is a sleaze, and if his behavior is inappropriate, he should be fired."

"Oh, that's just great. You think in man terms, both of you. If he comes after me in retaliation, I can't just beat him up, Collie!"

"He won't come after you. Aren't you being a little paranoid?"

"Maybe, but it's better than being para*lyzed*."

He rolls his eyes. "All right, drama queen. Whatever. But please promise me you'll think about it."

I give him my promise without any intention of changing my mind. I'll think about filing the complaint, because I said I would, but that's as far as it's going to go.

The instruction video I'm working on is still waiting where I left it; the program records my keystrokes—and thankfully not in real time—and then the designated narrator will voice over verbal commands in time with the video. Usually Hannah or Brooke adds the audio; they have those wonderful sultry voices that are suited to recordings. And now that I've been given the training on the Harper & Lyttle software systems, I feel much more confident and competent in my job duties.

The soothing chatter of my cube mates and the sounds of them going about their various duties soothe me. It takes about half an hour, but I finally relax enough to stop jumping anytime someone makes a sound behind me. By the time we close down for the tournament, you almost can't tell I had an asthma attack.

Gretchen gathers us together to dole out our responsibilities before the tournament officially begins—those of us who haven't signed up to golf, that is. Mostly it will be the senior execs putting through our various departments, but many of the staff signed up too, hoping to rub elbows with those of higher power and have their names remembered. Collie joined in—just because he loves golf, even of the miniature variety—and Lauren and Hannah as well. Gretchen has assigned herself to the refreshments table with Brooke, leaving me and Allie to act as hostesses.

"Sarah, I'd ask that you take Frannie's duties and make yourself available to the judges for any errands they need or specifics on the hole. I had Collie putt through to determine what par is on our hole."

She passes out a sheet with the participants and judges names. I scan the list, my eyes stopping on one name, and I send a sidelong glance at Collie.

He leans close to my ear and whispers, "Hey look, it's your boyfriend," and points to Gus's name.

I pinch the soft flesh under his arm in reply and he leans away, mock-glaring at me and rubbing his side.

But Gus keeps his distance from me for most of the evening,

either by design or because of the sheer volume of golfers coming through. I barely have time to sit for a minute straight; the entire evening is spent keeping the (slightly inebriated) golfers in line and dodging the videographer.

At one point in time I gain a reprieve; one of the divisions set up their hole in one of the elevators because their department is so small, and the golfers are all stuck on the fifth floor waiting for a whack at the hole when the doors open. I find a quiet spot to sit, enjoying the solitude, so I'm none too happy when Brooke, of all people, joins me.

"Busy night," she remarks.

"Yeah, who knew? I thought maybe a handful of people would golf through. I didn't know it would be half the company."

"Golf is popular among the white collar set. Listen, Sarah, I wanted to talk to you about something."

I turn to stare at her, my surprise showing plainly on my face. Brooke has not sought me out once for a private conversation; in fact, I had the strong impression that she rather detests me, probably because I'm the other half of the troublesome Collie-and-Quinn team.

"Sure. What is it?"

She pulls Stella's chair out of her cubicle and swings it around to sit by me. "I wanted to talk to you about what happened with Eric Edwards."

"Does *everyone* know already?"

"No. Collie mentioned in passing that you had some words with Eric and it caused you to have an asthma attack. What did he do?"

"He was just being a persistent asshole." I wave it off, but I can feel my chest tightening just thinking about it.

"Sarah, Collie said you weren't going to file a complaint against him."

"Gee whiz, can't everyone leave me alone about that?" I mutter crossly.

Brooke is silent for a moment, her head bowed so that her long blonde hair half-hides her face like a curtain. Sometimes I wish my hair were straight and sleek and shiny like hers; I have to spend an hour with a straightener every morning to achieve the results that come to her naturally. And then, with the slightest hint of moisture in the air, my hard work is decimated as my hair springs into loose, floppy, unruly curls.

"Sarah, what I'm going to tell you has to stay between you and me." She waits until I indicate my agreement. "Three years ago, I worked for a company that was not so...what would you say? . . . ah, security-minded. The office was located in a bad area of town, and it seemed to attract some not-so-desirable employees."

"I think I see where you're going with this," I interject, trying to stop her.

"No, I don't think you do," she persists. "One of the guys who worked there was a very dangerous man. He did things much like Eric did to you today, but eventually he—what do the police call it?—he escalated." She chews her lip for a moment. Her face is white as a sheet.

Alarmed, I lay a hand on her arm, bringing her head up. "Look, Brooke, you don't have to tell me this. It's obviously hard for you to talk about it."

"And obviously hard for you to hear it, because you keep trying to stop me," she points out. "Sarah, I didn't file complaints about his behavior. He cornered me all the time, made inappropriate advances, and I never said a word. I just let it go. And he escalated. He strong-armed me into a date one day. I was afraid to go, but I was afraid to say no."

She swallows hard, her eyes darting around the department for signs of eavesdroppers or golfers needing assistance. I'm hoping for an interruption myself, but we're completely alone. Gretchen is talking to Allison, and Gus, from all appearances, is playing a game on his iPhone.

Brooke's voice is small when she speaks again, sounding tiny and defeated. "He raped me. They call it date-rape, but rape is rape no matter how you term it. He made me feel like I'd asked for it all along, told me no one would believe me because I'd gone out with him; I'd never made any complaints about him."

"Jesus, Brooke!"

"And because I never reported him for raping me, he was loose on the streets to rape someone else. He beat her senseless, hospitalized her. And when she came out of her coma, she couldn't remember anything of that whole week, even the days preceding the rape. He told the police she'd cancelled on him, and phone records showed she'd called him at the same time he claimed she cancelled their date. His sleazy buddies backed him up, gave him an alibi."

"Holy shit," I mutter.

"Because I did nothing, she'll never be the same. She has trouble with her short-term memory sometimes, and she had to learn to walk and read again. She lives with her parents because she can't hold a job. She'll never be a wife or mother unless she finds a man who is willing to put that much time and effort into a wife who may not remember his name from one minute to the next."

"I get what you're saying." And I really do, but damn, I want this conversation to be over. It hasn't escaped my attention that perhaps there's a good reason Brooke is a bitch on wheels, and that perhaps I've judged her too harshly and too hastily, like I did Gretchen. Another of my character flaws.

"Do you?" she asks in a cold voice. "Because if you really do, you won't be the one to let Eric Edwards go unchecked. If you really do, you'll file that complaint before he escalates."

She reaches out and grips my hand, her movements convulsive and awkward; she obviously doesn't handle adrenaline spikes well. In contrast to her voice, her hand is very warm. "Please don't tell anyone."

I look up at her, surprised, and for a moment I can almost see us side-by-side, both of us tall, leggy blondes with blue eyes, athletic figures, and classic features. *It could have been me. I could be the damaged one, the one who lives in fear, mired in guilt.*

"I won't tell a soul," I promise.

She squeezes my hand and slides out of her chair, disappearing into the bathroom just as the elevator dings. The door slides open and in the crowd of polo-shirted men spilling out of the elevator car, I spy Eric Edwards, smiling his best smarmy salesman smile, slapping one of his buddies on the back as they roar in laughter at some joke whose punch-line I thankfully didn't hear. He looks up, catching my gaze, and his grin widens into a wolf's sneer as he tips a wink my way. His friends see and hoot their encouragement.

His sleazy buddies backed him up, gave him an alibi.

My flesh prickles into goose-bumps as his group makes their way to the other departments whose holes come before ours in the course.

You won't be the one to let him go unchecked. You'll file that complaint before he escalates.

"Yes," I murmur, standing abruptly. "I will."

Gus is deep in his game when I approach, but not so preoccupied that he doesn't know I'm there.

"Yes, Sarah?" he asks without looking up. His fingers fly over the keys, the phone makes a disagreeable sound, and he winces. "Damn!"

"I want to file that complaint."

Now I have his full attention. Those grey eyes bore into mine, seeming to read every nuance of my soul.

Finally he says, "Then I'll see you first thing in the morning in my office."

"Yes, sir." I'm four steps away when his voice comes again.

"And Sarah?"

I turn back. His fingers are working the phone keys again, but his eyes are on me. "No more of that 'sir' crap or I'll write you up for insubordination."

"Oh? How can that be when it's a term of respect?"

"Because I've instructed you to call me by my first name."

I raise my brows. "I don't seem to recall that."

"My oversight. Consider it instructed."

"Of course." I can't help my little smirk. "Sir."

His quiet laughter follows me across the room. I chance a look over my shoulder; his expression is anything but neutral as he watches me. I remember his words—*What makes you think it has anything to do with Collie?*—and I wonder what I've gotten myself into.

THE BEST LAID PLANS

"I'm sorry, Miss Quinn. Mr. Haldemann is in an unexpected meeting and isn't available to meet with you until later this morning. He asked me to tell you he'll call you as soon as he's free." Gus's administrative assistant gives me a bland, perfunctory smile, twirling her mechanical pencil between her fingers.

I swallow back my disappointment and offer her a fake smile of my own. "All right. Thanks." I back a step away from her desk, which stands like a stolid fortress between me and the inner sanctum, and scurry out the door. I don't have much courage—I think we've already established that—so to be postponed is not the ideal situation.

Not to mention the fact that I actually adhered to the Harper & Lyttle dress code today, and can find no complaint with my appearance: black slacks, slightly flared at the ankle, an azure, v-neck shirt layered over a copper, lace-trimmed tank, and wide-heeled black pumps that will put me nearly eye-level with Gus should I ever get to talk to him. Not that he was a factor in my choice of attire for the day. At. All.

I may not have dressed to impress (that's my story and I'm stickin' to it), but while I lay awake last night into the wee hours of the morning, waffling in my decision to file a sexual harassment complaint against Eric Edwards, I recalled overhearing Evelyn Harper (who Frannie calls Roxanne, for some unknown reason) mention to Frannie one day that dressing to the nines is like wearing armor when you have to face an unpleasant situation. Frannie looked skeptical, but I think Evelyn's onto something. So I donned my armor this morning, only to find the battlefield empty and the war delayed.

"Hey, Quinn, lookin' good!" Collie winks at me as he breezes past, a bulging leather business case slung by its worn strap from his shoulder. "I'm off to train a group of execs who won't remember a thing I say five minutes after the session's over."

"Have fun with that." I watch him round the corner, and when I turn to go into my cube, I find Allison and Hannah hovering in my way.

"So what happened?" Allie follows me to my desk, getting in my way as I reach for my file cabinet drawer to stow my purse out of sight. Hannah hangs back just outside the cubicle, no less curious but not quite as forward. I'm just happy that we know where she is for a change. Every office has one of those employees who just randomly vanishes to parts unknown without a word—a Happy Wanderer, if you will. That's our Hannah. Half the time we can't find her when we need her, and at those times no one can recall when she left or where she went.

"Nothing. He was called into an unexpected meeting. His assistant said he'd call when he's free."

Allie wrings her hands together. "Just great. So in the meantime, you have to fend off Eric Edwards and worry about being alone anywhere in the building."

Now I hadn't thought about things in those terms until now. "Well, thank you for that uplifting thought, Chicken Little. I can always count on you to let me know when the sky is falling."

"I don't mean to be a downer, Sarah, but you really should be careful."

"Geez, Allie. Hannah, what do you—" Allie and I both turn, but Hannah's already gone (and we don't see her for another twenty minutes).

"Someone needs to tie a cowbell around her neck," Allison grumbles.

"I know, right? Come on, O Pessimistic One, let's get some java before Marketing stampedes in there and takes it all."

But there's no coffee in my immediate future. As we round the corner into the hallway, Gus Haldemann comes out of the elevator. I could have imagined his step faltering, but I don't think I did. He doesn't smile as he closes the gap between us.

"Excuse me for interrupting, Allison, but may I borrow Sarah for a moment?"

Allie's expression registers her surprise that he knows her name, and then her eyes bounce from Gus to me and back again. I can almost see chunks of sky falling.

"Sure. I'll get your coffee, Sarah." She takes my mug and abandons me at top speed with no backward glance.

Gus takes my elbow, the movement serving to both turn me in the opposite direction and impel me forward. "Bad meeting," he says, stopping at my cube. "Get your inhaler."

I flick a glance at him, but his expression gives away nothing except a trace of expertly suppressed fury. I can almost feel it thrumming through him, like you can feel the hum of an electrical current if it's strong enough and you stand too close. A moment of rummaging in my purse unearths the albuterol, and then we're moving forward again, into Frannie's office where Gretchen is waiting, seated in a small grouping of chairs in the corner of the office. She doesn't appear to be startled by our sudden invasion, which tells me he called ahead. Gus twirls the rod on the mini blinds, closing off Fran's office from department view.

"You'll want to sit down for this, Sarah," he advises.

"What's going on?"

"Sit!" I sit. He huffs out a breath, runs a hand through his hair. "I'm sorry. I'm just so—"

"Fucking mad?" Gretchen supplies helpfully.

"That about sums it up."

"What *happened*?" I scoot to the edge of my chair, but a sharp glance from Gus pins me there before I can get up. He starts pacing the room like a caged lion.

"I can't believe this happened," he mutters.

"Sarah," Gretchen says, and all trace of her sarcastic humor is gone. "Eric Edwards tried to file a complaint of sexual harassment against you this morning."

The blood drains from my face, leaving me cold and faint. Predictably, my chest tightens. Gus drops into the empty chair beside me, his hands on my cheeks unnaturally warm.

"Sarah?"

"I'm fine. I'm *fine!*" I snap when he continues to gaze at me skeptically, although he takes his hands away. "How could he do that? You were there—you saw what he did!"

Complete silence settles in the room, and I don't miss the look that passes between him and Gretchen—and we won't even talk about the unreasonable, totally inappropriate swell of jealousy that sweeps through me at that silent communication. He takes a deep breath, starts to speak, sighs instead, and then takes another breath.

"He claims you came on to him, wouldn't take no for an answer, became angry when he refused to accept your proposition." He pauses. "Sarah, what I saw was two people talking. I couldn't hear what was said."

"But—he stopped me from leaving—and my asthma attack—"

"He says he thought you were collapsing, and he was trying to help you."

I can't believe it; I can't believe how easily Eric turned the tables. "How did this happen? He's done this before; how can anyone believe he's the victim?"

Another silent exchange moves between Gus and Gretchen. "It's my fault, Sarah," he says quietly.

"*What?*"

Vivid color blooms in his face. "Eric said that because of my personal interest in you, I'm not an impartial witness to the exchange. I'm sorry."

Gretchen looks away politely, and for the first time I wonder what she thinks of this. He's been with her for nearly three years, and now here she sits on the eve of their breakup, silently bearing witness to his admission of interest in me.

And on the heels of that, I realize what he just confessed. I look up at him, but he only gazes back impassively, that damnable poker-face fixed to his expression.

"So what do we do?" I ask numbly.

Gus grits his teeth, a flash of fury in his eyes. It's Gretchen who answers.

"Eric said he won't file a complaint if you don't."

I clench my fingers around the arms of my chair. I haven't been this angry in years—not since that makeup compact fight with my sister in my teens. Impotent emotion coils inside me, but I know the urge to rampage through the office in a violent rage will pass in a few moments, suppressed by habit and conditioning. That doesn't mean it won't stew inside me for days, making me sick to my stomach.

"Can I still have security assigned to walk me to and from the parking lot?"

Gus closes his eyes. "Edwards said he would construe that as the company siding with you, and he'd lay a sexual discrimination suit on top of the whole mess."

"So I have no recourse in correcting his actions, and no protection to make sure he can't do it again."

"I'm sorry, Sarah," he says again, his voice barely audible. "The company attorneys told him if you each filed a complaint, they would nullify each other—but they only did it because I pointed it out. It would turn into a he-said, she-said situation and waste a lot of time. That made him back off, but…."

But it doesn't help protect me at all.

The hideous unfairness of the situation hits me full force. My throat narrows. I grip the inhaler in my hands, its round contours somehow comforting, but I don't want to use it yet, not in front of them. *Show no more weakness than you have to, Sarah-Jane,* my mother used to say, instructing me to keep my inhaler out of sight and my asthma as concealed as possible because God forbid there ever be any public displays of my weakness.

"He—he was in our break room," I point out weakly. "He had no business being there!"

"There's no company policy on each department or floor using its own break area," Gus replies. "Can't use that, Sarah."

"He's done this before—he's gone through the training twice!

He—he was in there when he had no reason to be! He trapped me in there, called me a—I can't believe this! I can't believe there isn't anything I can do!"

"I'm sorry," he says yet again. "My hands are tied, and the decisions regarding this matter were made at levels way over my head. The Legal Division is adamant; they don't want a discrimination lawsuit."

"But how could they determine that this fast?"

"Edwards called my supervisor last night," Gus explains, a hint of red still in his cheeks. "Because, he said, he didn't feel comfortable voicing his complaint to me. I've been in meetings about this since seven this morning."

I chance a look at Gretchen, who is looking sympathetically angry. "They're hanging me out to dry."

"Company has a long record of *that*," she mutters. "Sarah, we'll take precautions. We just can't take official ones. All right?"

Precautions? I think dumbly. *That's all I get?*

"If there's anything I can do, Sarah…" Gus trails off, and I feel a flash of anger so intense it leaves me shaking.

"I think you've done quite enough," I manage to squeeze out through the pinhole in my throat. He lowers his gaze. I need to use my inhaler immediately. I stand up too quickly, nearly toppling my chair, mortified to find that my legs don't want to obey my brain's commands. But through sheer force of will, I make them carry me to the door.

"Sarah, wait!" Gretchen implores, but I can't—I'm pretty sure I'm going to be rather violently sick.

Through the cube farm, down the hall, and into the bathroom—finally the relief of albuterol. I collapse on the sofa, willing the nausea away, fighting for each breath until they come easier and plentiful. But my anger at Gus—that stays, reaching a level disproportionate to his crime. I hold onto it like a security blanket, using it to distance myself, because we all know that man is entirely out of my league, and I would never be able to measure up to his expectations, so it's better I put an end to these futile flights of fancy right now.

And that's the thought that makes me curl into the corner of the sofa and cry.

$$* \quad * \quad * \quad * \quad *$$

Half an hour later Allison pops in, stepping tentatively around the corner, obviously looking for me and not relief. I take a deep breath; Allie is somewhat of a stress puppy, and often when I need to calm down she winds me up instead. She thrives on the drama; adds excitement to her life, I guess.

"I've been sent in to bring you out," she says, perching beside me. "Are you okay, Sarah? What's going on?"

"Who sent you?"

"Gus Haldemann."

"Oh." My lips compressed into a tight line, I cross my arms, settling more firmly into the corner of the sofa. My terse, one-word reply leaves her in no doubt of who is the object of my displeasure.

She shrinks away, looking quite alarmed at my expression. "He said if you don't come out in the next ten minutes, he's coming in, and then there will be a whole host of *other* problems to deal with."

Yeah, such as the rumor mill; the grapevine would thrive on passing on the knowledge of a private tête-à-tête between the two of us in the ladies' room. And Collie…oh, Collie would flip!

"Gus can kiss my ass," I mutter. "This is all his fault anyway."

Not precisely true *or* fair, but anger rarely sees logic. I know I'm being unreasonable; it really isn't his fault at all—that dubious honor belongs to Eric Edwards alone—but I can't help feeling that had he been a little more discreet about his interest in me, Eric would not have been able to use it against me. Now I have to look over my shoulder everywhere I go and hope that when I do, I don't see the Sultan of Smarm behind me.

"What did he do?"

"Not important. I'll come out when I'm good and ready."

She looks uncertain. "He means it. I wouldn't put it past him. And Sarah…it *is* during work hours. Technically he's your boss, and if you refuse it's insubordination."

"Whose side are you on, anyway?"

"No one's. And I don't know why I'd be choosing up sides anyhow; I don't know even what's going on. Will you come out, or do you prefer humiliation?" I glare at her. "I think he just wants to know that you're all right. Er...*are* you all right, Sarah?"

"Peachy-keen," I growl.

"Well, come on then. We can try to go get that cup of coffee again."

"Oh, fine." I capitulate with ill humor.

Allie follows me out, wisely remaining silent. I'm not very often visibly grouchy, but this whole incident makes me so angry...angry and afraid, and being afraid makes me even angrier.

The man in question is lounging against the wall across the hallway from the bathroom door, ankles and arms crossed, expensive Italian leather loafers scuffing the carpet.

"Well, I see you're breathing," he says.

My eyes narrow, signaling my continuing displeasure with him. For a split second, his expression is resigned, and then his mask slips smoothly back into place, that iron control obviously holding him in good stead.

"That's all I wanted to know. Good day, ladies."

He pushes away from the wall and walks away without another word.

Allison watches him go, a thoughtful frown puckering her forehead. "Why do I get the feeling more just happened here than I know about?"

"It doesn't matter now, Allie," I reply quietly. The contrary being that I am, I experience a disquieting sense of loss, but with monumental effort I slam the door on my secret dreams involving Gus Haldemann and throw the bolt to keep them imprisoned.

My dilemma is solved. No more distractions or foolish school-girl crushes on men who outclass me. From now on it's just me and Collie—and Munchkin—and a large dose of reality.

You know what they say about the best laid plans.

THE THINGS I'VE LEARNED

Over the weeks following the Eric Edwards incident, I've learned several things, such as Allison has strange taste in men although she has the good sense to fish outside the company pond. The quirky guy she picked up in the dairy aisle at Wal-Mart at one in the morning (she always shops late at night because she detest crowds) seems to be a good fit though; their odd angles go together seamlessly like a jigsaw puzzle, and they both seem happy enough.

I've also learned that I'm never going to be a professional bowler. Collie and I joined a late-night league with Allie and her beau Thomas, and every Tuesday finds my skill depleting rather than refining. At this point in time, I believe Munchkin bowls better than I do. I'm positive the only reason the others haven't replaced me is it's a handicap league, and my handicap goes up as my average goes down.

Another home truth is that I can't play tennis for crap. Collie has been trying to teach me, and I'm sure by now—what with the bowling fiasco added in—he thinks I'm completely athletically challenged. But seriously, why can't the man ask me to play softball or basketball? And just because he played second position on the tennis team in both high school and college doesn't mean that I'm going to share his prowess on the netted court.

Possibly the worst thing to discover is that Collie genuinely likes animated Disney movies, not that he would ever admit it to my face. But you can tell; he doesn't protest much when Munchkin insists on watching them, and he wears a goofy smile for the duration of the film. Don't get me wrong; I'm not averse to watching a cute film every now and then, but after living on a steady diet of shoot-em-ups,

Disney fare seems excessively sugary.

Not surprisingly, I've discovered that I love babies. I love the solid weight of them in my arms, their powdery scent, their soft skin. Frannie frequently brings in little Noelle and I could spend hours holding her. It seems to make Collie nervous when I do, so I curb my natural instincts and push aside—as best I can—the niggling worry his discomfort causes in the pit of my stomach.

I've also learned how to look over my shoulder and plan my day carefully so that I never find myself in a situation where I can be cornered. Sometimes this isn't easy; once I found myself in the office with just Gretchen and Stella while the others went to an Excel training session (which, I'm pleased to say, I don't need because I've already passed my MOUS certification). On that particular afternoon, I went without coffee for four hours and finally had to beg Stella to let me go with her when she went to the restroom because I'd been holding it for two hours. She has what she calls "pee anxiety" and can't relieve herself if she thinks anyone else can hear. Silly, but we all have our quirks, I guess.

Eric Edwards is easy to avoid, since the Sales Division is two floors up, but there have been a few occasions when I found myself in the same room through unavoidable circumstances. Luckily, the room was big—either the lobby or the convention room that occupies a third of the basement—and I didn't have to be close to him. It doesn't stop him from sending me knowing smirks or tipping winks my way, trying to set me off-balance. I've schooled myself in ignoring them and showing no reaction, even though his persistence in needling me makes me very uneasy.

Another thing I've learned is how to admit when I'm wrong and how to apologize. It doesn't come easy to me; it's one of those people skills my hopelessly deficient parents failed to pass on to me because they don't possess it themselves. But as the days move slowly, agonizingly by, my conscience pricks at me to the point that I finally swallow my pride and apologize to Gus for blaming him for the harassment fiasco. He listens to my stammered apology (*way to go, Sarah; way to look like a complete social retard*), accepts it graciously, and ushers me out of his office so smoothly I don't realize until I'm in the elevator that I've been dismissed. His poker face never slips, and he's since put everything back on professional footing.

Which brings me to the most important thing I've learned: regret. I miss his surprising humor, the way his presence seems to engulf me. He's closed off now; aloof, unapproachable, and I know that I caused it—and that I can't fix it. And on the heels of those regrets I damn myself eight ways from Sunday because I shouldn't care so much. Collie should be my only focus, but like I said before—there's something about perfect, powerful men that makes you desire them, no matter how committed you are to someone else.

Another thing I've learned…testosterone drives men—and some women, I'm sure—to be competitive. When winning becomes more important than having fun, Sarah-Jane checks out. I don't find it fun to have people angry at me because I don't share their competitive drive or their athletic ability. Give me a basketball and I'd make you proud. Bowling, however….

This league has brought out a side to Collie that I'd never suspected existed; and coupled with the thread of unease that seems to be my constant companion lately, I'm beginning to get the feeling that what I thought is paradise is really only the trailhead, just a clouded glimpse of said mythical land.

"Sarah, you're up," Collie says curtly, nudging me as he sits down by me. I glance up at the auto scoring screen to see that he just rolled a strike. Figures. I'll be damn lucky to get six pins, which will frustrate everyone because the other team is ahead…but just barely. I'm not one of those people who performs well under pressure; in fact, the more pressure there is, the worse I do.

Which is what happens now. Did I say I'd be lucky to get six pins? Lady Luck has fled the premises; the ball rolls a wavering course toward the gutter and barely manages to hook back toward the pins to clip the ten pin. Allison giggles, Thomas pats me on the back with good humor…but Collie sighs and shakes his head. Which pisses me off. Which puts pressure on me. Which makes me sure I'm going to miss the other nine pins by a mile. Which *really* pisses me off.

111

I line up, draw in a breath, and hear Collie mutter to Allison and Thomas, "It doesn't look like we're going to win *this* game either." I lower the ball to my side, and turn to give him an eloquent look. He at least has the grace to look embarrassed if not contrite. I turn back to the pins, but I've lost all interest in caring how I do or if we win.

"Little bastards," I mutter to the remaining pins, and then I just walk up, fling the ball at them, and turn without watching. To my surprise, Collie's mouth drops open in surprise, and he pistons his arms into the air, letting out a whoop of elation.

"YEAH!" He catches me as I start to brush past him. "Tenth frame, Sarah. You have another ball." When I raise a brow inquiringly, he points behind me. "You got a spare."

Imagine that. At least he won't go home utterly disgusted with me. And tomorrow, perhaps, I might even hit a tennis ball that doesn't catch the net or go over the chain link fence surrounding the court. And perhaps I might even give a shit about my performance. And pink pigs will spread their little wings and fly.

I grab my ball, give another careless fling, eliciting another cheer from my teammates.

"A strike, Sarah! A STRIKE!"

"Cool." I brush past him and head for the lounge at the other end of the alley, ignoring Thomas and Allison calling my name. I have fifteen bucks in my pocket; that should be enough for a couple of Kamikazes. And that, perhaps, will be enough to mellow my nerves.

There are a few people in the lounge, both at the cocktail tables and at the bar itself, but I don't pay any attention to them. I slip onto an empty stool, fish out my money, and place my order. While I wait for my drink to come, I rest my head on my folded arms and will away the evening.

His scent announces him as he slides onto the stool next to me. I don't need to hear his voice to know it's him, and to know this is the last thing I need. I groan.

"Well, Sarah. You're not very good at bowling, are you?"

"*Thank* you for that observation, Mr. Haldemann. Perhaps you'd like to rub some more salt in that wound."

"No one can excel at *everything*...Miss Quinn," he responds with amusement. "Not even you."

I laugh, not with humor but with sarcasm, raising my head as the bartender slides the Kamikaze in front of me and takes my money.

"Gus, it goes beyond simply being bad at bowling...and tennis," I add in a mutter.

"Tennis too?" he mocks, grinning.

"I suppose you're good at both," I remark disgustedly.

"Passable to fair," he admits modestly. He signals the bartender, who sets an uncapped bottle of beer in front of him. He picks it up and tips it at me. "I think your friends are looking for you. Enjoy the rest of your evening."

A glance at the door tells me Allison and Collie have run me to ground. I turn back to watch Gus walk back to his table, where Frannie, Sam, and a woman I've never seen before are waiting for him. He gives the beer to the woman and claims his seat, his back to me. Frannie and Sam wave, and I wave back as though I didn't just take a massive blow somewhere in the region of my solar plexus.

"Sarah," Collie says meekly. I whirl on my stool in time to catch him directing a scowl Gus's way.

"Time to go?"

He runs a hand through his hair, looking both contrite and aggravated. "Look, I'm sorry. I'm just really competitive, and I get carried away."

"While you're getting carried away, Collie, you're making me feel like complete shit. So you know what? I'll pay for a sub for the rest of the season, but I'm done."

He throws his hands up in frustration. "Oh, come on, Sarah! Aren't you being a little melodramatic?"

Allie looks away uncomfortably and edges toward the door where Thomas is hovering uncertainly.

I grab my drink, shoot it in one gulp, and set the glass down a little harder than I meant to. "I should get home. I have to work tomorrow."

"Sarah," he says wearily as I slide off the stool and head for the

113

door.

The drive home is made in virtual silence. I'm angry at the way he's treating me, and he's angry at my reaction. And for the first time I realize the fun little things that attracted me in the first place have slowly, inexorably subsided. There's no more betting a dime, no more good-natured riposting, no gentle ribbing. I've no idea when it all stopped, which makes me squirm with guilt because my attention has not been on the state of affairs with Collie but has been indulging in fantasies involving another man.

When he stops the car outside my apartment, we sit for several long minutes, steeped in the silence that seems to have rendered us both virtually unable to speak. Finally I turn in my seat to look at him, swallowing over a lump of fear that threatens to paralyze my vocal chords.

"I need to ask you something."

He shuts off the engine and shifts to face me. "All right."

"Why are you with me when I appear to do nothing but frustrate and embarrass you?"

His mouth drops open. *"What?"*

"You heard me." My voice quavers, but you know me—I won't cry, no matter what. "I can't bowl for shit, Collie. And I can't play tennis. I never did either on a regular basis. You don't seem to have an interest in playing the sports I excel at."

"Sarah—"

"And what happened with betting a dime on everything? Or calling me 'Quinn' all the time? Or running off to the basement to make out when we're supposed to be working? Or making cookies together? You don't seem to even want to—"

"Oh, *Sarah*," he says softly. He slides across the bench seat and pulls me into a tight embrace. "I don't know what the hell I'm thinking. Sports make me so damn competitive and I just lose sight of everything else. I didn't mean to make you feel unimportant."

He sets me away from him a couple of inches so he can look at me, smoothing my hair off my forehead. "I'm an idiot. I'm sorry."

"It's all right."

"No, it's not." He tilts my face up so he can see my expression in the glow of the streetlamp. "And to tell you the truth, for a while I wasn't sure I wasn't going to lose you to Gus Haldemann."

I lean away, scrunching my face at him. "As though he'd have more than a flirtatious interest in someone like me. I'm not sophisticated or classy enough. You're silly."

"But you like him," he guesses accurately.

I shrug. "I like lots of people, Collie. That doesn't mean I want to hop into bed with them. Can we put all this behind us and do better in the future?"

He smiles. "I think we can manage that." He pulls me to him again, his lips finding mine in the kind of kiss we shared when we first started dating—and a huge weight lifts from my heart. I still love him. Not that I ever really doubted. Not in the slightest. No more room for doubts anymore, no more competitiveness, most of all no more bowling—

Who *was* that damn woman with Gus tonight, anyway?

Tales from the Water Cooler

Saturday, May 9
WTF Is Wrong with Men???

Posted by Sarah Quinn

Men. Every day, I come in to the office and find myself confronted with yet another odd, unexplainable specimen. They primp and preen almost as much a bunch of tramps at a night club—and while we're at it, what the hell is this "Got your tickets…to the GUN SHOW?" crap about? Those aren't GUNS, bub, those are BICEPS, and you need to work on them.

Then there are the ones who can't take NO for an answer. No means NO, dumb ass! It seems a simple enough answer: one syllable with negative connotations. You can't understand that? Are you just retarded or what?? And then after they corner you in the break room and get caught, they try to file complaints against YOU!! JERKWAD!!!

Now let's talk sports. I'm all out for a good game of softball or basketball. And a night of Monte Carlo bowling…yeah, I'm down with that. But league bowling…BOWLING?? And getting mad at me—I mean us—when we suck?! I oughta beat you with my tennis racket, since that particular athletic equipment isn't good for anything else! Yeah, you SAY you're sorry you acted like that, but I HEARD you talking to your brother about it, you oinker!!!

AND WHO THE HELL WAS THAT WOMAN *HE* WAS WITH????? AM I REALLY THAT EASY TO FORGET????

DID YOU KNOW:

There is no damn tip this month, just like there was no damn blog last month. You want to know how to do something? Try F1! And if you can't find what you need in the totally useless help files, find an online forum like I do!

Blog Archive

    2009

        May

            WTF Is Wrong with Men???

        March

            Love Triangles: Three- Pointed Pains-in-the…

        February

            Faces in the Crowd

        January

            Going Postal: A Career-Limiting Move

About Me

    Savvy Sarah

    I am an administrative office professional with several years' experience in office settings. I have an AAS in Administrative Office Management and currently work as a training specialist for a software development company in Los Angeles.

NEVER PUT ANYTHING IN WRITING

"Sarah, we need to talk about this." Lauren pulls out a chair and slaps a sheet of paper in the middle of the table. I glance at it and choke on my fettuccini, darting a look at Gus sitting three tables away. Allison grabs the printout of my most recent blog and folds it in half, sending a censuring look at Lauren.

"You *printed* it?" I hiss. "Are you *crazy*?"

"Oh, no one will know it's you," she scoffs.

"Of course they won't. It's only left at a table where I was sitting, with the name *Sarah Quinn* on it. No one will put *that* one together."

We all pause as Gus turns the page of his newspaper, shakes it flat, and subsides into silence. It's a strange thing he's been doing lately, eating in our break room at least three out of five days of the work week, and always at my lunchtime. I know why he's here; it supposedly gives me a chance to relax while I eat my meal, but the truth is I'm just as ill at ease with Gus's presence as I would be with Eric's, only for different reasons.

Lauren leans closer to me, snatching the paper from Allie and scooting the break room detritus to the edge of the round table: newspapers; salt and pepper shakers, those cardboards ones you take on picnics; defaced company newsletters; and a men's health magazine.

"What the hell are you doing?" she whispers. "I thought you were committed to Collie. Why are you pining after…" Her gaze cuts away to Gus and then back to me, and she waves the paper in my face. "…*him*?"

"I'm *not*."

119

"You *are!*" She unfolds the paper and reads from it: "...'And who the hell was that woman *he* was with? Am I really that easy to forget?' *Sarah!* What would Collie say if he read this blog?"

"Why?" I challenge. "Are you going to make sure he does?"

She looks pissed. "Of course not! But I don't want to see you crapping all over him either! And what's wrong with you, Sarah— don't you know you *never* put *anything* in writing?"

"Keep your voice down!" I hiss. I push my microwave dinner away from me, my appetite gone. "Perhaps you haven't been aware of the hell I've been going through, Lauren. Collie turned into some sort of sports megalomaniac, and I just got him to stop. If I...lost my head for a while, it's only because I was confused. I've come to my senses, and I don't need you screwing anything up!"

Lauren's eyes flash and her face takes on a positively frightening cast—we don't call her Tasmanian Devil for nothing. With cruel deliberation, she crumples the paper into a tight ball and with unerring accuracy tosses it right into Gus Haldemann's lap without ever looking away from me. He picks it up, lays it on the table in front of him, and goes back to his paper without missing a beat.

The only worse thing she could have done would have been showing that blog to Collie (thankfully he's out on a personal day today because Munchkin's sick). There's no way I can get it back without humiliating explanations. I scoot my chair back, legs screeching on the tile floor, making everyone in the room wince. My heels tap an angry staccato rhythm as I cross the room, and I can feel eyes boring into my back as I leave the break room, but I don't turn to see whose.

About an hour later, Allison comes into my cube and tugs on my chair, causing me to mistype.

"Allie! I'm recording a tutorial. Now I have to edit the code."

"Something's going on. Stand up."

I stand, finding my other cube mates prairie dogging out of their chairs as well, just in time to see Frannie disappearing into Gretchen's office. The door bangs shut behind her. I glance at Lauren and mutter to Allie, "This had better not be about that damn blog."

Allie tugs me back down. "Lauren was really sorry after she did it, but she couldn't get it back."

"Did she even try?" I ask coldly.

"He left right after you did. The paper wasn't on the table, so we assume he took it with him."

I sink into my chair and bury my face in my hands. "Oh, *great*. This is all I need." I have no trouble picturing him smoothing the paper out and reading my jealous maunderings. At least it might have been good for a laugh.

Frannie comes out of Gretchen's office a while later, and we all prairie dog again. She looks like she's been crying. Hannah, her cube closest to Fran's office, takes three steps toward her, but Frannie waves her off, shutting her office door behind her and twirling the blinds closed so we can't see in.

"What the hell?" Lauren murmurs.

I sit back down, a little worried. And a few minutes later an e-mail pops up from Gretchen. I open it immediately, figuring it's an explanation for Frannie crying, and in a way I suppose it is, but not how I expected.

"I have had a long career here at Harper & Lyttle, and have met many terrific people. It is with regret that I say goodbye to my work family. I will be leaving the company at the end of the week to pursue other opportunities. Thank you, everyone, for the wonderful memories and experiences. I will miss you all. Gretchen Clark."

* * * * *

Frannie seems to have gone into a period of mourning; the last two days of Gretchen's employment with Harper & Lyttle find her bursting into tears without warning. It could just be post-partum depression, but I'm pretty certain it's Gretchen's decision to quit, precipitated by her ex-husband's transfer to Houston. Contrary to popular rumor, she didn't move back in with James after leaving Gus. She moved into an apartment with the girls. But James asked her to go with him to Texas and told her if she said no, he wouldn't ask again.

So off to Houston she went, for better or worse. Fran isn't taking it well; I'm not entirely sure if it's because Gretchen's no longer close at hand or because she went back to James.

Collie has made a concentrated effort to tone down his testosterone, and we even went and played basketball for a couple of hours last night. Yeah, he's good at that too, the jerk, but at least I can hold my own and might have even raised his estimation of my athletic ability. Given enough time, I might even forgive him for griping to his brother about my bowling deficiencies while he thought I wasn't in my cube.

The last couple of weeks have been remarkably uneventful, which should have been my first clue that things were about to go sideways. But me—I've never been very good at picking up on vibes.

I'm keying in my handwritten notes from some new software that I've been testing when I hear Collie swear softly. It's not often that he uses profanity, so when his stunned "Well, fuck *me*!" floats over the cube wall, it gets my attention immediately.

"Win the lottery?" I ask cheerfully.

"Oh, he probably won some sports pool," Hannah remarks.

"Or Showtime cancelled his subscription," Allie chimes in.

Stella's cutting voice outdoes us all: "He probably just woke up and realized you all are *still* talking."

"Quinn," Collie calls out, his voice strange. "Can I talk to you for a minute?"

"Sure."

He's already waiting for me outside the cube farm, and I'm shocked to see his colorless face. Taking me by the elbow, he marches me to the break room, but finding that room occupied, he keeps moving until we find a vacant alcove by a window.

"Collie? What is it?" I tug his hand to bring him down to the bench to sit beside me, but he paces instead, running a hand through his hair.

"I got an e-mail." He barks out a laugh, a sound of bewilderment rather than humor. "Jesus, did I get an e-mail." He rubs a hand over his face and stops abruptly. "Megan's mother wants to see her."

"Oh my God, Collie! I thought you didn't even know where she is."

"I don't, and she didn't say."

"How did she know where you work?"

"She didn't send to my work. She sent to an old e-mail account I check every now and then." And for some strange reason, I get the feeling there are unspoken words hanging at the end of that sentence: *just in case she ever wanted to reach me.*

Not for the first time, I wonder about the exact nature of their relationship. Collie's never said anything conclusive, and I've always had the impression that if it wasn't a one-night stand, it wasn't a relationship that had lasted very much longer. Now I wonder.

I can't explain the strange feeling inside me, and I know it isn't anything compared to what he must be going through. Take my twisted gut and sudden, breathless panic and multiply it by a million, and that's where Collie's at right now. I get it; I really do. It sucks to be a single father. The courts favor the mother so often, even when the mother abandons the child and now wants to come back. I can read his fear like a billboard.

"What are you going to do?"

"Call my lawyer." He sits abruptly. "I don't want to lose Megan."

"I know."

He bounces to his feet again. "I need to make a call." He stalks away, quick strides taking him back to our division. And that's the beginning of Collie's abrupt personality change.

Over the following weeks, he's so stressed that I barely see him. When I ask if he's communicated with Megan's mother, he replies "Yes," in such a terse tone that I don't ask again. I tried several times today to broach the subject of dinner plans for my birthday tomorrow, but he was in such a foul mood I never managed to find the courage to push the issue. I console myself with the fact that I'll have lots of birthdays and he's fighting to keep his daughter, but it still hurts.

Frannie, likewise, is stressed and uncharacteristically curt as she goes through applications to hire someone for Gretchen's position. Stella has indicated a surprising reluctance to move up, stating that she

123

and Mario are happy working only forty hours a week and being ulcer-free, and she has declined a promotion. Frannie has finally narrowed down the applicant pool to five candidates, which she has me review as well to see if she's missed any indication of unsuitability. She hasn't been sleeping well—the baby gets her and Sam up a couple of times every night—and she looks exhausted.

"You should get home, Frannie; you're beat. Sam and little Noelle are waiting for you. I'll close up the office."

She cracks a tired smile. "You mean Sam and Noelle are sleeping on the sofa, taking advantage of mean old Mommy coming home late."

"I see how it is." I grin back at her. "But I'm serious. Go home and have a glass of wine and relax. Take a long bath. Go to bed early. But go!"

"Oh, all right. But I have to make cupcakes tonight. *Someone* has a birthday tomorrow."

I raise a brow. "I can't imagine who."

"Do you have any exciting plans?"

"I thought I did, but now I don't know. Collie's…really distracted right now."

"It'll be all right," Frannie assures me, patting my shoulder. "I'm sure he isn't so distracted that he forgets your birthday or blows you off." She shrugs into a windbreaker and picks up her leather brief bag. "I'll send Harold up to escort you to your car. You're an angel, Sarah. I'll see you tomorrow."

Once she's gone, I make my way around the office, turning off lights, cup warmers, and radios—things Frannie usually does after we go home. When I finally make my way back to my cube to grab my things and leave, I find a greeting card-sized envelope in front of my keyboard, my name written on the front in an unfamiliar, masculine hand. It wasn't there when I went into Frannie's office an hour and a half ago, so someone snuck up here and left it while we were occupied—which is kind of creepy when you think about it, especially with Eric Edwards running loose, but with Harold hovering unobtrusively by Fran's office, I'm not too worried about it.

I slit the seal with a letter opener (and let's talk about that for a second, shall we? Why the hell does a company whose Adminisphere regularly enrages its employees equip said employees with sharp, stabby objects?) and slide out the card.

Honesty is the best policy here; I think we've established that already. The truth is I barely even look at the card because my attention is riveted on the paper tucked inside. It's been crumpled and then straightened out again, but won't lay flat. Heart hammering like a bass drum, I unfold it.

And groan—"Oh, *no!*"—because it's the printout of my blog that Lauren had wadded up and thrown at Gus Haldemann. He's left his remarks in a bold, masculine hand at the bottom of my diatribe: *Thanks for the advice; you're right; the help files are anything* but *help. I've been in the online tech forums all damn day. The woman is my sister. And who says I've forgotten?*

A WHAT-DID-I-DO-LAST-NIGHT INCIDENT OF EPIC PROPORTIONS

I come in the next morning to a scattering of birthday cards and presents across my desk: a lace-trimmed tank and complementing shirt from Allie; a desk calendar of classic art from Hannah; a novel about a girl whose blog gets her into mishaps from Lauren (!); a silk scarf from Stella; a book called *15 Signs That He's Not Right for You* from Brooke (which makes me wonder what she's trying to tell me); a gift certificate to a local art supply store from Morgan; and a pair of tickets to a showing at an art museum from Frannie and Sam. Collie is late coming in, but he brings me a set of quality paint brushes in a handsome, cherry-finished box, and a very…ah…physical apology for being so distracted of late (which doesn't stop him, however, from continuing to be distracted).

There's no explanation for the truly gorgeous art book on the techniques of the great artists—Picasso, Rembrandt, Gauguin, Renoir, Degas, and Magritte, among others. It's simply there beside my monitor, its vibrant cover like a magnet to my eyes.

Between sporadic bouts of work and several hushed phone conversations, Collie comes into my cube to peruse my haul, examining each gift in turn.

"Hey, this is pretty nice," he remarks approvingly as he pages through the art book. "Who gave this to you?"

"No idea. It was just here when I got in this morning. No card, nothing."

Collie's face goes carefully neutral. It suddenly occurs to me what I should have known all along: when one is fond of a woman who is otherwise spoken for, a gift of this expense is given anonymously. And then I remember the card—the card I barely read because all my attention was focused on that damned crumpled paper tucked inside.

He lays the book down abruptly. "So Quinn, what do you want to do tonight? Dinner, movie. Bowling?" He waggles a brow at me and I smack him on the arm.

"Dinner and movie, yes. That would be nice."

He leans in for a quick kiss and murmurs, "As you wish," before going back to his cube. I bite my lip, troubled at his sudden display of attentiveness. I'm not sure I want him to abruptly morph into the consummate suitor when I'm torn and uncertain of who I really want.

And truthfully, it really bothers me that he never presses the physicality of our attraction to the limits of the boundaries we set. I understand his opinion, and completely agree with it, that sex shouldn't be the focus of our relationship and that we shouldn't risk an unplanned pregnancy, but I'd at least like to know he desires me.

When I'm sure he's staying in his cubicle (I know because he's on the phone again), I slide the birthday card out of my desk drawer where, out of an unprecedented sense of prudence, I'd stored it—no, that's not true. I promised honesty, didn't I?

I hid the card. I hid it because I knew that I'd be getting lots of people through my cubicle who might ask uncomfortable questions. I hid it because I know Gus Haldemann is one of Collie's buttons, and I didn't want that button pushed on my birthday. And because, above all other reasons, I didn't want Collie doing anything to deface the perfection of that card. I know, I know! You aren't thinking anything about me that I'm not thinking about myself.

The photo on the card is a forest on fire, flames reaching into the night sky, smoke coloring the moon a rich copper. The printed quote inside reads *"A great flame follows a little spark." - Dante Alighieri*. And in his own hand: *Happy birthday, Sarah-Jane Quinn*.

Oh, I know it's a stretch to make a big deal of such a card. But you tell me—honestly—that if a man who had professed a personal interest in you gave you a card talking about sparks causing great flames, you'd think he was talking about not starting forest fires.

The blog, in case you're wondering but think it indelicate to ask, is folded up in my wallet.

* * * * *

Collie is late picking me up; Munchkin had a hard time letting him go when he dropped her at his parents' for the evening. The emotional toll that her mother's return is taking on Munchkin makes me angry, and I don't fully understand why Collie didn't just tell whatever-her-name-is that she couldn't see Megan. After all, when eighteen consecutive months had passed and she'd attempted no contact with her child, the state terminated her parental rights and Collie was given full custody. That he seems to be bending over to accommodate her is irksome, but I'll go so far as to admit that as long as he does, I feel justified in my flirtation with Gus. Flimsy excuse, I know.

Dinner is fantastic; you can't go wrong with a good steak. We try the infamous Valentine's Day steakhouse again, and this time our evening isn't laced with drama. It is, however, punctuated with some not-so-comfortable silences that for some reason I'm sure have nothing to do with his obvious exhaustion.

And speaking of his exhaustion... Call me completely clueless or insensitive if you will, but it seems to me that his weariness far exceeds his daily activities. To tell you the truth, I'm not really sure anymore just *what* his daily activities entail. I see him mostly at work; he rarely comes by my apartment anymore, claiming he's too tired or busy. I know there's a lot of work involved in making sure he retains custody of his daughter, I'm sure the worry keeps him awake some nights, and I know I'm making this sound like it's all about me, but...damn.

And Easter—I haven't told you about that, have I? Collie, Munchkin, and I went to Collie's parents' house for Easter dinner. Or perhaps I should say Easter Dinner, for that's how the invitation was issued. Collie told me to dress nice—very nice—and even though I obliged, I looked and felt like a Pinto in a parking lot of Mercedes Benzes.

The Tates were polite and impeccably mannered, but chilly. And I, being Sarah-Jane Quinn, found myself retreating. By dessert and coffee, a thick silence had descended on the table. I know Collie was annoyed with me, and later when I tried to explain that I felt their judgment of me had found me wanting, he accused me of calling his parents snobs. All in all, it wasn't a fantastic evening. And now, lest you be completely in love with him and think I'm a terrible person for being torn between him and Gus Haldemann, let me disabuse you of the notion that he is always the sunny, carefree Collie I've presented previously.

After dinner, he begs off the movie—and I let him. He's so tired that he wouldn't have enjoyed it. If he'd fallen asleep during it, I'd have felt guilty for dragging him out when he's weary and stressed, and what fun would that have been? But I'm disappointed, bitterly so.

"Happy birthday indeed, Sarah-Jane Quinn," I murmur as I watch his tail lights round the corner at the end of the block. *What is it about me that makes it so I'm never at the top of anyone's list?*

And it's this thought, perhaps, that motivates me to swap my slacks and blouse for snug jeans and a trendy shirt that clings to my curves and leaves my bare shoulders peeking through artful cutouts. I'm going to Marty's to have a tall, cool Mojito or three. Maybe nine. Yeah, nine.

I call a cab because I know I won't be able to drive myself home. I resolutely refuse to think about the preceding half of the evening on the long ride to Marty's, and when I arrive I head straight for the bar in the corner, tunnel vision blinding me to everything except the promise of rum oblivion.

"Mojito, light on the mint."

Slapping my money onto the bar, I slide onto a vacant stool. A man at the end of the bar, looking a little unsavory with his day's growth of beard and his carefully mussed hair, stands up and starts my way. I beam a glare at him, satisfied to see him stop in his tracks and reconsider his decision to be ruled by his baser instincts.

"Make it two," I say to the bartender over a raucous cheer from a rowdy table on the other side of the room. He hesitates, and I add, "It's my birthday."

"Then happy birthday." He sets in front of me a perfect blend of mint, rum, and…whatever the hell else Mojitos are made with, and by the time he has the next one ready I've drained the glass. He eyes me as though assessing how much trouble I'm going to be as he whisks the empty glass away, but then flicks a glance over my head and moves off down the bar to tend to other tasks. I start in on the second drink, and the amused chuckle behind me makes me choke.

"Well, Sarah-Jane Quinn, you sure know how to make an entrance."

"Are you stalking me?" I don't turn to look at Gus as he leans against the bar between my stool and the one next to it, uncomfortably —intoxicatingly—close.

"I was here first." He pries the glass from my hand and takes an experimental drink—an unprecedented liberty that implies intimacy— and makes a face. "I think he made this a double. I hope you aren't planning to drive yourself home."

I scowl at him. "Came in a cab, going home in one. Can I have my drink back? I have some celebrating to do."

"Celebrating…all by yourself?" He pauses, grey eyes moving from my hand clenched around my glass to my eyes. "Where's Collie?"

"He was tired, so he went home after dinner. I wasn't ready to call it a night."

"Too tired to take his girlfriend out for her birthday?"

I frown. "He took me to dinner. He's just been…preoccupied with some personal issues. You know how it is."

"Mmmm," he answers noncommittally. "All I know is I'm not as careless as he is. Why don't you join us?"

"Us?" I start to turn to see who might be with him, and he stops my chair with a grin that makes me want to fling myself into his arms and pledge to be his sex slave for life.

"My sister's not here tonight or I'd be delighted to introduce you."

Hot color rushes into my cheeks. "A gentleman wouldn't bring that up."

"Who says I'm a gentleman? Come along, Sarah-Jane." He casts a glance down the bar to my ill-fated Romeo. "I obviously need to keep an eye on you since you're determined to drink yourself into oblivion."

"What are *you* up to tonight? Just out for a quiet drink with friends?"

"Nothing quiet about it; we're the noisiest table in the place. Frannie bought that *Pirates of the Caribbean Game of Life* and for some reason she seems to think it'd be fun to play it while drinking numerous margaritas."

"I don't want to displace anyone."

His hand curves around the glass, sliding over mine. "Sarah, stop worrying about offending people and start having fun. Come on."

He doesn't give me a choice this time. He takes my drink and tugs me off the stool, leading me by the hand across the room. I'm acutely conscious of his fingers curled firmly around mine, especially when we arrive at his table. Nothing escapes the attention of Sam, but he looks away discreetly, a smile tugging at his mouth. Frannie sends a pointed glance at our joined hands and another at Gus, who blithely ignores it. He drops my hand to pull out a chair for me, and sets my drink on a paper coaster a safe distance from the game.

"Sarah's on her own tonight. I invited her to join us."

"On your own?" Sam says, and now Frannie's gaze shifts to me, one brow arched inquiringly.

"Collie bailed early," I explain, feeling inexplicably embarrassed to admit that. Oh, all *right*—it's *not* inexplicable. It goes back to that question I asked myself earlier: *What is it about me that makes it so I'm never at the top of anyone's list?* And it *is* embarrassing to have to admit that even to my own boyfriend I'm unimportant, easily forgotten.

Who says I've forgotten?

Remembering Gus's comment written on my blog, I glance up at him from the corner of my eye, finding no pity in his expression. I relax marginally, finding courage in my Mojito, and as Fran reads the rules of the game I find myself wondering what sort of crazy universe I landed in. I should be with Collie; he's what I wanted. Yet there's that strange yearning I feel toward Gus, and Collie bailed on me. Here I sit, timid little Sarah-Jane, rubbing elbows with management—and indulging in dangerous daydreams.

"Sarah, you're the youngest. Rules say you spin first." Sam

motions to the board.

Ah, what the hell? I've done crazier things on my birthday than playing *The Game of Life* pirates' style. Such as playing Spin the Bottle in a cemetery at two in the morning one summer…

The Mojitos flow as captains and ships are chosen, booty is collected, and then lost again as calamity strikes. My last real moment of clarity finds me marveling that I'm so at ease with these people. At one point in time I think I even confide in them my deepest secret dream: to buy a bed and breakfast inn that I can vaguely remember vacationing at when I was a child. I can't remember the name of it, but I'm fairly certain it was in northern California. I've never before told *anyone* about that secret desire, and I'm hoping I didn't admit to them the main reason I want that place.

Oh, it's nothing really earth-shattering. I just remember a swing set in the immaculately landscaped yard and twirling up the swing so I could spin when a boy several years my senior came over and pushed me off. I skinned my knees and bumped my chin and hollered holy hell. Mom berated me for being a crybaby and Mary-Anne pressed her finger hard against my bruised chin, but the mistress of the inn cradled me to her cushy bosom and showered me with endearments I couldn't understand because they were spoken in another language. I'm pretty sure she was French. And later that evening as the sun set, she wrapped me in a hand-sewn quilt on the porch swing and shared with me a dish of homemade ice cream topped with fresh blackberries. Silly that that's one of the few treasured memories of my lifetime, but there you have it.

The rest of the evening passes in a blur. I'm not sure how many Mojitos I drank; I sincerely hope no one got stuck with my bar tab because I went with only a certain amount of money for drinks and an amount set aside for cab fare. I do recall not needing the cab fare; Frannie and Sam offer to drive me home, but Gus tells them not to be ridiculous; he has to go in my direction anyway, and they live the opposite way. I also remember a *big* truck, and being boosted up into it by strong hands. And something about a movie—one of the *Bourne* series, I believe—and I'm reasonably sure I wasn't talking to myself while lounging on the sofa, so I'm sure in my inebriation I invited him inside. Or perhaps he had to carry me (Jesus…is there no end to my humiliation?) and I invited him to stay.

Then there's the vague memory of looking up with a bleary gaze into grey eyes, but that would be ridiculous because it would mean that I was lying in his lap, and the potential for complete mortification over that is simply too much to bear.

But I push away the memories—hallucinations?—because my head hurts too much to think and the light peeking between the panels of the living room curtains stabs me like a thousand ice picks in my brain. I throw an arm over my eyes and groan, shifting my position to one more comfortable. I'm warm and lazy, albeit miserably hung-over, and I could lay here on this sofa forever enjoying the soothing comfort of the chenille blanket covering me; the firm cushions beneath me; the steady, strong beat of the heart against my back; and the soft stirring of breath on my neck—

Holy *shit!*

I twist around, only now realizing my precarious position on the sofa is made secure by muscular arms around me. The world tilts and my stomach heaves a mighty protest at the unwelcome movement, but those are nothing compared to the seizure my heart has when I see him.

Shirt half unbuttoned, revealing a muscled, tanned chest in which beats that rhythmic pulse I was so enjoying before I realized exactly what it meant. Long, black lashes fanned out against high, proud cheekbones, closed eyelids shielding those penetrating grey eyes.

A lazy chuckle rumbles in his chest, and without opening his eyes he murmurs, "Too late to run now, Sarah-Jane."

Oh. My. GOD! I JUST SPENT THE NIGHT WITH GUS HALDEMANN!

TAMING THE (TASMANIAN) DEVIL

There's a procedure called a Plexotomy that I'm considering having done. That's where a sheet of Plexiglas is inserted in your abdomen so when you have your head up your ass, you can see where you're going. I figure I'm a prime candidate.

I spend the rest of the weekend alternately burning with shame and anxiously wondering if anyone ever died from a Mojito hangover. I've heard of people *wanting* to die from a tequila hangover, and I imagine rum is much the same in after-effect.

Gus didn't stay long after I woke up and discovered we'd slept together on my sofa. Perhaps he sensed my utter horror at my discreditable conduct; I'm sure my tumbling off the sofa exclaiming, "Oh my God! Holy fucking shit! What the hell did I *do*?" probably clued him in to the fact that I was quite displeased with my behavior.

While I shower and brush my teeth, he makes coffee. Over a strong cup of java—and sitting on separate pieces of furniture—he assures me that nothing untoward happened. He'd stayed because it was my birthday and I'd asked him to, and watching a movie with me seemed harmless enough. Then I fell asleep and gradually slumped in my seat, ending up (in a drunken sprawl, although he doesn't say that) across his lap. In an instance like this, what's a poor, sexy bachelor to do but ease himself down beside me and stay the night?

"Not so much as a…I mean, we didn't even…"

"Not even a kiss," Gus insists, eyes gleaming, which makes me wonder if I'd tried and he begged off. I rather doubt he'd take advantage of a drunken idiot; he'd want his woman conscious and fully capable of enjoying his considerable charms.

I half expect to hear from Collie over the weekend, and I agonize about whether or not I should tell him. My friend Jennifer, one of my few remaining single pals, comes over Saturday night with a bag full of greasy burgers and onion rings, a sure-fire cure for a bad hangover. After scarfing a couple of the greasy burgs and a handful of onion rings, my stomach feels much better. My abject humiliation remains unabated, however, and Jennifer advises me not to tell Collie about Gus spending the night NO MATTER WHAT. But keeping this secret from him, especially considering what he's going through with Munchkin's mother, seems like a betrayal.

Betrayal. Could it be called a betrayal when nothing happened? And when Collie has made no exclusive commitment to me, or I to him? With the way he has been acting lately, it's almost like I don't exist anyway.

I still haven't decided what to do by Monday morning, and I go into the office with a trepidation I haven't felt since my first day. But Collie's so wrapped up in his own emotional upheaval that he doesn't seem to notice my mental turmoil. In fact, he doesn't even greet me until nearly nine-thirty, and then it's obvious something is occupying the majority of his attention…and it's equally obvious that it isn't me.

"Psst! Quinn."

"What?"

"Take a break? Gotta talk."

Oh boy.

I follow him down to the only place we can have a private conversation: the basement, although this spring it's been a regular hotspot. He leads me through the labyrinth—or perhaps by this time I should be saying The Labyrinth—and finds a couple of chairs so we can sit. Dark circles underscore his eyes, and his normally vibrant smile is gone. I realize I haven't seen it since Munchkin's mother e-mailed him.

I sit facing him, watching him closely. He sits with his hands clasped between his knees, staring at them.

"I'm sorry I've been…preoccupied," he finally says.

"I understand." And I do, that's the bitch of it. I understand that I will never top his list of priorities, and that's as it should be: he has a child, and she takes precedence. I have an unexpected epiphany and miss half of what he's saying: I don't know if I can be second in line for the rest of my life. Somewhere, someday, I want to be someone's first thought.

He looks up, his green eyes shadowed. "I haven't been sleeping well. I'm tied up in knots all the time. I'm so frigging scared they're going to give Megan back to her mother that I can't think straight."

"I know. It's all right."

"No, it's not. And last night, I just left you high and dry on your birthday. I'm sorry, Sarah. I haven't treated you right at all, and I wanted to apologize for it."

I squirm in my chair uncomfortably. Yeah, I'm a real piece of work—finally he's able to see above the horizon of his own personal hell, and I'm sleeping with Gus Haldemann. Well, not *sleeping* sleeping with him, but you know what I mean.

Collie reaches out to take my hands, holding them lightly between us. "I think I owe it to you to tell you what's going on."

"All right." I have a quivery feeling of anxious dread at what's coming, because while I may be torn between him and Gus, I don't want to let him go.

He draws in a breath. "I called my lawyer after I received Yasmina's e-mail."

I don't hear the next two sentences; now Megan's mother has a name: Yasmina. And I have to face the fact that she was once Collie's lover. I'm not certain whether it's jealousy I feel or that faithful old companion that's been with me most of my life: that feeling of somehow just barely missing out on all the best things. Yasmina knew him before he became a father; did she also know what it's like to be Collie's first priority?

"We set up a meeting with her, just to get a feel for what she was really after." He scuffs his shoe across the cement floor, kicking his toe lightly against the leg of my chair. "We came up with a plan to reintroduce her into Meg's life with the least possible disruption."

"And that entails?" I can see it all too clearly: every weekend taken up with ferrying Megan to or retrieving her from her mother; countless interruptions in our time together to deal with Yasmina. Am I ready for that kind of life—becoming third instead of second, because the child's mother must be appeased lest she file court action?

"She took a leave of absence from her job and is working for a temp agency while she's here. She'll stay for six more weeks, and then she'll go back to Seattle."

There's a catch, I know there is. Things like this never come without one. "And after that?"

"I have to reciprocate. In August I'll have to go to Seattle for eight weeks."

I swallow hard, feeling the first tightening in my chest, and for the first time I wonder why I'm always so nervous and uptight when I'm with him, never at ease. Shouldn't he be a safe haven, a place where I can wind down and relax? Wouldn't he be comfort and security if I really loved him—and were certain that he loved me in return?

"I'm…not sure I understand why you have to do this."

He flicks a glance at my face, and then looks back down at our hands, shifting his grip. "We're trying to determine where Megan would best thrive."

"Trying to determine custody, you mean?"

"Sort of. If she does best here with the support system she has, Yasmina will move back down here. If Megan does best in Seattle…"

"Then you move to Seattle." The words fall like a dead thing from my mouth. I can't believe this is happening, that my life is once again spinning out of my control. And what happens if he—no. I won't think about that right now. Yasmina abandoned their daughter at the daycare—the daughter Collie hadn't even known he'd created—and attempted no contact in the intervening two-plus years. How could I even think he'd want a relationship with her?

"I have to do this, Sarah," he rushes on desperately. "I'm fairly certain that Yasmina will end up moving back here; Megan's got a good support system here already. But I have to be prepared for any event."

I want to ask where this leaves us, but I can't force the words out.

So I remain silent, as always, trembling but unable to express the dread running rampant through my entire body. Surely he can see it, surely—

But he doesn't. He's so in the grip of his own panic that he can't see beyond it. I offer a smile that feels more like a grimace and words that I don't really believe: "I'm sure everything will work out fine, Collie."

He smiles in relief and some of the tension goes out of him. Don't worry, though—it didn't get lost; it found me, and becomes my almost constant companion.

"All right, then. I feel much better; I should have told you sooner." He tugs my hands, bringing me closer, and kisses me lightly, quickly. Distractedly. "We'd better get back to work. C'mon, Quinn."

I follow him back upstairs, and he leaves me at my cubicle with another perfunctory kiss. I sink into my chair, butterflies swarming in my stomach, and for a long time I simply stare at my screensaver, wondering why I'm always on the outside looking in.

But there's a saying I've heard bandied about all my life: No sense borrowing trouble. So I don't…or I try not to, anyway.

On Wednesday the company has a potluck in the convention room. Well, "potluck" is the generalized term; they tout it as a "Summer Social." Frannie eyes the flyers pasted everywhere—and I *do* mean everywhere, even inside the restroom stalls—with a mixture of amusement and disgust and mutters, "But what if we don't *want* to be social with people we work with?"

I don't mind these kitschy things for the simple reason of who I get to see at them. And speaking of… At the salad table, peering into a metal bowl with an expression that clearly wonders *what in the hell is this*, stands Gus. He elbows Sam; their heads go together as they collectively try to determine the nature and composition of the offering in the bowl. Then each shakes his head and they scurry away as though afraid the salad in question might jump from its confines and onto their plates without their knowledge or consent.

Frannie snorts her derision at this display of male bravery, and I suppress a smile, turning to find Lauren frowning at me.

"You're playing with fire," she hisses, and lapses into a phlegm-rattling coughing fit. She has a summer cold and is testy as hell. Oh, and let's add the monthly blight and its flood of bitch-creating hormones, and damn!

"Mind your own business or I'll be speaking to Stewart." I smile sweetly at her as she takes a cough drop from her pocket and unwraps it. The other pocket holds a couple of O.B. tampons. I hope she doesn't get her pockets confused.

"Fine. I'll reserve a room for you in the burn unit." And she flounces away, grabbing a startled Hannah by the arm as they pass each other. Hannah gives us a helpless shrug and allows Lauren to drag her off.

"What was that about?" Collie asks at my elbow. I jump, the butterflies taking frantic flight inside me.

"I threatened to tell Stewart Drummond she likes him, and she threatened to flame-broil me."

"Don't poke the Tasmanian Devil," he warns with a grin. "Although...bet you a dime—"

"Oh no you don't!"

"C'mon, Quinn. Live a little. Bet you a dime you can't get the two of them together today."

I frown. "That's moving a little fast, isn't it?"

"We men don't like to take our time."

"And we women have noticed. Why do you think we fake it?"

He winces. "Ouch. Touché. All right—not *together* together, but...at least to the speaking stages of the courting dance."

"I'm beginning to think the tectonic plates move faster than either of those two. But I'll take your bet."

The task proves not to be an easy one. I don't think I'll quit my day job to become a matchmaker. To start with, Lauren is suspicious by nature and vocal about it (Tasmanian Devil, remember?) so maneuvering her across the room to where Stewart stands in a clutch of programmer cronies takes a finesse I'm not sure I possess. Add to it Collie's devious and brilliant sabotage, and the difficulty of my mission increases two-fold.

It's Frannie who inadvertently comes to my aid and tips the scales in my favor. She apparently has no qualms about marching Stewart across the room, and Lauren damn near faints when she sees him coming. She would have bolted for the nearest 'fraidy-rabbit hole had I not clamped my hand around her arm tight enough to make her grimace.

"*Sarah!*" she grinds out, jaws clenched.

"Mmmm? Oh, sorry." Feigning innocence, I ease up the pressure on her arm, conveniently just as Frannie and our man Stewart join us.

"Sarah, you know Stewart, right? Tell him about that little bug you found in the new HR project—and that enhancement you wanted."

Stewart listens attentively as I explain the glitch I found and a couple enhancements I think would be beneficial to such a program. After several minutes I notice his attention is wandering. His gaze sneaks surreptitiously to Lauren, who blushes, and an answering blush blooms in his face. After noticing this phenomenon several times, I know I've bagged my dime.

I tactfully bring the discussion to a close, and then almost as an afterthought I say, "Stewart, do you know Lauren Douglas? Lauren, Stewart Drummond."

"We've met," Stewart says, his voice like a strangled duck. Lauren looks surprised, and his face flames. "Christmas party."

"Oh, yeah," she says dumbly.

My mental groan is so loud I'm sure she must have heard it, for she stammers for something more intelligent to say and ends up in a coughing fit. Into her pocket goes her hand as Stewart steps manfully up to the plate and raises his hand to thump her helpfully on the back. Indecision and self-consciousness stay his hand.

"Sorry!" Lauren gasps, her voice rough and phlegmy. "Terrible cold."

A wrapper rattles, and then Stewart's eyes grow big and round, and his shade of red turns Day-Glo fluorescent.

"Aaaaahhhhh," he says, and I'm sure he must be having a stroke. "Excuse me," and abruptly scurries away. I turn to Lauren, perplexed.

"What the—*shit!*"

Hurriedly, I close my hand over hers and shove it down to her

141

side, and over her shoulder I catch sight of Collie, who is smothering his laughter with his hand. He rubs the fingers of his other hand together in the age-old "give me money" gesture, and I rub my middle finger along the side of my nose. His grin widens; he knows I was *this close* to victory, and my success was shot down by Lauren herself, because half unwrapped and aiming for her mouth had been an O.B. tampon.

Tales from the Water Cooler

Friday, June 26
Choices

Posted by Sarah Quinn

Today we're going to talk about choices. You're going to have to make them, so no sense in dodging the issue. God knows I've tried that and ended up with a frigging mess—but enough about me.

As you go about your daily tasks you may find yourself confronted with the choice between two different programs. For the sake of example, let's say you're presented with the choice between Windows 7 and…MS-DOS.

Now MS-DOS is a tried-and-true program, no doubt about that. But let's examine its functionality. A bit slower to get anything done, what with all the commands to remember; there is no Undo if you make a mistake; response time is slower. Not to mention it's an outdated mode of operation and seems a little tired, and all its resources are being used elsewhere, so you aren't ever going to be its *numero uno*.

Windows 7, however, has all the bells and whistles. This baby is faster than the speed of light (figuratively speaking) and can process multiple tasks at the same time with no noticeable lag. Bright colors, crystal clear images, quality sound, and sleek style. It is hot, hot, hot! You can't wait to open it up and put it through its paces. You search with delicious anticipation for surprises yet undiscovered.

The decision should be easy to make, shouldn't it? There should be no confusion about which is the better product, which has more to offer. But you're used to that MS-DOS; you know its quirks and know how to cajole a response—most of the time. And although you're never quite at ease with it because you aren't sure what command is going to send all your data into the ever-after, you're not quite ready to let it go.

143

Damn you, Windows 7! Damn you for showing me what I never knew I wanted! I'm just a simple girl—I don't know how to handle this sophistication!

DID YOU KNOW:

WINDOWS TIP: If you hold down the Windows key (key with the Windows icon, usually near the ALT key) and press TAB, all the windows you have open will stagger at an angle on your screen in a smaller version. As you click TAB, you can scroll through them. When you find the one you want, just let go of the Windows key, and that window becomes your active one.

This is similar to ALT+TAB, which lets you tab through teensy icons (with captions, so you know what you're looking at) so that you can quickly change your active window without having to grab the mouse, only this is way cooler.

This only works with Vista and later versions of Windows.

Blog Archive
  2009
    June
      Choices
    May
      WTF Is Wrong with Men???
    March
      Love Triangles: Three- Pointed Pains-in-the…
    February
      Faces in the Crowd
    January
      Going Postal: A Career-Limiting Move

About Me

Savvy Sarah

I am an administrative office professional with several years' experience in office settings. I have an AAS in Administrative Office Management and currently work as a training specialist for a software development company in Los Angeles.

A SHIFT IN THE BALANCE

Over the next week I spend an inordinate amount of time with Stewart Drummond, going over the software I'm testing and chasing bugs. The product is a human resources management environment—or so says Stewart; to me it's a kick-ass database that links all pertinent data together in one convenient place. I wonder idly if Gus has seen it.

The few times Stewart comes to my desk to go over something, Collie manages to find something for Lauren to bring me or ask me. Try as I might to facilitate interaction between the two of them, Lauren turns into a stammering imbecile and all the blood in Stewart's body seems to find his face, which apparently renders him speechless. Frankly I can't see them ever getting to the speaking stage, let alone going out on a date. And I thought I was socially inept.

Three of the five applicants Frannie was considering for interviews have already found jobs, so I also spend a lot of time with her, going over the remaining apps to broaden the interview pool. Company policy states we have to interview five candidates unless fewer than five have applied for the job. I'm beginning to see what Frannie means when she says the oxygen gets thinner the higher up the corporate ladder you go, making logical thought difficult if not downright impossible.

"Oh, you're eating lunch today," Allison remarks caustically as she claims a seat at the table with me, motioning to my half-eaten Panini sandwich. The break room is empty but for us. "Are you looking for a new job?"

I give her an inquiring look, and she motions to the classified ads I'm reading. "Oh. No, I like this job just fine. I saw a listing for a bed-

and-breakfast a few weeks ago, and I was just seeing if it was still in here."

"You're going to buy a bed-and-breakfast?"

"Not just *a* bed-and-breakfast inn, but a particular one—not that I could afford it right now anyway. I spent a vacation at one when I was six. I saw one listed in here that might be it, but it's gone now, and I can't find the issue it was in; someone recycled it. I just wanted to know the name of it and where it's located."

"You don't remember?" Allison opens her insulated lunch bag and takes out a sandwich and an apple, staring at them dismally. "Why did this seem so enticing this morning when I made it, but I'm so disappointed to eat it now?"

I chuckle. "No lie. This looked better on the package than it tastes." I take another half-hearted bite and glance around the break room. I've felt wrong-footed since I came in; after my birthday, Gus stopped eating lunch in here altogether. I miss his quiet presence, and my apprehension over what Eric Edwards might do if he gets a chance to corner me again has reared its ugly head once more.

"Why don't you just call your parents and ask them where you stayed?"

I chew the sandwich, grimacing because it's gone cold and tastes even less appealing than it did warm. "Because I haven't talked to my parents since January."

Allie gapes. "Sarah! That's been—six months?"

"Almost seven."

"And *they* haven't called *you*?"

I send her a look over the top of my paper. "Get real. It's much more convenient for them to not to bother with me. Trust me; I'm perfectly fine with it."

Blatant lie number one. I am not *perfectly fine* with it. I don't know that I will ever even be *reasonably accepting* of it, but what's a girl to do? I can't force them to like me—either figuratively or literally speaking, and I'll never force the issue. You know me—charter member of Nonconfrontationists Unite.

Allie ponders this while making headway on her PBJ. "I knew

things weren't great between you guys, just from things you've said every now and then, but I didn't realize it was that bad."

"Well, now you know." I glance at my watch and fold the paper, setting it aside. "Gotta go. Stewart's coming by to test out that enhancement he's been working on. I have barely enough time to orchestrate some sort of matchmaking scheme with Collie to get Stewart and Lauren actually *speaking*."

I start toward the door, but Allie stops me again with an unexpected—and not entirely welcome—question.

"Have you kissed him?"

"Collie?" I'm baffled, because she herself has seen me kiss Collie on several occasions. And she certainly can't mean Stewart.

She fidgets in her chair. "Gus Haldemann."

A sudden chill douses my body. "No, I haven't. Why would you even ask that?"

She shrugs self-consciously. "I've heard things along the grapevine. I was just wondering what it was like if you had."

"Much like kissing any other man, I imagine," I remark uneasily.

Blatant lie number two. I doubt with every fiber of my being that it's like kissing any other man, because he's not just any other man. I recall thinking *the difference between men and boys* at one point in time, and I've been trying—with nominal success—not to compare the man with the boy. But Collie is one of those who will always remain boyish, and I'd bet—more than a dime—that Gus Haldemann has been a serious-minded fellow from birth, and he's proving to be an inescapable temptation.

"I wonder," says Allison dreamily, "what it's like to have his arms around you."

And I answer without thinking: "Extraordinary," my mind wandering back to the morning I woke up on the sofa with his arms securely wrapped around me.

Allie's eyes pop open wide, her mouth falls open in shock. I scramble hastily to cover my slip. "He hugged me after we delivered Frannie's baby."

"Oh," she says dismissively, although she shoots a speculative look my way. "That's not really what I meant."

"I know what you meant. And now I have only two minutes to set Lauren up with Stewart. Gotta run!" I beat a hasty retreat, hoping like hell Allison forgets all about that conversation. The last thing I need is any of it being repeated to Collie.

Lauren is ridiculously easy to hoodwink, as prickly people often are. She's so intent on being annoyed that she doesn't realize how unashamedly I've manipulated her—and I'm no expert manipulator. I quite detest people doing it to me, so I feel no less the hypocritical schmuck than I appear to be to you.

But this is for her own good, and honestly, I feel partially responsible for the tampon disaster at the Summer Social. I know how tongue-tied and flummoxed she gets around a guy she likes; I never should have allowed her to possess both cough drops and tampons on her person at the same time—although you can't beat the incident's comedic value. Collie came over that night for what's becoming a rare visit, and we howled until our sides ached.

"You going to come over and say hello when Stewart gets here, 'Fraidy-Cat?"

"I'm not afraid. I'm just not—forward." Lauren juts out her chin defensively.

"Well, all right. You just seem so uptight around him. I thought you were afraid."

"I'M NOT AFRAID, SARAH!"

"Really?" I arch a brow at her. "Then Truth-and-Dare. I dare you to ask Stewart out—cup of coffee, drinks, dinner, whatever."

She looks like she just swallowed a slug. Not just any slug, but one of those ginormous ones you find under rocks in the garden after a heavy rain. Super slugs.

"That's not fair!" she hisses.

"Like you making me kiss Collie at the Christmas party?" Got her there. Now she looks like a *guilty* slug-eating individual.

Her eyes shift away from mine. "That was Hannah."

"You think I haven't figured out that you were all in it together? It was too smooth to be a whim. And he wasn't at all surprised, so I'm

150

betting he was the instigator. So what's it to be, Laurie—take the dare or be the slave?"

"Don't call me Laurie!" she mutters just as Stewart comes up behind her.

"I thought your name was Lauren," he says, and promptly blushes like a nuclear explosion.

"It is," she squeaks and clears her throat. She's mostly over the cold, but she's still having some phlegm issues.

"I like Laurie. It suits you."

I'm marginally surprised when everything within a five-foot radius doesn't burst into flame from the intensity of the burning color in his face.

"Er…umm…thank…ah…wouldyoulikeacuppacoffee?" Her own face flaming, Lauren manages to spit the words out, sounding like an auctioneer on speed.

"Aahh," says Stewart, turning that Day-Glo red again. "I just had a Big N' Tasty from McDonald's. I probably shouldn't follow it with anything. But thanks."

Lauren looks excruciatingly embarrassed—and completely deflated. I can't believe they managed to muck up such a well prepared scheme.

"Ah, Stewart," I interject. "I believe she meant would you like to get a cup of coffee with her sometime."

He looks at me strangely, as though wondering how I translated *that* from her garbled squawk. "Oh. Ah. Sure. Tonight?" he stammers hopefully, sounding for all the world like Tarzan. *Me Stewart. You Lauren. Go tonight?*

"Sure!" Lauren squeaks again, her voice rising into the piercing tones of a coloratura soprano. A smile blooms on her face like a rare, exotic flower and he grins foolishly. I sigh mentally. How does Cupid stand his job? No wonder he shoots arrows at us; it's not to make us fall in love, but because we make him want to vomit.

My work with Stewart doesn't take long and I send him off to Lauren's cube, glad to resign as matchmaker. A few minutes later, a dime sails over the cube wall between Collie and me, landing on my keyboard and bouncing a jangling course toward my trash can. I catch it just in time.

"Nice to know you're not a sore loser," I remark.

"Yeah, whatever," is his good-natured rejoinder. A moment later he sidles into my cube, pulling his tie over his head and giving it a quick adjustment. "I have a meeting with my lawyer and Yasmina. I'll see you tomorrow." A quick kiss on the corner of my mouth, almost as an afterthought, and he's gone.

The remainder of the afternoon—and into overtime—is spent with Frannie, going over the other applications and trying to choose three more candidates who meet our qualifications. I get this fantastical chore not because of wisdom or seniority but because no one else wanted to do it.

We finally agree on three applicants and Frannie clips their application packets together, stuffing the rest into a folder. She pinches the bridge of her nose between two fingers and massages for a moment.

"Oh, I have a headache. I hate doing this."

"I know. It *is* kind of a pain—and terrible that it's Gretchen you're replacing."

"Yeah," she murmurs. "I miss her." She straightens abruptly. "Sarah, I don't think I could take one more step than I have to today. Would you mind taking these up to Gus's office? You can just slide them under the door; I'm sure he's gone home for the day."

"I don't mind. Go on home; I'll have Harold walk me out to my car."

"You're a gem, kiddo."

I smile. "I've heard that somewhere before."

I take the elevator up to the fourth floor where Human Resources is located. The quiet hush of the normally busy office is eerie. I stop three steps across the HR lobby. The Keeper of the Gate—aka Gus's administrative assistant, Leslie—has already gone home for the evening, and I have an unimpeded path to his office. He's at his desk, jacket and tie discarded, sleeves rolled up, top two buttons of his shirt undone. The overhead lights are off, and the desk lamp illuminates the center of his desk and the notepad he's writing on, glinting off his gold pen and setting fire to his hair. I rather suspect that he started life as a blond or a redhead; even now, his hair has persistent russet tones that refuse to give way to true brunette.

I knock, and his head comes up quickly, a fleeting look of guilt crossing his expression. "I didn't mean to startle you. Frannie asked me to bring these up to you."

"Thank you, Sarah. So she made her choices?"

"Yes. It was tough for her, though." I glance around his office, wondering if it's my imagination or if I really smell blackberries. The scent triggers a swell of emotion deep inside me, but I can't quite grasp the memory associated with it.

"I'm sure it was."

An awkward silence descends, and after a moment I offer a half smile and excuse myself. "I should be going. I'm late getting out of here."

He stands up, tossing the pen onto his notepad. "Would you like me to walk you out to your car? You shouldn't go alone after business hours."

"Harold is waiting for me in the lobby, but thanks. Goodnight, Gus."

"Goodnight, Sarah," he replies quietly.

I take a step out the door and on crazy impulse pivot on my heel, bracing a hand against the jamb to keep my balance. The words tumble out of my mouth like a wild horse making a break for freedom.

"May I ask you something?"

His posture shifts subtly; he's guarded now. "Certainly."

"The birthday card you gave me…what did you mean?"

"Exactly what the card said. I always say exactly what I mean, Sarah."

I bite my lip, frowning. "Why?"

Now *he* frowns. "Why do I always say what I mean?"

God, this is uncomfortable ground. I feel hopelessly naïve. What the hell am I doing, opening this door? Hadn't I closed it, slammed the bolt home, shut him on the other side of it?

153

"That's not what I meant. I just—I don't understand why a man like you would even bother with—" I stop abruptly, my face flaming *a la* Stewart. Undercurrents in his silence make me fear that I've misunderstood his intentions.

"Someone like you?" he finishes thoughtfully. He comes a couple steps closer but stops when I fidget uneasily. "How do you picture yourself, Sarah?"

I lift one shoulder in a shrug, dropping my eyes. "A girl who had an unhappy childhood and is hopelessly socially inept."

Gus closes his eyes for a moment, breathing in sharply through his nose as though my response has made him angry. He seems to be carefully considering his words.

"That isn't how I see you."

I force the words out, still unable to look at him. "Then what…?"

His voice lowers, his tone taking on that intimate quality that makes me quiver inside. "I see a beautiful young woman with an intelligent mind, a quick wit, and a personality that makes her damn near impossible to forget."

He closes the distance between us despite the keep-your-distance signals I've been sending and hooks a finger under my chin, forcing my head up, waiting to continue until I look at him. His grey eyes are the color of summer storm clouds, dark with emotion.

"What are you really asking, Sarah?"

"I don't know… I shouldn't have said anything. I have to go. Goodnight." Nonconfrontationists—unite!

I head for the elevators at a speed just controlled enough to not be called running, but before I can jab the call button, I hear him jogging to catch up with me. Oh God, I don't want to talk about this, can't he see that?

"Sarah, wait!"

I almost push the button—really, I almost do. I'm terribly embarrassed; why did I even broach the subject? What in the hell is wrong with me? Playing with fire, Lauren had said, and she's right, only it's not just matches I'm fiddling with but a friggin' wildfire that I can't control. What made me think I could move in this circle, that this man would ever be anything but more than I can handle?

But my hand falls away from the button and I wait like a paralyzed rabbit cornered by a hungry predator. All I can do is stand here and dread the killing blow.

He slows his pace as he approaches, but he doesn't stop outside my personal space. One arm slides around me, his hand pressing against the small of my back to keep me anchored to him; the other cups the back of my head, fingers twining into my hair. With the ease of experience, his lips find mine with no awkward bumping or searching. This is not a kiss like he gave me the day Frannie's baby was born. This is the kiss of a man who desires a woman—desires her tremendously.

His scent—musk, heady and intoxicating. His lips—warm and pliant, coaxing my uninhibited response. His mouth—moist and flavored with cinnamon, eliciting dark visions of consuming passion. His heart hammers a frantic rhythm against my chest, matching mine; our breath comes ragged and desperate. He gathers me closer, bringing me up on tiptoe to bridge our difference in height, the full-frontal contact electrifying and exhilarating. Beneath my hands, the muscles of his shoulders seem impossibly strong.

When he breaks the kiss, I feel a piercing loss on some elemental level of which I've never before been aware. His hands frame my face and he stares down into my eyes, his own wide and full of emotions I don't have the experience to name. His voice shakes when he speaks.

"If he can kiss you like that and make you forget me, then you belong with him."

It seems to take an eternity to find my voice, and it trembles like his and I can't force it louder than a whisper. "And if he can't?"

"Then we'll talk about this."

"I don't know what to do. I shouldn't…if I…"

"There's a difference between desire that comes from here," and he touches my temple gently with his finger, "and desire that comes from *here*." He lays his hand boldly over my heart, its heel a mere fraction of an inch from the nipple of my left breast.

A tremor quakes through me, making me tremble from head to

foot. If he lets go of me, I'll probably just melt to the floor in a puddle of liquid desire.

"I don't know how to tell the difference," I whisper, and then—God help me—all caution and propriety go out the window. "Show me."

My whisper hangs in the scant inch of space between us. Our lips are nearly touching. I raise my chin, shortening the space to a mere fraction, but instead of closing the distance, he pulls back.

"Be sure you want to walk through that door before you open it, Sarah," he whispers back. "There's no going back."

With sudden clarity, I realize that over the months since Valentine's Day, he's seduced me so completely, so expertly, that the physical act of making love will be just a formality. The precarious balance I've maintained between my desire for him and my feelings for Collie has shifted; truthfully it's been shifting since the day after the disastrous Valentine's dinner.

The moment spins out, laden with unfulfilled yearning...and passes. I can't bring myself to bridge that fraction of distance; to do so would mean being consumed. *He gives his all, Gus does, with no conditions.* And, if my estimation of the man is accurate, he would expect no less from a lover. If I lose myself in him...what becomes of Sarah?

I draw my hands from his shoulders, and this motion of retreat gives him my answer. He shows no sign of disappointment or regret; he simply holds my eyes in a steady gaze and reaches without looking to press the call button for the elevator. When the doors open, he guides me inside the car and stands, hands in his pockets, watching me until the doors start to close.

And then he smiles.

NOW *THIS* COMPLICATES MATTERS...

One wonders sometimes at the cosmic injustices of life. In the weeks following that soul-shattering kiss with Gus Haldemann, Collie turns into the perfect boyfriend: charming, attentive, thoughtful, and suitably ardent. I'm not sure what caused his change in behavior; I don't ask for explanations and he doesn't offer any, but as quickly as his decline started with Yasmina's e-mail, he's back to his old self again. I'm positive there's some explanation that I'm not going to like, but for now I'm enjoying the attention and the time he's spending with me even while part of me wishes he'd push me farther away and make my decision easier.

Through excursions to the beach with Munchkin—and sometimes without her—movie nights, and dinner dates, I'm being properly courted. I'm just not sure he's the one I want courting me. You can imagine my guilt. Or maybe you can't—maybe you're one of those people who have never been torn between two suitors, never experienced a single moment of disloyalty, although the question begs to be asked again: am I being disloyal when there's been no promise of commitment between Collie and me?

That's one for Doctors Phil and Laura, because I sure can't figure it out. All I know for certain is that when Collie kisses me, I have to keeping shoving Gus to the back of my mind. When Gus kissed me, Collie never even *crossed* my mind.

Perhaps that's my answer, but I'm not making that determination without a hell of a lot of consideration. My particular circle of friends is spread so thin that if I crash and burn, I'm likely to remain broken and bleeding for any number of days or weeks before anyone can come to my emotional aid. Allison spends all her time with Thomas, and Lauren and Stewart, against all odds, have been inseparable since their first date (which was full-on dinner, movie, and drinks, God bless him). Jennifer just started a new job and has been flirting with some guy there; she's been begging me to come out with them as a chaperone, but I've refused. Collie has to take Megan for visitation with Yasmina the evenings Jen has off, and I don't want to be a third wheel on Jen's date. She's getting impatient with me because she won't go out with a guy alone until she knows him really well; she's taking no chances of being date-raped.

My particular problem with Eric Edwards hasn't completely gone away—he still smirks at me and when he can get within earshot without anyone else hearing, he makes perverted innuendos—but since nothing has happened in the last four months, I've relaxed my paranoia. I don't call for an escort to my car anymore when I stay after hours, but I'm cautious. And I still steer clear of the stairs or any secluded area where he could corner me.

Stella gets married the last week of July, and it's at the wedding that I finally understand why Collie has been so attentive in recent weeks. The wedding colors are ivory and gold, with traces of black— yes, black, but it works well. Stella herself is a vision, her ebony skin glowing, her black hair pulled smoothly back from her face and then cascading from an elegant knot in spiral curls to her shoulders. She's put something in it to make it shine and then dusted it with large flecks of gold glitter. Mario seems star-struck; he can't stop staring at her.

Half of Harper & Lyttle appears to be in attendance; behind Stella's parents, siblings, cousins, aunts, and uncles in the middle section—reserved for relatives and friends of both bride and groom— are six solid rows of H&L employees. Sam and Gus occupy the seats at the other end of the aisle from Lauren, Stewart, Allison, Collie, and me.

Hannah, closer to Stella than any of the rest of us at the low end of seniority, is checking invitations and handing out programs, as well as attending the gift table and guest register. Frannie and Morgan are two of Stella's bridesmaids, and observing Morgan in her elegant gold dress with a scandalously low back I wonder at her unusual glow and her slightly rounded tummy.

Collie's noticed too, for he leans close to my ear to murmur, "Is it just me or does Morgan look like she's pregnant?"

I follow his line of vision to the end of the aisle, where she's talking to Frannie, likewise dressed in gold, and promptly encounter Gus's cool grey gaze. He doesn't seem perturbed to see me with Collie, and the brief glance he flicks at our linked hands is amused, as though he figures he's already won and it's only a matter of time until I accept it. This annoys me; it's bad enough he made his interest in me known *after* I'd finally caught Collie, but for him to assume I'm going to choose him… Arrogance supreme. I look away, frowning crossly, and when I chance a surreptitious glance at him again, he smiles at me with undisguised humor…and a little sympathy.

"I'm glad to see he's leaving you alone now," Collie says, still murmuring near my ear.

"Who?" He tips his head slightly in Gus's direction. "He was never bothering me."

Perhaps this isn't the wisest thing to say, because Collie's brow puckers and he leans back in his chair, effectively putting some distance between us. And just before the organist starts the wedding march, he leans back in and decimates my peace of mind with one question.

"I'm assuming he won't be sleeping over again anytime soon?"

I stare at him, the round-eyed gaze of one whose lie has been caught long ago but who is only now finding out. Then the pastor asks us to stand, and Collie offers me a lopsided, somewhat melancholy smile as we rise and face the aisle. After a moment his hands come up to rest on my shoulders, soothing the quivery nerves making me tremble. We turn as Stella progresses up the aisle past us on the arm of her father. We wait until he officially gives his daughter to Mario and the pastor asks us to be seated.

I send Collie a sidelong glance as we sit, and under cover of the rustlings and scrapings as people claim their seats on the long pews and arrange themselves comfortably, I whisper, "Who told you?"

"Doesn't matter," he whispers back. "We'll talk about it later."

What I really want to do is put Stella's wedding on hold while I resolve this matter here and now but that, of course, is impractical (besides, she'd kick my ass). So I face forward and try to calm those butterflies in my stomach.

After a moment, Collie takes my hand and squeezes it reassuringly. I give him a tense grimace that's supposed to be a smile, my explanation log-jamming in my throat, wanting desperately to tumble out yet held in check not by fear, for once, but by our present surroundings.

The ceremony takes for-freaking-ever. And *then* there's the throwing of birdseed (or, rather, black oil sunflower seeds, which are actually quite attractive in gold-net bags tied with ivory ribbon) and the throwing of the bouquet, a smaller version of Stella's actual bridal bouquet. I try to beg out of that, but Stella points her bony finger right at me and then at the group of single ladies gathered in hopes of becoming the next blissfully wed woman. I sidle up to the edge of the group, trying to remain unobtrusive.

And damn that black woman's hide—she throws that frigging bouquet right at me. It sails over the grasping fingers of those in front of me and into my arms. I barely mange to catch it because I'm not expecting it. The spectators hoot and holler and blushing furiously, I try to give it away. But I've won it fair and square; no one will take it. Collie extricates me from the knot of well-wishers as Stella and Mario get into the waiting limousine that will whisk them away to the reception. I feel eyes on me the whole way to the car but when I look, Gus is nowhere to be seen.

Then we're alone. Collie starts the car and joins the queue to exit the parking lot, and while we're at a stand-still waiting for traffic to let up so we can exit the parking lot, I ask my question again.

"Who told you?"

He shrugs, not looking at me. "Dunno. Doesn't matter anyway. But it's true, though, isn't it?"

"Not in the way you think."

Now he looks at me, his expression exasperated. "Sarah, his truck was seen parked outside your apartment at various times during the night. *And* he was seen coming out of your apartment the next morning. Don't tell me it isn't what I think. He spent the night with you."

"I'm not denying that," I reply, my voice tight, a rising blush in my cheeks making me certain I'm about to achieve that incandescent shade of red that so favors Stewart Drummond. "You're assuming that I had sex with him, but I didn't."

"A man like him—*all night*, Sarah! How can you expect me to believe that a man of his experience, who is obviously attracted to you, spent the night with you and never laid a hand on you? And you can't deny that *you* are attracted to *him*."

I swallow hard, feeling the increasing need for my inhaler. "I went to Marty's Lounge after you dropped me off. I drank the alcoholic equivalent of my weight in Mojitos. Rather than leaving me to the tender mercies of an L.A. cab driver, Gus drove me home."

"And came in, and—"

"*Stop it!*" My sudden shout startles us both. "Why don't you just come right out and call me a slut, Collie, because that's what you're implying. *Nothing happened!*"

He subsides into silence, chewing on the inside of his cheek. Finally he murmurs, "I'm sorry, Sarah. That wasn't my intention."

"Wasn't it?" He doesn't respond. "I invited him in to watch a movie. We did—one of the *Bourne* movies, I think. I fell asleep and woke up on the sofa with him—*fully dressed*. Now you know as much as I do."

"And you're going to take his word for it that you didn't—you know?"

I have no trouble meeting his gaze. I'm positive of the answer to this particular question. "Yes. He's an honorable man."

Collie barks out a laugh, sounding for all the world like his namesake. "*Honorable?* Honorable would have been leaving *before* you passed out. Honorable would have been not going into your apartment in the first place."

"Now you're sounding like a prude. If you want to talk about honorable, let's talk about how you ditched out on me on my birthday. Perhaps if you hadn't, I wouldn't have felt the need to go to Marty's lounge and he never would have spent the night at my house."

His eyes practically bug out of his head in surprise. "So it's *my* fault?"

"Well, I'm a slut and Gus is a dishonorable lecher, so why not make it your fault? I want to know who told you."

"What's it matter?"

"Someone was watching my apartment if they saw his truck outside at various times during the night, as you worded it. Was it you?"

"*What?*" He looks outraged. "Why would I watch your apartment? I had no reason not to trust you until *after* that night."

True, that. After a moment—during which we actually advance forward by three car lengths—I fumble my inhaler out of my purse and trigger foulness down my throat. Collie offers me a cinnamon Altoid, but cinnamon reminds me of Gus and I refuse the tin. After a moment he puts it away. My only other option to cleanse the foul aftertaste is a chewy Rolaids, so I eat one. He sighs at what he sees as cutting off my nose to spite my face.

"Now you're angry."

"No."

"Sarah—"

"I'm fine, Collie," I say mildly. "I just wasn't aware until now of the incredibly low opinion you have of me."

He huffs out an impatient breath. "You took it wrong."

"I don't believe I did."

"And it wouldn't matter even if you *did* have sex with him. I'd understand. I wasn't there for you. Can we get past this now?" He rolls the car forward as another two cars escape the queue, and when the motion stops I consider popping the door open and hopping out. But I don't, because—well, because I'm me. Instead I offer a scant twitch of my lips that can by no means serve as a smile but seems to satisfy him.

But me—I'm not satisfied. I can walk away from this at any time—really, I can, and why shouldn't I? A relationship that always has you tied in knots can't be healthy, can it? And while we're talking about any indiscretions that may or may not have happened between Gus Haldemann and me, how about we talk about the numerous hours spent in, and undisclosed events of, his meetings with Yasmina? Yup, completely hypocritical moment of jealousy.

We sit in the line, waiting to get out. And we go to the reception. We even dance, and Collie makes a point of kissing me when he knows Gus is watching (and is unable to completely hide his annoyance when Gus seems unaffected by this public display of affection). We kiss the bride and congratulate the groom, eat our cake, drink our champagne, laugh at the best man's toast (or is that roast?), and blow bubbles as the happy couple departs.

He delivers the coup de grâce of this fine day once I've drank enough champagne to nearly eliminate my anger with him.

"I'm going to Seattle in two weeks. I'll be there for two months."

We've left the reception by this time and are at my apartment. I'm having a rather rare moment of feeling girly, so I'm reluctant to take off my spaghetti-strap azure dress. Its skirt is flouncy and edged with lace and I like the way it swirls around my legs just above the knees. I do shed the shoes, however, because my feet are killing me. At Collie's casual statement, I whirl around from the bookshelf—where I'm trying to find a movie he'll watch—hard enough to give the bottom of my foot friction burn.

He's standing behind the sofa watching me, hands in his pockets, his gaze searching my face as though he's hoping for a particular reaction.

"Oh." I don't know what else to say. That sensation of feeling things slipping out of my grasp—or perhaps it's that I'm slipping down a steep incline into the abyss of the unknown—presses in on me again. I turn back to the videos, but I don't see them. In my mind I'm picturing Collie in a lip-lock—and more—with a sultry Latino beauty, which is ridiculous since I've never even seen Yasmina.

"Sarah." His arms come around me from behind, his hands sliding over mine and prying my fingers from their death-clutch around the edge of the shelf. "It will be all right. Bet you a dime."

He turns me around in his arms, holding me close, and in his eyes I can see the Collie that so captivated me from the day I met him. A surge of fierce emotion makes me raise my chin and kiss him. After a moment, he kisses me back. If my sudden attack of affection perplexes him, he doesn't dwell on it. In fact, he takes full advantage of the fact that I'm not yelling at him or pointing out his obvious failings as a boyfriend.

His hands slide down my back and over my buttocks, his fingers catching the hem of my dress and ducking under it. I lean away from him to protest—oh, *fine*, not protest, more like question—but he follows me, bending me back over his arm, his biceps bunching against the middle of my back. He deepens the kiss, his tongue sliding insistently against mine, tasting faintly of the cinnamon Altoid he'd popped in his mouth before we came in the apartment. And God help me—it's this more than anything that causes me to abandon any self-restraint and give in to my libidinous urges.

I barely notice when Collie's fingers find the zipper pull of my dress and yank it down. The garment floats to the floor, my panties following seconds later, and I'm naked before him. I watch, biting my lip self-consciously, as he sheds his own clothes, and then he's gathering me to him, the touch of his bare flesh against mine startling. His lips move from my shoulder to the curve of my neck, where they linger long enough to drive my arousal to the point of no return, and then up along my jaw to my ear.

"All I need to know, Sarah, is that you don't love him."

I try to pull back, to put some distance between us when I answer, but one hand holds me securely against him, the other works magic in regions too long neglected. Logical thought is impossible at this point; I can barely stand on my own.

Dizzying motion, the world tilts, and I feel against my back the soft, cushy pile of a fleece blanket; somehow he's managed to drag it off the sofa and has lain me on it on the floor. His arousal presses insistently against my leg, but he's still waiting for my answer, withholding the fulfillment I want so badly.

"Collie—" I arch against him, and he closes his eyes, drawing in a shuddering breath.

"Tell me, Sarah."

Just surrender, Sarah. "I don't love him."

I close my eyes against his triumphant smile, and for a long while I let his body make me forget how those words feel like an utter lie.

FRACTURE

"I wonder where it came from."

"It looks brand new."

"What *is* it?"

The knot of onlookers (truthfully only Allison, Hannah, and Lauren) huddle at the entrance to my cubicle, peering in at some fascinating specimen I can't see because they're in the way.

"Whatcha looking at?"

They break apart to let me through, all talking at once. "What is it? … It was there when we got here … Is that the thing you've been looking for?"

And sure enough, beside my monitor sits a Dictaphone in pristine shape with its cord neatly coiled and secured with a zip tie. No note to explain its presence, which smacks of only one person. His *modus operandi* is unmistakable.

As dubiously thrilled as I am at finally having a Dictaphone intact—I don't really like transcribing, but I equally don't mind being in the direct-contact sphere of Evelyn Harper—I have to shelve the little bugger for the next week because Concept Development delivered a product early and we now have to bust our asses to produce user manuals for an earlier-than-anticipated release date. In case you haven't figured it out, I'm basically a technical writer. A little more than that, but no less.

Add to the early deployment stress Collie's impending two months' leave of absence; the sum of *that* equation is more work for the rest of us and a Sarah who is easy to irritate and quick to snap. For some reason, I have a terrible feeling of foreboding about his going to

Seattle, but I don't breathe a word of it to him. He seems tense enough about it himself.

While he's gone, Collie's sublet his apartment to a friend who just moved into town, so he and Munchkin arrange to stay with me the week before they're to leave. She's tearful about their trip but I spend an hour or so one night showing her where Seattle is on the Google map (and how tiny the distance looks from there to Los Angeles reassures us both) and telling her all the things there are to do in Seattle, and she actually falls asleep with a smile, looking forward to riding the ferries and visiting Pike Place Market.

During the time they stay at my apartment, I learn the whole story about Collie and Yasmina, and it brings me no comfort. If anything, it heightens my anxiety. Munchkin falls asleep watching a show on Nickelodeon; we just leave her in the living room for the night instead of carrying her into my guest bedroom, which she doesn't like sleeping in anyway. We move the coffee table and put the back cushions from the sofa on the floor to catch her if she falls off, throw a blanket over her, and she seems comfortable enough.

But it displaces us for the rest of the evening—it is, after all, only eight o'clock—so we end up watching TV in my bedroom. I say watching TV, but really it's only on as background noise. I'm reading and Collie is taking care of some last minute things for work, his finger flying deftly over the keyboard of his laptop. Okay, I'm not *really* reading; what I'm doing is watching Collie and trying to define the exact source of my dread.

It comes to me as he frowns over something on his laptop screen. The light plays over his face, making him seem Picasso-ish, which makes me think of the art book I keep locked in the cabinet at work with the Dictaphone, which makes me think of Collie's revelation at Stella's wedding, which makes me realize that my dread is two-fold: what is he going to be doing with the mysterious Yasmina, and am I going to be able to resist any contact with Gus Haldemann while Collie is away? Not that Gus has done more than greet me in passing since he kissed me, but who knows what the man will do once his competition is safely tucked away in the drizzly Pacific Northwest?

So I swallow the fear that has stayed my hand and struck me mute all my life and I ask, "What is Yasmina like?"

He slants me a look from the corner of his eye, finishes what he's typing, and gives me his full attention. "You're finally asking—three days before I leave?" His tone is exasperated and amused.

I shrug a shoulder. "You never offered any information, so I assumed you didn't want to talk about it."

"You can't wait for other people to bring things up, Sarah. You just have to ask what you want to know." He skates his finger across the touchpad, navigating his electronic folders, and taps twice.

"So I'm asking."

"I'm working on it." He flashes me a grin, scrolls some more, and then taps twice again, this time turning his laptop toward me. The screen fills with a photograph. Skin a shade darker than Munchkin's, the young woman has the same dark coffee eyes and nearly black hair. She's attractive but not the raging Latin beauty I'd expected. She also looks very young.

"That's a recent picture?"

"No." Collie turns the computer around, scrolls again, and finds another selection, turning it back toward me. "Here she is now. That was her senior picture I showed you first."

"You've known her since high school?"

He shrugs negligently. "More like since grade school, though I didn't do more than pull her hair until high school."

"So she's your childhood sweetheart." I feel a flash of anger that he hadn't told me this. A brief, casual fling that produces a child happens frequently. The ties that bind two people together in instances like that are not as strong as those that bind a man to a girl he's known most of his life who bears his child.

"Kinda, I guess. We dated for a couple of years in high school and then broke up. Found each other in college again, dated for a couple of months, and then she just vanished on me." He lifts a brow. "That was when she found out she was pregnant with Megan."

I stare at the recent picture of Yasmina. Her face is more mature, she sports a more sophisticated hair style, and her clothing indicates she's some sort of office professional.

"Was she afraid of what you would do?"

He sees he's not going to be getting any more work done, so he closes the laptop, slides it under the bed, and shifts his position so he's lying face-to-face with me. His fingers stroke my cheek, brushing my hair back behind my ear.

"Fear does strange things to people. I suppose my attitude at the time made her think I wouldn't take responsibility for Megan. She did the best she could."

"Abandoning Megan at the daycare was the best she could do?" I remark caustically. "Thank God she gave her all."

"Sarah," he says, censure edging his voice. "Try not to judge her too harshly. She left Megan at the daycare, yes. But she left all the contact information she had for me so they wouldn't have trouble locating me. She was overwhelmed and scared."

"She made it through the pregnancy and a year-and-a-half of Megan's life, and *then* she got scared?"

He twines a curl of my hair around his finger, turning it this way and that to catch the light. "Her family had all relocated to Washington State; migrant orchard workers. A settlement from a car accident allowed them to buy an orchard up there, and they've become a pretty affluent, respected family. They're also very strict, with very definite limitations on acceptable behavior. Becoming pregnant, especially by a white Irish boy who's never picked an apple from a tree in his life, was *not* on their agenda for her. She was afraid of what they would say, of how they would treat Megan. But she'd lost her job, was two days away from being homeless, and had enough money for a bus ticket to Wenatchee and a couple of meals along the way. She thought leaving Megan with me would be best for Megan."

"But she didn't leave her with you. She left her with the daycare, essentially leaving her to the mercies of social services."

"It worked out, Sarah, so I'm not complaining."

"No, but you seem to be excusing."

He frowns, irritated. "Why are you getting so upset? If I choose to forgive Yasmina and to try to understand the mindset that made her do what she did, what difference does it make to you?"

I flush. "None. I just have a hard time seeing it from your perspective."

The frown smoothes away, but he still looks wary. "You've been really touchy lately, ever since Stella's wedding."

"Yeah, well, that wasn't the most fantastical day, now was it?"

"It ended well." He grins, scooting closer, his arm snaking underneath me to haul me against him. His other hand plucks the book from my grasp and tosses it aside.

"You just lost my page."

"You'll find it again." He kisses the tip of my nose. "Do you want to know a secret?"

"I'm not sure. Will it make me want to kick you in the shins?"

Collie hooks his leg around both of mine and rolls onto his back, rolling me on top of him. "Now *that's* more like it."

"Don't try to distract me. What's your secret, Tate?"

But he draws me down for a kiss first, and it's a long, fuzzy time later that he answers. "Someone gave me some advice. I wouldn't have taken it, considering who gave it to me, but since it concerned you I decided to give it a shot. Turns out he was spot-on."

I don't follow at first; my attention is focused on his hands, which are edging ever lower down my back. "Mmm?"

"You have a one-track mind, woman," he teases. "Gus Haldemann told me that if I wanted to keep you, I needed to put in the effort to show you mattered to me. He also said he'd stand down while I tried to fix things."

I gape at him. *"What!* Things weren't broken, Collie; why would either of you think they needed to be fixed?"

"Ah, *Sarah,*" he replies, his smile sweet but resigned. "You're a terrible liar, which is why I'm glad you don't try it too often. Things weren't exactly *right,* now were they—not if you ended up sleeping with him on your sofa."

"Sleeping," I stress. "Nothing more."

"We've been through this already."

My turn to frown. "Fine. So am I to assume Gus is the one who told you about that night?"

"Actually, he didn't mention it. Some photos with time stamps on them were left in an envelope on my desk. I know the time stamps are accurate because of the light in the sky. I know it was your apartment because they showed the front of the building with the address. I know it's his truck because I checked the license plate at work the day after I received the prints."

"Photographs again." I'm sure I'm not the only one here reminded of Gretchen's compromising position caught on film.

"I know, right?" Collie laughs. "It's okay, Sarah. It woke me up to a few things." His hands slide over the curve of my backside, pressing me hard against him.

Unfortunately, that night with Gus woke me up to a few things too—well, at least the morning after did, since I barely remember the night of—and one of those things is how much I secretly enjoyed being the one he woke up with. Another is how much more relaxed I am with Gus than I am with Collie, as though he's inviting me to show my humanity and make a mistake, whereas I'm always afraid that my mistakes will tarnish my image in Collie's eyes.

Perhaps it is an instinctual fear, one that something deep in my subconscious tells me is justified and is only a matter of time until it's proven out.

I have these rare moments of profound intuition where for one golden second I simply know something I shouldn't otherwise know. I had one of those moments while my sister was stealing my prom date, which is what urged me home early and launched the war of all sibling wars.

And I have one right now regarding Collie. Although he's holding me, touching me as only a lover would, half his mind or more is elsewhere. I remember reading in a novel where someone notes that it's no good being with a woman who has one guy between her ears and another between her legs. That phrase is completely apropos in this situation. He may be making love to me in actuality, but I'd bet my last dime I'm not who he's making love to in his mind.

And therein he has my complete understanding, because I'm just as guilty of that particular sin.

* * * * *

The next two days fly past with barely a second to take a breath—at least for Collie. For me they crawl because I'm dreading this so much. Everyone in the company seems to want to talk to him before he leaves, which annoys me to no end, and when toward the end of the workday we catch our first moment alone, I'm thoroughly disgruntled. Even Collie looks a little harassed.

To catch an uninterrupted interlude, we have to go to the employee lounge on the top floor, a nicely appointed, glass-walled room not nearly big enough to accommodate all who want to use it. Comfortable sofas and arm chairs are laid out in clusters around the room, and three sofas are arranged in a U in front of a large, flat-screen TV which seems permanently tuned to a tiresome soap opera. At this late hour of the day, the room is empty but for us.

"Popular boy," I grumble as Collie slides his arms around me from behind. We're standing at a window on the west wall, looking out over the city. The light has taken on that late-afternoon hue typical of summer days. For some reason, this particular summer light has always struck a chord of melancholy inside me, and today is no different.

"It's really starting to get annoying," he replies. His reflection in the window smiles at me, and mine smiles back at him, tense and tired.

"Are you excited?"

He shrugs. "Excited to get this over and done with so I know what to expect for my future."

I'd like that as well. And to tell you the truth, it might make things simpler if he decides to stay in Seattle and take up with Megan's mother. But that's the coward in me speaking; I dislike confrontation so much that I'd rather not have to make a decision between him and Gus Haldemann, because it requires me telling one of them that I've chosen the other. I'm no good at stuff like that.

My second all-time secret dream, on the list just after the bed-and-breakfast of my childhood, is to be completely swept off my feet by a

173

man, unable to resist his seduction even though I'm not one of those mushy romantic types. I want a man who desires me to distraction, who thinks the sun rises and sets on me and who doesn't mind if I hang the moon on him. Okay, so maybe I *am* a bit of a mushy romantic after all. And honestly, Collie's never indicated he's the one who is willing, ready, and able to be that man.

We stand in silence for a long while, his chin resting on my shoulder, his breath stirring my hair, my arms folded over his. And in our reflection I can see the shadows of the other people who occupy the corners of our hearts but who really deserve the whole of them.

"Collie," I say, surprising even myself. I hadn't intended to speak out loud.

"Mmm?"

Don't ask! Don't you dare ask! But I've never been very good at taking advice, including my own. "Do you want to have a relationship with Yasmina?"

I'm sure I'm not imagining the tension that suddenly coils through him. "I'll always have to have a relationship of sorts with her because of Megan."

"That isn't what I meant. I meant a relationship with her outside of her role as Megan's mother."

He's silent for a long time, withdrawing slightly as he straightens. "You mean a romantic or sexual relationship."

"Yes," I say, relieved he caught on. My relief is short-lived.

"Is that what your undies have been all in a bundle over?"

"Attractive phrase," I remark. "I just wondered."

"Hoping I do because it excuses your dallying with Gus Haldemann?" His arms drop away and he steps back. "I've kept my hands to myself with Yasmina, thank you for your vote of confidence. I rather thought we were in a relationship, but I can see your idea of one differs from mine."

I turn around slowly to face him, but I can barely meet his eyes. He's right about Gus Haldemann, but there's something in his expression, a furtive guilt, that makes me certain this isn't the complete truth.

"You're the only woman I have feelings for, Sarah. Can you say the same thing?"

I manage to find my voice. "I don't have those feelings for *any* woman." I chance a look at him; he is *pissed*.

"This is just a joke to you? I can't believe you're doing this on the night before I leave. What the hell is the matter with you?"

"Many have asked, none have had answers," I reply cryptically. I can't seem to stop the steady stream of sarcasm running through my mind. "Something just…changes in your voice when you talk about Yasmina. Maybe you've done nothing with her, but that doesn't mean that you don't want to."

A shutter closes over his face, presenting me with a blank, expressionless mask. "I'll see you when you get home." *And it isn't going to be pleasant.* I can almost hear the words even though he doesn't say them. With one last cool glance, he spins on his heel, his purposeful strides carrying him out the door with quick efficiency.

I don't need anyone to point out that I could have handled that better.

He seems to be over the worst of his anger by the time I make it home. Dinner is halfway done and he doesn't protest when I step in to help. Munchkin sets the table (with help) and chatters through dinner, covering our silences. And because they're leaving in the morning, we put her to bed early, letting her watch a video until she falls asleep. Collie sits with her for so long that I suspect he's going to sleep on the sofa with her or in the guest room, but eventually he comes into my bedroom, pausing to lean against the jamb and watch me as I lay on my back staring at the ceiling, covers pooled loosely in my lap.

He sits on the edge of the bed, his back to me, as he sheds shoes and shirt. And he stands, his back to me, to shed the rest. And he slides under the covers, his back to me, until I reach out to shut off the lamp.

"Don't."

My hand falls away from the switch. "All right."

After a moment he rolls over to face me, his green eyes startlingly vivid in the glow of the lamp. He reaches across the distance between us, and I wonder how we went from betting a dime over the number of times George Stuckey would say "umm" to watching our relationship fracture before our very eyes.

His hand slides into my hair, his caress gentle and sweet, encouraging me to roll onto my side facing him, so I do. His eyes move over my face as though seeing it clearly for the first time in forever.

"You're so beautiful, Sarah," he murmurs. He skates his thumb across my lower lip. "But you're so far away all the time. In here," he clarifies before I can ask, tapping my forehead with one finger. "I never know what you're thinking or feeling. Sometimes I'm not sure I even know who you really are, what your dreams are."

"I can't have dreams?"

"Everyone has dreams. It's just that yours seem to be top secret."

I raise a brow. "And that's bad?"

He sighs. "It's your secret dreams that scare me." His arms slide around me, reeling me in until we're nose-to-nose, chest-to-chest, pelvis-to-pelvis. His leg curls around mine to hold me there. I try to reach behind me to click off the lamp—the glow from the sodium arc light outside my bedroom window seems much more conducive to the relaxation of inhibitions and the promotion of intimacy—but he stops my hand.

"Leave the light on. For once I want to be sure you see *me* when you make love to me." I open my mouth to protest, and he presses his finger against it, and then his lips.

There's a hesitancy in his kiss that I've never experienced, not even at the Christmas party when we kissed for the first time. Everything about our interlude tonight has a surreal quality that I can't define until much later, when I lie sleepless and staring at the darkened ceiling as he sleeps.

It felt like a goodbye.

Tales from the Water Cooler

Friday, August 14
RSS Feeds: Really Simple, Stupid

Posted by Sarah Quinn

It was brought to my attention that this blog has slipped slightly off topic. Oh, all *right*, more than slightly. I took a hiatus in July to pull my focus back to helping you all be better office professionals. My humblest apologies for the digression.

I can't say enough about RSS feeds. I love 'em. I subscribe to many of them from current world news to Microsoft Office tips to happening in the art world to celebrity gossip columns. And I don't have to leave Outlook to keep track of them.

RSS stands for Really Simple Syndication. In other words, an RSS feed is a really simple way to get a site, be it blog, article, etc., into "syndication"—multiple publication, in other words.

The beauty of Outlook is that your RSS feeds, when you subscribe, are shown in your Outlook RSS Feeds folder, making them easy to read and manage. When there is new activity in your feeds, it will show in your Unread Mail folder, and once you're done with it, you can delete it. No more opening multiple windows and hunting for those bookmarks every morning.

It doesn't matter what browser you use; MS Internet Explorer will automatically show your subscriptions in your RSS Feeds folder. If you use Firefox or Safari browsers (or any other non-Microsoft browser), in the drop-down box beside "Subscribe to this feed using," simply select **Microsoft Office Outlook**. Your feed will automatically appear in your RSS Feeds folder in Outlook.

So go out there and click those RSS feed buttons for all your daily reads. You won't regret it!

DID YOU KNOW:

MS OFFICE 2007 TIP (all relevant programs): We've all done it—highlighted a word or sentence so that we can move it to another location...only to find that annoying little Mini Toolbar in the way. So instead of moving the text, we end up boldfacing and applying yellow highlighter to it. Thank God for the Undo button.

There *is* a way to turn off that little annoyance. I wasted no time finding that OFF option, and as a result I curse a little less often.

Click the Office Button.
Click Word Options.
Deselect **Show Mini Toolbar on selection**.
Click OK.

Your troubles are over.

Blog Archive
  2009
    August
      RSS Feeds: Really Simple, Stupid
    June
      Choices
    May
      WTF Is Wrong with Men???
    March
      Love Triangles: Three- Pointed Pains-in-the...
    February
      Faces in the Crowd
    January
      Going Postal: A Career-Limiting Move

About Me

Savvy Sarah

I am an administrative office professional with several years' experience in office settings. I have an AAS in Administrative Office Management and currently work as a training specialist for a software development company in Los Angeles.

THE SULTAN OF SMARM

A box of tapes is delivered to me just before ten in the morning a couple of weeks after Collie goes to Seattle. Frannie leaves a Post-It on the sealed box, her tone seeming a little curt: *I know Evelyn wants these transcribed as soon as possible, but with Collie gone we are short-staffed. Please only spend a couple of hours on these each day and then go on to the rest of your workload.*

She's feeling the pinch, as are we all, of Collie's workload in addition to the rush for early deployment of the new HR software. I also think she's not sleeping well—curse of having a new baby— because there are dark circles under her eyes and she's been napping on her leather sofa during her lunch hour. Sam comes up to see her frequently, looking tired himself. Brooke, surprisingly, points out to me one morning that he approaches her like one would approach a restless, foul-tempered tigress: cautiously and damn near subserviently. It never fails to amaze me the way Sam can placate almost anyone.

Collie communicates with me via e-mail at least every other day; even Munchkin has sent me notes. Collie's mother, an English professor (hence his and his brother's names: Coleridge and Emerson, after the poets), has been teaching her to read and write, and she's able to send me short messages, usually spelled phonetically.

"What's that, Sarah? A present from Collie?"

I turn around to find Allie and Hannah behind me, holding their coffee mugs. "No, just the tapes Evelyn Harper wants me to transcribe."

"Doesn't she have an administrative assistant?" Hannah frowns.

"Yeah, but Evelyn doesn't give dictation. She writes out a rough draft and sends it via e-mail to her assistant. Hardly anyone dictates anymore, and when they do, it's electronic and transcribed from an audio file online."

"So lucky you—you're the only one who knows how to use one of these things?"

"Or Frannie was the only supervisor willing to spare a staff member who can transcribe. I get the feeling there's not much she would refuse to do for Evelyn Harper."

Allison takes a sip of her coffee and makes a face. "Ugh! Cold. Let's go get a warm-up."

I grab my mug and join them on their quest for hot java. Allie has been a gem and is standing in as protector while Collie is gone—and since Gus seems to have relinquished that role even in Collie's absence. There have even been a couple of times that Brooke has taken her lunch in the break room with me rather than at her desk, which is her usual routine, and after these past two weeks I'm starting to suspect they've been put up to it. That they do so willingly and without complaint—at least, no complaint within my hearing—gives me one of those rare, warm-fuzzy feelings.

"Have you noticed how Frannie calls her Roxanne? I wonder what that's about." Hannah takes my mug and fills it, and then Allie's, leaving herself for last. She always does this. I've also noticed that when people are going out a door, Hannah will hold it and go out last. I don't know if it's part of her upbringing—I've never gotten the impression that she was raised in a traditional Asian home—but she's very self-effacing. That she seems cool with it and even seems to enjoy putting others first is admirable. Some lucky guy is going to enjoy having her as a wife—if indeed she's hetero. I'm still not certain.

"I think it's her real first name. Have you ever seen her business card? It says *R. Evelyn Harper*." I sip my coffee tentatively as we head out of the break room—and then it sloshes over the rim, burning my hand, as I stop short at the door.

Eric Edwards, the Sultan of Smarm himself, is passing by, listening to one of his Sales cronies drone on. His eyes meet mine and his customary smirk curls his mouth. He flicks a glance at Allison and

Hannah and then at me, obviously dismissing my guard detail as unimportant. Then they round the corner, disappearing from view.

Allie gasps when she sees my hand. "Jesus, Sarah! We need to get some cold water on this."

I don't protest as she drags me to the sink and stuffs my hand under the coldest damn water she can muster from the faucet.

"I really don't like that man," Hannah mutters at my other elbow. "I wish you could have gotten him fired."

"Had I been a little quicker to file a complaint, he would have been. I gave him time to get the jump on me. Never again."

But the confidence behind his dismissal of my escorts worries me, and I make a mental note to make sure I'm never alone anywhere at any time. It's not fair that I have to always be on my guard and never feel safe in my place of work, and I damn Eric to eight eternities in hell for the cat-and-mouse game he's playing.

Some aloe vera gel with Lidocaine helps ease the burn and allows me to start transcribing the tapes. I manage to complete two full tapes in the two hours I'm allotted. They are literally crammed with letters and memos, and I save them onto a flash drive Stella gave me. When I lock the tapes in my overhead cabinet with the Dictaphone, I indulge myself for five minutes, losing myself in the pages of the art book Gus gave me for my birthday before shutting it away with a lingering sense of guilt. The book is fantastic and I would love it no matter who had given it to me, but I rather suspect my fierce attachment to it stems as much from its giver as from its content.

My routine is set for the next week and a half: transcribe for two hours, a quick sneak peek at my art book, and then nose to the grindstone to complete the documentation for the HR software. That is, until that project grinds to a screeching halt. The software, for inexplicable reasons, simply stops working. I try everything I can think of before calling Frannie to my desk. She claims my chair, her mouse-clicks lightning fast—but to no avail.

"Nothing for it but to call Stewart," she says with a sigh. She's looking better this week, like she's finally been sleeping at night. "I'll make the call. He'll have to look at code from his office."

183

"Do you want me to take some of Collie's projects off someone's hands in the meantime?"

"No, that's all right. Allison, Hannah, and Brooke have it well in hand. Go ahead and go back to Ro—er, Evelyn's transcription."

There are thirty-two tapes to transcribe; thirteen of them labeled in neat caps, all by the same hand. The remaining nineteen are scrawled in different handwriting. I've sorted them by handwriting and then by date; I've found transcribing all the dictation from one dictator to be easier than mixing and matching dictator styles and inflections. Once you get into the rhythm of that person's speaking patterns, the flow is smooth and quick.

I finish up the first thirteen in a week. My software still isn't fixed, although Stewart's had me test a couple of things for him, so I pop the first of the remaining nineteen tapes into the machine, thinking I have just enough time to key a letter or two before quitting time. The handwriting on the label is obviously masculine and has none of the time stops noted like the other tapes. It doesn't take long to learn why.

The by-now familiar voice of Garland Harper, founder of Harper & Lyttle and former CEO, comes through the headphones, but he's not dictating a business letter this time. In fact, although he addresses it like a letter, it sounds more like an audio journal than it does personal correspondence.

"My dear Carolina, what would you have me do? I have given Malia a job in the Training Department—the supervisor there is quite patient and easy-going; it was the best fit I could think of. Yet...still there are problems. She's drinking again. The stress is too much for her, and she's crumbling."

"Sarah!" Hannah's voice yanks me abruptly away from the taped discussion. "Are you going home?"

"Yeah, in a little while. I just want to finish up here. I won't stay long."

She looks dubious, but a glance at her watch tells me she has plans and probably won't harp on me too long or she'll be late for them. Allison is already gone to an afternoon dentist appointment, and Brooke called in sick today. Stella and Frannie are out at some stupid seminar, which has left us alone this afternoon, and the new office manager won't start work for another week. It's fine when the building is busy and full, but after the mass exodus at quitting time, it gets kind of eerie.

"All right. Just be sure and have security escort you out."

"I won't be long. I'll call Harold to walk me out."

"Okay, then. Goodnight." Still looking troubled, she heads down the hall. I put my earphones back on and start the tape again.

"I've kept our relationship secret—she has enough to handle without others crying nepotism and making snide remarks about being the boss's daughter. Evelyn has graciously invited her into our home several nights a week for dinner, hoping that we can minimize her alcohol consumption if we keep her busy and show our support. Malia responds with insults and ingratitude. At work she causes friction, steals ideas, and mismanages her workload.

"I have done the best I can, and yet she relays to me your grumblings and complaints. What else can I do but what I've already done? You know I am right—she belongs in an inpatient treatment facility that can dry her out and help heal her mind. You were wrong to remove her when she was sixteen, and you are wrong to refuse to help her now.

"Regardless of what you think of me, Malia is your daughter too, and she deserves your compassion and care, not your mind games in a pointless attempt to vex me. Please, think of Malia for a change."

Abruptly I stop the tape. I can't believe I've been avidly, unashamedly, eavesdropping on Garland Harper's private matters. I rewind the tape and take my foot from the pedal, removing the temptation to continue prying.

Malia—that must be Malia Moreno, Sam Harrison's first wife. The date on the tape is nearly seven years ago, but I don't know if that precedes his marriage to her. I don't have all the particulars of the story, but what has whispered through the grapevine indicates he was tricked into marrying her and a couple of years later had an affair with Frannie, which resulted in Malia shooting him and then wrecking her Porsche at a high rate of speed. From all accounts, she was hucked into the looney bin afterward, which only goes to prove my suspicion that men will drive you crazy if you let them.

I put the tape in the box, bundling the nineteen with his

handwriting separately from the others. Evelyn may want to hear these, but I have no business knowing any of this. In fact, tonight I'm going to indulge several alcoholic concoctions involving rum just to erase the memory of what little I heard so I won't be tempted to repeat it.

The tapes and the Dictaphone safely locked in my cabinet, I start shutting down. I make my rounds through the department, checking everyone's coffee warmers and space heaters and other such potential fire hazards while Windows shuts itself down. And I ask you, while we're on that topic, why the hell does it take so long to shut down? I can practically groom an English sheepdog before that sucker closes. And GOD FORBID it wants to install updates upon exit. Might as well grab a good book and a pot of tea for *that* blessed event.

I'm in Allie's cube, shutting off her radio and her coffee warmer, when I hear a sound in Marketing, which is around the corner from Training's cube farm. I don't think too much of it at first—I'm not the only one prone to working late.

The department sorted out, I go back to my cube. Windows is now installing 3 of 6 updates. Fan-freaking-tastic. It's going to be a while. But at least I'm not alone; the Marketing employee is still knocking about, no doubt also trying to shut down.

Installing update 4. The sounds—a quiet rustling, like someone sneaking, have moved into the far reaches of Training. I tidy my desk, putting away errant paperclips, Post-It pads, and writing instruments, and check to make sure my overhead cabinet is locked.

Installing update 5. A stealthy footstep on the other side of the cube farm. I have a sudden rush of irrational fear, one of those flashes of intuition that something is terribly wrong. I listen carefully, thinking I hear someone breathing two or three cubes away, until the frantic pounding of my pulse in my ears obscures all other sound.

I lean under my desk and hold in the power button; Windows can fragment all it wants; I don't really care. I grab my purse from my desk drawer and pause, hunched down in my cube, to determine if the breather is still present, and then I duck-waddle out of my cube and move to the left, where I can circle around the back of the elevators and go down the hall to the front stairs.

I wriggle my cell phone out of its pocket on the side of my purse and dial security as I creep around the cube farm. It's too early for Harold, but one of his flunkies should be manning the desk. The line rings once…twice…three times…and goes to voicemail.

"Are you freaking kidding me?" I hiss onto the recording. "This is Sarah-Jane Quinn in Training on the second floor. Someone is stalking me through the department. I want someone up here *now*! My cell is 555-4872. I'm trying to make my way to the main stairs."

I turn off the ringer using external buttons, trying to muffle the sound in my armpit. My stalker is somewhere near Allison's cube now—just past mine and on the other side. I'm petrified he heard the bleeps from my phone. Why the hell can't the manufacturers design phones that don't make sounds while you're trying to shut off the ringer? Don't they know you might someday be stalked and you could live or die because of one errant bleep?

Careful step after careful step, I edge to the hallway, peering around with one eye just enough to see if it's clear. It is. I stoop to remove my shoes, thanking God I didn't opt to wear hose today. My bare feet should find enough traction on the steps once I make it there, and I'll be faster in bare feet than in backless clogs.

The elevator dings and the rattle of a cleaning cart comes as a staggering relief. I will my heartbeat to calm so that I can hear over the thundering pulse in my ears, and I tiptoe down the hallway, coming to the intersection just as the janitor Barry disappears into the elevator, earphones firmly embedded in his ears, hacking and breathing heavily with a late summer cold. The door closes on his wheezing, and I slump in relief and not a little shame.

"Sarah, you are an idiot," I admonish myself. Scared senseless by the cleaning guy. I press the button to call the elevator car, leaning against the wall beside the door to fire escape stairs as I watch the indicator move from 3 to 4 to 5. Barry is going all the way up, it seems.

Drifting up the stairs from the lobby comes a faintly whistled tune like an ethereal melody from another dimension—and meant solely for me: "Me and Sarah Jane" by Genesis.

Oh, shit!

The elevator doesn't seem to be coming any time soon. My exit from the main floor is going to be hindered by the fact that my stalker—and yes, I do indeed have one—is in the lobby. There's no other way out of the building, and as long as he's down there, I'm stuck up here.

The whistling comes closer; he's standing at the bottom of the main stairs. This is a strategic spot; it's in full view of the elevators and the fire stairs. I won't be able to get past him. My only hope now is safety in numbers; I have to go up and find Barry, and have him escort me to my car since the entire security division seems to have taken a vacation.

I slip silently into the fire escape stairs, catching the door before it snicks shut and easing it soundlessly closed. This stairwell always seems creepy to me, even though it's brightly lit, perhaps because you can't see more than a segment ahead of you. The stairs go up to a landing, turn to the left, up again to another landing, turn to the left, etc. Visibility sucks, in other words, and what you want when you're being hunted through a building is visibility.

Up the first segment, peek around the corner. Clear. Up the next segment, peek around the corner. Clear. Up the third segment, peek around the corner. Clear. Up the—

Without warning he hits me from behind, and we crash onto the cement steps with bone-jarring force. My purse and shoes fly out of my hands, hitting the wall at the head of the landing. My startled scream echoes up and down the confines of the stairwell, but I have little hope of being heard; the janitors run the vacuums while listening to their MP3 players.

I barely have time to register that the squirrely stalking bastard snuck up on me from below before the seriousness of my situation hits me: I'm alone in a secluded stairwell in a mostly empty building with little chance of being heard if I scream, and I'm pretty seriously injured. I am in big trouble.

The impact has stunned him as well as me. I manage to scrabble halfway out of his grasp. He swears and grabs the back of my blouse,

188

dragging me back down. The buttons pop off, clattering on the cement stairs. One side flaps open and his weight falls on me, pinning me down and mashing the bare upper swell of my breast against the rough sandpaper non-skid treads on the stair. Blood soaks into my bra and puddles on the stairs. He winds his fingers into my hair and yanks my head back. My cry of pain seems to excite him.

"Did you think I forgot all about you, Sarah?" he rasps in my ear. Eric Edwards. I hate being right. "You think I'm going to lose my job because of some little company whore?"

He shoves my head down, grinding my left cheekbone against the edge of the step, stunning me again. Starbursts explode in my vision. A warm trickle of blood flows to my chin and drips onto my fingers. I scream again, but my voice has lost most of its power as my throat closes in panic; only a breathless, high-pitched whistle comes out, like a tea kettle.

His hand gropes around, finding my bloody, half-bared breast and freeing it from the confines of my bra. Pinching, bruising pain sets off swells of nausea in my stomach, the salt from his skin like acid in the wound. My panicked mind can focus on only one thing: I do not want to be raped.

"GET...OFF...ME!" I shriek, slamming my elbow backward, connecting with his shoulder. The impact jerks his hand off my breast.

"You fucking bitch!" Fingers twined in my hair, he yanks my head back again with such force that I'm certain he must have cracked a vertebrae. Panic flares again like a solar explosion. Being paralyzed and at his mercy would be infinitely worse than being out-muscled and at his mercy. At least I can fight back if I can move.

I reach with my right hand for the tread on the next step up, trying to drag myself away. Eric only laughs. He twists my left arm up behind my back, sending screaming pain through my wrist.

"Just be a good girl, Sarah, and mind your manners. This is gonna happen whether you fight or not, so just save yourself the trouble."

My throat closes to a pinhole. Tears run into the raw wound on my cheek and burn. I open my mouth to scream and he yanks my left arm up so high my shoulder pops out of joint. Excruciating pain like white lightning blazes through me. I can't get enough air to do more than whimper. I'm afraid I'll never wake up again if I pass out. My purse is three steps up, its contents strewn across the risers, my inhaler just out of reach.

"No!" I gasp. "Can't breathe. *STOP!*"

"You're done calling the shots," he replies coldly. He grips my earlobe between his teeth and bites down hard, his hot breath fanning into my ear. I grab for the riser above me again, for the life-saving albuterol, and he drags me back down, punching me in the ribs. I claw desperately at the step, catching the sandpaper traction strips. Pain like fire at the tips of my fingers as two fingernails peel back from the nail beds and hang by the cuticles. My vision goes grey around the edges. Blood wells and drips onto the scuffed cement.

"How do you like it, Sarah? How do you like being at the mercy of someone with more power than you? Think I was going to let you do that to me, that I was going to give you the upper hand? You should have just said yes the first time. I *always* get what I want."

He reaches around me, popping the button of my slacks and sliding the zipper down. I twist away, clawing at the step above me again despite the electrifying pain it causes through my tattered fingers, but he's holding onto me too tightly, his strength more than I can escape. His hand plunges down the back of my panties, groping fingers clenching painfully on my bare buttock as they inch forward.

"*NO!*" Barely a whisper, and it just makes him laugh.

Like a wild animal cornered and terrified, I reach deep inside for my survival instinct. Flight is impossible, which leaves only fight. And I come out fighting. I rear my head back, head-butting him with blinding force.

"*AAAAGH!*" His hand clenches, his nails raking bloody furrows in my right buttock. My world goes dark as I hover on the edge of a faint, but I don't dare stop even if I can't see clearly. I kick backward, my heel connecting with the meaty part of his thigh where a cluster of nerves is located. The impact sends blaring pain from my ankle to my hip. He screams the high-pitched, agonized shriek of a little girl. I lunge for my inhaler. Eric grabs my ankle. I twist in his grasp and trigger the albuterol directly into his eyes. He screams again, letting go.

Waste no time, Sarah. Not like those stupid women in the movies. Don't hang around to let him recuperate enough to rape you or kill you…or both.

I skitter backwards, my back finding the wall. I stagger to my feet, using the wall behind me as support, and mostly stumble down the risers to the next landing. My left arm hangs useless. Blood flows from my buttock down the back of my thigh, and from my cheekbone and off my chin, staining my blouse with a crimson bib. My right leg barely holds my weight, pain screaming from ankle to hip as I force it to perform. My head clangs like a Klaxon alarm. I trigger the albuterol down my throat, trying to suck it in; my breathing doesn't come any easier even after three doses. But I keep going, shambling like a zombie in a bad horror movie toward the exit, aware of the rustling noises of his recovery behind me.

I lurch out of the emergency stairs on the first floor into the empty, darkened lobby, my eyes focused only on the glowing red EXIT sign hovering like an apparition over the glass doors. My right leg drags, mostly useless. Dark splotches of blood mark my inexorable passage across the tiled floor to the front doors, which are locked and alarmed for the night. I lean against the push bar, falling halfway outside onto the sidewalk, face turned up to the twilight sky, relieved by the knowledge that the silent alarm is alerting security and law enforcement.

Running footsteps pound the tile. Shouted exclamations. A horrified brown face hovering over me, brown eyes peering anxiously into mine. Harold. Security. *Safety.*

The world spins away, taking me with it into painless oblivion.

20

A LIFETIME OF TEARS

"…find who did it?"

"No, not yet. How he made it into and out of the building is anyone's guess."

The muted conversation flows around me, but I can't make sense of the words. A thumping headache makes me certain someone used my head as a battering ram. Pain flares like a violent bonfire through my entire body.

"Sarah?"

A deep masculine voice, anxious and scared. I should know this voice, but my headache is so excruciating that I can't think. Panic flutters, making my heart race.

"Shhh," he says when I whimper, stroking the back of my right hand, which seems to be the only part of me that doesn't hurt. "I'm here. You're safe now."

"Gus, is she awake?" A familiar female voice. I dismiss it, clinging to his voice, now identified as someone trusted.

"Not really, Fran. Why don't you and Sam take Noelle home? You need some rest; you look wiped."

"*I* look wiped?" she replies. "You've been here for nine hours without a break. *You* should go home and get some sleep and let either me or Sam stay here."

"No. I'm fine." There's something reassuring about his implacable reply. Gratefully, I let go of consciousness.

I wake again to the poking and prodding of a doctor. His white coat is like a nuclear blast and I see two of him, so I close my eye again and wonder if I've been blinded in the other one. I can't seem to find my way past the booming in my head to care. A moment later he peels one lid open, shining a bright light into it, sending shooting stabs through my brain. I grumble a protest.

"I know that hurts, Sarah. Just bear with me." He moves the light around in both eyes—holding open the left one with his other hand—and then clicks it off. "How's your head?"

"Hurts." My voice rasps, barely intelligible.

"Moderate concussion. You might experience double vision for a few hours. Do you know where you are?"

My mind struggles for the word, finally finding it. My tongue has trouble saying it. "Hops...hopsital?"

"Indeed. Can you tell me your full name?" I do. "The president of the United States?" It takes a moment, but I come up with the correct name. "Your mother's maiden name?" I produce one. I sincerely hope it's the right one. He doesn't seem to find anything amiss with it. "Do you know what happened to you?"

"Doc, is this necessary right now?" Gus interjects in protest.

Doc changes tack without missing a beat. "Can you stay awake long enough for me to give you a prognosis?" he asks me. I nod slightly, even though I can't quite bring up the definition of that word, and immediately regret the motion as nauseating pain explodes from my neck up through the back of my head and down my spine.

"Don't try to move, Sarah. We have your neck immobilized while the swelling goes down. You have a nasty case of whiplash. You also have a concussion. Your left wrist is fractured, as are three of your left ribs. Your right ribs are severely bruised and may hurt for a while. Your left shoulder was dislocated. That's been fixed, but there is usually damage to the tendons and ligaments with a dislocation. It will be sore for a while and you'll need physical therapy."

"That's all?" I force the words out. My throat is raw and dry. "*Everything...*hurts."

"I'm not done, Sarah," he replies in a somber tone. "Two nails have completely detached from the nail beds. They were still attached by the cuticles; we pushed them back down and taped them, but you will lose them. For now, they protect the nail beds while the new nails grow."

Just the thought of it makes nausea curl through my stomach.

Doc continues, "You have an abrasion on your left cheek; I don't think it's deep enough to scar. Your left eye is swollen shut; the bone is bruised but not fractured; your eye is not damaged. You also have a large abrasion on your right breast as well as a deep contusion—a bruise." He pauses now and flicks a glance at Gus. "The gouges on your right buttock required nineteen stitches. They *will* scar."

"Ax...axes..." I close my eye and fish for the word. "Accident?"

Movement on my right tells me Gus has come closer. My breathing space is filled with musk and cinnamon, and for the first time in a decade I find myself on the verge of purely emotional tears.

"Sarah," he says softly. "You were attacked and beaten very badly. Do you remember anything?"

I cast around in my scrambled brain and receive only flashes of panic, of not being able to breathe, of spraying someone in the eyes with my inhaler. The memories crowd, all wanting to be freed at once, and I frantically push them away.

"A little," I croak. "My throat...hurts."

"The EMTs had to intubate in the ambulance," Doc chimes in. "You had a severe asthma attack and stopped breathing. We injected you with epinephrine to stop the attack. Your chest may be a little sore from the shot. You're on oxygen now as a precaution."

"Did I die?"

Gus draws in a sharp breath, but Doc smiles gently. "Almost, Sarah, but lucky for you I was on duty in the ER when you were brought in. Now that you know the extent of your injuries, can you tell me who did this to you?"

Unbidden a voice hisses through my memory—*Did you think I forgot all about you, Sarah?*—and I shudder convulsively, sending pain screaming along my raw nerve endings.

"It's all right, Sarah," Gus says soothingly, his fingers stroking my hair with a delicate touch I would never have expected from such a large man. "You're safe. It's okay to remember."

"Eric caught me in the emergency stairs."

"Eric Edwards?" he clarifies, his voice hard as steel now. I nod, sending screaming pain up the back of my head from my neck. "No more right now, Doc, all right? She's not ready."

"All right," Doc says, agreeable but dubious. "An advocate for victims of sexual assault will be by to talk to you later today."

My eye flies open now, dread filling my heart. "Was I…" I choke on the words, unable to force any more out. Gus's teeth audibly grind together.

"Raped?" Doc fills in matter-of-factly. "No, there's no evidence of it. But the assault was very sexual in nature, hence the advocate. You don't have to discuss anything you don't want to, but sometimes it helps." He sends another glance at Gus. "I think that's all for now. Get some rest, Sarah; you'll heal better with lots of sleep—it's the best pain killer there is, and the only one I can offer besides Tylenol because of the concussion."

"Stellar," I murmur, already drifting toward exhausted slumber. The soothing motion of Gus lightly stroking my hair invites somnolence, and I'm too weary to fight it off.

The blinds are prudently closed against the bright daylight outside when I next open my eyes—or, rather, eye. The headache has abated some—not much, but enough that I can remember names. And I can remember what happened to me, every last detail no matter how much I want to hide from it and forget it.

A dim light casts enough glow into the room that I recognize Sam Harrison in the chair next to my bed, reading a novel. When I turn my head his way, he looks up, smiling.

"Hi, Sarah."

I swallow, and find my throat better if not a little dry. "Where's Gus?"

"Fran and I sent him home a couple hours ago to get some sleep. He'll be back in a few hours—too few hours," he mutters as an afterthought. "Frannie's getting coffee in the cafeteria."

"Okay."

"Sarah, Gus told the police that Eric Edwards attacked you. They're going to be here in a while to take your statement. Can you handle it?"

"I'll manage."

And I do. Gus is back by the time the cops arrive, and it's probably only by virtue of his presence that I make it through the tale without the logjam of emotion in my chest stopping the words or my throat closing to a pinhole. In their wake they leave a 'victims of violent crime' pamphlet with my case number written on the front…and a whole lot of dread and anxiety.

The sexual assault advocate, a thirty-something African-American woman with a wonderful deep-pitched voice and soothing manner, arrives shortly afterward, and since I'm already feeling raw and exposed I see no reason not to tell the tale again. This time Gus isn't allowed to remain in the room. He assures me he'll be nearby, and I suddenly wonder if he and Sam are taking it in shifts to stay with me so Eric can't make a second attempt. It's ridiculously easy to find someone in a hospital.

When the day is over, I feel like Eric Edwards has beaten me up all over again.

I'm in the hospital four days, and the whole time I view my release with a mix of terror and relief. With Eric still on the loose, I'm afraid to go home, but I hate being confined. And I'm bloody tired; the nurses keep telling me to rest, yet it seems they're waking me every hour to take my vitals. How the hell can you rest when someone keeps interrupting your sleep cycle? Some-damn-body needs to clue in the medical profession to this fact.

"Are you ready?" Gus asks, and I grip the arms of the chair beside my bed, take a deep breath, and nod.

"Did you call Allie? Can she stay with me? I don't think I can manage on my own."

"You're not going home."

I look up at him (one-eyed; the other is still swollen mostly shut), moving slowly. My head is still apt to excruciating pain if I move too quickly, and whiplash has stiffened my movements. My neck isn't fractured, though, so I guess that's a plus, although it's hard to look at things in a positive light when everything on your body aches fiercely.

"Where am I going, then?"

He studies me without expression. "My house."

"Oh, Gus, I don't think… I don't want to be an inconvenience."

He lifts a brow. "Eric Edwards has not been caught, Sarah. You're mistaken if you think I'm going to let you go back to your apartment in your condition while he's on the loose."

And so I'm packed into his truck, which is not a joyful experience, and carted off to parts unknown. Every road seems to sprout canyon-like potholes just for me, and by the time we reach his house every nerve ending in my body is shrieking in protest. I insist on trying to walk in, but halfway up the walk from the driveway my leg gives out, and he carries me the rest of the way. My head is throbbing again, so I don't notice much of the house as he navigates his way carefully through to his bedroom.

My relief is enormous when he lays me on the bed, and I think I fall asleep (pass out?) for a while because the next thing I know I'm covered with a thick, warm blanket and he's bringing me Tylenol and a bottle of water. He's changed into sweats and a tee-shirt, and he looks angry.

I drink half the bottle, watching him pace beside the bed. "What's wrong?"

He turns, his hand raking through his hair and leaving it ruffled. "Don't worry about it. You should go back to sleep."

"Is it about what happened?" I persist, even though going back to sleep sounds like a fantastic idea.

Sighing, he perches on the edge of the bed beside me. "Your call to security went unanswered because the guard on duty in the dispatch room deliberately ignored it."

For a moment, his words make no sense. And then I realize that I was set up not only by Eric, but by one of his smarmy friends—a guy I barely even know.

"Why would he do that? I don't even know him! How could he just—" Predictably, the words clog in my throat and choke into silence. There is no explanation that makes sense.

"Eric asked him to whistle a particular song at you from the lobby while Eric snuck up the emergency stairs toward you." He looks down at his hands, clasped between his knees. In one of those surreal moments where you notice every minute detail, I see a wicked cut on the forefinger of his left hand. Looks like a file folder cut, and must hurt like a mother.

"He saw nothing wrong with Eric beating the ever-loving shit out of me?"

"His defense is that he thought Eric was only going to scare you, and he had no idea it would go so far. Shit for brains, that one." He slants a humorless smile at me. "You'll be relieved to know he has been fired, and the police are charging him as an accessory.

"Eric timed his attack according to the change of shift, and your unfortunate habit of staying late played into his plans. Harold Martin, the senior guard who found you after you triggered the alarm system, was just coming on duty."

The Tylenol seems stuck in my throat. Either that or it's another of those lumps of emotion I can't swallow, breathe, or speak past. I should have been more careful. I knew he hadn't forgotten, and he seemed too smug that day our paths crossed a couple weeks ago.

My self-recrimination must show on my face, because he says quietly, "It's not your fault, Sarah."

Letting down my guard and allowing Eric Edwards to get the drop on me *is* my fault. But I don't say it. I simply nod once—all I can manage—and close my eye again.

After a moment he sighs again and gets up.

"Will you stay with me? Just for a little while?"

"Sure. But you have to go to sleep." He moves to the empty expanse of bed behind me. He doesn't touch me but lays close enough that I can feel his warmth.

The last dose of Tylenol is wearing off and the latest yet to take effect. Pain sings through my body, an unrelenting misery. My whole frame trembles with it. I can't describe how I feel except to say it's like such a high level of anxiety that I can't stand being inside my own skin. After a moment, Gus lays his hand on my hip, careful not to jostle my left arm, which is immobilized in a cast and held in a blue canvas sling.

"Sarah, it's okay. I'll keep you safe. I promise."

I shake my head mutely, pressing my face into the pillow. He moves carefully closer; it wasn't easy getting comfortable, considering all of my injuries, and he's mindful that he doesn't cause undue pain. His arm goes around me, strong and comforting.

With wonder, relief, and utter horror, I begin to cry—a lifetime of tears dislodged from my battered heart and bruised body, an emotional storm of frightening proportions that goes beyond the events in the stairwell at Harper & Lyttle—that, in fact, reaches back in time to the events that shaped me and allowed a man like Eric Edwards to find me easy prey. The intensity of my breakdown should have had Gus running for the nearest exit.

But he stays through it all, holding me and murmuring German words that I don't understand. His voice is soothing, his comfort patient and unconditional. It's obvious from how he ignores the persistent ring of the telephone, the waning light of the day as the hours pass, the rumbling of his stomach as it protests missed meals, that I'm his first priority.

Finally, I'm number one on someone's list.

BREATHE IN. BREATHE OUT. MOVE ON.

Over the next three months as I heal, I have a lot of time to reflect on my life and the decisions I'm making—and why I'm making them. Which, in turn, leads to a lot of reflection on whether I'm really making the choices that I *want* to be making.

A Gus-Frannie-Allison conspiracy to allow me time to process what's happened to me—and to be able to sit upright without the undesirable result of a thumping, queasy headache and excruciating pain in my ribs and my ass—has buffered me from all phone calls directed to my cell. Frannie and Allison have kept Collie updated concerning my condition since the moment they received word about the attack, but neither of them thought it prudent to mention where I'm staying following my release from the hospital.

Therefore, my first conversation with him after the assault does not go well. Although he doesn't say it in so many words, he's peeved I didn't call him before now. It doesn't seem to matter to him that I was in no condition to call while I was in the hospital or that I've slept twenty hours of each day since being released…or that I had no idea where my cell phone was until this morning. I find it conveniently located—and ringing, which is what wakes me—on the night table by my bottle of water and a prescription bottle of Vicodin that I'm reasonably sure wasn't there last night.

"You're not staying alone, are you?" Collie asks. "You should have Allie or Jen come over, or go to your parents."

I experience a little twinge of guilt, because Gus has spent every night beside me on this bed—*all* night and just as platonic as the first time—and my clothes and hair smell of his musk cologne. "I'm not staying at the apartment. Eric Edwards hasn't been arrested yet, and I'm pretty sure he knows where I live."

"*I'm* pretty sure he's the one who took those pictures left on my desk, to be honest," he says, surprising me. This is the first time he's mentioned his suspicion. "It seems like a stalker thing to do. Who's staying with you? Someone who can defend you, I hope. Doesn't Jen have a gun?"

"No gun needed. There's plenty of muscle." The line goes silent, and for a moment I think we've been disconnected. "Collie?"

"Not again, Sarah," he says wearily.

"What do you mean, *not again?*"

The silence that fills the phone line between us is full of tension and accusation. I think he'd rather anyone but Gus nurse me back to health—even Eric Edwards himself.

"You had nowhere else to go? What about your parents?"

I take a deep breath, fighting a wave of pure fury that is not the first I'll have in the aftermath of the assault. I can't even roll over without help, I've come damn close to being raped, and he's worried about me having wild, passionate sex with Gus Haldemann? All concern for my physical and emotional condition has been shunted aside in favor of male territorial posturing, and I can't believe he's being so insensitive.

"What do you think is going on here? I can barely walk to the bathroom by myself. In case you've forgotten, Collie, I was viciously beaten and almost raped. Even if, by the farthest reaches of imagination, I had the urge to participate in those kinds of activities, I'm not exactly able to follow through with them or attractive enough in present condition to inspire any sexual interest whatsoever."

"Men don't care, Sarah," he counters impatiently. Now it's *my* silence that fills the line, and then his resigned sigh. "I'm sorry. I just…can't stand it that I can't be there." *That I can't be there and he can,* is what he's really trying to say. "If I wasn't in the middle of this visitation…"

"I know. I'm all right," I repeat. I don't know why but it's important for me to make him think that I am.

Collie's voice softens. "Are you really? You would say that just to make me not worry, you know."

"I know."

Silence fills the line. After a moment, he says, "You sound tired, so I'll let you go so you can sleep." It could be my imagination, but it sounded like he stressed the word *sleep*. "I have some things I have to get done today, but I'll call you later this evening or tomorrow, okay?"

"Okay." Sudden tears cling to my lashes. I try not to sniffle, because he'll ask why I'm crying and I have no answer. What can I say, really? *I'm crying because even now, broken and bruised and battered, I'm still not your number one and I can't summon the strength to be more than regretful about it?*

He disconnects and I close my phone, dropping it on the bed beside me. I lay staring at the wall until Gus comes in twenty minutes later with a tray of food I rather suspect will be bland in nature and nothing I want to eat. He makes room on the night table and sits on the edge of the bed next to me, looking from me to my phone and back again.

"Didn't go well?"

"He's more concerned with where I'm staying than with how I am."

Without responding, he helps me sit up in a semi-comfortable position, which takes some doing to find, and hands me a cup of heaven: strong black coffee, brewed from espresso beans just like I do at home.

He starts arranging things on the tray and says without looking at me, "Frannie and I discussed it with Allison, and we all figured it would be better if you told Collie where you were staying rather than one of us. I'm sure it wasn't welcome news."

I stare at him through the steam rising from my cup, wondering if that's really a blush on his cheeks. But when he looks up, he smiles without any self-consciousness.

"Cheese and fruit; Jennifer told me your favorites. You need something in your stomach to be able to take the Vicodin."

"So I'm allowed painkillers now?"

"Yes. You can take one when you feel you need to, so don't just lie there in misery because you're too stubborn to use them."

"I'm not—"

"You are." I crack a small smile, and he seems smug that he was able to coax it. "Frannie and I went to your apartment and got the things you asked for. I raided your video collection while I was there and brought some movies I haven't seen. A couple I *have* seen which I like and want to see again."

"What movies?"

"Here's the catch. You have to get up and come into the living room to see." He doesn't miss my look of dismay. "I know you hurt all over, Sarah, but you have to get out of bed and start moving around as soon as possible. Not just because you'll heal faster physically, but because you'll heal faster psychologically."

I scowl at him. "I'll watch two movies *and* eat dinner out there if I can have a shower."

"No shower—you have a cast and stitches. But Jennifer's coming over in a while to help you with a sponge bath, if that's acceptable."

I sigh, yielding to the lure of being somewhat clean if not as clean as I want to be. A shower would feel heavenly, almost as heavenly as a long, hot bath—but both are weeks in my future.

The next twenty-some days settle into such a routine. The painkillers make me throw up, so my doctor switches me to Percocet, which makes me throw up even more violently. My broken ribs ache fiercely after two days of experimenting with dosages, and I finally toss the bottles, opting for Tylenol and dealing with the residual pain as best I can.

Gus lures me out of bed for longer and longer periods of time—which I find fantastically ironic considering Collie's apprehension that he's luring me *into* bed. I try not to think about the fact that Gus has spent at least seventeen out of the last twenty-two nights sleeping beside me, usually because we fall asleep watching a movie. The nights he attempts to sleep in the guest room, I have such horrific nightmares that my screams bring him running, and he holds me while I calm down—and a few times while I cry—and ends up sleeping beside me

204

anyway.

Jennifer, Allison and Frannie come by three or four times a week to keep me company and help me maintain a level of cleanliness. During these visits Gus leaves on what he refers to vaguely as "appointments." It's not until I ask Frannie where he goes that I learn what's happening at Harper & Lyttle in my absence.

The aftermath of the assault has shaken up the company's security policies and procedures. The whole of said division is under intense scrutiny, and nearly all of the guards have been replaced (one happy exception being Harold Martin, which pleases Frannie for unknown reasons—other than the fact that Harold is a genuinely nice man). Evelyn Harper has authorized the expense of a security system overhaul, which includes closed-circuit cameras in the emergency stairwells. Gus, although having taken some vacation time and arranging to work from home during my recuperation, attends all meetings pertaining to the assault, and Frannie tells me he's a formidable force. I don't doubt it.

"I hear he reduced Lynn Geraghty nearly to tears in yesterday's meeting," she informs me with obvious relish, helping me shrug into a clean, button-up shirt, which is easier for me to manage than pullovers. Lynn Geraghty is one of the corporate lawyers in the Legal Division who caved to Eric Edwards' pressure after he cornered me in the break room in March. She's well-known to be a completely unsympathetic individual who bases her actions solely on the odds of winning rather than on the morality or virtue of the argument.

"Oh? How'd he manage that?"

"Completely maligned her ethics and values and threatened her with legal action eight ways from Sunday for failing to give you adequate protection and thereby indirectly sanctioning Edwards' attack. Or at least that's how Gus worded it. She may be an iceberg in the court room, but Gus is no slouch himself."

"He's a lawyer?" I'm stunned; I had no clue, although in retrospect I suppose it's not that uncommon for a human resources director to have a background in law.

Frannie chuckles. "He'd be terribly offended if he heard you call him a lawyer. He says he has too much respect for truth and compassion, which is why he took a job with Harper & Lyttle after passing the bar exam." She sends me a look from the corner of her eye. "You have a strong ally in your corner, Sarah, and he's shaming them into an out-of-court settlement."

"Settlement!" To be frank, my physical and mental conditions have not been conducive to thinking beyond recovery. And Gus, although we spend a lot of time together and much of it talking, has not mentioned legal action against Harper & Lyttle whatsoever.

"Sarah, through their refusal to act when Eric Edwards was caught harassing you, they allowed this to happen. Let them learn their lesson—and the way to make a corporation this size learn anything is by hitting them in the pocketbook."

She's sitting cross-legged behind me, brushing and braiding my hair, which I can't manage on my own. I can take my left arm out of the sling now for several hours at a stretch, but my cast and my healing shoulder don't allow me to maneuver my arm into the correct position to work the braid. It's more comfortable sitting now, though—the stitches came out of my backside a week ago, and the gouges are healing and itching like fury.

"I didn't mean to eavesdrop," Fran says tentatively, "but it sounded to me like you and Collie were fighting when you called him earlier."

I bow my head, but she pulls gently on my hair to bring it back up so she doesn't lose the ends of the braid.

"Not your imagination." I don't mention how hurtful it is that I had to call him; he was supposed to phone me eight days ago and never did. When I asked why, he completely blew off the question.

"Mmm." Her deft fingers skim through my hair, the tug and twist somehow comforting. "Men don't always know how to handle these things. I'm sure the advocate who comes to see you has talked to you about that."

"Yes, she has." The advocate comes once a week while I'm laid up. When I'm able to get around, I'll have to go see her if I want to continue our sessions, which I'm not sure I do. It seems to me that continually talking about what happened just drags the scab off the wound and never allows it to heal.

"But then again, you *are* living—however temporarily—in the house of a man who could quite easily take Collie's place if you found yourself willing, and who has not been shy about making known his interest in you. I can see where Collie would be very threatened by that."

I tamp down another wave of that irrational, disproportionate anger. "He thinks this is some sort of cover for a secret sexual liaison. Like I'm in any condition for those kinds of activities."

"And if you *were* in adequate physical shape?"

"Then perhaps Collie would have something concrete to worry about."

Frannie laughs. "You're looking at it all wrong, Sarah. He's not worried about you having a physical relationship with Gus—in fact, if the grapevine has it right, he assumes you already are. Collie's more concerned with your emotional attachment to Gus."

"He should be." The words are out of my mouth before I can stop them. Fran's fingers pause, and when she speaks there's a definite note of amusement in her voice.

"Can't be any more plain that that," she replies cheerfully. "Holy shit, Sarah—this braid looks like a blind man did it. D'you care?"

I laugh. "Not really. I'm only going to end up sleeping on it anyway."

"Well, good. My work here is done then, and just in time—my arms are killing me!" She scoots off the bed and helps me up. "Let's go watch a movie."

We've come to an agreement on acceptable movie standards, she and I. Frannie is definitely chick-flick lady, whereas I'm truly happy only when watching some ever-loving asshole get the living hell beaten/shot/tortured out of him or her, which are the kind of movies Gus routinely brings from either my collection or from the local Blockbuster—those and some damn odd, quirky movies that quickly become favorites.

A week before Halloween, Collie calls to tell me he's extending his stay in Seattle until just after Christmas. I meet this news with silence, more because of his defiant tone than anything else. I miss him very badly and—oh, all *right!* I promised honesty long ago. Fine. Okay. I *do* miss Collie, but in an abstract way. I have to confess that being vulnerable to Eric Edwards is only one reason I dread moving back to my apartment. Gus Haldemann has eclipsed every other man I've ever met, and I'm loath to give up the life with him to which I'm rapidly becoming accustomed.

"Sarah?" Collie prods sharply. "Did you hear what I said?"

"I heard. What…ah…made you decide this?"

"This wasn't as cut and dried as I thought it'd be." In other words, either Megan is thriving…or Collie is. I draw in a breath to voice some acceptable answer, but he goes on before I can speak, his voice taking on an edge. "Besides, since you're virtually living with Gus Haldemann…."

Am I the only one thinking *que la chinga* here, because it certainly is a what-the-fuck moment. I consider and discard various responses—*aren't you just a bright little ray of trust, fuck off and die,* and *bite me, asshole* being just a few—and finally settle for silence.

Eventually it becomes apparent that neither of us is going to breach that silence. With a thoughtful frown, I close my phone, severing the connection. Seconds later it rings again, and I send the call—and the three that follow it—to voicemail. The last time he tries calling, he actually even leaves one, to which I listen with a jaded ear: *Look, I'm sorry, Sarah, okay? Try seeing this from my perspective—you're living with a man who has made it clear to both you and me that he's a rival. Why would you think it wouldn't bother me that you're staying with him, of all people?* (Of all people? This makes me grind my teeth.) *When I come home, we'll sit down and talk about everything, all right? We can get through this.*

But I don't think we can, and I'm less sure that I want to.

I don't hear from my mother until two days before Thanksgiving, and it goes about as well as my last conversation with Collie (who has tried to call at least once a week since I hung up on him. I always send his call to voicemail.

When I call my home answering machine to retrieve my messages (and wade through reporters' requests for interviews, telemarketing calls even though I'm on the Do Not Call registry, and a few hangsups that make me sweat and shake, wondering if Eric Edwards had been on the other end of the line), I find a message from my mother left a week ago, imperiously asking about Thanksgiving. Eight months with no contact, and surely she's heard about the assault by now, but not a word about where I've been or how I am.

My lips compressed into an angry line, I hang up on my answering machine and dial her number, muttering under my breath. Gus is making dinner in the kitchen behind me, and he looks up from his task but wisely keeps his mouth shut.

"Hello." Mother's voice across the line is haughty.

"It's Sarah-Jane. You called."

"Sarah-Jane. It's about time. I left that message more than a week ago—"

My chest tightens just hearing her voice. "Six days ago," I correct her.

She goes on without pause. "I really need to know what time you plan to be here on Thanksgiving. We will be having several guests, and I'll need you to be here early. If you get here by nine o'clock, you and I just might have enough time to get everything done."

"Where will Mary-Ann be?"

I can almost see her blink in surprise. "Why, here, of course."

Of course. "I don't think I can make it."

An impatient huff, and then her long-suffering, what-did-I-do-to-deserve-such-children tone. "Of course you can make it. It's Thanksgiving—where else would you be?"

With no warning, with no conscious decision to oppose her, I simply snap. *"Mother."*

Even Gus stops what he's doing, wary of my tone.

"Sometimes I don't know what you're thinking, Sarah-Jane. What am I supposed to do if you don't come?"

"Perhaps you can make Mary-Ann do something for a change. I'm not your beast of burden. And in case you haven't been paying attention, it's been eight months—*eight months*—since we've spoken.

209

During that time my birthday, Mary-Ann's birthday, and your and Dad's anniversary have all passed. You didn't even notice I wasn't there."

She sniffs. "Of *course* I noticed! After your atrocious behavior the last time you came for dinner—"

"*My* atrocious behavior! I dropped some spaghetti sauce on my shirt. Hardly a capital offense. I won't be coming, Mother, because I'm still recovering from the assault."

"It's been three months, Sarah. You can't keep using it as an excuse to neglect your—"

"*Stop it! Just fucking stop it!*" Her disapproving, shocked silence is a palpable presence on the electronic connection between us. "I am so sick of this. Stop pretending that you even care about me showing up. All you want is someone to shoulder the work."

"Of course I care," Mother says, affronted.

"Yeah? Really? Where have you been for the past three months, then? You didn't even bother to send a goddamn get-well card."

"Sarah-Jane, really!" she huffs, angry now. "If you didn't always act like such an ungrateful child—"

The fury comes out of nowhere, unreasonable, deeper than the situation warrants. "Fuck you," I say, coldly and deliberately.

Dead silence reigns both on the phone and in the kitchen, broken only by the clatter of Gus dropping his santoku knife.

"You're dead to me." I hang up, pressing my hand to my mouth and my cast to my suddenly heaving stomach.

I barely make it to the bathroom in time. My ribs ache, the straining muscles around the fractures pressing on healing bone. My embarrassment surpasses endurance as I become aware of Gus kneeling beside me, gathering my hair out of the way.

When I'm done, he helps me stand. I brush my teeth and stare at myself for a long moment in the mirror, wondering for the gazillionth time what it is about me that makes me fade into obscurity even with those to whom I should matter the most.

"Sarah, don't cry." Gus turns me around to face him, his fingers swiping at the tears on my cheeks. I'm a regular waterworks lately. I'm amazed the man hasn't thrown up his hands and sped away in disgust. His hands settle on my shoulders.

"I wondered why the hospital called me first, and why your parents haven't made an appearance yet—I even called your mother myself to tell her what happened. If you only listen to one thing I ever tell you, make it this."

He waits until he's sure he has my undivided attention, and then he looks me square in the eye and gives me an invitation to let it all go and not look back.

"A lot has happened in your life that you have to learn to live with. Agonizing over it will change none of it; doing so only tells people you're easy to manipulate. You're the only one who's miserable with things the way they are. So breathe in." I do. "Breathe out." And I do. "Now move on and take what you want from life, Sarah. I can't imagine anyone who deserves it more."

He bends and kisses me, his lips clinging to mine for a timeless moment, and then leaves me to mull it over as he goes back to dinner preparations.

We eat in silence, but it's a comfortable one, full of unspoken communication. And later, while we're watching a movie in the darkened living room, I pull my fleece blanket up to my chin and lean against his shoulder, liking the feel of his muscles beneath my cheek. He smiles down at me, and I close my eyes, feeling that strange anger ebbing and finally disappearing altogether.

More weeks pass. My cast comes off the day after Thanksgiving. Gus lets me pick his Christmas tree after the appointment, probably to take my mind off the disconcerting fact that the lower half of my left arm looks like the underbelly of a dead fish.

Frannie comes over to lament that the new office manager—which, I might remind everyone, *she* chose from a crap-ton of applicants—has magenta highlights in her hair, wears combat boots under her gauze skirts, talks to the staff in a hipshot manner, and got her eyebrow pierced as an early Christmas present. She's also frighteningly efficient and the staff relates to her rather well, which leaves Frannie floundering about what to think.

We watch more movies. A week before Christmas, the doctor clears me to go back to work following the holiday. We celebrate with too much rum and a day of the *Die Hard* series.

I wake well into the third movie to find myself sprawled in his lap again. He isn't watching the movie; he's watching me, twirling my hair around his forefinger. When he bends to me, he doesn't kiss me but whispers in my ear, a suggestion that steals my breath and tempts me beyond resistance.

We sit for a long moment, staring at each other with his words hanging between us. And finally I whisper back: "All right."

Breathe in. Breathe out. Move on.

Tales from the Water Cooler

Sunday, November 29
Beware of Bosses Bearing Transcription

Posted by Sarah Quinn

I'm back—finally—after a long illness. Thank you, blog followers, for the well-wishes and the pleas for more office tips. It's nice to be appreciated.

Today let's discuss transcription. It used to be the bane of the administrative professional's office life (unless you're one of those who dearly loves to transcribe, in which case I suggest intense therapy with substantial quantities of Thorazine).

Recently I was asked by our CEO to transcribe some tapes left in storage by her predecessor. "Some tapes" turned out to be 32. WOWZA! I reminded myself that I'm at work for eight hours no matter what; it doesn't matter what I do in that eight hours.

So I organized the tapes according to the handwriting on the labels (it's easiest to transcribe all tapes from one dictator rather than mixing and matching. Mix and match and you will be heading for that Thorazine post-haste) and started happily (?) typing away. Of the 32 tapes, only 13 contained letters and memos, most of which were already saved in dead-tree form in the CEO's file cabinet or various other places around the company campus. All these tapes were labeled in a decidedly feminine hand.

I then popped in the first of the remaining 19, following the date order as listed on the labels, which are written in a definite masculine hand. Two sentences into the dictation, I realized that I'm not hearing letters dictated, but a recorded personal journal. I will not tell you the subject matter, although let me just say that I was not aware of such shenanigans going on in this company, and why do I always miss out on all the excitement?

The lesson: If your boss comes at you with a box of transcription, discreetly ask him or her if he or she has screened the tapes before blindly handing them over. Also inquire whether his or her administrative assistant can transcribe, and if not, why was he or she hired? Those of us at the bottom of the admin pond should NOT have to know about the seedier side of office politics.

I am now going to go consume numerous Mojitos to erase what I learned.

DID YOU KNOW:

WORD/EXCEL MAIL MERGE TIP: A well-known fact amongst office professionals is that mail merge using an Excel document as a data source does not always go smoothly. When you have a number with a decimal derived from a formula, you sometimes end up with 49 places behind the decimal (or so it seems). This does not import well into Word, which like a faithful dog will do whatever you ask it to in a merge (unlike any other time you're trying to accomplish something).

The trick to making sure your figures show with only two decimal places is simple but obscure. It is called a **Numeric Picture Field Switch.**

- Open your main merge document.
- Press ALT + F9 to show the merge field coding. It should look something like this: **{MERGEFIELD "fieldname" }**
- At the end of the field name, leaving no spaces and adding no quotes, type \#0.0x (to round to two decimal places; 0.00x for three decimal places, etc.)
- Press ALT + F9 to toggle out of field code display.
- Your numbers will now import into the merge with the correct number of decimals.

Blog Archive
2009

November
Beware of Bosses Bearing Transcription
August
RSS Feeds: Really Simple, Stupid
June
Choices
May
WTF Is Wrong with Men???
March
Love Triangles: Three- Pointed Pains-in-the…
February
Faces in the Crowd
January
Going Postal: A Career-Limiting Move

About Me

Savvy Sarah

I am an administrative office professional with several years' experience in office settings. I have an AAS in Administrative Office Management and currently work as a training specialist for a software development company in Los Angeles.

EVERYTHING I NEVER KNEW I WANTED

"Are you sure they're expecting us?"

"You asked that an hour ago," Gus replies, taking his eyes from the snowy road for a brief second to smile at me. "Nervous?"

"I'm mostly nervous about *not* arriving, which is why I wondered if they knew we were coming. If we don't show up, I'd like to think someone will be searching for us before spring. We have only one candy bar left, not enough to last until May."

He grins. "Don't worry. I grew up in this. I know what I'm doing."

"*I* don't know what you're doing, which is where my anxiety comes from."

"Trust me. I'm a capable man."

Capable indeed, I agree silently. I can't argue his point; he handles the truck with remarkable ease as it plows through the snow, and I understand now why he owns a 4 x 4 crew cab truck when he lives in Los Angeles. He makes the trip up here to Grants Pass, Oregon, three or four times a year, and in snowfall like this, four-wheel drive is necessary. In some places, I can barely see over the berms the plow has left at the sides of the road. We've been swallowed by a forest of white-draped pines and mountains, and the flakes are still coming down.

"We'll be there in an hour or so, long before the worst of the storm hits," he predicts.

He guides the truck around a curve that would have had me shaking and crying, and the dashboard lights glint off the gold ring on his left-hand finger. *My* ring.

To this day I can't tell you with one-hundred percent certainty just what we vowed to one another. All I remember with crystal clarity is his gaze holding mine, his unwavering confidence in this insane venture somehow reassuring me that this is anything *but* insane; the warmth of his skin as I slide my ring onto his finger; the feather-light caress he gives mine as he places his; and the clinging kiss we share as we're pronounced man and wife—a Las Vegas wedding that he says is going to make Sam Harrison shit his pants.

You think *you're* surprised? The enormity of what we've done doesn't hit me for a few hours. I'll probably never know what possessed Gus to suggest we go to Vegas and get married, just like I'll never know why "yes" seemed like the most natural response in the world. And the biggest mystery is how he managed to get the chapel— let alone a room—at the Bellagio Hotel on such short notice at Christmas.

After the ceremony he takes me dancing because he wants to see my dress swing. And swing it does, as we travel a circuitous route from hotel bar to hotel bar, eventually making our way back to our room at the Bellagio. We've had more to drink than we should—everyone seems to want to buy newlyweds copious amounts of alcohol—and we've made many friends we'll never see again, which is kind of funny when you consider the fact that we're both a bit introverted.

"Did you see the look on that guy's face when I told him we'd just met yesterday?" he says as we spill into our room, laughing.

"And what he said… 'Good God, man! It's not too late to fix things!'"

I shed my shoes and whirl around, sending my dress swinging again. No white for me; I saw this green confection in a shop window on our way to lunch. Its colors flow from dark spring green to gold and on a whim I tried it on. The look on his face when I came out of the dressing room was enough to tell me the $750 price tag is well worth it—not that I paid for it. A discreet word from him to the saleswoman secures me coordinating pumps, purse, and golden velvet wrap; he doesn't even blink as he signs the receipt.

I could have afforded it myself if only for the simple reason that

Harper & Lyttle has me on paid leave-of-absence (Gus's doing, according to Frannie), and in spite of all my monthly bills being paid on time and in full, the balance in my bank account only grows with each paycheck deposit (Gus's doing again).

Gus shed his tie some hours ago, and the tail of it is hanging from his left trouser pocket. Our eyes meet and the laughter dies as he slides his arms around me. With the force of a hurricane, it hits me: we've joined our lives—legally, emotionally, financially, and—if you're of this mindset—spiritually.

Alone for the first time since the wedding, facing the husband I never expected to have by year's end, I have only one thought: I want to be out of this dress very badly and not because it's uncomfortable.

His hands are hot through the chiffon layers and scorching on my skin as the dress floats to the floor. He touches me with reverence and wonder, as though lost in a dream he can't quite believe is real. Our bodies entwine, his bare skin against mine electrifying every nerve ending in my body. His lips follow a path his hands blaze, trailing feather-light kisses that set fire to my skin. When I touch him, he stops breathing. And when my hand moves lower, he loses his English and a stream of murmured German pours out, sounding both fierce and exotic. *Mein Gott* is the only thing I understand, but it's encouragement enough to continue my explorations. He turns the tables, and I lose *my* English, but I have nothing to replace it with but breathless sighs and gasps of pleasure.

Making love with him for the first time is like finding everything I never knew I wanted, treasures unknown but more precious than any ever discovered. The kiss we shared in June outside the Human Resources elevators was not even a glimpse of what was to come. By dawn I can't remember the name of any other man on the face of this planet, and it occurs to me that Dante Alighieri was right: a great flame does indeed follow a little spark, and we've both been consumed in the fire.

"You keep looking at me like that, I'm going to have to throw you in a snow bank," he remarks conversationally. "Or in the back seat."

I jump, realizing I've been staring at him while remembering. "It's your own damn fault, you know."

His grin now is absolutely sinful. "I aim to please."

"Nothing like an overachiever."

We're on our way to his parents' house for Christmas, in case you're wondering why we're driving around the wilds of southern Oregon in the dead of winter. And no, they don't know we got married. No one does except the two of us, the minister at the Bellagio Hotel's wedding chapel, and the hapless couple we conned into being our witnesses after sharing drinks in the lounge.

And you might rightfully ask where Collie fits into this. He doesn't. From the moment Gus whispered to me while we were watching movies (you were probably thinking he was talking me into his bed, not that it would have taken much talking), I have not spared more than an uneasy thought for Collie, and only then because his reaction is likely to be less than pleasant and probably highly unflattering toward me, and I'm not looking forward to it.

Not that I could blame him; I *do* love him—no, don't shake your head like that; I truly *do*—but there are many degrees of love and mine for him is like a distant flame. My fear that losing myself in Gus would be losing my identity has proved unfounded; I've never been more aware of who I am than at the moment I agree to marry him. I'm Sarah-Jane Aubrey Quinn, a desirable woman and first on this incredible man's list of priorities.

"So what are they going to say when you show up with a wife, Gus?"

He chuckles. "Nothing I do surprises them anymore. They won't say anything in front of you, but I'll get an earful." He considers. "Except from my sister."

"She'll be all for it?"

"She's all for anything that makes me happy." His right hand leaves the wheel, snaking across the bench seat to pluck mine up. He kisses my finger just below my wedding rings—oh, and let's talk about *those*. Also seen in the window of a shop as we passed by, he suggests we go in so I can try them on for kicks and giggles. We walk out with the bride and groom wedding bands in ring boxes in his pocket and the engagement ring on my finger—thank God I have "showcase hands"—and I make damn sure there's insurance on this baby, because a rock this size…

"It's going to be chaos when we get there," he warns as he slows the car to turn left onto a road that, for all appearances, leads directly into the thick of the forest and up a mountain. It's been a long damn day, and I'm a little sorry that we decided to drive instead of fly. The trip to Vegas from Los Angeles isn't very long, only about five hours; it took us six and a half because of the frequent stops to let me walk around. My right leg still aches fiercely sometimes when I sit for too long, and my left side from shoulder to waist fares no better.

This leg of the trip, however, has been sixteen hours so far. I drove part of it, but once we got off Interstate 5, I relinquished the wheel because I've never driven in snow before.

"Will all your brothers and your sister be there?"

"And their wives, and my sister's husband, and all their kids."

I mull this over for a moment. "We're going to end up on a sleeper sofa somewhere, aren't we?" I guess morosely. My shoulder is still stiff and sore even on his very comfortable bed at home.

"Nah. Worst case scenario is we end up in the attic bedroom. It's really nice, but a bit chilly in the winter, which I don't mind myself. You might get cold, though. Mom keeps a heater up there, and once we kick it on it'll warm up fast."

I personally don't mind sleeping in a chilly room; not only do I sleep better, but it also allows me to cuddle up to him without us bursting into flames.

"How many kids?"

"Too damn many when it comes to buying Christmas presents," he replies ruefully. "Joe has five; Dee has three; Kasey has two; Nick and Sebastian have four each; and Liesel has one and is working on the second. Hence the limited space for our luggage in the back seat."

"Jesus!"

"Told you."

"And you're the last to get married."

"Yep. But I'm not the youngest. I'm the third child—also the third boy. Liesel is smack dab in the middle, right after me, and then come another three boys."

I digest this silently, mentally adding up my new extended family. Counting his parents, I'm walking into a crowd of thirty-three established relatives, all in one house. "All I have to offer are two snobby parents and an evil sister."

"Shades of Cinderella?"

"Now that you mention it…"

"Don't worry. My mother will have you peeling potatoes and telling her your life story in no time, and my sisters-in-law will be quizzing you about orgasms within a day."

Hot color floods my face. "I have to tell them about those?"

This makes him laugh so hard he almost drives off the road. "Please don't! Keep 'em guessing, that's my motto. For a long time, I think they speculated that I might be gay because I was the only one not married. I'm sure some money changed hands over it, too," he adds thoughtfully.

I'm stunned. Discussing orgasms and their bachelor brother-in-law's sexual orientation—and betting on it? "What kind of people *are* they?"

He smiles with genuine fondness. "They're family."

A few minutes later he turns off the main road—if it can be called that; I think every one of my teeth has been jarred loose and my shoulder is throbbing just like after my physical therapy sessions—and onto a one-lane drive. Through the trees I can see the warm glow of lights, and then a large farmhouse comes into view. Not a pristine, urban replica like my parents' but a *real* farmhouse. Gus parks the truck next to a line of others in front of a barn and turns in his seat to look at me before shutting off the engine.

"A couple of things. They'll speak a lot of German—both Mom and Dad are Mannheim transplants. We grew up with a mixture of English and German that made it *damn* difficult when we started school." He flashes a grin. "Don't take it personally; just know beforehand that they *are* talking about you, but it's probably flattering—though beware of the words *die Schlampe* coming from

Maggie, Dee's wife. And if she calls me *der schwanz*, just pretend like you didn't hear. She and I don't exactly get along."

"And what might those two phrases mean?"

"*Die Schlampe* means bitch. *Der schwanz* means prick."

"And does she perhaps call you a prick because you call her a bitch?" I arch a brow at him and he laughs.

"You're priceless. More like the other way around. We had a falling out long ago—like the day I found out Dietrich asked her to marry him and I voiced my opinion. Are you ready?"

It doesn't matter if I am or not, because the rumble of the truck engine and the headlights flashing in the windows of the house as we came up the drive alerted the occupants of the house to our arrival. Several kids of varying ages spill out the front door and race pell-mell toward us, followed by a couple of adults who remain on the covered front porch and out of the snow.

"Ah. A welcoming party." He grins with relish and without further remark pops open his door and hops out into the snow. I follow more slowly, waiting for him to come around the truck and join me. He's mobbed by delighted kids shrieking "Uncle Gus! Uncle Gus!" and is lost in a snow bank under the weight of at least six miniature Haldemanns.

"Who are you?"

Surprised by the innocent question, I look down at a girl no more than five-years-old with strawberry blonde curls, freckles across her pert little nose and cheeks, and solemn blue eyes. An older boy bearing a strong resemblance to her hangs back, watching.

I discard several answers, finally opting for the simple yet obscure, "I'm Sarah."

They exchange a look, and the boy is triumphant. "Told you!" he says to the girl, who sticks out her tongue at him. He lopes off toward the house shouting, "He brought a girl! He brought *Sarah*!" and vanishes through the front door, to spread the news far and wide.

"So much for arriving discreetly," Gus laments, brushing snow— and children—off his coat and jeans. He gives them a command in German and they rush off, laughing and pushing each other into the snow.

"He speaks fluent German," I remark out loud. "Is there nothing you can't do?"

And bless his heart, he replies straight-faced, "I can't bowl, and I can't play tennis."

That's the last moment we have alone until we go to bed. The adults who came out with the kids have gone back in with them, leaving Gus and me to come in unescorted. The front door opens up to a staircase dead ahead, leading upward. French doors on the left lead into a dining room with the largest table I've ever seen, adorned with dishes in varying stages of use. A few people still clustered around it smile at us, but weighted down into apathy by good German cooking, they don't do more than call out greetings.

A coat closet beneath the stairs opens up on the right, with a long bench along the wall and a large sisal rug to catch the snow and mud. French doors on the right lead into a large family room where most of the adults and kids have congregated following dinner—which I'm sorry to say we've missed; it's just past eight-thirty.

We shed boots and coats and go into the family room, and everyone starts talking at once. The little blonde girl from outside takes my hand and tries to lead me away, but Gus ruffles her hair.

"*Nein, Liebchen.* I have to introduce her before I throw her to the wolves." She accepts this silently and attaches herself firmly to my leg.

"Out of my way! Out of my way!" A plump, sixty-something woman makes her way through the throng, drying her hands on a dishtowel that she uses to swat various family members in her path. Her hair, once up in a very European bun, has let loose several tendrils of graying blonde hair that curl around her flushed face.

"My mother, Katja," Gus murmurs to me, and then she's upon him, smushing his face between her damp hands. She bestows a kiss on each plumped cheek and speaks with a clipped German accent.

"Gustaf! I thought you would be later. Papa has gone to bed already."

"He's all right?"

"Ach!" She waves away with question. "He chopped wood today.

He thinks he's a young man. I hope you drove carefully."

"As carefully as I could. Precious cargo." He draws me in front of him (clinging child and all) and rests his hands on my shoulders. The occupants in the room fall quiet after much shushing of each other. "Everyone, I'd like you to meet Sarah. My wife."

Five seconds of shocked silence, everyone exchanging looks with one another—with everyone but us, it seems—and then they all start talking at once, shouting over each other. Men get up, shoving each other out of the way like children, to come thump their brother on the back. He's carried away from me as though caught by a riptide, and my last glimpse of him for the next half an hour is the rueful, apologetic smile he sends over the shoulders of his siblings.

For a moment I'm nonplussed; they're congratulating him—or berating him, not sure which since they keep lapsing into German— but they say nothing to me. Then I realize that the bulwark presence of his mother is between me and them; she obviously gets the honor of being first. She's a couple of inches shorter than me but she seems a giant as she scrutinizes me with a sharp eye.

"Liebchen." Then her hands smush up *my* face and she kisses me on each cheek. *"Willkommen Zuhause."* Whatever that means. She takes my right arm, drawing me (and the child still attached to my left leg) into the chattering mass of her family.

I eventually wind up in the kitchen, happily eating reheated sauerbraten with dumplings and potato cakes topped with applesauce, chased with strong dark beer (and still accompanied by my new best friend, who now has a name—Stefanie—and parentage: Gus's brother Josef), and this is where I'm reunited with my husband. His cheeks are red and he looks a little harassed, but he's in good spirits.

"Hey, can I have some of that?" He gestures to my beer, and I hand it over reluctantly, which makes him grin. "There's more where this came from, if I know my father. Good stuff." He drinks deeply and hands the mug back as Katja sets a plate in front of him and smacks him on the shoulder with a wooden spoon.

"Sit and eat!"

He obeys without argument, which cracks me up because the

employees at Harper & Lyttle have exactly the same reaction to him when he gives a command. He fixes his niece with a glower.

"Don't think I'm sharing a room with you tonight," he says gruffly. "It's bad enough I have to share with Sarah. She hogs the covers." Little Stefanie—which everyone pronounces SHTE-fanie—giggles.

"I do not!"

"Do so. Might I remind you…aaaahhh." He breaks off, coloring again. My own face flames. That particular night—just last night, in fact—wasn't so much hogging the covers as it was wrecking the bed.

Another swat on his shoulder makes him wince. "Bedroom talk is for the bedroom. Eat up! It's a long day tomorrow—Christmas Eve—so everyone is getting up early." Her eagle eye swoops over my face and passes judgment. "And Sarah looks exhausted."

This sobers him, serving as an unwelcome reminder of my still-recovering body—and why it's recovering. I wonder how much his family knows about that. "Yes, she does."

"I've put you in the attic bedroom—the only empty one."

Gus tips me a wink and mouths, "Told you so."

It's almost ten before we finally make it there, and it's nothing like I expected. Rather than being some stuffy run-down closet, it's spacious and cedar-paneled, decorated with homey rag rugs on the wood floor. White-washed furniture brightens the room. I'm pleased to see a goose-down quilt folded at the foot of the bed, and two dormer windows that will make me a little less claustrophobic. A small bathroom adjoins the bedroom, another welcome relief.

His preteen nephews carried our luggage up earlier, so everything is waiting for us. Gus turns on a space heater that looks like a radiator, churning heat into the room, and advises me to wear something to bed because the possibility exists that we'll have a kid invasion in the morning. Fantastic. Our teeth brushed (cinnamon toothpaste is his secret to always tasting like cinnamon—just FYI) and faces washed, we climb into the squeaking bed.

"Is this a joke?" I ask as the springs squeal.

He pulls me against him, tucking one arm beneath his head. The springs lodge their protest at the movement and he laughs helplessly. "We're in for it now. They're gonna hear it every time we roll over and assume…well, we *are* newlyweds."

I turn off the lamp and roll over to face him. Blue light fills the room: the moon shining off the snow and colored by the night, filtering in through the sheer white curtains. The creaks and muted conversations of a house bedding down for the night lull me toward sleep, but I resist for a while, content to lay with my cheek against his chest and his hand stroking my hair.

I speak into the silence, surprising myself. I've never told anyone this dream, either, not that it's top secret or anything. It's just kind of silly.

"I've wanted a blue bedroom since I was a little girl."

"Yeah? Why's that?"

The steady *thump thump* of his heart against my ear invites intimacy. How can I not reveal my most secret dreams when I'm listening to the very life inside him, which is much more mysterious than my desire for a blue bedroom?

"We stayed in a blue room at that bed and breakfast I told you about, the one my family went to when I was little. I wish I could remember the name of it."

"It'll come to you someday, out of the blue—pun intended. I'm sure it will be sometime around three in the morning. Try to remember it, because if you wake me up…"

I pinch him. "Smart ass. The walls were a beautiful cerulean with white trim, the ceiling a soft cloud-white. There were rag rugs on the floor with all kinds of country colors in them, and elegant French furniture—what do they call it?"

"Baroque? Rococo?"

"Rococo. The lines were clean and curving and it was all white-washed. I remember one piece in particular, a small chest of drawers with a toile design painted on it."

"You want a bedroom like that?"

"I do."

"I'll see what I can do."

I shift so I can look up at him. "Your house is too modern for it. It's more suited to this house, or that inn where I saw it."

"*Our* house, and we're only renting. I sold my house after Gretchen left with the girls; haven't bought a new one yet."

"Why not?"

Now he shifts, making the bed creak and me giggle, and then we're nose-to-nose. "I was waiting for you to make up your mind."

I smile faintly. "You already knew what I would choose."

But he shakes his head. "Not really. When Collie came to talk to me about you, I did what I thought was best for all involved: I told him how to keep you because that's what you seemed to want."

"But what about what you wanted?"

"That wasn't important. You seemed happy. That was all that mattered to me."

I consider this for a while, marveling at the difference between the two men I had to choose between. Collie, who warned away the competition; and Gus, who bowed out gracefully to let me decide without pressure, letting the irresistible pull of his personality speak for him. Even then I was his first consideration.

"Do you miss Gretchen?"

"Do you miss Collie?" he counters.

I shrug. "I miss certain things. And I'm *really* dreading his reaction when I tell him we got married. But I chose who I really wanted, deep inside, all along."

"Gretchen and I were over long before you came on the scene, Sarah. But she's such a mess that I would have stayed with her for the next fourteen years until Beatrice, the youngest, was grown up just to give those girls a stable home, regardless of my feelings for you."

I hadn't even known he knew my name, let alone had any interest in me. Or perhaps because I was blinded by infatuation, I never saw beyond Collie.

He tilts his head and kisses me, pulling me out of my introspection. "What do you say we give the family something to talk about?"

"Since they're going to talk anyway, you mean?" I grin back at him.

"Exactly."

"You're a hard man to resist."

His answering grin is wicked. "Ah, but they say a hard man is good to find."

"I'm not arguing that point."

He rolls onto his back, pulling me atop him, and flings his arms wide. "Have your way with me. Just be gentle."

"No mercy," I warn, bending to him.

We make love slowly, almost furtively, trying not to make the springs creak and snickering when we do. And then we lay curled together in a tangle of limbs, spent and satisfied. Sleep catches him first, and I lay drowsy and content, listening to the hush of the winter woods around us.

I fall headlong into slumber, and for the third night in a row my sleep is untroubled by nightmares.

STANDING IN THE GAP

Morning breaks (don't expect me to fix it), bringing brilliant blue skies, sunlight that reflects blindingly off the snow, and a warm furnace behind me in bed, faithfully putting out BTUs. My eyes shut against the brilliant beam stabbing in through the open curtains and falling directly across my eyes, I huddle more securely against Gus. The bed in front of me dips, and I open my eyes, startled, to find him sitting before me, grinning.

"Who's behind me?"

"Stefanie. The furnace is out, and while the other kids are huddled around the fireplace in the family room, no doubt roasting marshmallows by now, she wanted to come up here with you, so I brought her."

"How long have you been up?"

"Long enough to regret getting up so early—Pop is swearing a blue streak in the utility room—and to realize that even while you are one of the most beautiful women I've ever known, you still sleep with your mouth open and drool running down your cheek and into your pillow."

I poke him in the knee just under the cap, making his leg jerk. "A gentleman wouldn't mention that."

"I told you before," he reminds me, eyes gleaming, "I'm not a gentleman." He slaps me on the rump, the sting absorbed by the blankets. "Come on, get up. Coffee's waiting. There are still some potato cakes left from last night. And Mom's going to make Christmas cookies."

"What about small stuff here?" I jerk my thumb over my shoulder

231

at his niece.

"We'll take her with us."

I'm loathe to leave the warm bed, especially considering the fact that the furnace isn't working, but the kitchen is likely to be the warmest room in the house since Katja is baking. And as much as I enjoy spending time in bed with my husband, he is not *in* bed at present time, doesn't appear to be returning to it any time soon, the bed is occupied by one too many people, and I equally enjoy him fully clothed.

A thorough scrub of teeth and face wakes me up. A quick comb raked through my hair tells me there will be no taming my curls without drastic measures. I wet my brush and drag it through the unruly mess, then fluff it with my fingers. It falls into damp ringlets and looks much more attractive.

Gus is bent over my suitcase, sorting through the winter clothes we bought me in Vegas. I didn't own anything appropriate for the mountains in Oregon since I've lived all my life in southern California, and the lure of a shopping expedition with a man of impeccable taste and apparently unlimited funds was irresistible. He pulls out a tee-shirt and a long belted cardigan, tossing them on the bed with a pair of clean jeans.

"If you pick out my underwear and socks, I'm going to smack you." I turn my back to make the bed as best I can around Stefanie, whose interrupted slumber and journey upstairs don't appear to have affected her ability to achieve that almost comatose level of sleep only small children seem to enjoy.

"I never realized what a violent streak you have." He zips the soft-side case, sticks it back against the wall, and gets up from the floor. "I like that in a woman."

"You say so now."

His arms come around me from behind, and I lean into him, folding my arms over his. His cheek pressing against mine is rough with stubble; he didn't shave this morning.

"Why cinnamon?" I ask out of the blue.

"Why was my number first in your cell phone directory?"

"Totally unrelated question."

"You didn't specify any rules for this Q&A, so it's a fair question."

"You try my patience."

He nuzzles my neck, sending a flood of signals to regions of my body best left dormant considering our miniature chaperone. "Why not? I've tried everything else you have."

"Lecher," I accuse mildly, even as I let his hands slip lower.

Voices calling up the stairs halt his exploration, and he moves his hands to a more publicly acceptable position a nanosecond before his brother Dietrich knocks courteously on the jamb of the open door.

"I hope I'm not interrupting," Dee says stiffly. Of all the Haldemanns, he's the most uptight and formal—at least according to Gus. "Everyone is getting ready to head into town—Dad needs a part for the furnace and everyone else wants to do some last minute Christmas shopping. We just needed to see who doesn't want to go so we don't have to take all the children."

"We're all done with our shopping," Gus says. "Unless there was something you needed, Sarah."

"Nope. I'm good. We did all our shopping in Vegas, Dee."

"So we can stay with the kids," Gus offers. Bless his little heart—how many kids are there again? Oh, yes—nineteen.

Dietrich looks a little apprehensive—perhaps my alarm at governing nineteen children shows on my face—and Gus snorts impatiently.

"I'm responsible for more than a hundred and forty employees, Dietrich. I think I can handle my nieces and nephews."

His brother looks a little mollified. "Well, all right. You want to bring Stefanie down with you?"

"Sure." Gus scoops her up, and down the two flights of stairs we go.

The kids are mostly gathered in the family room around the fire. I'm not surprised to see some of them are toasting marshmallows just like their uncle predicted. The next twenty minutes is a flurry of adults throwing on winter gear and giving us last minute—and completely unnecessary instructions—and then we're on our own.

233

It's not nearly as bad as I thought; the older kids are already schooled in watching their younger siblings and cousins. Gus and I retreat to the kitchen for coffee and reheated potato cakes. A steady procession of kids comes through while we eat and clean up, and eventually the older boys drag Gus out back to excavate the basketball court while I get hauled into the family room to learn the finer art of video games.

We're both still occupied when the rest of the family tumbles in, shaking off snow, shedding jackets and scarves and coats, laden with packages that they scurry off to private places to wrap. Oskar, Gus's father, retires to the utility room with his furnace part, and in short order warm air begins pumping through the house.

The rest of the day passes in a blur of baking cookies, shredding potatoes for more potato cakes, making applesauce, and dozens of other chores. I'm most comfortable with Katja and Nick's wife Angela, and for a long while it's just the three of us in the kitchen. Gus is outside again shoveling the court (his nephews abandoned him hours ago; he took advantage of their defection to grab a nap in the sitting room, waking with butterfly barrettes in his hair courtesy of Stefanie and her female cousins), but it's fast going since his brothers joined him. I take a short break to watch them; their voices drift in through the window Angela opened a while ago to keep us all from spontaneously combusting. It doesn't take long for me to wish I had decided to sit in the family room with the kids.

"I'm just saying—"

"I know what you're saying, Dee," Gus replies. There's an uncharacteristic bite in his voice. "You're saying it was fool-hardy and a financial risk—which I think is really the crux of your problem with this and—"

"You have to admit this could put everything at risk," Dietrich insists. "If you suddenly find yourself insolvent, it affects us all."

"Insolvent? Why would I find myself insolvent?"

"I think he means to say," Nick interjects, "that he thinks you'll be divorced within the year, she'll take all your money, and you won't be able to uphold your part of the family venture." He says this laconically, giving me the impression that he's poking fun at Dietrich. Nick is the most laid-back, or so says my husband.

"Thanks for your vote of confidence, Dee." Gus stops shoveling and trades Dietrich the shovel for the basketball. Dee takes up snow duty where his brother left off as though they aren't in the middle of a disagreement.

"I'm not saying anything against your wife, Gus. She's perfectly lovely. But you have to admit this was sudden."

The set of Gus's shoulders tells me Dee struck a nerve. "There was nothing sudden about it."

"Oh, come on. You can't tell me that some fairy-tale happily-ever-after—"

"Oh, give it a rest," Kasey chimes in with weary impatience. "The worst thing that ever happened to you is that damn uptight accounting degree you got. Apparently when you pass the CPA exam, they ram a stick up your ass and suck all the fun out of you."

Dietrich stops shoveling and turns around to fix him with a haughty glare. He's standing under the snow-laden basket, and even I can see this is a colossal lapse of judgment on his part.

"You can't deny Gus has a problem maintaining a relationship for any length of time, Kasimir."

"That was a low blow, Dietrich," Kasey replies.

Dee has pushed Gus too far now. Wrists turn, palms go out, and a neat chest pass into the headboard knocks the snow from the basket and onto Dee's head. He bellows angrily, and his brothers fall over each other laughing.

"You're an asshole, Gus!"

"Yeah? So far in this conversation, you've predicted me being cleaned out in a divorce practically on the eve of my wedding *and* said I have a problem with commitment although I do believe I just made one of the biggest commitments of my life. And *you're* calling *me* an asshole?"

"Three years with Gretchen and you never committed to her. You can't deny the facts."

"Three years with Gretchen because of the kids, Dee, and you damn well know that whole situation."

"So along comes a pretty face and off you go to Vegas? I'm a sucker for blonde curls and blue eyes too, Gus, but you're chasing a fantasy, and you're never going to find—"

"I *did* find her. And I married her."

A hand falls on my shoulder and I jump, embarrassed at being caught eavesdropping. I'm troubled by the conversation, not because of his brother's skepticism regarding the potential longevity of our marriage (as a matter of fact, we discussed it before leaving Vegas and expected to meet some resistance), but because there seems to be a lot I don't know. What fantasy might my husband have been chasing, and what joint financial venture does he have going with his family? I suddenly realize how little I know about the man I married.

"Don't take it wrong, Sarah," Angela says gently. "Dee's always a bit of a wet blanket, but he means well. He's just concerned Gus rushed into something and is going to be hurt."

"He won't be."

Angela merely smiles, drawing me away from the window and back to the cooking. Troubled, I allow myself to be distracted, but the disquieting sense that everyone knows something of import that I don't, that I'm deliberately not being told, is unshakeable.

Dinner is a frenzy of platters and casserole dishes being passed pell-mell; shouts for the salt and pepper or the relish tray or the cranberry sauce fill the room. The younger kids eat in the kitchen at the huge butcher-block that doubles as a table, their feet dangling from the bar-height chairs. I don't know what trick of time makes it so that you spend all day cooking a fantastic meal and thirty minutes—tops—consuming it, but all too soon it's over and you're left with a monumental cleanup and a horrific case of heartburn and indigestion.

The kids clean up and we adults spend the rest of the evening playing a chaotic and sometimes confusing round of Mexican Train dominoes. Because there are so many of us we use two eight-port hubs and four sets of double fifteen tiles, and keeping track of what trains are open and whether you can play on them is a craps shoot at best.

With much hilarity, we draw when we don't have to, try to play on trains that aren't open, and foil one another's carefully laid plans. Oskar and I are neck and neck until the opening of one round finds me without a tile, and I have to draw until I get one I can play. Thirty-seven dominoes in one sitting—*thirty-seven!* Even Dietrich and his equally uptight wife Maggie are howling with laughter.

Around midnight, the kids are shuffled off to bed (or futon, or sleeping bags on the floor of the family room, or sleeper sofa in Oskar's den), and the adults retreat to Katja's formal sitting room where we indulge in hot mulled cider heavily laced with brandy and watch the snow falling outside the mullioned windows. Christmas carols play on the stereo, turned low to allow conversation, and in short order I'm barely able to keep my eyes open.

A little before one in the morning, Gus nudges me, jolting me out of a near-doze. "C'mon, sleeping beauty, let's go to bed."

"Newlyweds," Josef remarks to his wife, rolling his eyes. Everyone laughs.

"Speaking of," Sebastian chimes in, "do you think you guys could move it to the floor? We're right under your bed, and the springs…." More laughter. My face is about to burst into flames. So far I haven't been asked about orgasms, and I sincerely hope Gus was joking when he warned me about it.

"Yeah, what'd you guys do? Put the damn bed frame outside in the spring rain to make sure it rusted? That thing is really noisy. I can't scratch my ass without the whole house thinking…." He sends a sidelong glance at me, and I elbow him in the ribs.

"All right," I say loudly. "This is getting highly personal. I say if they're going to *think* we're up to something, we might as well *be* up to something. Let's go, Romeo."

"She's already forgotten his name!" Liesel exclaims, *sotto voce*, and their laughter chases us up the stairs.

I let Gus have the bathroom first, since I take longer, and when I come out after brushing my teeth and washing my face, he's sitting with his hands behind his back, waiting for me.

"I have a present for you."

"Oh?"

"Yeah. It's something I took care of earlier, just for you."

"Is that right? What is it?"

He brings his hands around, holding out a can of WD-40. "All oiled and mostly silent. They can stick *that* in their pipes and smoke it," he says with satisfaction. He sets the can aside and snags my wrist, pulling me down on top of him as he falls backward on the bed. He's right; the bedsprings are mostly silent now. And things are getting truly heated when he suddenly breaks away and holds me away from him.

"Why *was* my number first in your directory?"

"Why cinnamon toothpaste and not mint?"

He grins, recognizing the parry. "All right, then. I don't like mint. Just the smell makes me want to hurl, so I use cinnamon instead. Your turn."

"I didn't want anyone calling my parents in the event of an emergency. I'm sure they wouldn't waste an opportunity to pull the plug on me." I smile wryly, but it hurts. I thought they'd at least call to wish me a happy holiday, or perhaps even send a card, but so far they've been silent. Mother is not precisely a forgiving person.

"Sarah," he murmurs gently, brushing his thumb across my cheekbone.

I go on quickly before I have a chance to turn maudlin. That just wouldn't do on Christmas Eve. "After you put your number in my cell phone on my birthday, I added the asterisk to bump it to the top of the list, figuring you would be the first person someone called if something happened to me. I don't trust anyone as much as I trust you." I pause, and he waits through the ensuing silence. "What's that say about a person when she doesn't even matter to her own parents?"

His eyes blaze, and his arms tighten around me, bringing me closer. "It doesn't say anything about you, but it speaks volumes about how much they don't deserve you. You have my family now, Sarah. Let them stand in the gap."

"Yeah, I heard how happy *they* are about us getting married. They already think we're going to get divorced."

"Angela said you heard Dee. Don't let it worry you. We'll be fine,

Sarah." He draws me down to him until I can feel his heart beating against my chest. "We'll be as good together as we want to be."

"Then let's be good," I suggest, and kiss him.

He seems surprised but quite agreeable to my uncharacteristic initiative; until now he's been the sexual aggressor, but since he first made known his interest in me I've wanted to just pin his wrists to the bed and dispense with gentleness, sweetness, and restraint. And now I do just that.

No amount of WD-40 can silence old and weary mechanics when pushed to their limits. The bedsprings sing, and I don't think anyone in the house is going to believe he was just scratching his ass.

* * * * *

We wake early the next morning despite our late night. We expected the kids to be up swarming the Christmas tree and rousting the house, but most of them are still sacked out. Sebastian is in the kitchen, one hand curled around a cup of coffee that smells divine, the other holding a folded newspaper in front of him. His youngest son Johann (Jon for short) is sitting on the stool next to him, holding his comic and hot chocolate in precisely the same way as his father.

"Good morning," Sebastian greets us without looking up. Gus gets us both coffee and we climb onto the stools opposite his brother and nephew.

"Yes, it is." I don't miss the sidelong glance my husband sends me, and neither does Sebastian.

"Indeed," he mutters, a smile tugging at his mouth. He looks amazingly like Gus, and his son shows every indication of being a heartbreaker himself.

"Uncle Gus, will you say grace over my hot chocolate?"

Perplexed, Gus shrugs. "Sure, buddy. Didn't you already say it, though? You're halfway done."

"But Dad said you're a really holy man and that's why you kept saying 'sweet Jesus' last night in your room. He said you were praying."

Gus chokes on his coffee and snorts it out his nose. I clutch my head, my embarrassment too much to bear while maintaining eye contact with anyone.

"And to think you *used* to be my favorite brother, 'Bastian."

"Bummer." Sebastian's grin widens behind his newspaper. I peek at him and he winks. Flirts, the lot of them.

We're saved further humiliations by the stampede of suddenly roused children through the house. Breakfast seems to have been cancelled in favor of Christmas cookies, fudge, nut brittle, and fruitcake (don't laugh; this stuff is actually good. Katja must have the only recipe in the world that doesn't suck).

Festively wrapped presents are passed every which way, and no one opens until every single item is doled out to its recipient. I'm surprised to find a growing pile beside me, but when I nudge Gus and raise a questioning brow, he just smiles and puts his arm around me.

Paper rips, bows fly, and delighted squeals fill the air. I didn't expect anything other than what Gus bought me while we were still in Vegas, and now I understand the sudden mad dash into town yesterday for last minute shopping. While part of me feels uncomfortable that they felt they had to get me anything, another part—the larger part—is thrilled.

I go more slowly than the kids (and some of the adults—namely Nick and Josef), unwrapping my treasures. A silver picture frame, engraved with wedding bells and sketchy silhouettes of brides and grooms from Nick and Angela; a Fabriano Quadrato artist's journal and a set of carbon pencils from Liesel and Joel; various bits of vintage jewelry—brooches, clip-on earrings, necklaces, and bracelets—that I wouldn't have thought to purchase for myself but which suit me perfectly from Sebastian and Wendy; a clever, expandable book for holding recipe cards from Josef and Karen (each page holds three cards in plastic sleeves so when someone gives you a recipe, you can just tuck it into an empty sleeve. A number of family recipes are already inserted); a collection of silk scarves, one for every day of the week, from Kasey and Inna (I pick one out that goes perfectly with my turtleneck and wrap it artfully, making Inna smile happily); a family scrapbook just waiting for memories to be recorded, from dating to marriage to births to children's marriages, from Dietrich and Maggie.

I hold this one the longest, understanding its underlying meaning: an apology of sorts and an expression of faith that my and Gus's marriage will last. My fingers move over the tooled leather cover, and when I look up Dee smiles without an ounce of artifice. I smile back.

A larger package is addressed to both Gus and me from Katja and Oskar. Gus lets—or should I say makes—me open it. I think he already knows what's in it. The bright paper covers a cardboard box taped shut. Kasey slits the tape for me, his knife ever at the ready in case someone needs his help (it's a Swiss Army and he just got it for Christmas. It does everything but perform surgery—although I bet it could do that in a pinch, too).

Layer upon layer of tissue-wrapped items fill the box. One by one I unveil them: a blood-red linen tablecloth with intricate cutwork and detailed hand-embroidery; matching placemats, each one with a different embroidered motif—the set is obviously antique. Hand-tatted doilies; embroidered sheet sets and pillowcases; a hand-quilted bedspread with initials and a date embroidered on the bottom-most corner: GS 1897—this jogs my memory for some reason, a random association that I can't define; Depression glass candlesticks in the traditional rosebud shape and pink hue; an old cookbook of German recipes with notes written in Katja's and others' hand.

We've been given a box of family heirlooms. I know it's silly but I can't even describe the feeling it gives me deep down inside. I've been given a piece of their heritage. This is more than just being accepted by my husband's family, more than simple approval; it's inclusion, and so much more than my own family has ever given me.

When I raise my eyes, I don't see their expectant faces, waiting anxiously for my reaction. I simply see them standing in the gap like Gus said they would. I look up at my husband, who looks back silently, steadily, the corner of his mouth tugging upward.

Again I feel a strange familiarity, a nudge from an ancient memory that I can't bring to the surface. A revelation, waiting to become an epiphany, hovers at the edge of conscious thought—and then vanishes as Stefanie and Jon pile into my lap. The room erupts in exuberant noise, and the moment is lost—for now.

Something has changed when I look at Gus; it's strange and terrifying…and absolutely wonderful.

BABY STEPS

We've told no one back at home about our marriage except Frannie and Sam because we both thought I should have a chance to tell Collie myself rather than letting him hear it through the grapevine. I'm not sure that Collie's going to care one way or another, anyway—he hasn't called since before Christmas. But to say Frannie and Sam were shocked is an understatement, although Sam took it rather better than his wife.

"You did *what*? Are you freaking *crazy*?" Frannie explodes, popping off the sofa. We'd dropped by to see them the day after we got back to Los Angeles; Gus didn't want his best friends hearing about his marriage through the grapevine, either.

"Fran," Sam says, placating her even though he looks stunned himself. She's not to be stopped, however. She rants and paces and mutters to herself. I send Gus a worried glance, but he's watching her with amusement.

"I thought you'd learned your lesson from *him*!" She stabs a finger at her husband.

Sam groans and flings himself back on the sofa cushions, sending his best friend a betrayed glare. "Here we go."

"Frannie, it's not like we went to Vegas and decided to get married on a whim. We planned it before we got there." Yeah, two days before we got there. "And neither one of us was roofied or otherwise incapacitated."

"Still…"

"Is this about Gretchen, then?"

Frannie stops pacing and drops onto the sofa beside Sam. "No, it's not. It's about Sarah. Gus, it just seems so…"

"Naughty?" he suggests with a piratical grin. I elbow him in the ribs but he pays no more attention to my agitation than he does Fran's.

She nods. "Exactly. What are people going to think? First you take her home from the hospital with you, and then suddenly you marry her."

She's said the wrong thing. My revelation of the moment is that my husband very definitely does not care about popular opinion. It is, perhaps, why he made it to a senior executive position at Harper & Lyttle by the tender age of twenty-eight.

Gus's mouth tightens just a fraction, and some of the warmth and laughter leaves his eyes. "I really don't give a damn what anyone thinks."

Her dark eyes swing to me, but before she can launch her campaign to make me see reason, Noelle begins to cry in the other room. Torn, her eyes dart from me to the nursery door and back to me again. Sam starts to get up, but Gus motions him back into his chair.

"I'll get the baby."

Frannie's protests fall on deaf ears. Sam doesn't bother, perhaps knowing his friend well enough to see that it's pointless to argue. He looks back at me, his eyes narrowed thoughtfully, and something makes him smile.

"Samuel, this is *not* funny. It's very serious!"

"Fran, I'm not making light of the situation. I just think it's none of our business. Gus and Sarah obviously want to be married. Who are we to argue?"

"It's just…Sarah's so young…and right on the heels of…people are going to say the worst!"

"They talked about us," he reminds her gently. Her scowl softens. "Frannie has some understandable issues with Las Vegas weddings, Sarah," Sam tells me. "It's made her biased against them."

She fumes. "It's not just—"

"He didn't force me to marry him," I chime in, and she falls silent. "And he didn't seduce me into it, either. We discussed it thoroughly

244

and it's what we wanted."

She fidgets in her chair, twisting her fingers together. Her wedding rings send little rainbows around the room. A flick of a glance toward Noelle's nursery, and then she asks the question I'm sure occurred to her first. I'm amazed she was able to repress it until Gus was out of the room.

"What about Collie?"

"What about him?" I ask evenly. "I haven't spoken to him in weeks. He was more concerned about with whom I was staying than about my well-being."

"But Sarah..." Frannie sends a helpless look at Sam and he shrugs, his face unreadable. "Do you love Gus?"

I promised honesty, remember? I've given no less to everyone else than I've given to you. "I don't know what it is that I feel. But I know I have no intention of living the rest of my life without him."

Sam sits up suddenly, slaps her on the knee, and climbs to his feet as Gus comes out of the nursery, bouncing Noelle in his arms. "Well, that's good enough for me. We don't have any champagne, but how about a glass of blackberry brandy?"

Gus misses a step and his gaze narrows on Sam's face for a fraction of a second. But he only says, "Blackberry brandy is fine." He taps Noelle's nose lightly and she gurgles, her eyes crossing. "You look like your mom when you do that."

"*Thank* you, Gus," Frannie replies smartly. Her tone is sharp but she smiles at him again, so I figure she's over being angry with him. Much like Sam, he's hard to stay mad at.

Sam has filled four small snifters with blackberry brandy and he passes them out. Gus shifts the baby so she fits in the crook of one arm, looking impossibly small.

"May you be poor in misfortune, rich in blessings, slow to make enemies, quick to make friends, but rich or poor, quick or slow, may you know nothing but happiness from this day forward." As Sam finishes the traditional Irish toast, we clink glasses and drink. At least, I *think* Frannie takes a drink. Her eyes cut away from mine to rest briefly on my and Gus's wedding rings, and she looks worried.

The sweet brandy fills my mouth, the fumes pervading my senses. A memory tugs insistently at me. *A hard shove, skinned knees and bruised chin, a boy triumphantly taking my swing. Mom swooping down on me, her mouth an angry hyphen, swiping roughly at my face and fingers. Blackberries, both sweet and tart, bursting in my mouth. Dark smears of purple juice on my fingers, seeds crunching between my teeth.* What was the name of that damned inn?

Then Gus is passing the baby to me, and the moment of remembrance passes.

* * * * *

I stare up at the building, a knot of dread in my stomach. My breath fogs the window of the truck, and when Gus shuts off the engine I jump.

"You don't have to do this today, Sarah. I can take you home."

I grip the door handle so hard my knuckles go bloodless. "No. If I can't come back today, I don't think I'll ever be able to. It'll just get easier to stay away."

He gets out and comes around the truck, but I pop the handle and open the door before he gets there, sliding out on my own. It's important that I do this on my own. I must walk in under my own steam, despite the fact that my legs are shaking—my whole body is shaking, a fine tremor that is barely noticeable but sets my nerve endings on edge.

Walking the short distance from his executive parking spot to the front doors of Harper & Lyttle seems to take an eternity. Gus doesn't touch me, knowing that I need to rely solely on myself. By the time we step into the lobby I've broken out in a cold sweat. Right there, the door I just walked through—that's where I fell, triggering the alarm.

My step falters halfway across the lobby; my suddenly nerveless legs are considering resigning. There, by the elevators: the emergency stairs where Eric Edwards snuck up behind me. I wobble, then teeter, but although he reaches out automatically to steady me, Gus still doesn't touch me; he draws back before he makes contact. I've given him his orders, and for the time being he's obedient.

Despite the fact that my leg still aches fiercely when over-exerted, I veer toward the curving staircase behind the reception desk that leads to the second floor, avoiding the elevator alcove. *Baby steps*, I keep telling myself. *Take baby steps. Eventually you might even be able to go into the stairwell, but today's not the day to be anywhere near there.*

Gus prudently trails a couple of steps behind me, ready to catch me if I lose my balance. But I make it, even though I'm quaking with effort by the time we reach the top.

"The elevator would have been easier," he remarks.

"Physically, perhaps."

Around the corner and into the hall past the elevators. I flick a glance at the stairwell door. And right there—that's where I sought escape and ended up in the clutches of a would-be rapist. I stop suddenly, bringing a frown of concern to his face.

"He tried to rape me."

A muscle jumps in his cheek. "Yes."

"Don't you think it's a stretch that he goes from two incidents of sexual harassment in two years to an attempted rape?"

"It occurred to me."

"And no one noticed any escalating behavior?"

He's frowning in earnest now. "Are you trying to tell me you don't think he did it? I thought you saw him, Sarah."

Other than the police and my friend Jennifer, Gus is the only one who knows every detail I can remember from the attack, confessed reluctantly in the dead of night after sweat-drenching nightmares in the first weeks of my recovery. His silent strength and unconditional comfort are solely responsible for keeping me from losing my mind in the aftermath.

"I'm not saying it wasn't him; it was. I'm just saying it seems strange to me that he goes from inappropriate remarks to an attack like that." I motion vaguely toward the door.

"Sarah, let's get you to your desk and think about everything else later. You're white as a sheet. I'll make some inquiries," he assures me as Allison comes around the corner from the cube farm, glancing at her watch.

"You're here!" She smiles in relief, ignoring my pallor and quaking limbs. "I've got it from here, Mr. Haldemann."

He sends a glance heavenward. "Gus, please. Remember what I asked you?"

She nods, her expression as pleased as a child who remembers her recitation perfectly and can't wait to perform. "She won't be left by herself for a nanosecond," she promises.

The elevator opens conveniently behind him, and he gives me a two-fingered salute and steps back into the car. The Suits and Skirts inside make way for him without protest. His eyes hold mine until the doors close, and then I'm alone with Allison, whose presence is a comfort but which doesn't give me the same feeling of security as my husband's.

Hannah and Lauren are waiting in my cube along with a huge bouquet of flowers. Lilies, freesias, coral bells, and a few other species I can't name sprout from a vase that appears about to burst from the sheer volume of the stems it contains. With a feeling of trepidation, I reach for the card attached to a deep green ribbon. The last thing I need is a bouquet like this from a man who doesn't know yet that I'm no longer his.

"You can relax. It's not from me," Collie says behind me, a trace of irony in his voice. I look at him in surprise, and his mouth crooks into a half-smile. I'm grateful that I wore a light-weight turtleneck with extra-long sleeves that cover my hands almost to their fingertips. I want him to hear the words from my mouth, not see the evidence on my hand.

But we don't have time to talk before my cubicle is invaded by well-wishers. Morgan and Stella crowd in with hugs and cards (Morgan gives me a Starbucks card for fifty bucks. She's my new favorite!), and Hannah, Lauren, and Allison are determined to catch me up on all gossip before the staff meeting.

The new office manager, Loralei—yeah, the 1980s will never be eradicated, I guess—arrives in a swirl of gauze and the clump of heavy boots, not gentle as a butterfly nor soundless, as the song implies, but brash and uncomfortably direct, forward and with little regard to personal space. She blazes through the office, leaving us breathless and excited and exhausted.

We love her.

We're ushered into the meeting shortly afterward. Frannie stays off personal topics altogether, her apprehensive glance passing from me to Collie, who sits two chairs away. And after the meeting Brooke seeks me out, going with me to the break room for a cup of coffee.

"I'm sorry you had to go through what you did," she says quietly as she pours us each a mug. "I'm just grateful you fought back and got away before it got worse."

"It was bad enough," I reply, accepting my cup from her. "I wish I had filed the complaint right after that first incident instead of waiting. He might not have gotten the chance to do what he did had I been braver."

"You were brave enough, Sarah. Don't sell yourself short."

"I shouldn't have stayed alone. If I had gone home when Hannah did, he wouldn't have had the chance to corner me."

"It isn't your fault."

"Whose fault is it, then? I relaxed my guard, thinking that after months had passed he'd just leave me alone."

"Do you blame Hannah?" Brooke asks, her eyes hard and glittering.

"Of course not!"

"But she left you here alone."

"She had an appointment, and I needed to stay and finish a project."

Brooke sets her coffee aside and rests her hands on my shoulders. "Sarah, I can't stress this enough. Blame the person who is responsible: Eric. You have the right to work late without being assaulted."

When I don't answer, she lets go of me and steps back a pace, taking up her coffee again. "I have some numbers I want to give you. I hope you make use of them."

Halfway back to my cube, she puts her arm around me and gives me a one-armed hug, much like Frannie does. I wonder suddenly who was there for Brooke after she was raped. I'm willing to bet she didn't have someone like Gus Haldemann to take care of her wounded body and shattered soul. Extraordinarily lucky, that's what I am.

I put my arm around her and hug her back, and she smiles in surprise—the first real smile I've ever seen her give.

Finally I'm alone with my flowers, and I open the gift card with a surreptitious look to make sure no one is hovering. But the flowers aren't from my husband; they're from Evelyn Harper. I suddenly remember the tapes I'd been transcribing before the attack; since they weren't of import to current events in the office, I'd put them completely out of my mind while I was recovering. I retrieve the key to my cabinet from my purse, open it up, and lift the box.

"Sarah, can we talk?"

I suck in a huge breath and spin around, cowering backward against my desk. The box drops from my hands and tapes scatter across the plastic mat under my chair. Collie holds his hands up as though gentling a wild horse as our coworkers prairie-dog out of their cubes.

"I'm sorry. I didn't mean to scare you."

"Jesus, Collie, what were you thinking?" Hannah scolds, pushing past him. She kneels and gathers all the tapes, and stuffs them into the box. "Sarah, breathe."

Only then do I realize I've been holding in the breath I took and little black motes are dancing before my eyes. Hannah pushes me down into my chair, forcing my head toward my knees.

The commotion brings Loralei and Frannie out of their offices; Fran waves off Loralei, who despite of her lack of regard for personal space goes out of her way to not step over authoritative boundaries, and she takes command of the situation with a skill I wonder if she picked up from Sam because it's so smooth and flawless.

"Oh, are those Rox—er—Evelyn's tapes? If you're done with them, Sarah, we can take them up to her. I wouldn't mind chatting with her for a few minutes." Frannie grabs up the box of tapes, takes my arm, and pulls me from my chair.

In the elevator, she sends me a sidelong look and murmurs, "You haven't told him yet."

"I haven't had a chance."

"The grapevine's starting to buzz. Someone noticed Gus is wearing a wedding ring. It won't take them long to put two and two together. Collie should hear it from you, Sarah."

"I know."

The doors open into a plush lobby on the executive floor. Frannie seems comfortable in such rich surroundings. The receptionist greets her by name and with easy familiarity rather than the cool impersonal tones the higher exec support staff seems to use with us peons.

Then we're ushered into Evelyn's office, where we spend a surprisingly comfortable, enjoyable half an hour. The CEO seems pleased with Gus's and my marriage, and rueful about his involvement in the aftermath of my assault. When Frannie presents her with the box of tapes, she asks if I had a chance to transcribe them all.

"The ones labeled in your husband's handwriting are personal. As soon as I realized it, I stopped listening and put them away."

She holds my eyes for a thoughtful moment, the hands resting on the top of the box, which is perched on her knees, and then she sets it aside. Fran gives it a speculative look, but then Evelyn asks her a question—quite deliberately designed to take her attention off what might be recorded on the tapes—and conversation resumes about my recovery, my wedding, Noelle, anything but Garland Harper and his crazy daughter. The tapes are forgotten, or so I think.

Frannie is silent, troubled, on the way back down. Just before we reach our floor, I punch the emergency stop, bringing the car to a halt.

"Sarah, what—"

"I heard enough of the tape to get the gist of what Malia Harrison was like."

She smiles. "It's all right, Sarah. You don't have to tell me anything you heard. You did the ethical thing handing them back over to Evelyn without listening to them."

"Do you know who Carolina might be?"

"No. Why?"

"Because those were personal letters he was dictating, at least the one I heard was." I pause a moment, noting the tension that tightens her face at any mention of Malia Harrison. "Harper knew she needed mental treatment, appealed to this Carolina to get her into inpatient care. I think he gave Malia a job here to keep her close in case she fell apart."

"That's all in the past. Sam's mine, and she's never getting out of that mental institution. She's just a bad memory." She reaches for the button to start the car. I stay her hand.

"Frannie, I see the way you tense up when she's mentioned. I just thought you should know that Garland Harper seemed very scared for his daughter. I thought maybe...maybe if you knew that, you would be able to see her in a more sympathetic light, and you wouldn't be so bitter about her."

"Bitter?" Fran says, incredulous. "I'm not bitter."

"Sure. Okay. We'd better get back to work." I reach for the button to start the car, and this time she stays my hand.

"Since we're indulging in confessions, I should tell you before you hear it from someone else. Before I married Sam, I went out with Eric Edwards once."

My face must say everything I'm wondering, for she rushes to explain.

"I didn't know what he was like. And even after that dreadful date, I never would have expected this from him. He's smarmy and sleazy, but what he did to you goes beyond anything he tried with me."

"You couldn't have known."

She jabs the button and the elevator lurches into motion. "No. And neither could you," she says pointedly.

But it sure doesn't feel that way.

Collie finally runs me to ground in the break room after lunch. Allison prudently excuses herself, but I can hear her skulking about in the hallway, waiting for me. After a minute I hear her talking in low, excited voices with someone else. I'm more concerned with Collie at the moment to worry about what's going on.

"You've been avoiding me ever since we got in that argument. Do you ever plan on talking to me again, Sarah?" He's tapping a pencil against the table, and it's making me nuts.

I sit back in my chair, my arms folded under my breasts. My back is to a wall, and the door and the open expanse of room beyond is in my direct line of sight. I guess it will take me a while to feel safe again.

"I'm not avoiding you. It's just been a really busy day. A lot to catch up on."

"You're still angry with me."

"You were very insensitive. But I'm not angry."

He clenches his fist around the pencil. "It's just…he's so…"

"Collie, I—"

"I was confused for a while, really messed up about what I wanted, but I had a lot of time to think after you stopped talking to me, and I got my head on straight. Sarah, I love you."

"Please, Collie, I have something to—"

He starts to reach across the table for my hand and thinks better of it. "It doesn't matter if you were involved with him. I understand. I'm just asking for another cha—"

Allie pops into the door, her eyes avid with the fervor that comes only from hearing the juiciest gossip. I want to stop her before the words come out of her mouth, for I'm sure I already know what her news is, but she's too fast for me.

"You'll never believe what I heard! Gus Haldemann got married! Were you at the wedding, Sarah? Who is she? I didn't even know he was seeing someone, and so soon after Gretchen!"

Collie sees the truth written on my face, and a dawning look of horror crosses his. I don't stop him when he grabs my left hand and shoves my sleeve up over my wrist. The diamonds catch the light and sparkle, the gold bands putting several vows and all they imply between him and me.

Allie's mouth pops open, and she realizes belatedly that she inadvertently brought our conversation around to its most important topic. Muttering profuse apologies and working hard to hide her shock and burning curiosity, she backs out of the break room. Collie doesn't notice; he's sitting in his own haze of disbelief.

"Can you…" His throat works hard to swallow, and he lapses into silence for a moment. "Can you undo this?"

"I could, but I don't want to." He winces. "Collie, we aren't good together, you and me. It doesn't work."

"So you just ran off and married Gus Haldemann? Jesus, Sarah, if you were feeling pushed into a corner, I could understand you sleeping with him! But marrying him? Are you *crazy*?"

"Apparently, since everyone seems to think so." I draw my hand back across the table, fiddling with the pencil he discarded. "Do you understand one bit of what I went through?"

"Yes, but—"

"Collie, I was stalked, beaten, and almost raped. You called and rather than express concern with what happened to me, you picked a fight with me over where I was staying, implying that I was sleeping with Gus with no regard to how that accusation sounded on the heels of an attempted rape."

He flushes. "I already apologized, Sarah. What do you want me to do, crawl?"

"No. I want you to understand. It's more than just how you were after I was attacked. It was how *we* were before you left for Seattle."

He levels an angry, accusatory look at me. "Do *you* understand what *I* went through?"

"Yes, I do. Or as much as I can understand, not being a parent. That's not necessarily what I meant, though. I meant that there will always be someone ahead of me in order of importance."

"I'm a father, Sarah! Jesus, what do you want me to do? Put you ahead of Megan because of your insecurities?"

That rankles, but I don't back down. "No. I would never ask you to do that. It wouldn't be right. But therein lies the problem with you and me as a couple. My *insecurities*, as you put it, make it extremely hard for me to always be the last priority."

"So you married him because I have a kid who comes first." His voice has taken on an ugly tone I don't much care for, but I suppose I can't blame him.

"I married him because I wanted to," I reply, my tone steely. He holds up his hand in a placating gesture. "Look at it from my viewpoint, Collie. You went to him to warn him away; he backed off because he wanted me to have whatever it is that I wanted. You extended your stay in Seattle after the attack; he took vacation time and arranged to work from home while I recovered so I would have help and so I wouldn't be alone. Every step of the way, I've come first with him. It's not just that he's *able* to do it, but that he's *willing* to do it."

"So it's all about you, then. All about what *you* want and what *you* need."

I consider this for a minute that seems to stretch out for years. "Tell me how that's different than anyone else, even you. We all look for something that's personally fulfilling, and when we're lucky, we fulfill the person who is fulfilling us."

"Did Confucius say that?"

"No. It's just something that I've come to understand since September."

"And just like that, Gus Haldemann is what fulfills you."

"It wasn't 'just like that,' although I can see why you would think so. I think you know I've been torn between the two of you for a long time now."

"And because he makes you queen of the world, you chose him." Sarcasm drips from his voice.

"No. Because he is who he is, and because of what I need from a relationship, I chose him. I didn't plan this, Collie. I wavered a long time, I want you to know that. But in the end, I realized that he and I are better together than you and I could ever be. I'm not what you need, Collie. You should go find what you really want."

His green eyes bore into mine with uncomfortable intensity for a long, tense moment. "You didn't marry him because he took care of you, Sarah. Or because you're not first with me but you are with him. You married him because you're in love with him." I don't reply. "Have you told him? Have you even realized it yourself?"

"Collie, this isn't about that feeling of being in love. That goes away. This is about commitment, and respect, and—"

"Sex?" he interrupts angrily, which pisses me off.

255

"Yeah, and about sex, too," I reply savagely. "That make you happy?"

He barks out a laugh totally devoid of humor. "No, not really. Oh, this is priceless. Just fucking *priceless*. What do I tell Megan, Sarah? She loves you! She thinks that you and I…"

"You tell her that I love her, no matter what. Collie, I'm not the one. Go find the one and be happy."

I leave Collie sitting there, stunned and angry, and try my best not to think about what he said. I've never tried to analyze my feelings for Gus in terms of love and romance. It just seems good—and right—to be married to him. It goes beyond being happy, beyond being "in love." It's about connection, about how we fit together, move together, think together.

I join Allison in the hallway. I can almost see all her questions building up behind the dam of respect for me—a dam that will hold for only so long.

"Yes," I say with weary patience. "I married Gus Haldemann."

She smiles, her smile turning into a foolish grin. "I thought you seemed very smug and satisfied."

I flush brightly. "Allie!"

She hooks her arm with mine, chattering excitedly as we head down the hallway past the elevators. I almost don't notice when we pass the door to the emergency stairs.

Almost.

Tales from the Water Cooler

Sunday, January 17
Singing the Praises of OneNote

Posted by Sarah Haldemann

Please forgive my delay in posting the new blog and the lack of a post for December. I know my upkeep recently has been sketchy, and I promised to keep this on topic—on Office tips, that is—but... I got married! Yes, it was totally unexpected, but I'm very happy. Now, back to business!

OneNote, an often overlooked but wonderfully useful tool. I never realized until recently just how useful it is. I opened it up on a whim, and voila! There it was, my virtual notebook. No more running to the store to pick out one that meets my needs. No more wasting money on tabbed dividers that don't fit my project. Just click here, click there, and customize OneNote to fit your needs.

Want to save some research but don't want to print it—or don't have a printer available? Send it to OneNote. OneNote has a print driver that will print the contents of the page to a OneNote page. You can then give the entry a title and move it to a proper section of your notebook.

I can't urge you enough to make use of this tool. Save a tree or two and print your Internet finds to OneNote. One notebook, one file, one location for all your precious information. Who could ask for more?

DID YOU KNOW:

WORD TIP: Using Quick Parts. These little snippets of text semi-automate entries you make on a regular basis. You will find in Building Blocks any auto-text entries you create.

- Go to the Insert tab on the Ribbon
- In the Text group, click Quick Parts
- Click Building Blocks Organizer
- Scroll down until you find the entry you want
- Click on it for a preview; double-click to insert

You're ready to go!

Blog Archive
    2010
        January
            Singing the Praises of OneNote
    2009
        November
            Beware of Bosses
            Bearing Transcription
        August
            RSS Feeds: Really
            Simple, Stupid
        June
            Choices
        May
            WTF Is Wrong with Men???
        March
            Love Triangles: Three-Pointed Pains-in-the...
        February
            Faces in the Crowd
        January
            Going Postal: A Career-
            Limiting Move

About Me
    Savvy Sarah
I am an administrative office professional with several years' experience in office settings. I have an AAS in Administrative Office Management and currently work as a training specialist

for a software development company in Los Angeles.

THE CALM BEFORE THE STORM

The days settle into a routine. Not necessarily a *good* routine, but one nonetheless. An atmosphere resembling that of an armed camp has descended on the office, and the tension that permeates the very air we breathe is almost a living thing. If it were any more real, I'd give it a name and a food dish.

Frannie, while outwardly polite and friendly, has created a deliberate distance between us and is downright short with Gus on the few occasions she's deigned to talk to him. I've heard enough about her and Sam from the rumor mill—rumors resurrected because of my and Gus's Las Vegas wedding, no doubt—to comprehend her reaction to our marriage, but I can't deny it rankles on my nerves.

Gus seems to take it in stride; he and Sam still meet for their workouts and their boys' night out, and Sam seems to have no qualms about the suddenness—or location—of his best friend's wedding. But Gus mentioned the other night that his once-a-month standing invitation to Sunday dinner was cancelled this month, and Sam's amusement with his wife's cold shoulder is turning to frustration.

Collie tried to talk to me several times in the first days after he learned I married Gus, but the conversations all ended the same way—"Can't you fix this?" and "I can't believe you did this to me!"—so finally I told him that I didn't wish to discuss it with him anymore. He's lapsed into sullen silence, and the grapevine is thrumming about his request to transfer to another division—a request made through one of Gus's subordinates.

I've also noticed a low level of hostility aimed at me by the single females from ages too-freaking-young to should-know-better. I've not only taken an eligible, well-paid bachelor off the market, but a drop-dead gorgeous, sexy one to boot.

"I don't get it," I say one day in late January when we have a rare minute alone at work. I've also noticed an odd phenomenon lately that seems aimed at making sure we don't have much time at work to converse.

"Don't get what?" He fishes one of my chicken fingers out of a foil deli wrapper and swabs it through the last of my ranch dressing.

"It's a good thing I like you so much or I'd have to be irritated," I remark, resorting to sprinkling the remaining half of my chicken finger with salt. I've learned from sad experience that the chicken shouldn't be eaten without a condiment of some sort.

"It's not my fault the cheapskate deli gave you only one packet," he says mildly.

"Bastards," I agree. "Anyway, what I don't get is why everyone's so upset with us."

He chuckles. "When you do something people don't expect, you kill their expectations and aspirations. It'll pass."

"Women I don't even know are being absolutely vile to me!"

He chuckles. "Ah, Sarah. And I've been told no less than nine times how much better than me you could do."

I sniff. "I disagree."

"Me too," he quips. He glances at his watch and pushes to his feet, leaning over to kiss me. Cinnamon and musk. My heart accelerates, but he's already drawing away, a knowing gleam in his eyes. "I have a meeting in twenty minutes. Come on, I'll walk you back to your desk."

And so the days pass. After a couple of weeks a lot of the hullabaloo of our sudden wedding dies down, but many conversations still stop when I come into the room. I'm not sure if it has to do with Gus and me or if it's because of the assault. Either way, I do my best to ignore it even though it makes me feel isolated in a way I haven't felt in many years.

A few days after I returned to work, Gus posed some pointed questions to the detective in charge of my assault case which caused her to start questioning just what we know about Eric Edwards. We get unwelcome information in just a few days: in all his previous jobs, Eric Edwards had performed admirably, was respectful to all his fellow colleagues, and never had a complaint lodged against him. It was also a well-known fact that he was openly, unapologetically gay.

More investigating uncovers the startling information that Eric Edwards quit his previous job six years ago via telephone and moved with no forwarding address. His former roommate—and no one is certain if this was just a roommate or a lover—left the area a few weeks before Edwards. This fellow, one Daniel Jackson, was a convicted sexual predator out on parole and fell completely off the grid shortly after Eric quit his job. He also bears a likeness in build and coloring to Eric Edwards, according to those who knew both of them. When shown photographs of Eric Edwards taken at Harper & Lyttle functions—and curiously, there are damned few—former coworkers were unable to say for certain whether it was the same man they'd worked with.

Detective Morris puts forth the possibility that the man I know as Eric Edwards is actually Daniel Jackson—which then begs the question: to where did the real Eric Edwards vanish? Gus immediately calls a security company, and they came out last Monday to install a security system in the house.

It's this added stress, perhaps, that prompts me to make a standing date every Friday night at Tony's with Hannah, Allison, Lauren, and my friend Jennifer. Not all of us make it every week, and sometimes Brooke or one of the office assistants in Marketing joins us, but one thing never varies: I *always* show up. It would be easy to sink completely into introversion, build a wall around myself with my considerable collection of books (I won't repeat some of the things Gus said as he hauled box after box of novels out of my apartment), and make my husband my world because it would be a safer life. At least it *seems* it would be safer.

But that wouldn't be fair to him, and it wouldn't be fair to me either. I force myself to be active and self-sufficient in spite of the fact that I'm never left alone. I rather suspect Gus would never let me retreat from the world anyway, and sometimes I think he's silently pleased that I haven't succumbed to the temptation.

The girls—including Brooke— are all gathered by the time Jennifer and I get there; there's a Mojito waiting for me and a Sex on the Beach waiting for Jen. As the waiter breezes by, I motion him over and request an ice pack for my shoulder, which has been bothering me since my last physical therapy session. Another lingering effect of the assault is a numbness along the outside of my left thumb, indicating nerve damage from my fractured wrist. My physical therapist says that probably will never go away.

Midway through my third Mojito (which is the third or fourth drink for everyone else but Jennifer) Brooke reaches into her purse, rummaging around.

"Is that a bra stuffed in there?" I ask, peering through the darkness into her equally dark handbag. A wisp of lace pokes out of the top.

Hannah whips it out before Brooke can stop her, and we stare for a surprised moment at a barely-there Victoria's Secret brassiere. At least I think it's a bra—there isn't much to it, to be honest. Brooke turns eighteen shades of red, making a grab for it. Hannah holds it out of her reach and waves it like a flag of surrender.

"You never know when you're going to need a backup," she says, avoiding my gaze.

The guys at a nearby table are hooting and encouraging us to whip off more clothes. Brooke yanks the scrap of lace from Hannah's hand and stuffs it into her purse, blushing furiously.

I've copped a pretty good buzz by now and have abandoned Mojitos in favor of the Redheaded Slut shots that Lauren and Jennifer keep ordering everyone. Those go down so smoothly that when Brooke orders me an Irish Car Bomb, I down it with hardly a qualm because I'm too inebriated to know better. I grin triumphantly—albeit drunkenly—at Brooke, who is just as shit-faced as me. She grins back at me, giggles (yes, Brooke; I'm shocked too), and leans over to whisper to me.

"I'm in love with Collie." I stare at her, surprised. The alcohol has flushed her cheeks and leant a false sparkle to her eyes. "Are you angry?"

I think about it. My time with Collie is like a distant, pleasant dream, but nothing I long to get back to. In fact, I'm too busy counting the minutes until I'm home with Gus again, which are far too many; it's poker night with his buddies and he's usually not home until after one in the morning.

"No."

Brooke's revelations are far from over. "I knowed . . . knewn . . . knew! I knewed it when you guys weren't gettin' along. I said—I said Collie—"

She motions me closer, bathing my face in tequila fumes. I return the favor by bathing her in whiskey, rum, and schnapps fumes. She hooks her hand around my neck, bringing us forehead to forehead.

"I said 'Collie'—"

"You said that already. Like eight times."

We both snicker.

"I said 'Collie, you gotta make up your mind. You can't keep comin' over and spendin' the night when you're with Sarah, 'cuz I'm in love with you.'"

I draw back, shocked. "You were—while I—with Collie?"

She nods, the awkward, over-exaggerated nod of a drunk person. "I know!' She pats my arm, and then pets it like it's a cat. "He said you were doing it with Gush...I mean Guz...so that meant you had an open relashentip."

"Relationship, you mean." Inside I'm fuming. Collie, you lying sack of shit! The day before he went to Seattle, he looked me right in the eye and said— But what *had* he said, really? *I've kept my hands to myself with Yasmina*, and *You're the only woman I have feelings for, Sarah*, but he said nothing about me being the only woman he was sleeping with.

"'S what I said."

"I didn't sleep with Guz...I mean Gus...'til we were married."

"Yeah, you did. You just didn't..." She peers around to make sure no one is watching or listening, which everyone is, and makes the age-old motion of her finger moving through a circle made by her thumb

265

and forefinger of the opposite hand: the universal sign-language slang for sex.

"But Collie thought we were…." I make the same motion and she snickers, leaning her forehead against my arm and drooling down my arm.

"Yes!" she squeaks. "I thought you and Collie weren't seriesous. Ooops." She tries to stifle her laughter and it snorts out her nose.

Again I just stare at her for a long moment, and then we start laughing hysterically. I don't know why this all strikes me as so funny, but it does. No wonder Collie was so understanding when he thought I'd gone to bed with Gus—he was sleeping with Brooke the whole time. Suddenly the presence of the bra in her purse makes sense—no doubt she left it at his apartment and he returned it to her at work.

I don't know how many more hours pass. I've managed to keep track of my purse and money, so I'm not nearly as annihilated as I could have been, but Jen and I are far enough gone that when we share a cab home, we completely forget that she was going to come home with me and stay the night since Gus didn't want me coming home alone so late.

The long cab ride sobers me enough that when I totter up the walk after paying off the taxi, I barely stagger and I find my key with no problem. I insert it into the keyhole with some difficulty, which for some damn reason makes me think of Brooke and Collie (damn Brooke for making that hand motion!) and cracks me up.

I drop my purse in the living room, stopping to read the note Gus left propped against our framed wedding picture on the bookshelf. The photographer could not have come cheap on short notice anyway, but the quality of the pictures tells me he wouldn't have come cheap no matter what.

I'll be home around 2 a.m. Make sure you set the alarm and lock all the doors and windows, the note says. No greeting—it's like he's resuming a previously abandoned conversation. And likewise no closing, just a quickly sketched "G" that incorporates a sketchy heart into its curves.

Smiling faintly, I lay the note down and pick up the photograph. When we received the prints, I immediately selected this one and put it in the frame Nick and Angela gave me for Christmas. At the time I didn't know why this one called to me so strongly, but now I see it clearly. This is what love looks like.

I wonder just when it happened; I can remember no "aha" moment, no sudden revelation, no tidal wave of desperate emotion. Just suddenly, one day—today—the realization hits me that the man whose ring I wear is the other half of my soul. And looking at him in our wedding photograph, I can see he's known it all along. I wonder why he's never told me. I intend to find out when he comes home. It should prove an enlightening conversation, if we're lucky.

I set the photograph back on the bookshelf, retrieve my inhaler and cell phone from my purse, and head to the bedroom. A quick change into tank top-and-boxers pajama set, and then bed. I leave a dim lamp on the dresser burning, pull a fleece blanket over myself, and fall asleep waiting for my husband to come home.

✳ ✳ ✳ ✳ ✳

A hand caressing my hip brings me reluctantly out of slumber. I was having the best dream—blackberries and blue bedrooms with wispy, sheer white curtains at open windows, a warm summer breeze billowing them into the room like surrender flags unfurling—and I'm loath to leave it.

But the lure of my newly realized feelings for Gus bring me awake as his hand winds into my hair and exerts pressure to bring my head back. I murmur something incomprehensible—to this day I'm not even sure what I tried to say—and then the wrongness permeates my brain: the wrong smell, the wrong feel. Not Jovan Musk for Men, but Grey Flannel. A smaller, more compact musculature, and the left hand tangling into my curls and pressing against my scalp wears no ring. *Oh, God!*

Eric Edwards croons in my ear, "Miss me, Sarah-Jane?"

26

THE KINDNESS OF STRANGERS

Cold steel against my temple—the barrel of a gun. My mind freezes, and I frantically try to scramble over its blank wall. No time to be paralyzed. He nearly killed me last time; he won't fail given a second chance. The clock reads 1:07 a.m. Gus won't be home for another hour. He'll be an hour too late.

"How did you get in?" I try to keep my voice steady, but there's no disguising the tremor in my voice. It seems to please him.

"It was ridiculously easy, Sarah. You locked all the little doors and windows, but you forgot to set the alarm, didn't you? Just the opportunity I've been waiting for. They've been very careful with you, especially your proud groom."

"Not careful enough, apparently." I try to move an inch or two away from him, hoping to get just a bit closer to my inhaler…and then I realize both the inhaler and my cell phone have been confiscated.

He chuckles nastily. "We won't be having a repeat performance of September. I thought you'd blinded me. Now be a good little girl and don't fight me. You know how bad it can be if you struggle."

My chest wheezes, and I try desperately to calm myself. An asthma attack could be fatal without my albuterol. He shifts onto his knees and pulls me onto mine by my hair, still holding the gun. His other hand snakes around me, skating over the ribs he broke four months ago to clench my breast.

"I figure I have about forty minutes to discover the delights of Sarah-Jane Quinn—oh, pardon me: Sarah-Jane *Haldemann*—before he gets home." His hand moves from my breast ever lower, his fingers snaking under the waistband of my boxers.

269

I remember Brooke's halting confession about her rape, the phone numbers she gave me when I came back to work after Christmas, and God help me, I don't want to be some shell of a woman sitting in a victim's support group because I'm unable to bear even the touch of my own husband.

His warm fingers against the bare skin of my belly galvanize me. As unexpectedly as I fought the first time, I fight now. An elbow to the ribs, a bite on the biceps, and I'm free—for a second. My legs tangle in the blanket and I fall face-first off the bed; the carpet rubs the skin off the tip of my nose and forehead. Eric stifles his bellow of rage and pain—this isn't an isolated stairwell in an unpopulated business building, after all, but a house in suburbia that sits too close to its neighbors.

He grabs me by my foot and drags me back onto the bed. A hand against the nape of my neck and his knee in the small of my back guarantees my submission, at least for the moment.

But it isn't the hair-pulling that makes me suddenly freeze. It's the rumble of a truck engine outside, an engine I know well. *Oh sweet Christ, he's home early—but not early enough!* Eric cocks his head, listening. His hand against my neck is also holding the gun, cold steel pressed tightly against my head. His other hand swiftly moves its crushing grip from my arm to seal firmly over my mouth just as I draw in a breath to scream.

The jingle of keys, the turn of the lock. The front door squeaks open and then closes. I can see his routine in my mind: shrug out of the jacket and hang it on the coat tree inside the door; drop keys, wallet, and cell phone in the dish on the bookcase; move through the house, turning off lights and making sure everything is locked up; coding in the password to set the alarm system.

Footsteps come down the hall, their pace measured and purposeful but not urgent. *Oh dear God, don't let him do anything stupid. Let him realize before he gets in here that something is wrong. Let him realize the alarm wasn't activated when he came in.* Eric lets go of my neck, leaning on his hand, the gun an inch from my eye.

Gus takes two steps into the room before he comprehends the

270

scene before him. He stops abruptly, drawing in a sharp breath.

"Well, well, well," Eric sing-songs. "If it isn't Gus the Great himself."

"Eric," Gus says calmly. His gaze is sharp, watchful; he hasn't been drinking tonight like I have. "Or is it Daniel?"

"Pieced together a lot, have you? Well, close but no cigar. Eric Edwards from birth. I've just been very good at disguising my...ah...extracurricular habits. Funny how you tell people you're gay and they automatically think you couldn't possibly hurt someone. But hurt someone—badly—is exactly what I'm gonna do."

Gus flicks a glance at me, trapped under Eric's weight. My eyes keep going to the gun—the gun I'm sure is going to take my life before the end of this very long night.

"Just let Sarah go."

"Not gonna happen. Now there's the small problem of you to deal with it, but that's easily resolved."

His hand moves on the weapon. My mind's eye sees the gun spit a bullet at my husband, sees him crumple lifeless to the floor.

"No!" I buck upwards, throwing off his aim. The gun booms and the bullet thunks into the door jamb above Gus's head. Gus charges, launching himself off the ground halfway to the bed. He hits Eric like a missile, and for a terrifying minute their combined weight presses my face into the mattress and I can't draw a speck of air.

And then they roll off the other side, fists and curses flying. The gun flies as well, bouncing off the end of the bed to the floor. I drag in a laborious breath as Eric rolls to his feet and Gus pistons himself off the floor. They crash into the window, shattering the glass. Jagged shards rain down on them.

Eric shoves Gus away, clutching a wicked piece of broken glass in front of him that slices into his fingers. The blood makes it hard for him to keep hold of it. He sends a longing glance at the gun. I'm closer to it; he isn't sure what I'm going to do so he doesn't make a move for it. He rocks onto the balls of his feet, preparing to lunge, and I can see a whole vista of nightmarish endings to this horrific scenario.

I scramble off the bed toward the weapon. Eric makes a feint at

Gus, who dodges the wrong way; the glass slices through the sleeve of his tee-shirt and blood blooms in a spreading stain through the fabric and runs down his arm.

With no further hesitation, I aim the gun and pull on the trigger. Nothing happens. I pull again and again, but the trigger won't depress.

"The safety, Sarah!" Gus shouts as Eric lunges at him again.

A precious second to find the safety and flick it off. I aim again and this time the trigger pulls, firing a wild bullet. It misses Eric, lodging into the plaster wall behind him. He ducks instinctively, and then charges Gus with head lowered.

I fire again as he raises the shard and stabs it toward my husband. The bullet hits home in the side of Eric's head. Blood, bone, and brain splatter my bedroom wall. He topples to the floor, the glass shard falling from his bloodied fingers. The gun drops from my hand. My stomach heaves with rolling nausea, and I barely control my gag reflex in time.

Gus takes one step toward me, wobbles, and his legs collapse under him. Blood pours from a wound in his neck—too much blood. Eric's last lunge at him with the glass punctured his skin. He puts a hand to his throat but it's like trying to stop a flood with a handkerchief.

"Oh no! No no no!" My legs spill me onto the carpet beside him. I slide my fingers under his and apply pressure, but there's still too much blood. "Oh God, what do I do? Tell me what to do!" But he can't answer. I press harder, to no avail.

For some reason, my mind hurtles me back in time to the days after I was released from the hospital. Frannie and I, watching movies and eating popcorn. A chick flick. War. Explosions. Blood. A nurse…and it comes to me. I slide my finger through the blood, seeking the opening. It's too small to ease my finger inside; I move around to find the right pressure point and press on it hard to close to wound, making him cry out in pain. Finally the flow slows dramatically—it must be just a nick—but he's pale and shaking, his breathing shallow, and he's murmuring in German: *"Brombeere. Sarah, Ich liebe Dich. Brombeere. Ask Liesel."*

He's already in shock, and I'm too far away from the phone. *Think, Sarah, THINK!*

I draw in a shaky breath and find my chest tight. I need a phone to call for an ambulance. Gus usually leaves his in the dish in the living room. We have no landline.

THINK!

And I remember. Eric took my inhaler…and my phone. I close my eyes and send up a brief prayer: *Please let me be strong enough to do this!*

Turning carefully, keeping my finger steady on Gus's wound to keep the nick in his artery closed. Eric is barely within reach; I gulp in a breath, the thick, coppery scent of blood triggering my gag reflex again. I snag the hem of his shirt and yank him closer. He slides through his own blood with a sickening squelch. Gus moans and shudders convulsively as my finger moves.

A bulge the shape of my inhaler in Eric's front pocket points the way. Closing my eyes and praying for strength, I slide my hand in, fishing out the inhaler. The inert weight of his body makes gooseflesh ripple out on my skin. In again, deeper, to find my phone. My control slips and a stream of alcohol-diluted bile spews from my mouth and into the carpet, splattering in his blood.

And then the phone is in my hand. I dial 9-1-1, and bathed in my husband's blood and my tears, I wait for rescue.

* * * * *

The memory of the rest of the night always presents itself in surreal flashes: the police and paramedics, each vying for my attention; the argument between both as the EMTs try to take me with them, my finger still socked tightly against the wound in Gus's artery. The paramedics win, and the police have to be satisfied with processing the scene and removing Eric's body, and finding me later for my statement. I remember nothing of the journey to the hospital except leaning close to Gus's ear, his blood soaking into my tank top, and murmuring all the reasons he needs to hang on to life. I desperately fear none of them will prove enough to keep him with me.

Eventually I find myself ushered out of the operating room as the surgeons take over. Gus has lost a dangerous amount of blood; much of it is dripping from my hand and soaked into my shirt. A passing orderly takes pity on me and shows me to a restroom, where I'm able to wash my hands and rinse out my shirt. But the cold water is not enough to take out all the blood and I have nothing else to wear, so I dry it as best I can under the hand dryer and put it back on.

In the ER waiting room, I make the necessary phone calls. Both Nick and Liesel live in Los Angeles suburbs, so I expect them at any time. When I call Frannie and Sam, I ask her to bring me a clean shirt. Fran promises that she and Sam are on their way.

I wedge myself into a chair in the corner, shivering, trying not to think, a steady flow of hot tears running down my cheeks until my eyes hurt. My mind hurtles into dismal fantasies of a barren future, and finally I close my eyes and sink gratefully into numb oblivion.

A tap on my shoulder brings my eyes open. A man leans over me, holding out his hoodie. I start to refuse on grounds that I don't need it, but my flesh is prickled into goosebumps the size of marbles; I suspect he'll see through the lie. Gratefully I take it and shrug into it. He touches my shoulder again and asks if I'm all right. I tell him I am, and he goes back to his seat. I drift away again.

Time passes. I'm not sure how much, but not enough to have brought Sam and Frannie, Nick, or Liesel. A tug on my sleeve brings my eyes open again, this time to find before me a small boy no more than four, clutching a stuffed alligator. We stare at each other for a moment, his dark eyes solemn and unblinking, mine bloodshot and desperate. He holds out the alligator to me, and after a moment I take it. His grin blooms big and wide, full of innocence, and he dashes back to the proud, safe embrace of his mother.

I stare at the alligator, and the kindness of these strangers hits me full force. I have no idea why they're here; obviously they have troubles of their own. But they reached past their own sorrows to comfort me. I press my face into the alligator and breathe deeply. It smells like Stefanie.

My tears come again, which seems to be the cue for my support system to arrive. First Frannie and Sam; Frannie, bless her heart, brought not only a clean shirt but sweatpants and socks as well as a battered pair of sneakers. After I change clothes, I try to return the hoodie, but the man refuses to take it back.

"You look like you still need it." He's right; the goosebumps are back. I thank him and pull it back on, returning to my seat, now flanked by Sam and Frannie. After a moment Sam's arm goes around me, and I lean my head on his shoulder. Another moment passes, and Frannie takes my cold hand between both of hers.

We wait.

Nick arrives, pale and frantic, and takes the chair adjacent to Sam after hugging me. When Liesel arrives, she brings with her the scent of rain, and for the rest of my life I'll associate it with this night.

Frannie moves over a chair, and Sam transfers me from his shoulder to Liesel's. She murmurs to me, a mixture of English and German, and after a while I raise my head and look at her.

"He said I should ask you something, but he kept speaking in German. I don't know what he wanted me to ask."

A ghost of a smile touches her mouth, and she darts a glance at Nick. "Do you remember the words?"

"He said something like broom beer. And ish-leeba-dish or something like that. And he said to ask you."

Sam shifts uncomfortably in his seat, exchanging a look with Liesel. He knows whatever Gus has kept from me. Of course he does—he's Gus's best friend.

Liesel draws away from me and takes my hands. "*Brombeere*," she says. "Was that the word?"

"Yes."

"Blackberry," she says randomly.

"What?"

"*Brombeere* means blackberry." She frowns, biting her lip. "I don't know where to start, except to say that you made him the man he is today, Sarah."

But I shake my head. He was extraordinary before I came into his life, and no doubt would be extraordinary had our paths never crossed.

275

"You misunderstand. You remember the inn you stayed at as a child?"

"He told you about that?"

She draws in a breath and rubs her eyes. She looks tired and scared. "He didn't have to. That's our inn. My parents owned it, and now my brothers and I do. Your family stayed there when you were really small, probably only in kindergarten. He pushed you off the swing and you skinned your knees and bumped your face. Do you remember?"

At last the dam blocking my memory breaks loose, and the past floods in. *Blackberry House Bed & Breakfast*, my mind finally supplies. *A creaking swing, the favorite of the grey-eyed boy. A demand to get off, a shove when I refuse. Pain in my chin, blood running down my knees. Mother scolding. Mary-Ann laughing. Katja clucking her tongue and murmuring German endearments, pressing my cheek against her ample bosom and drying my tears with her apron. And later, a peace offering: freshly picked blackberries, held in a hand stained with purple juice, solemn grey eyes waiting for my acceptance of the implied apology. Katja calling out the back door: "Gustaf! Lass sie in Ruhe! Let her be!" Plump, wild blackberries, tart-sweet juice bursting in my mouth. And later still, homemade ice-cream while rocking on the porch swing, sandwiched between Katja and Gus and wrapped in a quilt—the quilt she gave me for Christmas this year—watching stars shoot across the inky night sky.*

Katja's greeting to me when we announced our marriage—*Wilkommen Zuhausen*—suddenly makes sense. *Welcome home*, as though a treasured child had been returned to the bosom of a pining family.

"Sarah, are you all right?" Liesel nudges me, concerned.

"He pushed me off the swing and later gave me blackberries," I say faintly.

Liesel smiles in relief. "You *do* remember. Mom chewed him out and thrashed him with a wooden spoon, and then she made him watch while your mom chastised you and your sister poked at your wounds to make you cry. He was a handful as a child, kind of mean, set on becoming a bully by junior high. Kids used to walk a mile out of their way to avoid him on their way home from school.

"But he changed after that day. He became kinder; he stuck up for the smaller kids. He became the man he is today because of the child you were, Sarah."

I digest this silently. Blackberry House Bed & Breakfast. And here it is, three in the morning just like he said it would be when I remembered. *Try to remember it, because if you wake me up…* A clawing panic grips my heart.

Nick takes up the story. "He's looked for you all his life. We used to worry that he was chasing some fantasy, and when he did find you, you'd be nothing like he'd imagined all those years. His fairy-tale, we called it. He wanted to be sure you were all right, that you'd managed to grow up happy despite your family."

Liesel continues. "And then he called me last August when you applied for a job at Harper & Lyttle and said he'd found you—at least, he was fairly certain it was you. He wasn't completely sure until your birthday, when you told him about the inn you stayed at as a child." She smoothes my hair. "*Ich liebe Dich* means 'I love you.' He's loved you almost all his life, Sarah."

All his life—the life that now hangs by a thread—and he doesn't know that I love him back. I stand up abruptly and then stop, confused. I can't just rush in and tell him. I look at Nick, but movement in the hallway just past him catches my eye.

The surgeon. He sees me and his step falters. In that shattering hesitation, I see all the things that will never be: I'll never bear his children or feel his arms around me again. He'll never hear the words "I love you" from my lips or know that by my changing his life when he was a child, he changed mine when I became a woman.

I surrender to the swirling darkness, and pray that I never wake up.

ICH LIEBE DICH

"I think we've ran over on time," I say in surprise, looking up at the clock. My listeners are staring at me, slack-jawed and teary-eyed.

"You can't just leave the story there, Sarah!" Carmen, our group leader, sends a look around the circle. "Does anyone mind staying late?"

No one does. I sigh. This story has not been easy to tell and after the last bit, I'm drained. That wasn't a day I ever wanted to relive for any reason, but the whole purpose of this group is catharsis and healing. God knows I need to heal.

There's a hush in the Community Center today that seems appropriate for the current topic of the Thursday afternoon Grant's Pass Victims Support Group, as though the very air currents are honoring those who have suffered.

I finish my tale, and cry a little myself. But it feels as though something poisonous has been drawn out of me. February isn't that far behind me; five long months with this violent memory roiling inside me, screaming for release. My paintings aren't enough to contain the surges of wild emotion that often overwhelm me, hence the group. Katja directed me to these women who have quickly become my greatest emotional supporters outside my family.

We all hug and go our separate ways, and I hope that my story speaks something positive into their lives. Love can be fleeting or forever, but it is never wasted.

I lift my face to the sky, letting the warm July sunshine bathe it, and breathe in the clean mountain air. Oregon is my home now; I live at Blackberry House Bed & Breakfast, which is just weeks away from its grand re-opening. It's been a lot of work and promises to be more, but I wouldn't want to be anywhere else. The creaking metal swing-set has been replaced due to the threat of tetanus, but I spend a lot of time there anyway, swinging and remembering. Introspection is good for the soul, they say, and it seems to be having positive effects on mine. I know Sarah-Jane Aubrey Quinn Haldemann backwards and forwards, and for the first time in my life I completely love who she is.

But for now…duty calls. I turn from the sunshine reluctantly and get into the truck, guiding it out of the parking lot and onto the highway that will take me home—the home I've been trying to get back to since I was six.

The drive is pleasant, with tall pine woods flanking the highways. The air up the mountain is cooler than down below, not that the inn is at a high elevation. Just in the foothills, really. I'm both looking forward to and dreading winter; I've seen firsthand the amount of snow that can accumulate in this area. But I'm determined to learn how to drive in it, and my brothers-in-law and their wives have all promised to teach me to ski. I hope I don't end up in traction.

I guide the vehicle around curves with a confidence I pray I'll have in December, and I remember the drive through the swirling snow last Christmas, the berms so high we couldn't see over them, on our way to tell his family that it had grown by one. The memory makes me smile.

I slow the truck to turn off the highway as the dirt road to the inn comes into view. It's much easier to navigate without the snow, and Oskar just had it graded and oiled so it will be smooth and not throw up clouds of dust. I honk as I pass their house, and continue farther up the road—up the foot of the mountain, really—to the inn. It's within walking distance of Oskar and Katja's via a well-maintained footpath. A path lined with blackberries.

A man sits on the porch in a wicker rocker, reading the newspaper. I'm surprised to see him; I wasn't expecting him to be here today. I park the truck, retrieve my packages from the passenger seat (I went shopping before my group met), and skip up the steps.

"Did you spend all your money?" he asks mildly without looking up from the paper.

"A good portion of it, but these were all on sale and absolutely necessary for the inn."

I grin and take my treasures inside to my bedroom—my blue bedroom. Cerulean walls with white molding, colorful rag rugs on the polished wooden floors. I set my purse on the whitewashed Ambale chest with its hand-painted toile. A wayward breeze flutters the sheer white curtains, unfurling them like sails.

And then I see the gift left for me on my bedside table: a glass dish with seven plump wild blackberries. Always seven, because that's what he gave me as a peace offering that day when I was six and he was twelve and our lives made an eternal connection.

I pop one into my mouth and roll it across my tongue, then crush it against the roof of my mouth. Juice spurts, both tart and sweet, flooding me with memories almost too intense to bear.

"Good, are they?" he asks from behind me. His arms slide around me and he nuzzles my neck. The scents that evoke the strongest emotions in me fill my space: musk, cinnamon, and wild blackberries.

"Delicious. Aren't you supposed to be at Sebastian's?" I turn in his arms to face him, and reach up to brush the scar on his neck, pressing my fingers against the pulse of his life.

"Mmmm," he murmurs. "That's tomorrow."

It had been so close, his dying, close enough that I don't waste any chance to enjoy what we have together. After I fainted, I regained consciousness to Frannie chewing out the surgeon for scaring me half to death. He'd only come to tell me that Gus's vital signs had stabilized, and with transfusions of blood to replace what he'd lost, he should make it through just fine. He'd paused when he saw me because he at first didn't recognize me; I'd been in a bloody tank top and boxer pajamas the last time he'd seen me.

My relief had been so intense I almost fainted again.

Gus made a full recovery after depleting the hospital's supply of O-negative blood—and a good portion of Nick's as well. We never went back to the house after he was released; I sent a moving company to pack our things and we stayed with Nick and Angela until we had decided what we wanted to do.

Eric Edwards turned out to be just who he said he was, and the people he'd worked with previous to Harper & Lyttle were shocked to find out that he was neither gay nor a pleasant person. His roommate resurfaced—in prison for a sexual crime, and he confessed that he knew of several unreported incidents of Eric assaulting other women while they shared a dwelling, although he hadn't beaten them half as badly as he beat me.

No charges were filed against me for killing Eric; no one ever doubted it was self-defense, especially after they searched his apartment and found literally hundreds of digital photographs of me from the time I started work at Harper & Lyttle (including the photos Collie had received after Gus spent the night at my apartment), as well as hundreds of others taken of unknown women the police are now trying to identify. In my darkest moments, I wonder about the other women he assaulted, the ones who haven't come forward because they're so frightened of him.

Our decision to leave Harper & Lyttle and make a full-time go of the inn wasn't easy. We hashed out budgets, argued over necessary expenses, ruthlessly cut back on spending. I've immersed myself in my art and have sold a few pieces for handsome prices, the money boosting our savings account, and Gus used his capital gains from selling his previous house to pay off his portion of the inn and all the credit cards. We have very little overhead but also a limited income, although my pending settlement from Harper & Lyttle should be in the six-digit range. That will give us a nice little nest egg to help raise the children—and we plan to have several in typical Haldemann fashion.

A good advertising campaign has assured us that we'll see plenty of business all four seasons, and so far we've not been disappointed— and we haven't even "officially" re-opened yet! This Thursday afternoon in July is a rare day that we have alone together. One of his brothers or Liesel relieves us every couple of weeks and we travel to Los Angeles to see friends, or in other directions to make new ones, or we just go to a cabin we bought a short distance away—far enough that we aren't tempted to meddle in the inn's affairs while we're off duty.

Tomorrow will bring Frannie, Sam and little Noelle; I'm looking forward to seeing them. Frannie apologized to me at the hospital for her reaction to the news of our marriage, and while I may never know the full story behind it, she did give me just a little insight: "It was just too sudden and reminded me too damn much of when Sam married Malia." Fran and I are fine now, and she stayed beside me nearly every hour of Gus's confinement to the hospital.

Gus leans down to kiss me, and cinnamon mingles with blackberry, making me suddenly want a blackberry cobbler.

"Any secret dreams I should know about, Sarah-Jane?"

"Nope. Well, maybe the one about having blackberry cobbler, since you can be of immediate assistance with it."

He chuckles. "I thought you might like that. I already have the blackberries crushed and sugared."

"Well then. I can think of only one other thing I've been dreaming about."

He lets me tug him toward the bed, a wide grin curving his mouth, and he follows me down, his body warm against mine.

He whispers to me: "*Ich liebe Dich*, Sarah-Jane Haldemann." *I love you.*

"*Ich liebe Dich*, Gustaf Haldemann," I reply softly, and show him with body and soul just how much.

I've no more need of secret dreams. Everything I could ever want lies here in my arms this very moment: a man worth loving, a love worth dying for, and the future stretching before us, full of hope and promise, and sweet wild blackberries.

ABOUT THE AUTHOR

Sharon Gerlach was in training to be a ninja, but a dismaying lack of physical grace and balance—not to mention the inability to keep her big mouth shut—ended her ninja career before it had really begun. Now she writes. She doesn't write about ninjas because that's obviously a sore subject. But she writes about other really cool things and figures someone else will cover the ninjas. Life's really not all about ninjas, anyway.

Sharon lives on the dry side of the Pacific Northwest with her husband (who must really be fond of her as he hasn't left her yet despite her ninja failings); her three kids and numerous grandkids (none of whom possess ninja qualities either); and three cats. Yes, you guessed it—ninja cats!

Website:
sharongerlach.com

Twitter:
@SharonGerlach

Facebook Fan Page:
www.facebook.com /AuthorSharonGerlach

Facebook Beta Readers Group
(by approval only)
https://www.facebook.com/groups/SharonsWordWarriors/

HARPER & LYTTLE BOOK 3

Honor and I unwrap our presents at the same time, and each of us holds up a beautifully hand-tooled leather-bound book with blank pages. The front cover of Honor's says UNWIND; there's no mystery there, either. Honor is as tightly wound as a Swiss clock, and obviously Gus believes she can find some peace and relaxing with a little journaling.

The meaning behind mine, however, eludes me. REDEFINE.

"Thank you," I say uncertainly. He simply smiles at me as though understanding my confusion but willing to leave me wallowing in it.

"I'm going to call it an early night, ladies. I'll see you at work tomorrow."

Deb watches him wind his way through the crowd to the exit, stopping often to return greetings. "What the hell is wrong with *him*?"

"I thought we covered this already," Kaya replied. She stows her dreamcatcher safely back in the gift bag; I notice over the next hour how often she reaches in to stroke it. "Trouble in paradise."

Elke says, "I wonder why he thinks I need luck. Don't you usually give one of these to someone who moves into a new house?"

Deb snorts, no doubt formulating a sarcastic reply she never gets a chance to voice, for Kaya jumps in, sending a sharp look at our skinny friend.

"I think he's just wishing you luck with your new beau."

"Unwind," Honor says on a breath. From the look on her face, I can tell she just wants to grab a pen and let her stress bleed out onto the pages.

I run my fingers over the tooled cover of my book, tracing the letters embossed into the leather. REDEFINE. In my mind, I replay his smile as I thanked him, and suddenly I understand.

All that remains on my plate is a dollop of ranch dip and a few strings I pulled off celery stalks. Despite the mound of veggies I downed, all I have to show for my snack is a rumbling tummy and gas building in my gut from so much greenery.

"This is ridiculous."

Eyebrows shoot up into various hairstyles as they all goggle at me.

"You…you don't like your gift?" Elke asks, tentatively. It's a first in her book; she would like dog crap wrapped in cellophane if it came from Gus Haldemann.

"I love my gift," I snap, making her wince. "Let me reword. *We* are ridiculous. Well, all of us but Deb, anyway. What are we doing? Eating ourselves into the grave? Sitting on our rapidly expanding butts when we could be walking, or doing aerobics, or Zumba?"

"Zumba?" Kaya says. "Isn't that dancing?"

"It's better than dying!"

I stand up and slap my hands down on the table. The effect is somewhat ruined by the fact that I'm barely taller standing up than I am sitting down. The ladies all blink like startled owls.

"I'm going to shed this blubber, and you guys are going to shed yours too. Enough of this waddling, plus-sized crap!" They all stare at me, mute. "I'm going up to my office for a minute. I have a book I want to show you."

The elevators are those polished steel jobbies that reflect back at you every damn thing you don't want to see. Usually, I try not to look, and press myself into a corner behind others so I don't have to see what I really look like: a baby beluga whale stuffed into a business suit.

But tonight is different. I need to look, need to see, need to fix in my mind what I've become to see if what I was is still visible. My dress tonight is a silk sheath covered with a lace overlay, both brick-red; the bodice of the overlay is dotted with seed beads that exactly match the color of the fabric and catch the light.

"You look like a tomato," I say to my reflection. I'm suddenly, desperately aware of how much weight I've really put on, and how much I really want to be thin again. Or at least, thinner than I am now.

The doors open and I hurry down the hall to HR, where I stop abruptly. The front of HR's suite of offices are walls of glass, and through these I see Gus, elbows on his desk and head in his hands. *Sarah Quinn…if you only knew.*

I stop in his doorway and lean against the jamb. "Why don't you just tell her, Gus?"

He answers without looking up. "It's complicated."

"Whose doing is that? I advised you against getting involved with Gretchen Clark."

"What was I supposed to do, Chelsea? Let those kids suffer because their mother is a wreck? And how could I ever have known that Sarah would apply for a job here?"

"You've only been searching for her since you were twelve," I remind him. "And those children aren't your responsibility. As soon as you were certain things couldn't work out with Gretchen, you should have ended it. We both know that was well before you moved in together."

"Yeah, yeah," he replied, a trace of uncharacteristic impatience in his voice. "None of it changes the fact that I did move in with

Gretchen, I did find Sarah after all these years, and now my life is fucking complicated."

"Gretchen knows?"

"I told her."

"And she's all right with it?" I arch an inquiring brow at him, unable to believe Gretchen Clark is as supportive of his quest for his dream woman as he's making her out to be.

He shrugs, fiddling with the gold pen lying on his desk blotter. "Did I ever tell you she moved into the spare bedroom?"

"No. How long ago?"

"Two years." He looks up at me for the first time, and I see a trace of humor in his face at my expression. "We're just roommates, Chels. But she doesn't know how to be a single parent—or how to be a single woman—and she's terrified to break things off. And you know me."

"Sir Galahad," I say softly, and he chuckles.

"What brings you up here? You should be enjoying the party?"

"Enjoying working my way toward a diabetic coma, you mean? No thanks." We're silent for a moment, and then I ask quietly, "How did you know?"

"Know what?"

"That I don't particularly like what I've become."

He gazes at me for a moment, then gets up from the desk and crosses the room, stopping in front of me, his hands coming up to cup my face.

"Chelsea, you're so capable and strong that it's nearly impossible to tell you anything. You're not particularly happy, and you're desperate for a change, but so damned determined not to admit it. I had to find a circumspect way around you to *get* to you, to show you a way out."

I lean my forehead against his chest. "I don't know why you bother with us, Gus."

He chuckles again and hugs me tightly. "Well, you put up with me. It's only fair that I do the same for you. Now you should go on back to the party."

"I came up for a book." I start across the lobby to my office and pause. "You should come back down, Gus. Enjoy the party."

"Nah, I'm good. Really," he insists at my skeptical look. "Goodnight, Chelsea."

"'Night, Romeo."

I snatch the book from my office and head back toward the elevators, looking back at him once. His head is back in his hands, but this time there's something on the blotter between his elbows, a jar of some sort. Then he reaches for a pack of matches and strikes one, sticking it into the neck of the jar.

A moment later, I step into the elevator, chased inside by the scent of blackberries.

OTHER RUNNING INK PRESS BOOKS

MALAKH

Suzanne Harper had wielded supernatural abilities and super-athletic prowess while she was the lover of an angel. When a string of gruesome murders points to her former lover, Suzanne teams up with Icarus, an angel who hunts those of his kind who have fallen, because the choice of victims tells a terrifying tale: the next murder will be hers.

OFFICE POLITICS

Malaria is nothing a good dose of quinine can't handle, thinks Frannie Freeman when her vile office manager Malia—aka Malaria—marries their boss Sam, whom Frannie has loved for years. When Sam suddenly confides that he believes he was roofied the night of his surprise Las Vegas wedding, Frannie prepares for battle with a woman's three best weapons — a loyal heart, a willingness to fight dirty, and the strongest margarita money can buy.

THE WYCKHAM HOUSE

The Wyckham House has stood for centuries, its origin unknown, its history black and bloody. When Kimberly Owens' father disappears in Aaron Schaefer's town, all evidence points to the Wyckham House. Only one man has gone there and returned alive. But even if Aaron could remember what happened to him, he doesn't want to. For there are worse things than death.

CONDEMNED

Tools that relocate themselves. Shadows glimpsed from the corner of one's eye. The feeling of being watched when no one's there. Rachael Payne is delighted to be involved in renovating Bayview Manor for its new owner, Geoffrey Windsor. It doesn't bother her that the mansion's dark history is shrouded in rumor and legend, because she doesn't believe in ghosts. Geoffrey doesn't share her enthusiasm for his house. From its mysterious origins to the strange current events, he's certain something walks in Bayview Manor, unseen by the human eye. And he wonders if Rachael's faith in God protects her from the forces within the mansion...or blinds her to them.

BLINK OF AN EYE

One wrong blink sparked a global outbreak that mutated humans into brutal, conscienceless killers called Revenants. The Father of the

Apocalypse, Ren Leonard is a legend whom Mackenzie believes is their only hope for survival. She appeals to Leonard to turn the tide against the Revenants. She is about to learn that everything can change in the blink of an eye and Revenants aren't the worst danger.

WHERE I BELONG

In the follow-up novel to *The Secret Dreams of Sarah-Jane Quinn*, the perfect storm descends upon Sarah and Gus Haldemann, bringing a quarreling sibling, estranged family, a mother-daughter feud, and old lovers together under one roof - theirs.